SPELLS
TROUBLE

Also by P. C. Cast and Kristin Cast

SPELLS TROUBLE

P. C. Cast / Kristin Cast

WEDNESDAY BOOKS
NEW YORK

First published in the United States by Wednesday Books,
an imprint of St. Martin's Publishing Group

SPELLS TROUBLE. Copyright © 2021 by P. C. Cast and Kristin Cast.
All rights reserved. Printed in the United States of America. For information,
address St. Martin's Publishing Group, 120 Broadway, New York, NY 10271.

www.wednesdaybooks.com

Design by Jonathan Bennett

Map by Sabine Stangenberg

Library of Congress Cataloging-in-Publication Data

Names: Cast, P. C., author. | Cast, Kristin, author.
Title: Spells trouble / P. C. Cast [and] Kristin Cast.
Description: First edition. | New York : Wednesday Books, 2021. |
    Series: Sisters of Salem ; 1 | Audience: Ages 12–18. |
Identifiers: LCCN 2020053265 | ISBN 9781250765635 (hardcover) |
    ISBN 9781250765642 (ebook)
Subjects: CYAC: Witches—Fiction. | Sisters—Fiction. | Twins—Fiction. |
    Magic—Fiction. | Monsters—Fiction. | Mythology—Fiction.
Classification: LCC PZ7.C2685827 Sp 2021 | DDC [Fic]—dc23
LC record available at https://lccn.loc.gov/2020053265

Our books may be purchased in bulk for promotional, educational, or business use.
Please contact your local bookseller or the Macmillan Corporate and
Premium Sales Department at 1–800–221–7945, extension 5442, or by email at
MacmillanSpecialMarkets@macmillan.com.

First Edition: 2021

10 9 8 7 6 5 4 3 2 1

To Monique Patterson, our longtime editor.
Thank you for being our champion. This one's for you!

Goodeville

1. Norse Tree
2. Hindu Banyan Tree
3. Japanese Cherry Blossom
4. Greek Olive Tree
5. Egyptian Doum Palm
6. Goode House
7. Goode High School
8. Goode Lake
9. Corn & Bean Fields

SPELLS
TROUBLE

Prologue

Salem, Massachusetts

Sarah Goode didn't open her eyes when they began to test the gallows. Though Procter's Ledge was a goodly walk from the courthouse where Sarah was jailed, the breeze carried the sound through the bars of the glassless window above her head. It was ghastly. The metallic *creeeeak—snap* of the lever that opened the trapdoor splintered the night followed closely by the *thunk* of the burlap bag of sand they used in place of a falling body. The sarcastic guffaws and muffled comments from the men who witnessed the test flitted wasp-like to her through the otherwise silent night.

Beside her mother, little Dorothy stirred on the narrow cot and Sarah stroked the child's thin back comfortingly. She drew a deep breath, and the taste of rosemary filled her. She held in check the anger she felt at *them*. Bad enough that they had fabricated a reason to arrest her for witchcraft, but they'd jailed her four-year-old daughter as well because they'd found a fleabite on her little finger—*a fleabite!*

Sarah had paid attention to omens that warned she was in danger— the raven that had called through her window three mornings in a row—the mandrake roots she'd unearthed that were filled with

1

rot—and especially the rabbit she'd found dead on her doorstep. Sarah had heeded their warning and she had prepared, though she had underestimated how swiftly the town would move against her, or how her own husband would add to the accusations.

Still, she hadn't panicked until the day Constable Locker appeared at the close-set bars of her jail cell with Dorothy's small hand in his—and then opened the door and pushed the child in to her mother, saying, "Aye, well, 'tis true. The child confessed to witchery like her mother and showed Satan's mark as well. So she will abide with ye." That was the day Sarah knew the town would not overcome the hysteria that gripped it. They would not see reason and allow her or her precious child to go free—and if they did, where would her daughter go? Back to her treacherous father?

Sarah had to get her away.

Creeeeak—snap! Thunk! This time the men's laughter was punctuated by a smattering of applause.

Dorothy murmured restlessly against her mother's side, and Sarah hummed a familiar lullaby under her breath while she stroked her back. Normally she would sing to her daughter, but not that night. That night Sarah soothed the child just enough to keep her silent and sleeping. Her main focus—her true intention—was on the sprig of fresh rosemary she chewed slowly, carefully, into a fragrant pulp.

The time was nigh. The testing of the gallows confirmed that it was the night before she, along with four others—Goodwifes Martin, Howe, Nurse, and Wilde—were to be hung at dawn.

Why test the gallows in the deep of the night?

Sarah's full lips tilted up as the answer filled her mind. *'Tis because of cruelty mixed with their fear.* The small-minded men who ruled Salem called midnight The Witch's Hour—but they knew little else. Their show of bravado was meant to frighten away Satan should he stride into town, forked tongue flashing, to rescue the women Reverend Noyes called Satan's handmaids. They'd jailed each woman in different parts of the courthouse—to keep them from joining to call their master.

Sarah snorted. Fools—every one of them.

The other four women meant to hang that day were no more witches than Reverend Noyes was a warlock. *May that monstrous man's God give him only blood to drink for the misery he has caused,* Sarah thought. *And me? If I be a handmaid, it is for the Earth Mother Gaia.* Sarah Goode no more believed in Satan than she did in fairies.

Creeeeak—snap! Thunk!

Dorothy reacted less to the sound each time it came. She snored softly, her restlessness abating, which left Sarah to focus completely on the spell. She had surreptitiously palmed a sprig of rosemary during the brief trip she and Dorothy had taken to the outhouse to relieve themselves. Sarah continued to silently recite her intent, over and over as she chewed the rosemary.

> *Unaltered the fragrance aids memory*
> *I muddle—I chew—I alter thee three by three by three*
> *So that befuddled with sleep he shall be . . .*

"Yowl!"

The cat's cry sounded just outside the door to the courthouse jail, eerie accompaniment to the macabre gallows music, though to Sarah's ears the cat's lament was water to a parched desert. Gently, she shook her daughter's shoulders.

The child opened her moss green eyes immediately.

Sarah pressed her finger to her lips and Dorothy nodded, her eyes bright with intelligence. The child didn't move. She didn't speak. She also didn't go back to sleep.

"Yooooowl!"

"God's teeth!" Constable Grant, the junior guard, who went from room to room throughout the night to watch over the condemned, stood at his great oak desk. He set his cheap cigar on the fireplace ledge and closed his Bible abruptly, holding it in his bony hands as he stared at the door.

"Yowl!"

The constable jammed the cigar between his teeth and strode to the entrance of the courthouse's jail, which held three small cells along the rear wall, though only one was occupied. "Begone, foul beast of Satan!" he said around the cigar as he threw open the door and waved the Bible into the night.

The huge cat slipped lithely around him, ear tufts bobbing as the feline padded directly to the cell that held Sarah and her daughter. Constable Grant slammed the door and turned, only then seeing that the cat had snuck inside. He spat out the cigar, dropped the Bible, and stared incredulously as the large black-and-tan-striped feline rubbed itself languidly along the bars of the cell and purred riotously.

Sarah squeezed her daughter's shoulder. It was time.

Immediately Dorothy sat, holding her arms out and saying, "Mommy! Odysseus! 'Tis Odysseus!" Then, just as they'd practiced earlier, the child trotted to the edge of their cell where she sat and reached through the bars with both hands to caress the cat who was so unusually large he dwarfed—and intimidated—many of the village dogs.

"Get the child back! Back, I say Mistress Goode! I shall not abide Satan's beast!" Constable Grant grabbed an iron fireplace poker and held it menacingly aloft as he threatened the purring cat and grinning child.

Sarah squeaked a sound of motherly distress through the ball of masticated rosemary she held in her mouth and rushed to her child—and as the constable loomed over the massive cat, Odysseus met Sarah's gaze. She nodded. The feline familiar drew a deep breath and then squeezed between two bars until, like a cork freed from underwater, he popped into their cell to curl up contentedly in Dorothy's lap.

Constable Grant banged the poker against the bars, red-faced and repeating, "I shall not abide Satan's beast!"

At the same moment Sarah reached the bars. She looked up at the florid young man who was only a handspan away from her and then spat the mouthful of rosemary—filled with intention and saliva—directly into his face.

He dropped the poker. It clanged against the stone floor as he made odd squeaking noises while wiping frantically at the green goo that bespeckled his face and filled his watering eyes.

Sarah lifted her hands and grounded herself. With all of her being she reached down, down, down through the stone floor to the fertile earth below and drew to her the power that rested there as surely as the moon drew the tide. She felt the heat of the earth warm her skin and raise the small hairs on her arms and then Sarah Goode spoke urgently, her voice filled with the confidence and authority that had so intimidated the men of Salem that they had felt the need to hang her.

Rosemary muddled through the mid of night,
Shall now make thee fumble—make thee lose sight.

Grant gasped as she began the spell. His face blanched to milk while he staggered and wiped frantically at his eyes. Blindly, he stumbled back. His gait was awkward—as if he could not quite make himself awaken from a nightmare. He dropped heavily to his knees while he continued to wipe at his face.

Heavy are thy thoughts
Upon waking you shall remember naught.

"Satan's whore!" he slurred, and lurched to his feet.
Undaunted, Sarah continued her spell.

Deep shall be thy sleep
But first thrice I say to thee—drop the key, drop the key, drop the
key!

"I shall not succumb to you!" Constable Grant reached blindly into his pocket for the iron key ring as he stumbled backward, toward the door. "Witch! You shall never get—" His words broke off as his feet tripped over the Bible he'd dropped. He fell, arms windmilling. Grant's head hit the corner of his desk and he collapsed unmoving to the floor. The constable's hand opened and with a musical jingle the keys dropped against the stone.

"Hurry, Odysseus!" Sarah spoke to the feline, who bounded off Dorothy's lap, drew in another deep breath, and squeezed back through the narrow bars. He padded to the ring of keys and picked them up with his mouth, carrying them to the jail cell.

It took only moments for Sarah to open the door. She and Dorothy rushed out and Sarah locked the door again before returning the keys to the constable's deep pocket.

Odysseus growled softly.

Sarah nodded. "Yes, yes, I know. But he will awake with no memory of what happened and an empty jail cell. He shall spread the story of how the Goode witch and her spawn magically flew through iron bars and disappeared into the night—likely on the back of Satan's steed—which would be you, my Odysseus."

The huge cat purred as he wound around her legs.

"His tall tale will do more to make the townsfolk pause before tracking me than if I tied him and locked him away."

Odysseus chirped contentedly as Sarah took Dorothy's little hand and cracked open the door.

The night was dark and still and filled with the scent of rosemary. Sarah waited impatiently for the next ghastly *creeeeak—snap! Thunk!* of the gallows. Predictably, the men's laughter and applause followed, covering any sound she, her child, and their faithful familiar might make as they darted from the jail. They hugged the side of the courthouse, then dashed from shadow to shadow, making their way from the center of town.

"Mamma! Mamma!" Dorothy whispered urgently and tugged on her mother's hand.

Barely pausing, Sarah bent and picked up her daughter. "What is it, little love?"

"You are going the wrong way."

Sarah jogged across another dark dirt road and past two clapboard houses before she answered. "We are going to a new home—one that is far, far away."

"Is Father not coming with us?"

Sarah's jaw set. She caressed her daughter's matted curls and reined in her anger. "No, love. Your father did not keep us safe. So forevermore that will be my job."

Beside them Odysseus chirruped up at Sarah. She smiled and corrected, "My job and Odysseus's."

Dorothy's expression was somber and she suddenly appeared much older than her four years. "We shall keep each other safe."

"Indeed we will, little love. Indeed we will."

The predawn gloaming had begun to turn the sky the gray of a dove's breast when the three fugitives finally made their way to the apple grove that divided the west side of Salem from the farmlands and forests beyond. Sarah slowed, then, and allowed Dorothy to walk beside her while Odysseus trotted with them, weaving between the fruit-laden trees as she made her way to the oldest of the apple trees.

At the heart of the grove Sarah approached the ancient tree respectfully. She placed her hand against the rough bark and whispered, "Merry meet, old friend. I give thanks for you to our great goddess, Gaia." Sarah smiled up as the leaves above her quivered in response, though the lazy night breeze had completely died. She walked to the north side of the tree, where two massive roots had broken through the surface to form the V of a divining rod. There she dropped to her knees and, using a sharp stone, began to dig.

It didn't take long for her fingers to touch the wooden box. Sarah didn't bother to pull it free. Instead she cleared the dirt from it, opened the lid, and pulled out the cloth satchel she had buried the day before they'd come for her. It held her treasures—the means to a new future: travel cloaks for herself and Dorothy as well as a change of clothes, a leather purse filled with every coin she had saved, and her grimoire disguised as a prayer book. Beneath the book was a piece of cloth, carefully dyed the deep green of moss and of her daughter's eyes. Within it was wrapped a tin of salt and a precious walnut-sized opal that glimmered lazily in the wan predawn light.

"Sit here at the base, little love," Sarah told her daughter as she poured a circle of salt around the ancient tree. Then, with Dorothy by her feet and Odysseus beside her, Sarah drew three deep breaths and held the opal to the center of her forehead as she invoked.

> *By stone and salt I call to thee,*
> *Guide mine steps from this fair tree.*
> *Gaia, goddess good and kind and just—*
> *In you I have always placed my trust.*
> *Now I beseech, show me thy way*
> *I am yours to command—yesterday, tomorrow, today.*
> *Lead me to a place of power*
> *Where never again will your daughters fear and cower!*

With the last word of her spell Sarah closed her eyes and imagined that she peered out through her own forehead, into the flaming opal, and past it—to the magic it revealed.

"Oh, goddess be blessed! Thank you, Gaia! Thank you!" The words rushed from Sarah as green light lifted from the floor of the grove. Under her feet a ribbon of emerald pointed westward. As Gaia's power channeled through the opal to enhance her sight, the path blazed and pulsed with energy, building in intensity in the distance. She felt its pull as if she had been tethered to it.

Sarah opened her eyes then and bowed her head reverently. "I shall follow your path—now and always. Blessed be, Earth Mother." She kissed the center of the opal and then turned to the ancient oak. On tiptoes Sarah reached up to press the stone into a niche in the bark. "Thank you, Mother Apple. I shall always remember how you stood sentry over my future." Again, the leaves above her shivered in response.

Only then did she gather their supplies, rebury the now empty box, and—with her daughter's hand in hers and the feline familiar at their side—Sarah Goode broke the salt circle and headed west, following the ley line of power that thrummed like a heartbeat beneath her feet.

Present Day

GOODEVILLE, ILLINOIS – SALEM COUNTY

One

Goode Lake was postcard perfect with its tree-lined banks and sandy shores that gradually sloped into the crystal blue water. The lake always looked good, but somehow today it looked better. Maybe it was because today was Hunter Goode's sixteenth birthday. Or maybe it was because Hunter was looking for a reason to procrastinate. Either way, she had charged down to the edge of the water, towel in hand, shimmied out of her T-shirt and shorts, and now waded into the calm blue.

Goose bumps crested against her skin and she stared down at her feet as the gentle waves consumed more of her. The water reached the high neck of her swimsuit top and she could still see her toes, blurry pale orbs against the camel-colored sand. Another few steps and they were gone, swallowed by the rich navy of the deep water, and Hunter was floating.

She lifted her legs, stretched out her arms, tipped her head back, and closed her eyes against the piercing sunlight. Her ears plunged beneath the surface as she drifted on her back. The dull *whoosh* of water was an active kind of quiet. The sort of roaring silence that made drifting off to sleep more of a command than a choice. And, for Hunter, this forceful silence was always welcome. It kept her from her thoughts. Better yet, it kept her from her memories.

A boat motor stirred the water and roared through Hunter's reverie. She shielded her eyes and let her legs sink back into the water. The red-and-black boat circled the far side of the lake before it returned to the center. Its belly smacked the water as it jumped its own white-capped wake. A chorus of whoops and cheers erupted as the boat slowed and bobbed on top of the surging water.

A wave slapped Hunter in the face, and she wiped her eyes before squinting at the boat and its passengers. Its *five* passengers. Hunter blinked more water from her eyes. Five *male* passengers. And one of them was waving at—

"Hey!" The only shirtless member stood on the row of seats flapping his arms like a goose. "You go to Goode High, right? You're a Mustang."

The boat drifted closer to Hunter. She stared back at the five young men who looked at her expectantly. She opened her mouth to speak, but no words came out. Her heart was lodged inside her throat and her pulse hammered against her eardrums. She dove under the water and swam back to the safety of the sand and her towel and the clothes she'd stripped off when she knew no one was watching. Her chest ached for oxygen, but she kept swimming. She could hear them laughing. It rang louder than her pulse and the roaring silence. In middle school, she'd been everyone's favorite joke. Two years later, she still expected to be.

Hunter's lungs forced her above water. She gasped for air and crawled from the lake, nearly collapsing onto her neatly folded towel and pile of clothes. She didn't want to look back at the boat, at the boys, and see them pointing and staring, but she had to. The joke wasn't complete until she did.

Hunter's eyes burned. She shook away the tears. Crying only made things worse. She plucked her thin rope cord from the pile and squeezed the T-shaped opalescent pendant in her fist as she swept her gaze over the settling waves and back to the boat. The guys were dancing. Another had removed his shirt and was twirling it over his head. They turned up the volume and a fast, staccato beat reached Hunter as the motor roared and they took off.

Hunter's pent-up breath came out in staggered wheezes, and she dropped to her knees. They hadn't been laughing. Not at her, at least. The tears came then, and she let them. They splattered against the shore, painting the sand a deeper shade of tan. Maybe this next phase of her life would be different.

She dried her eyes, wrapped her hair in her towel, and tugged her shorts on over her swimsuit bottoms. Her necklace dangled from her fingertips as she threw her T-shirt over her shoulder and headed toward the dock. She was alone again, and it was perfect.

The weathered boards of the dock creaked as she shuffled to the row of three chaise lounge chairs and the faux leather–bound journal she'd abandoned for the blue waters of Goode Lake. Hunter shook out her towel-dried hair and pulled it back into the high ponytail she always wore before tugging on her T-shirt and collapsing into her chair. She opened her journal and fastened her necklace around her neck. She smoothed her fingers over the pendant and stared down at the blank unlined pages, unnervingly white under the bright April sun. She slid her pen from its holder and clicked and unclicked the retractable top. In the three weeks she'd owned the faux leather–bound book, all she'd managed to write was one sentence underneath her name, which she'd erased, written again, erased again and finally written it, *HUNTER GOODE,* in black marker on the worn page. She hadn't written her name incorrectly, it just wasn't . . . *right.*

That's what held Hunter back now, the not *rightness* of everything she wanted to say. She was supposed to author the next great American novel and, until she'd purchased the journal from the cute paper and craft store on Main Street, she'd thought she'd be at least halfway finished doing exactly that. She had already chosen a title and character names. Weren't those the most difficult parts?

Hunter rubbed the opalescent jewel hanging from the thin rope cord around her neck. The dip in Goode Lake was supposed to clear her head, but it'd only managed to stir up feelings she so desperately tried to keep tamped down. The deep purplish-pink core of the pendant spun like a top. It always did when she was this perplexed, like her confusion was a blender, her body the power source, and her budding magic a milky purple-pink smoothie.

She pressed the swirling gem against her palm and gazed up at the sky. Puffy white clouds floated above the lake. There were too many for her to see the moon's ghostly imprint against the pale blue. Without the moon, *her* moon, daytime often felt like Hunter's nemesis. She never should have left her tarot cards at home.

Hunter sighed and let her necklace drop against her chest. It stopped churning as soon as it left her fingers. It was weird how it couldn't sense her magic through a simple layer of cotton. Perhaps there wasn't enough of it. She smoothed down a few frayed strands of rope. After tonight, she'd be practically overflowing with enough magic no T-shirt would be able to get in its way.

A sharp, chittering meow lifted the hairs on the back of Hunter's neck. Seconds later, a brown, black, and white Maine coon pounced on the end of Hunter's chaise. She curled up next to Hunter's feet and yawned, the points of her sharp teeth glistening in the sunlight as she stretched her large paws and kneaded Hunter's shin. Xena was always popping up around town to check on Hunter. It was as comforting as it was stalkerish.

"Thanks for getting me back on track, Xena." Hunter set the point of her pen against the white page. After all these weeks she was finally doing it. She wrote the word *title* in loopy cursive and dotted the *i* with a perfectly drawn star.

When Darkness Rises.

She wrote that in block letters and didn't dot the *i* with anything. From here on out, it was serious author business only. And now her title was final. She nodded to herself and underlined the three words. Yep, it was set in stone forever.

She tapped the end of the pen against her round chin and leaned forward and combed her fingers through the cat's soft fur. "And then there are my main characters, Maisie and Mitchell, who will overcome all odds and fall deeply and madly in love with each other . . ." Hunter stared out past the end of the dock at the rippling blue surface of Goode Lake as she continued to scratch Xena. "Maybe they're causing my writer's block . . ." she mused. "Maisie and Mitchell . . ."

Hunter's fingers tingled as her thoughts shifted. Maisie and Mitchell weren't really the problem. Tonight was the problem. Tonight topped her list of *things not to think about*. It had for the past three weeks. The dedication ceremony and the gate . . . It was all *so much*. Her life was about to change, in an amazing and magical way, but still. Change was big. Change was difficult. And Hunter wasn't sure if she was ready.

Xena chattered her displeasure as Hunter's fingers stilled on the cat's back.

Hunter shook her head, clearing away the doubt to focus on the task at hand. "What if I change Maisie and Mitchell to Maisie and *Madison*?" Hunter wrote the names below the title and underlined each twice before turning her attention back to the disgruntled cat. "After all, don't they say to *write what you know*?"

The dock groaned and Xena's ears pinned flat against her head as the *slap, slap* of flip-flops drew near. Emily Parrott waved as the breeze caught the flowing skirt of her sunflower yellow dress and tangled around her legs. "Damn nature!" she hissed, and pushed her sunglasses on top of her head before gathering the silky lengths. "You

Goodes and your *always wanting to be outside* weirdness." She paused and adjusted the shoulder strap of her oversized neon pink bag before continuing. "There are perfectly good venues *in* town where you could've thrown *the best* birthday bash. Venues that have a/c and free Wi-Fi that would make your ridiculous midnight curfew more bearable." She wrinkled her nose and cocked her pointed chin. "More bearable for me, at least."

Hunter closed her journal and fastened it shut with the buckle she'd found in her mother's basket of Kitchen Witch Accoutrements. "It'll still be *the best,* Em. Even without air-conditioning and Wi-Fi and with us leaving at midnight." Hunter's throat tightened and she scrubbed her fingers along the thick trunk of her pendant.

Before Hunter could wrangle the giant Maine coon, Xena jumped off the lounger and stalked toward Emily.

The contents of Emily's bag clanked as she thrust it in the cat's direction. "If you don't move out of my way, I'm going to skin you and make you into a scarf."

The tabby arched her back and hissed. Her puffy black-and-brown-striped tail twitched in the air like a fly-fishing line.

Hunter tossed her journal and pen onto her empty seat as she stood and scooped up the mound of irritated fluffiness. "It's okay, Xena," she murmured, and rubbed the tufts of fur sprouting from the ends of the cat's pointed ears. "It's just mean ol' Emily Parrott. And she would never make you into a scarf."

Emily sneezed into her balled-up dress and rubbed her watering eyes. "I would, cat. Just try me." Another sneeze. "She knows I'm allergic and is trying to kill me." She wiped her nose on her dress and frowned. *"See?"* She held out the fabric as evidence. "That cat is making me leak!"

Xena melted against Hunter's fingertips as she scratched under the cat's chin. The Maine coon had been slinking around Goodeville, monitoring the town of five thousand Illinoisans, since before Hunter was born. Xena had even been there on the very day Hunter arrived in the world—quiet and doe-eyed (so her mother said), fifteen years, three hundred and sixty-four days and nineteen and a half hours ago. But who was counting?

The Maine coon's long body vibrated with a round of purrs while Hunter stroked her long back. "You should go, Xena." Hunter kissed the top of the cat's brown-and-white head. "Thanks for checking in."

Xena nuzzled Hunter's chin a final time and leapt from her arms. She landed at Emily's flip-flop clad feet, glared up at the tall, lanky brunette, and hissed before padding away toward the end of the dock.

"Begone, cat!" Emily shouted as Xena jumped onto land and twined herself through the wildflowers rimming the shoreline. "That cat is practically a dog, following you and your sister around all the time."

Hunter gathered her journal and pen before plopping back down into the chaise. "She really wouldn't like that you said that."

"She's a cat. Unless your mom has some kind of *cat-talking* spell, Xena has no idea what I'm saying." Emily dropped her bag and it landed on the dock with a clatter. "Not that I'd be surprised if your mom *did* have a cat-talking spell. I mean, that cat *has* been alive for a million years . . ."

Hunter picked at her fingernail. There were some things even Emily shouldn't know.

"Oh my god, your mom has a cat-talking spell!" Emily kicked off her flips and pushed them under the empty chaise next to Hunter. "I can't believe you've been holding out on me! Spill!"

The blaring speakers of a nearing ski boat saved Hunter from having to tell a lie Emily would have seen through before it left Hunter's lips.

Emily's back stiffened and she craned her long neck to get a better view at the boat's passengers. "Well, well, well, would you look at that."

Hunter tucked her chin into her shirt and followed Emily's gaze. The black-and-red boat was back. The five guys stood in the center, bobbing in time to the pulsing music. One of the shirtless members crouched down. Silver cans glinted in the sunlight as he tossed one to each of his friends.

Emily rose to her tiptoes and slid the thin straps of her dress down her russet brown shoulders. When she turned on the charm, appeal poured from Emily like a tapped tree poured sap.

Hunter chewed the tip of her fingernail and watched as, one at a time, each guy stopped bouncing and turned like a mob of meerkats to face the dock. The lump returned to the back of her throat and she sank farther down into her seat.

Emily continued her show, adjusting her strapless bikini top before smoothing the dress down her narrow hips and letting it pool around her feet. Not once did she look at the boat or the guys or even Hunter. She was alone. An island enjoying its own beauty. She didn't bother picking up her discarded dress. Instead, she stepped out of it and settled into the lounger. "I just love a good view, don't you?" She slid her sunglasses down to the rounded tip of her nose and stared out at the boat.

Hunter smoothed her fingers over her pendant. "I'm Hunter, not Mercy." She said the words without thinking. It was a line she'd spoken more than any other. It was a line that usually ended a conversation.

With a sigh, Emily eyed Hunter. "Well, yeah." Emily's golden eyes swept over Hunter's damp ponytail, closed journal, plain white tee, and plain jean shorts. "You two may be identical to most, but I've known you since second grade. Plus, there's no way Mercy would be caught dead without some sort of . . ." Emily waved her hand in front of Hunter, her gesture taking in every bit of the twin. "Bedazzlement. Your sister also wouldn't arrive half an hour before her party even started." She twirled a long curl around her finger. "I mean, Mercy practically *is* the party, so I guess it won't officially start until she gets here anyway."

Hunter tugged her shirt from her chin and clutched her journal against her chest. It pressed against the pendant of Tyr hidden under her shirt as she resumed chewing her nail and stared past the boat at the sunlight glinting off the lake's gently pulsing waves. "Why are *you* here so early, Em?"

Emily hefted her bag onto her lap and pulled out a stack of red cups. "My mom just flew back from her trip to DC and my dad doesn't leave for some gross embalming conference in LA for a couple days." She plucked a cup off for herself and offered the stack to Hunter. "So, both of my parents are home. Occupying the same space at the same time. And we all know how well they do that."

Hunter stared at the stop sign–red plastic cups and swallowed. She didn't want one. She also didn't want to be rude. "I'm sorry, Em," she said and took a cup.

"Don't be. They did it to themselves." Emily shook her head and set the tower of cups on the deck before reaching back into her bag. She wiggled her shoulders as she pulled out a glass bottle and unscrewed the cap. "Let's toast to divorce."

Hunter grimaced. "Is that vodka?"

Emily's brow furrowed. "I brought mixers, too. I'm not a savage." The clear liquid whooshed as Emily poured some into Hunter's cup and even more into her own. "I have OJ, tonic, cranberry, something called lemonberry spritz that I took from my mom's minifridge . . ." She shrugged. "Pick your poison, Miss Goode."

Hunter's stomach twisted. "I'm fine. I'll just hold on to this until you need another drink."

"Unclench, H. You know, live a little." Emily took out a plastic bottle of orange juice and poured far less juice into her cup than she had vodka before doing the same to Hunter's. "As someone who's been sixteen for, like, six months now, I'm going to give you some advice." She took a drink, grimaced, and took another. "Guys, girls, *whoever,* want to be with a girl who's free and relaxed, not rigid and uptight. Look at Mercy. She got Kirk because she's wild and breezy and weird, but in the best sort of way, like a kite, or a unicorn." She took another drink, motioned for Hunter to do the same, and settled against the chaise.

"Whether or not any of us *really* dig Kirk doesn't change the fact that all that stuff is what people want."

Hunter ran the edge of her ragged nail against her shorts. "People want a unicorn kite?"

"Exactly." Emily grimaced and downed the rest of her drink before she reached out and tapped Hunter's. The orange-tinged contents sloshed over the side of the cup and onto Hunter's fingers. "I'll also add some cran. It'll make it a smidge less brutal," Emily said, too busy rummaging through her bag for the mixer to notice the mess.

Hunter dried her hand on the bottom of her shirt. Just because it was simple white cotton and not covered in splashes of color or fringe or sparkles didn't mean she was devoid of personality. It meant she was different from her sister. And she liked being different than Mercy. It meant she could be there for her impulsive, trouble-making sister. If they were both irresponsible and spontaneous, the entire town would end up in flames. She was Mercy's counterbalance, and Mercy hers. They were perfect together, perfect for each other. Jax understood that about the twins. Sometimes it felt like he was the only one of their friends who did.

Emily poured a splash of scarlet juice into Hunter's cup and stared at her expectantly. Hunter brought the cup to her lips and closed her eyes. It smelled like rubbing alcohol and brunch. She tilted the cup back and swallowed. The liquid burned her throat and slid, fiery and hot into her stomach. Her eyelids flew open and she thrust the cup at Emily. "It's—terrible," she said between coughs.

"Well, yeah." Emily shrugged, took a sip, and refocused on the boat full of boys. She whooped as another peeled off his shirt and shook out his dark hair. "Don't you just love watching animals in the wild?" she asked, leaning into Hunter.

He performed an exaggerated bow before walking to the edge of the boat and jumping into the water.

"They're not there for you to ogle, Em. They're people." Hunter brought her nail to her lips and grimaced. Her fingers smelled like alcohol.

"Sorry. Meant to be here earlier, H, but football practice was hell, and then I was stalking my mailbox for your—" Jax paused and dramatically lifted a smallish rectangular box from behind his back. It was wrapped in swirly blue paper that had stars all over it and tied with a silver bow. "Birthday present! Ta-da!"

"Ooooh! You shouldn't have, but I'm glad you did!" Hunter squealed and bounced on her toes.

Emily bumped Mercy's shoulder. "I will forever think it's weird that your sister's bestie is a dude."

Mercy shrugged. "Well, as *my* bestie, I'm expecting you to gift me an awesome birthday pressie with tons of girl power that will put Jax's to shame."

Both girls watched while Hunter tore open the box and then shrieked in pleasure as she held up a gorgeous fountain pen made of something that seemed to glow.

"Ohmygod! It's opal! You got me a pen made of my favorite stone! You're the *best*, Jax!"

Mercy looked at Emily and held out her hands expectantly. "Gift me."

Emily shrugged and handed her the red plastic cup she'd just filled. "Happy birthday."

Mercy took the cup, sniffed it, and sipped it. "It's vodka and cranberry."

"I know, right?" Emily said. "Your fav!"

"Em," Mercy sighed. "You're gonna have to do better at Yule. You can't keep letting a dude out-gift you."

Emily's full bottom lip stuck out as she pouted. "But it *is* your fav."

"True, so you do get some bestie points for knowing that." Mercy handed the cup back to Em. "Which you immediately lose 'cause I cannot drink this—not tonight. You know H and I have to meet Mom in just a few hours for our special fam celebration thing—and I cannot be toasted for that. Gotta stick to beer—and just a little."

"Well, shit. Sorry," said Em. "Good thing my sparkling personality gift itself."

Emily blinked at Hunter from above the rim of her cup as if waiting for the punch line.

Hunter sighed. "They're people out here enjoying the lake just like *we're* out here enjoying the lake."

Emily pooched out her glossed lips and adjusted her long legs until she was stretched across the chaise like a cat. "And I expect to be ogled." She pushed her sunglasses back up her nose and readjusted her pout until it was duck lip perfection.

Hunter's chest warmed in the comforting way it did when her sister was near. Like she'd just taken the first drink of hot chocolate on a snowy winter day. It was one of the best feelings in the world.

"Mercy's here," Hunter said as she clipped her pen to the cover of her journal. Another writing day gone with nothing to show. At least tonight, if she could muster the courage to get through the midnight ceremony, would more than make up for it.

Emily lifted her cup to the sky and tipped her chin toward the sun. "Let's get this party started!"

Two

"Girlfriend, those jeans *slay*!" Emily said as she unfolded h
from the lounger she'd been sunning on and bent to mix Me
drink, displaying a whole lot of firm round ass, which had the
ball players who hadn't already followed their quarterback to tl
crowding the dock behind Mercy and cheering.

Mercy turned and narrowed her eyes at the herd of footba
ples. "Bloody buggering hell! It's just a girl in a bikini. Pic
tongues up off the dock. The keg is over there by the bonfire
needs to be lit so we can toast wieners and marshmallows. Sc
or I'll do a little bibbity-bobbity-bitch and the veggie wienei
replaced by a meatier variety." Mercy raised her hands and fl
fingers at the football team, aiming for just below their belts

As expected, the players backed off fast—heading to th
the heap of kindling and firewood as they rearranged thei
non-vegan wieners and sent her suspicious glances like th
entirely sure she was kidding.

"You know Mom would lecture you about teasing the
She'd say, '*What you put out into the world returns to you, and
thoughts, acts, and energy.*'"

Mercy grinned impishly as she turned to face her twii
Abigail's *not here.*" She threw her arms around her sister—
person in the world, though their mom was a close sec
birthday, little sis!"

"I seriously don't think being three minutes older m
little sister." Hunter repeated the line she'd been saying
both twins could remember, though she hugged her s
whispered, "Happy birthday."

"Aww, twin love." From a few feet behind them on
raven-haired player grinned a familiar crooked-tooth
sisters.

Hunter broke the hug instantly and hurled herse
friend's arms like she hadn't just seen him at school a

"Jax! Finally! I thought you'd never get here."

L et's get this par-tay started!" Mercy danced her way down the
dock to where her bestie and her sister were stretched out in
the chaise lounges. She raised her hands over her head and rolled
her hips back and forth in a classic belly-dancing move that had
the fringe belt she'd made and slung low on her hips rippling like
water over the boyfriend jeans she's spent *months* freehand embroidering vines and flowers all over. Her shirt was a retro halter top—
the same pink as the fringe around her waist, and her long, dark
hair was thick and loose around her shoulders—her fav way to
wear it. The big, worn leather boho purse she always carried was
over her shoulder and her hip bumped it like a tambourine. Mercy
felt as good as she looked, and she knew how good she looked
because Kirk Whitfield—and most of the football team that'd followed them to the dock—couldn't keep their eyes off her.

"Going to get some red Solo!" Kirk yelled as he trooped off with
the guys to find the keg.

"Okie dokie!" Mercy said as she blew him a kiss and dropped her
purse with a seismic *plop* into an empty chair.

22

23

"It's something, that's for sure."

"Mercy, isn't it perfect?" Hunter waved her new pen around.

Mercy grinned at her sister. "Yep." She looked up at the guy who had been her sister's best friend since second grade and shared the grin with him. "Way to go, Jax. You #nailedit."

"And I got you this." Jax ran his fingers through his black hair and tossed a tiny plastic baggie to her.

Mercy opened it and out slid a button that quoted, "I ask no favor for my sex. All I ask of our brethren is that they take their feet off our necks."—RBG. She looked up at Jax. "I love it. Seriously. Thanks, Jax!" Mercy pinned the button to her giant purse and then hugged her sister's broad-shouldered bestie tightly, enveloping him in her signature scent of spring lilacs as he grinned and patted her back affectionately.

A deep voice boomed with mock heartbreak down the dock at them. "Hey, whoa! I'm gone for, like, two minutes and I've been replaced?"

Mercy moved out of Jax's hug and turned to grin at Kirk. He carried two full cups of beer. Somewhere between the keg and the dock he'd taken off his shirt and the waning light of the setting sun caught the chiseled ridges of his pecs and biceps. His blond hair was shaggy and thick, and a lock had fallen over his face to obscure one of his perfect cerulean eyes.

"Oh, please Kirk. It's *Jax*." Mercy met him and tiptoed for a kiss before she took the beer he offered her.

"Who has been our friend for literally years before you managed to acknowledge Mercy even existed," said Hunter with an eye roll.

Kirk lifted the hand not holding his beer in surrender. "Ow!! I was just kidding around. Right, Jaxie?" Kirk leaned over and punched Jax in his shoulder, which had Hunter frowning and putting her hands on her hips. Jax let out an awkward laugh and furrowed his thick eyebrows.

"Of course Kirk was kidding!" Before her sister could start *another* argument with Kirk, Mercy stepped between them. "Guys, check out what Kirk gave me for my birthday." Mercy fished the cheap stainless steel ball chain out from under her shirt—making a mental note to swap it for something nicer when she got home—and lifted the ring that dangled from it. "As of this afternoon I am wearing his class ring."

"That's right, babe. You and I are official!"

"I'm your girlfriend, not your property. Remember? We talked about how saying that makes you sound douchey," Mercy said.

"That's why I don't." Kirk opened his arms while his blue eyes sparkled mischievously. "Come here, beautiful."

As Mercy melted against the quarterback's perfect body she heard her sister mutter, "Nice. A present that cost him nothing, but gets him everything."

Mercy ignored her sister's typical grumble—wishing that for once she could just get along with her boyfriend without constantly picking at him. Over Kirk's shoulder she saw a flash of orange and yellow. She unwound herself from him. "Hey, the bonfire's lit!"

"Oooh! Yeah!" Emily said. "Let's start roasting some of those wieners!"

"Good idea. Football practice made me puke, which means I'm starving," said Jax.

"Eww," said Hunter. "I don't understand why you'd play something that makes you hurl."

"What doesn't kill you makes you stronger!" said Kirk. He wrapped his arm around Mercy, barely giving her time to snag her giant purse before he led her from the dock. As the large group followed him to the picnic grounds that overlooked the placid lake, Kirk said, "Hey, babe, I got your wiener right here."

Mercy giggled and elbowed him. "Stop! And you know I'm a vegan."

"I'm hoping I can add a little more protein to your diet." He pretended to whisper, but his comment easily carried behind them to Emily, Hunter, and Jax.

Emily made retching sounds. Hunter didn't say anything, but Mercy knew she'd hear about Kirk's silly comment later and made a second mental note to remind Kirk—again—to watch his mouth. He didn't pose and bluster when it was just the two of them. He was sweet and sensitive and funny, but add a few people and his insecurities crept out in the stupidest ways.

It's okay, Mercy told herself. *He'll be better after we've been together for a while and he knows I'm not gonna take off like his mom did.*

"Happy birthday, Mercy and Hunter!" The growing group that was congregating around the bonfire greeted the twins with a planned shout.

"Veggie wieners, chips, and marshmallows for everyone!" Mercy shouted. "Let the music play!" She pointed at Emily.

"Syncing!" Emily pulled out her phone and then shouted victoriously when Taylor Swift's latest blasted from the Bluetooth speaker perched amongst the bags of chips.

"Ooooh, Come on, H! Let's dance!" Mercy grabbed her sister's wrist, but Hunter shook her off, laughing.

"Um, no. I will not dance with you because you stripper dance."

Mercy backed toward the bonfire where football players coupled up with cheerleaders and the pom squad, who'd just arrived amidst a lot of squeals and whoops.

"I do *not* stripper dance," Mercy said as she gyrated her hips and flung her hair around—like a stripper. "Plus, it's our birthday! Dance with me, woman!"

"She's definitely stripper dancing," said Jax, smiling crooked teeth at Hunter.

"As always," laughed Hunter, and she looked up at her tall best friend. "There's no way I'm going out there."

Jax leaned into Hunter. "Stop turtling and go and birthday dance with your sister!"

Hunter frowned and stared down at her feet as if the earth below would supply her with answers. She shook her head and sighed, the corner of her mouth lifting a little as her hips began to twitch. As

Hunter started to dance her way toward Mercy the music abruptly changed and "Witchy Woman" blasted across the campground.

"Yaaasss! That's my song!" Mercy twirled around, getting closer to the fire.

"That's right, it is, babe! That's why I played it." Fireside, Kirk crooked a finger at her.

As Mercy danced to him she surreptitiously stuck her hand into an outer pocket of her purse and spun her way closer to the fire. She flicked a handful of club moss quickly into the blaze as she raised her hands over her head and moved liquidly with the music, whispering to the fire, "By tree and leaf—wood and fire—burn bright, burn brilliant then fade to ghostly wisps of what you once were and what you shall be again." Mercy felt earth energy lift around her, like fireflies darting into the night sky.

There was a big flash and a fireball shot up, making everyone—except Mercy and Hunter—gasp.

"Come here, my little witch!" Kirk danced with her as the fireball gave way to white smoke that billowed up from the bonfire, forming the outline of the big oak that the logs had once been.

"Hey, that's cool! Doesn't it look like a tree?" someone shouted over the music.

Mercy smiled to herself as she let Kirk run his hands down her hips to cup her ass. Gracefully, she spun away from him, and as she did she caught a glimpse of her sister's face. Hunter had been watching the smoke with a knowing smile, but that smile suddenly changed to openmouthed shock. Her eye found Mercy and she jerked her chin at the bonfire as several of the kids shouted.

Mercy turned to the fire in time to see that the smoky outline of the oak had changed to become a nightmarish face that looked like a slavering wolf—or worse. Something with impossibly long teeth that shouldn't exist in this world. Quickly, Mercy plunged her hand back into the outside pouch of her purse and snagged the little bag of copper chloride she'd prepared for later. While everyone was gaping at the fanged thing in the smoke, Mercy threw the bag into the fire. Instantly the flames changed from yellow to blue, dissipating the smoke and sending the creature back to whatever hell it came from.

Mercy spun around, meeting her sister's gaze again. Hunter gestured for her to *come here,* but Kirk was there again. He pulled her against him and nuzzled her neck while he sang, *"Oooh, oooh, witchy woman,"* out of key into her ear. Over Kirk's shoulder she mouthed to Hunter, *I don't know what that was! Hang on—be there in a sec!*

Hunter rolled her eyes and mouthed, *never mind.* Before she turned her back on Mercy to take a hot dog from Jax she pulled Tyr's pendant out from under the collar of her tee and let it fall against her chest like it was a shield.

Well, she's pissed, but how am I supposed to know what that was? Mercy stewed as Kirk moved her around the bonfire. *Probably something to do with what's happening with our powers tonight, but I don't know any more than Hunter about it. Goddess! She's such a worrier. I really wish she'd learn to loosen up.* Instantly Mercy felt crappy about being frustrated with her sister. Of course Hunter worried—that's what happened when girls got bullied. Even when they weren't so little anymore they still had to deal with the emotional garbage left by jerks and assholes. Mercy sighed. *I tried to protect her, but I was only a kid, too . . .*

"Hey, are you not into dancing?" Kirk asked as he pulled a little away from her.

"I am. It's just . . ." Mercy's gaze automatically found her sister.

Kirk took her chin in his hand and gently turned her face up. "Don't let Hunter stress you out. I'll try harder to make her like me. Promise. And you know how charming I am." He kissed her then, softly—sweetly.

"I absolutely do and you absolutely are."

"Sorry I was kinda douchey before," he whispered as they swayed together. "I'm a dick when I'm nervous."

She pulled back to look into his eyes. "You were nervous?"

His blue eyes pulled her in and trapped her. "Yeah, of course. I know I'm not your sister's favorite person and I wanted everything to be perfect for you tonight. I shoulda gotten you something besides my ring. It was stupid of me to think that—"

"Shh." Mercy cut his words off by pressing her finger against his lips. "I *love* that you gave me your ring. Best present *ever*. And don't worry about H. She'll come around. Now I need a wiener!" He opened his mouth to say something she was sure would be douchey—again—and she pressed her finger back against his lips. "This is one of those learning experiences we talked about. Every time I say wiener you don't have to make a dick joke."

He laughed. "Got it! Now let's go get you some sausage!"

Mercy decided that was an improvement, albeit small. She searched for Hunter as she and Kirk made their way to the grills and the hot-dog dressing station, but her sister had her head together with Jax and didn't look her way. Mercy squelched a sigh. *It's going to be okay. Hunter will get used to Kirk and Kirk will get used to Hunter, and I'll get my happily ever after.*

Emily blinked at Hunter from above the rim of her cup as if waiting for the punch line.

Hunter sighed. "They're people out here enjoying the lake just like *we're* out here enjoying the lake."

Emily pooched out her glossed lips and adjusted her long legs until she was stretched across the chaise like a cat. "And I expect to be ogled." She pushed her sunglasses back up her nose and readjusted her pout until it was duck lip perfection.

Hunter's chest warmed in the comforting way it did when her sister was near. Like she'd just taken the first drink of hot chocolate on a snowy winter day. It was one of the best feelings in the world.

"Mercy's here," Hunter said as she clipped her pen to the cover of her journal. Another writing day gone with nothing to show. At least tonight, if she could muster the courage to get through the midnight ceremony, would more than make up for it.

Emily lifted her cup to the sky and tipped her chin toward the sun. "Let's get this party started!"

Two

Let's get this par-tay started!" Mercy danced her way down the dock to where her bestie and her sister were stretched out in the chaise lounges. She raised her hands over her head and rolled her hips back and forth in a classic belly-dancing move that had the fringe belt she'd made and slung low on her hips rippling like water over the boyfriend jeans she's spent *months* freehand embroidering vines and flowers all over. Her shirt was a retro halter top—the same pink as the fringe around her waist, and her long, dark hair was thick and loose around her shoulders—her fav way to wear it. The big, worn leather boho purse she always carried was over her shoulder and her hip bumped it like a tambourine. Mercy felt as good as she looked, and she knew how good she looked because Kirk Whitfield—and most of the football team that'd followed them to the dock—couldn't keep their eyes off her.

"Going to get some red Solo!" Kirk yelled as he trooped off with the guys to find the keg.

"Okie dokie!" Mercy said as she blew him a kiss and dropped her purse with a seismic *plop* into an empty chair.

"Girlfriend, those jeans *slay!*" Emily said as she unfolded herself from the lounger she'd been sunning on and bent to mix Mercy a drink, displaying a whole lot of firm round ass, which had the football players who hadn't already followed their quarterback to the keg crowding the dock behind Mercy and cheering.

Mercy turned and narrowed her eyes at the herd of football sheeples. "Bloody buggering hell! It's just a girl in a bikini. Pick your tongues up off the dock. The keg is over there by the bonfire, which needs to be lit so we can toast wieners and marshmallows. So, light it or I'll do a little bibbity-bobbity-bitch and the veggie wieners will be replaced by a meatier variety." Mercy raised her hands and flicked her fingers at the football team, aiming for just below their belts.

As expected, the players backed off fast—heading to the keg and the heap of kindling and firewood as they rearranged their personal non-vegan wieners and sent her suspicious glances like they weren't entirely sure she was kidding.

"You know Mom would lecture you about teasing them like that. She'd say, *'What you put out into the world returns to you, and that goes for thoughts, acts, and energy.'*"

Mercy grinned impishly as she turned to face her twin. "True, but Abigail's *not here.*" She threw her arms around her sister—her favorite person in the world, though their mom was a close second. "Happy birthday, little sis!"

"I seriously don't think being three minutes older makes me your *little* sister." Hunter repeated the line she'd been saying for as long as both twins could remember, though she hugged her sister back and whispered, "Happy birthday."

"Aww, twin love." From a few feet behind them on the dock, a tall raven-haired player grinned a familiar crooked-toothed smile at the sisters.

Hunter broke the hug instantly and hurled herself into her best friend's arms like she hadn't just seen him at school a few hours ago.

"Jax! Finally! I thought you'd never get here."

23

"Sorry. Meant to be here earlier, H, but football practice was hell, and then I was stalking my mailbox for your—" Jax paused and dramatically lifted a smallish rectangular box from behind his back. It was wrapped in swirly blue paper that had stars all over it and tied with a silver bow. "Birthday present! Ta-da!"

"Ooooh! You shouldn't have, but I'm glad you did!" Hunter squealed and bounced on her toes.

Emily bumped Mercy's shoulder. "I will forever think it's weird that your sister's bestie is a dude."

Mercy shrugged. "Well, as *my* bestie, I'm expecting you to gift me an awesome birthday pressie with tons of girl power that will put Jax's to shame."

Both girls watched while Hunter tore open the box and then shrieked in pleasure as she held up a gorgeous fountain pen made of something that seemed to glow.

"Ohmygod! It's opal! You got me a pen made of my favorite stone! You're the *best,* Jax!"

Mercy looked at Emily and held out her hands expectantly. "Gift me."

Emily shrugged and handed her the red plastic cup she'd just filled. "Happy birthday."

Mercy took the cup, sniffed it, and sipped it. "It's vodka and cranberry."

"I know, right?" Emily said. "Your fav!"

"Em," Mercy sighed. "You're gonna have to do better at Yule. You can't keep letting a dude out-gift you."

Emily's full bottom lip stuck out as she pouted. "But it *is* your fav."

"True, so you do get some bestie points for knowing that." Mercy handed the cup back to Em. "Which you immediately lose 'cause I cannot drink this—not tonight. You know H and I have to meet Mom in just a few hours for our special fam celebration thing—and I cannot be toasted for that. Gotta stick to beer—and just a little."

"Well, shit. Sorry," said Em. "Good thing my sparkling personality is a gift itself."

"It's something, that's for sure."

"Mercy, isn't it perfect?" Hunter waved her new pen around.

Mercy grinned at her sister. "Yep." She looked up at the guy who had been her sister's best friend since second grade and shared the grin with him. "Way to go, Jax. You #nailedit."

"And I got you this." Jax ran his fingers through his black hair and tossed a tiny plastic baggie to her.

Mercy opened it and out slid a button that quoted, "I ask no favor for my sex. All I ask of our brethren is that they take their feet off our necks."—RBG. She looked up at Jax. "I love it. Seriously. Thanks, Jax!" Mercy pinned the button to her giant purse and then hugged her sister's broad-shouldered bestie tightly, enveloping him in her signature scent of spring lilacs as he grinned and patted her back affectionately.

A deep voice boomed with mock heartbreak down the dock at them. "Hey, whoa! I'm gone for, like, two minutes and I've been replaced?"

Mercy moved out of Jax's hug and turned to grin at Kirk. He carried two full cups of beer. Somewhere between the keg and the dock he'd taken off his shirt and the waning light of the setting sun caught the chiseled ridges of his pecs and biceps. His blond hair was shaggy and thick, and a lock had fallen over his face to obscure one of his perfect cerulean eyes.

"Oh, please Kirk. It's *Jax*." Mercy met him and tiptoed for a kiss before she took the beer he offered her.

"Who has been our friend for literally years before you managed to acknowledge Mercy even existed," said Hunter with an eye roll.

Kirk lifted the hand not holding his beer in surrender. "Ow!! I was just kidding around. Right, Jaxie?" Kirk leaned over and punched Jax in his shoulder, which had Hunter frowning and putting her hands on her hips. Jax let out an awkward laugh and furrowed his thick eyebrows.

"Of course Kirk was kidding!" Before her sister could start *another* argument with Kirk, Mercy stepped between them. "Guys, check out

what Kirk gave me for my birthday." Mercy fished the cheap stainless steel ball chain out from under her shirt—making a mental note to swap it for something nicer when she got home—and lifted the ring that dangled from it. "As of this afternoon I am wearing his class ring."

"That's right, babe. You and I are official!"

"I'm your girlfriend, not your property. Remember? We talked about how saying that makes you sound douchey," Mercy said.

"That's why I don't." Kirk opened his arms while his blue eyes sparkled mischievously. "Come here, beautiful."

As Mercy melted against the quarterback's perfect body she heard her sister mutter, "Nice. A present that cost him nothing, but gets him everything."

Mercy ignored her sister's typical grumble—wishing that for once she could just get along with her boyfriend without constantly picking at him. Over Kirk's shoulder she saw a flash of orange and yellow. She unwound herself from him. "Hey, the bonfire's lit!"

"Oooh! Yeah!" Emily said. "Let's start roasting some of those wieners!"

"Good idea. Football practice made me puke, which means I'm starving," said Jax.

"Eww," said Hunter. "I don't understand why you'd play something that makes you hurl."

"What doesn't kill you makes you stronger!" said Kirk. He wrapped his arm around Mercy, barely giving her time to snag her giant purse before he led her from the dock. As the large group followed him to the picnic grounds that overlooked the placid lake, Kirk said, "Hey, babe, I got your wiener right here."

Mercy giggled and elbowed him. "Stop! And you know I'm a vegan."

"I'm hoping I can add a little more protein to your diet." He pretended to whisper, but his comment easily carried behind them to Emily, Hunter, and Jax.

Emily made retching sounds. Hunter didn't say anything, but Mercy

knew she'd hear about Kirk's silly comment later and made a second mental note to remind Kirk—again—to watch his mouth. He didn't pose and bluster when it was just the two of them. He was sweet and sensitive and funny, but add a few people and his insecurities crept out in the stupidest ways.

It's okay, Mercy told herself. *He'll be better after we've been together for a while and he knows I'm not gonna take off like his mom did.*

"Happy birthday, Mercy and Hunter!" The growing group that was congregating around the bonfire greeted the twins with a planned shout.

"Veggie wieners, chips, and marshmallows for everyone!" Mercy shouted. "Let the music play!" She pointed at Emily.

"Syncing!" Emily pulled out her phone and then shouted victoriously when Taylor Swift's latest blasted from the Bluetooth speaker perched amongst the bags of chips.

"Ooooh, Come on, H! Let's dance!" Mercy grabbed her sister's wrist, but Hunter shook her off, laughing.

"Um, no. I will not dance with you because you stripper dance."

Mercy backed toward the bonfire where football players coupled up with cheerleaders and the pom squad, who'd just arrived amidst a lot of squeals and whoops.

"I do *not* stripper dance," Mercy said as she gyrated her hips and flung her hair around—like a stripper. "Plus, it's our birthday! Dance with me, woman!"

"She's definitely stripper dancing," said Jax, smiling crooked teeth at Hunter.

"As always," laughed Hunter, and she looked up at her tall best friend. "There's no way I'm going out there."

Jax leaned into Hunter. "Stop turtling and go and birthday dance with your sister!"

Hunter frowned and stared down at her feet as if the earth below would supply her with answers. She shook her head and sighed, the corner of her mouth lifting a little as her hips began to twitch. As

Hunter started to dance her way toward Mercy the music abruptly changed and "Witchy Woman" blasted across the campground.

"Yaaasss! That's my song!" Mercy twirled around, getting closer to the fire.

"That's right, it is, babe! That's why I played it." Fireside, Kirk crooked a finger at her.

As Mercy danced to him she surreptitiously stuck her hand into an outer pocket of her purse and spun her way closer to the fire. She flicked a handful of club moss quickly into the blaze as she raised her hands over her head and moved liquidly with the music, whispering to the fire, "By tree and leaf—wood and fire—burn bright, burn brilliant then fade to ghostly wisps of what you once were and what you shall be again." Mercy felt earth energy lift around her, like fireflies darting into the night sky.

There was a big flash and a fireball shot up, making everyone—except Mercy and Hunter—gasp.

"Come here, my little witch!" Kirk danced with her as the fireball gave way to white smoke that billowed up from the bonfire, forming the outline of the big oak that the logs had once been.

"Hey, that's cool! Doesn't it look like a tree?" someone shouted over the music.

Mercy smiled to herself as she let Kirk run his hands down her hips to cup her ass. Gracefully, she spun away from him, and as she did she caught a glimpse of her sister's face. Hunter had been watching the smoke with a knowing smile, but that smile suddenly changed to openmouthed shock. Her eye found Mercy and she jerked her chin at the bonfire as several of the kids shouted.

Mercy turned to the fire in time to see that the smoky outline of the oak had changed to become a nightmarish face that looked like a slavering wolf—or worse. Something with impossibly long teeth that shouldn't exist in this world. Quickly, Mercy plunged her hand back into the outside pouch of her purse and snagged the little bag of copper chloride she'd prepared for later. While everyone was gaping at the fanged thing in the smoke, Mercy threw the bag into the fire. Instantly the flames changed from yellow to blue, dissipating the smoke and sending the creature back to whatever hell it came from.

Mercy spun around, meeting her sister's gaze again. Hunter gestured for her to *come here,* but Kirk was there again. He pulled her against him and nuzzled her neck while he sang, *"Oooh, oooh, witchy woman,"* out of key into her ear. Over Kirk's shoulder she mouthed to Hunter, *I don't know what that was! Hang on—be there in a sec!*

Hunter rolled her eyes and mouthed, *never mind.* Before she turned her back on Mercy to take a hot dog from Jax she pulled Tyr's pendant out from under the collar of her tee and let it fall against her chest like it was a shield.

Well, she's pissed, but how am I supposed to know what that was? Mercy stewed as Kirk moved her around the bonfire. *Probably something to do with what's happening with our powers tonight, but I don't know any more than Hunter about it. Goddess! She's such a worrier. I really wish she'd learn to loosen up.* Instantly Mercy felt crappy about being frustrated with her sister. Of course Hunter worried—that's what happened when girls got bullied. Even when they weren't so little anymore they still had to deal with the emotional garbage left by jerks and assholes. Mercy sighed. *I tried to protect her, but I was only a kid, too . . .*

"Hey, are you not into dancing?" Kirk asked as he pulled a little away from her.

"I am. It's just . . ." Mercy's gaze automatically found her sister.

Kirk took her chin in his hand and gently turned her face up. "Don't let Hunter stress you out. I'll try harder to make her like me. Promise. And you know how charming I am." He kissed her then, softly—sweetly.

"I absolutely do and you absolutely are."

"Sorry I was kinda douchey before," he whispered as they swayed together. "I'm a dick when I'm nervous."

She pulled back to look into his eyes. "You were nervous?"

His blue eyes pulled her in and trapped her. "Yeah, of course. I know I'm not your sister's favorite person and I wanted everything to be perfect for you tonight. I shoulda gotten you something besides my ring. It was stupid of me to think that—"

"Shh." Mercy cut his words off by pressing her finger against his lips. "I *love* that you gave me your ring. Best present *ever*. And don't worry about H. She'll come around. Now I need a wiener!" He opened his mouth to say something she was sure would be douchey—again— and she pressed her finger back against his lips. "This is one of those learning experiences we talked about. Every time I say wiener you don't have to make a dick joke."

He laughed. "Got it! Now let's go get you some sausage!"

Mercy decided that was an improvement, albeit small. She searched for Hunter as she and Kirk made their way to the grills and the hot-dog dressing station, but her sister had her head together with Jax and didn't look her way. Mercy squelched a sigh. *It's going to be okay. Hunter will get used to Kirk and Kirk will get used to Hunter, and I'll get my happily ever after.*

Three

Mercy finally spotted her bestie coming from the direction of the porta potties and hurried to intercept her. "Hey Em, have you seen Hunter?"

"God those things are *so fucking gross.*" Emily grimaced and wiped her hands delicately on her jeans. "Sorry, what'd you say?"

Mercy sighed. "Hunter. Have you seen her?"

"Oh, yeah, she's been with Jax all night." She fluttered her fingers at the lake. "I think they're taking pics of the moon over by the dock, which is weird, but definitely the norm for your sis."

"Mom's present to her was a bunch of attachments for her phone so Hunter can take night sky pictures." Mercy dug into her bottomless bag and checked her phone. "Sod it! It's eleven thirty! We gotta get outta here now so we can be home before midnight." Quickly, she texted:

WHERE R U?!

Then Mercy looked around the groups of semi-drunk kids. Some danced by the fire—some made out in the shadows—and a big group of the pom squad was skinny-dipping—or whatever it was called when you left your panties and bra on and jumped, squealing, into the lake from the dock. "Oh, bloody buggering hell! Is that Hunter over at the edge of the dock? She's not skinny-dipping, is she? She'll never dry before Abigail sees her!" Mercy started to rush toward the water, but Kirk's big hand on her shoulder stopped her.

"Did I hear you sssay those two magic words—ssskinny-dipping?" He leaned heavily on her and slurred his words.

Mercy turned to frown up at him. "Not tonight." *I asked him not to get wasted!* She shrugged his hand off her shoulder. "I gotta get Hunter and go. You know Mom wants us home before midnight."

He bent and booze-scented breath wafted over her. "Can't you be a little late?"

"No." Emily stepped between them and put her fists on her hips like Wonder Woman. "They can't. Abigail is cool, but when it comes to family traditions she does not play—just like she doesn't play about dudes who drink too much when they're out with her daughter. Go away, Kirk. Sober up. Byyyye." She hooked her arm through Mercy's and pulled her around Kirk.

"I'll text you tomorrow. Be sure you don't drive home." Mercy blew him a kiss and waved.

"Hey! I thought I was taking you home!"

"Not drunk you're not," Mercy said, but she smiled at him. "It's cool, though. Stay. Have fun. Just don't drive. Later!"

Emily didn't say anything, which made Mercy sigh. "You hate him, too, don't you?"

"Nope. He's tall and hot and captain of the football team. Nothing to hate about that."

Mercy waited and when that's all Em said she prompted. "But?"

"No buts. I'm your bestie. If you want him I've got your back. I've also got your back if he tries to do something stupid like drink and drive with you in the car—I mean, I knew I was driving you two home before midnight so I switched to water hours ago. If he can't figure out how to be responsible, too, then you don't get in the car with him. That's all."

"I wish Hunter felt like you do. I hate that she's such a bitch to Kirk."

Emily stopped and faced her. "Hunter is your twin. She's just protecting you—like you've always done for her. That's what you two do. You're there for each other. I know. I've been jelly of it since the first day of second grade when we met. Stop being so hard on her about it and start working on Kirk making a better impression."

Mercy chewed her lip. "That's what I tried to do tonight."

Emily snorted. "Girl, try harder. I could see that Kirk was being super sweet with you, but with the rest of us? Not so much."

"Okay, I get it. And you're right. I just—"

Hunter hurried up. "There you are. Let's go! We're gonna be late."

"H, I've been looking for you all night," Mercy said.

"Be serious. Your face has been smooshed against Kirk's all night." Hunter strode past them, heading to the grassy lot where Emily's car was parked and waiting for them.

Mercy didn't say anything. The fact that Hunter was right didn't help, but she wasn't sure *why* it didn't help. She wrenched open the front door and started to toss her boho bag to the floorboard, but Em reached around her, pulled the passenger's seat forward, and then pointed at the empty backseat of the 1966 Thunderbird convertible that had been Emily's sixteenth birthday guilt gift from her parents three months after her actual birthday, which they had both forgotten.

"Nope. You two sit back there. Together. Now," Emily said firmly.

Mercy and Hunter climbed into the backseat and remained silent as Em took the windy road that followed Goode Lake around to the two-lane blacktop that led to downtown Goodeville.

"Okay. I'm so over this." Emily glanced in the rearview mirror at the twins. "Mercy—Hunter, I hate it when you two fight. Do you know why?"

"Uh-uh," Mercy said softly.

"I hate it because you two almost never fight, and when you do it's like the fucking earth shifts on its axis and shit is not right. So, fix this right now and stop it. Jesus! It's your birthday."

Mercy gave Hunter a sideways glance. She was picking at her fingernails, her tell for being upset.

"H, I wish you'd give Kirk a chance," Mercy said.

"And I wish you'd get over your hormones. He's a douchebag," Hunter shot back.

Mercy slid to the side so she could face her sister. "He's only like that around you guys because you make him nervous."

"Riiiiight. I make him nervous. He told you that?"

"Yes. H, underneath all that—"

"Toxic masculinity."

"*No,* under all that pretend macho act is a really sweet boy who misses his mom. A lot." Mercy sighed. "Plus, now that I'm with Kirk we've totally made it! H, we get invited to all the cool parties and have lots more friends."

Hunter rolled her eyes. "You mean *you* get invited to all the cool parties and *you* have lots of new friends."

Mercy threw her hands up in frustration. "Oh my goddess! All you'd have to do is actually *participate* and you'd be included, too."

"I don't know if I want to participate." Hunter shook her head. "Not with them."

Mercy chewed her lip. *Why couldn't Hunter just leave the past in the past? She hadn't been bullied in ages. Can't she just get over it?* Mercy sighed again. "Look, I don't want to fight with you, especially not today."

Hunter's sigh was a mirror of her sister's. "Yeah, me, either. Sorry. I just don't like how Kirk talks to you."

"He *doesn't* talk to me like that when we're alone. Do you trust me?"

Hunter's gaze snapped to hers. "Of course I trust you."

"Then trust that I'm right about him."

Hunter picked at her fingernails some more. "I'll work on it. Promise. And I'm sorry I avoided you tonight."

"I'm sorry I let some guy come between us. I promise not to let that happen again. And if Kirk really is a douchebag, I promise I'll dump him faster than Xena makes Em sneeze—Goode guarantee?" Mercy lifted her hand.

"Goode guarantee!" Hunter's ponytail bobbed as she nodded and extended her pinky, which Mercy caught with her own—pinkies still hooked, the twins tapped their knuckles together before their hands separated, fingers fluttering like birds as they shouted, "Sisters of Salem!"

"Hugsees?" Hunter said.

"Total hugsees." Mercy grabbed her sister and squeezed her tightly.

"Yaaasss! Now *those* are my twins!" Emily grinned at them in the rearview mirror. "And it was a super fun party, though I don't know what the hell happened with that scary beast thing in the smoke. And Mercy Anne Goode, I'm talking to you."

"Hey, I don't know, either! I just did a little witchy stuff to the wood. You shoulda just seen the cool oak tree. No clue what happened."

"Wait, I think I know what went wrong," Hunter said. "You only called on oak?"

Mercy nodded. "Yeah, I checked out the woodpile before they lit it—well, from a distance—but it all looked like that old oak that split from lightning last spring. They cut it up and left it at the campgrounds for people making campfires."

"It wasn't all oak. Remember the apple grove just after you turn in to the lake drive?"

"I know what you're talking about. That's Mr. Caldwell's grove," Emily said. "Mercy and I got super sick the summer we were thirteen from eating too many green apples from there. Remember, Mercy?"

Mercy shuddered. "I'll never forget."

"Last winter that ice storm killed the oldest tree out there." Hunter tightened her ponytail as she explained. "Mom told us about it. Mr. Caldwell called her to see if she could save it, but it was too late. I remember she said that the apple wood was being chopped up and given to the campsite."

"Huh. I got the wood wrong. Still weird," said Mercy.

"And *super* weird that it was *apple* wood." Hunter touched her T-shaped pendant and shared a *look* with her sister. Neither needed words to understand the significance of that particular type of tree this particular night.

Emily waved her hand around, redirecting the twins' attention. "Hey, did you two ever consider that what happened might have just been a fluke and more about the weird smoke caused by your exploding moss fire bomb than anything remotely witchy? I mean, no offense, but that makes way more sense than saying that you actually *conjured* something from smoke."

Mercy and Hunter locked their gazes and smiled knowingly.

"You're right, Em," said Mercy.

"Makes *way* more sense," added Hunter.

"Well, anyway, it was a super cool party! And now that you two are back to your normal psychic-level closeness, all is right in the world."

"Oh, sod it! I'm a wanker! I didn't give you—" Mercy began.

"Your pressie!" Hunter finished.

"Mercy, you're *not* British." Emily tossed her mass of tight, dark curls back from her face as she glanced in the rearview mirror at her bestie.

"Neither are you!" Mercy giggled. "Me first!" She fished into her bag until she caught the little box she'd wrapped in silver foil and handed it to her sister.

Hunter shook it and then tore into it. She opened the box and her eyes went huge. "Holy Tyr! They're unbelievably gorgeous! Mag, you shouldn't have. They're way expensive." The moonlight that came in through the car's windows glistened off the moonstone studs that were set in white gold and circled by little diamonds.

"The look on your face was worth every second of the six months of babysitting I had to do to pay for them."

"Seriously? *That's* why you've been so cheap for the past six months?" Em said. "Why didn't you tell me?"

"Because you suck at keeping presents secret!" said the twins together. Then they laughed and, at the same moment, said, "Jinx!"

"I am so good at keeping secrets," Emily grumbled.

"Yeah, you are—as long as they're not about presents," said Mercy. "But don't worry. We love you anyway." She held out her hands to her sister. "Okay, now me!"

"You're super sure I got you something and I have it with me."

"Of course you did and of course you do. It's probably something little that you can fit into that ridiculously small cross-body you carry."

"Oh, please. What's ridiculous is that suitcase you lug with you everywhere." Hunter bent and felt around under the bucket seat in front of her.

"Yeah, but if the zombie apocalypse happens I'm set." Mercy patted the bulging bag at her side.

"Do not tell me that you hid her pressie in my car and *did not tell me about it,*" Emily squeaked.

"Okay, we won't tell you," Hunter and Mercy said together.

"Stop with the creepy twin speak," Emily said, and added, "and I can *so* keep a secret."

"Happy birthday." Hunter handed a narrow box to Mercy. She'd wrapped it with green paper covered in vines.

"Ooooh, the paper is awesome!" Unlike her sister, Mercy carefully peeled every piece of tape off and then smoothed the paper as she freed the box. She opened the lid and gasped. "Hunter! It's perfect!" Mercy caressed the slim stack of squares of vintage lace, then lifted each to study their unique beauty. "Ohmygoddess! I'll make such cool stuff with these!"

"I can't wait to see what you come up with," said Hunter. "Happy birthday. Love you twin."

"Happy birthday, love you, too, twin."

In the rearview mirror Emily smiled at them all the rest of the way home.

Mercy loved everything about the old Victorian home that had housed Goodes since the mid-1800s. It was the last house at the northern most edge of Main Street, backing onto acres and acres of cornfields or, depending on the year, bean fields. This was a corn year and the stalks were already as tall as the twins. Mercy loved it when the mature corn secluded their house and the expansive gardens that filled their five acres, which included a koi pond with a fountain of Athena, their mother's patron goddess, complete with plumed helmet, an owl on her shoulder, and a dolphin beside her spouting water from its mouth. And, of course, in one corner, surrounded by lilacs and framed by a wrought-iron fence covered with wisteria, was the meticulously tended Goode family cemetery.

It was over the top, but the entire Victorian house was gloriously over the top. The majority of the house was butter yellow, with its ornate trim painted highlights of purple, fuchsia, and dark green. The double front doors were the same bull's blood red as the wraparound porch. *Literally* bull's blood red, as their mom liked to remind them. Every time the house had been repainted, actual bull's blood, as well as protective spells, were mixed into the paint.

"There are my birthday girls! And right on time. Was the party fun?" Abigail Goode hugged each daughter in turn as they came inside. Without giving them a chance to respond she hurried on. "You need to get upstairs and change. Quickly. Then meet me in the kitchen and we'll gather the rest of the supplies together for the ritual." Abigail pushed them gently toward the stairs when they didn't move fast enough. "Quickly! Tonight is too important to chance being even a minute late."

The twins sprinted up the winding staircase to their side-by-side rooms. Mercy rushed to her closet. She'd hooked the hanger on which her ceremonial dress hung on the outside of her closed closet door, and she couldn't help taking a moment to reverently run her fingers over the intricate design of vines, flowers, and falcon feathers—one of the goddess Freya's favorite symbols. It had taken Mercy an entire year to finish the embroidering. The cut of the dress was simple—cream-colored hemp jersey flowed long and free from a teardrop neckline. Mercy stroked the material. "Soft as silk, but a lot easier to embroider," she murmured to herself. It was her artistic hand at embroidery that made the dress special and Mercy had meticulously decorated the neckline, sleeves, and the hem of the full skirt with symbols that celebrated the earth and her chosen goddess. She didn't wear an amulet that represented her goddess, like Hunter did her god. Instead Mercy imagined Freya as part of the earth itself, so every flower and tree, even every blade of grass symbolized her goddess.

Mercy hurried out of her clothes and then sighed happily as the dress slid over her head and down her body with the smoothness of water. Quickly, she brushed out her hair, put on big silver hoop earrings she'd saved for this night, dabbed more of the homemade lilac scent she loved so much behind each ear, and then slathered on her favorite pink lip gloss. Mercy blew her reflection a cheeky kiss, hefted her bag over her shoulder, and almost ran into Hunter as she bolted out the door.

"Sheesh, Mag, be careful!" But Hunter's annoyed frown turned into a soft smile. "Wow. I haven't seen it since you finished it."

"Do you like it?" Mercy twirled so that the full skirt of the dress swirled around her long legs.

"Yeah, I really do." Hunter cleared her throat and nervously smoothed her hands down her dress. "What do you think? Too plain?"

Mercy cocked her head and studied her twin. Hunter had chosen a short-sleeved tunic dress that looked like a long T-shirt. The color of the fabric was unusual. It brought to mind newly blooming purple pansies washed with the silver of a full moon. Her legs looked slim and strong—and appealingly cute, especially because she was wearing simple high-top canvas sneakers. The dress had no embellishment, which only served to highlight the T-shaped amulet that was her only jewelry.

Mercy touched Hunter's sleeve gently. "This color is absolutely perfect, H. Seriously. It's exactly like the very center of your amulet."

Hunter's smile was a beam of sunshine. "You really think so?"

Mercy nodded. "Yep. Totally. We look fantastic! Abigail is going to be so happy! Come on." She grabbed her sister's hand and together they raced downstairs to the kitchen. Before they walked in, Mercy pulled Hunter back and whispered, "Wait. Don't you love watching her putter around in the kitchen?"

"Yep. She's beautiful, isn't she?" Hunter said, keeping her voice low.

"Like a goddess," Mercy agreed.

The sisters stood, hand in hand, and watched their mom as she hummed a tune and collected supplies from her expansive pantry, placing each carefully in the basket that never seemed far from her. Mercy used to think her mother was an actual goddess, and then as she got older she understood that she was a mortal who worshipped a goddess, but that didn't diminish her beauty or the magic aura that hovered around her like the scents of cinnamon and spice she cooked with so often.

Abigail Goode had just turned forty-six, but she could easily have passed for a decade younger, especially dressed as she was that night in her favorite ritual garb—a dove gray floor-length silk dress that was as simple as it was flattering. Over her left breast was the only adornment on the dress—an owl that Abigail had painstakingly painted on the silk. Her long, brunette hair was usually pulled back in a cute French knot, with only a few tendrils allowed to escape. But tonight, as every ritual night, it drifted free around her waist—dark and wavy.

Without turning around she shouted, "Girls! We must go!"

"Jeeze, Abigail, you don't need to shout," said Mercy.

Their mom startled and pressed her hand over her heart. "Athena's shield! You're going to give your old mother a heart attack!"

Hunter snorted. "*Old?* You did not just call yourself old."

Mercy shoved a gingersnap cookie in her mouth and around it said, "Abigail, you won't be old until you start wearing a bra."

Their mother looked down at her perky though ample breasts. "Well, then, I'll never be old." When her gaze returned to her girls a smile blossomed across her face. "You two look perfect. Absolutely perfect. Hunter, the dye job on your dress is exquisite, and a wonderful match for Tyr's amulet. Mercy, I was worried your dress would be too plain because it's just an off-white flowy thing, but your embroidery is lovely. I particularly like the addition of your goddess's falcon feathers. Both deities will be well pleased tonight by my magnificent daughters." Then she turned all business. "Mercy, your apple pie has cooled nicely. It's still on the rack there by the window. You'll need to collect it and your candles quickly. Your basket is on the counter." Abigail fired instructions at the girls as she continued to gather items from her spacious pantry. "Hunter, your beer is on ice in the sink. It's going to be so interesting to invoke a god. I've been rereading our ancestors' grimoires and I couldn't find one instance where any of them chose a god. Huh. It's actually surprising that's never happened before."

Hunter picked at her fingernail. "Are you sure it's okay?"

"Sweetheart, as I told you three years ago when you chose Tyr as your deity—it is *your* choice. There is no wrong answer. And today I'll add to that by saying that it's about time a Goode chose a god instead of a goddess. It'll keep things interesting." Abigail paused and brushed a long, thick lock of hair from her face. "Now, stop worrying and get your candles together. And don't forget the opener for the beer bottle." She tapped her foot as she stared into the pantry. "Ah! Matches! That's what I was forgetting." Abigail looked over her shoulder at her daughters. "Go on! We need to leave in the next five minutes to make it to the tree in time. Shoo, my little chickies! Shoo!"

Mercy and Hunter grinned at each other.

"That's what we were waiting for," said Mercy.

Hunter nodded. "Yep, to be called your chickies and shooed."

"Are you making fun of your mother?" Abigail put her fists on her curvy waist and tossed back her thick hair that was artistically streaked with a blaze of silver gray that looked professionally created, but was actually as natural as their mother's sweet smile and brilliant green eyes.

"Us?" Hunter said with mock surprise.

"Perish the thought, Abigail!" Mercy added, clutching her pearls.

"Xena! The girls are making fun of me again," Abigail called.

In a heartbeat the huge Maine coon padded into the kitchen to wind around their mother's legs as she chirped and mewed accusatorily at the twins.

"Okay! Okay! We're getting our stuff together." Mercy backed away like the cat might explode all over them.

"Yeah, call her off! Call her off!" Hunter tried to keep up the pretense of horror, but when Xena plopped her fluffy butt down and began berating them in earnest, she dissolved into giggles.

"I know, they don't always respect their elders properly," Abigail soothed the big cat while she stroked her from her black-tufted ears to the tip of her bushy tail. "Yes, I'm not surprised by that, Xena sweetheart."

As Mercy packed her basket she asked, "What'd she say?"

"Not important," said Abigail, taking a white candle poured into a tall, clear glass from the pantry and adding it to her basket. "What is important is that she told me half the school showed up for your party—which means it was a success. Oh, and it seems one of my daughters is now going steady." Xena and Abigail sent Mercy pointed looks.

"I swear that cat spies on us," muttered Mercy.

"For sure," said Hunter.

"Well?" asked their mother.

"Abigail, it hasn't been called *going steady* for decades. Literally," said Mercy.

"Oh, I don't care about your hip teenage talk. When a boy gives you his class ring you're going steady. Let me see!"

With a grin Mercy lifted the class ring that dangled from its chain. "Kirk gave it to me tonight right before the party."

"Mag!" Her mom used the nickname she'd been shackled with since first grade when Hunter had figured out what her initials, Mercy Anne Goode, spelled out. "That's adorable of Kirk." Abigail studied the ring and then smiled slyly. "Ooooh, what big fingers he has. Which reminds me. There are condoms in the pantry. Be sure some of them make their way into that suitcase you schlep around with you—and also make their way onto Kirk's penis."

"Yes, Abigail, I know."

"Do I need to schedule a gynecological appointment with our na-turopath?"

"No, Abigail." Mercy tried to breathe through the heat spreading across her face as she stoically packed brown and green candles in her basket beside the apple pie.

"Sweetheart, would you like to discuss your clitoris—again?" her mother asked.

Hunter tapped her chin contemplatively. "Yes, Mag, would you?"

"No. Thank you. One clitoris discussion is all I needed."

Her mother sighed. "Well, if you have any questions you know I'm here with answers. Your pleasure is just as important as his. Do *not* for-get that. Oh, and you're welcome for your multiple orgasms. They're familial, you know."

Mercy buried her burning face in her basket. "I do now."

"Thanks, Mom!" Hunter said cheerfully.

"You're most welcome sweetheart," said their mom happily. "Oh, I need to get those quilts. Now, Xena, where did I put them after the Yule ritual?" Chirping nonstop, the Maine coon trotted from the room with Abigail following.

"If you encourage her to talk about my clitoris again I am going to cut off all your hair while you sleep."

Hunter grinned. "But you know how she likes to feel helpful."

"I do *not* need clitoris help!" She almost hissed the words at her sister.

"Mag, if you're *going steady* with Kirk, I'm pretty sure you do."

Abigail hurried back into the kitchen, carrying a slender pile of three vintage quilts—each the perfect size to wrap around their shoulders. "Xena knew where they were. Now, where were we? Did I hear you say you needed help with Kirk?"

Hunter was still grinning, but she came to her sister's rescue. "No, Mom, we were talking about the ritual."

Mercy grasped onto the change in subject like a lifeline. "Yeah, shouldn't we be setting our intention?"

"Oh, yes. Absolutely." Abigail hooked her laden basket in the crook of her arm. "But let's do that as we walk to the tree. Come, girls! Carry your baskets and let's go write another page of Goode history!"

Four

Mercy and Hunter, with Xena padding along somewhere beside them, followed their mother through their backyard and to the little iron gate that opened to a hedgerow that divided two massive cornfields. The family of four slipped through the gate and began walking along the hedgerow. It was late—almost midnight—but the full Pink Moon, named by settlers hundreds of years ago after early blooming wild phlox—made it easy for them to find their way.

"To set our intention let us begin by remembering the past. On July 29th, 1692, our ancestress, Sarah Goode, was convicted of witchcraft and sentenced to hang in Salem. Thankfully, unlike many of those poor, persecuted women, Sarah was, indeed, a powerful witch. Hunter, how did she escape?"

"She bespelled the jail guard so that he fell asleep. Then Sarah's familiar, a cat named Odysseus—" She paused as Xena meowed loudly, causing them all to laugh, before continuing, "brought her the keys to her cell so she and her daughter, Dorothy, could escape."

"Excellent. Mercy, how did Sarah and her daughter find their way to what would become Goodeville?"

Mercy and Hunter knew every word of their history. They also knew how to set their intention for a successful ritual, but they loved telling the story of their ancestress, especially because the telling of it made their mother so happy.

As Mercy answered she spread one arm wide and let her fingertips touch the slick, green edges of the nearby corn leaves that were already damp with dew. "Well, because Sarah had listened to omens of warning sent to her by her goddess, Gaia, she had buried money, clothes, and spellwork things outside town. The night she escaped Sarah made her way to her buried stash and, using a large opal, Gaia illuminated a path for her. So, she, her daughter, and her familiar started walking southwest, following a strong ley line of earth power. Eventually, they joined a wagon train that was happy to have a healer ride with them. The journey was long and dangerous, but Sarah kept heading west, following the ley line, and it kept getting stronger, until it brought her here, to what would eventually become central Illinois."

"Well told, Mercy." Her mother nodded appreciatively. "Sarah Goode stopped here, along with several families she'd become close with during the journey, because Gaia revealed that this was a site where five power-filled ley lines converged. Hunter, why was this beautiful, fertile land unsettled and avoided even by the aboriginal peoples?"

"Because they were freaked out by the monsters that roamed around here, slaughtering anyone who got too close to where the ley lines converged."

Abigail smiled over her shoulder at her youngest daughter. "You are an excellent storyteller, Hunter. Mercy, why were there literal monsters loose here?"

"Because at the apex of each ley line was the entrance to what we describe as a different mythological Underworld, though that never made sense to me."

"Why not?" her mother asked.

"Well, Abigail, if the Underworlds were mythological, the oogly-booglies"—she winked at Hunter—"wouldn't be real. And they definitely were."

"*Are,*" her mom corrected her. "We must never forget that what is on the other side of each of the Underworld gates is all too real."

"Good point, Abigail. It also supports my point about those places not being myths," said Mercy.

"I agree," said her mother. "Hunter, what did Sarah do then?"

"Sarah used her witchy wisdom and figured out how to close each of the entrances with a kind of a gate. Each gate is marked by a tree she planted, and each tree is from the area of the world the oogly-booglies were from," said Hunter.

"Correct," Abigail said. "But never forget that the trees were steeped in magic from their inception. Sarah was a Green Witch." She smiled at Mercy who grinned proudly back at her. "So first Sarah called forth the saplings magically. They were formed from the fertile earth below our feet mixed with her powerful magic. At the Norse gate the sapling that grew from her invocation spell was an apple tree. At the Greek gate an olive tree sprouted. For the Egyptian gate the magic chose a doum palm tree, and for the Japanese gate there appeared a very young, very supple weeping cherry tree. For the final gate, the Hindu one, a banyan tree lifted from the verdant ground. And when she was done calling forth the trees and casting the spell that sealed the gates with them, what did she discover, girls?"

Together the twins said, "That the trees created a giant pentagram!"

"Exactly! So she and the families that had stopped with her founded our town within the pentagram, and, in honor of their beloved healer, named it Goodeville. And every High Feast Day Sarah returned to one of the trees and performed a powerful protection ritual to be sure the gate remained sealed. During the rest of the year, what did she do, Hunter?"

"Exactly what you do, Mom. Sarah tended the trees to be sure they thrived and grew," said Hunter.

"Yes. Then Sarah settled here and worked as a midwife and healer, and she lived a full life to a very old age. She trained her daughter, Dorothy, to take her place after her own body returned to the earth, tasking her and each female from the Goode line that followed with tending to the trees, which close the gateways to the Underworlds beyond. So, as Sarah did all those generations ago, we also do. Our intention for tonight has not changed. We shall use the energy carried through the ley lines in the earth to strengthen the apple tree that guards the Norse gate. As we do that we imagine that the tree *is* a gate, and its strength is what keeps the Underworld gate closed.

"In addition, tonight my beloved daughters will speak aloud the type of witchcraft they have decided to practice in the name of their goddess—and god." Abigail smiled over her shoulder at Hunter. "Ah, and here we are! Right on time."

The hedgerow had ended in a grassy meadow where four fields converged. In the center of the meadow stood a thick-trunk apple tree whose gnarled branches spread like an enormous spiderweb. Some of the boughs were so huge and heavy that Abigail had placed wooden posts with padded Ys beneath them for support. Spring had been unusually warm, and the tree had bloomed early this year, but even though most of the blossoms were already turning into hard little green balls, the air around the tree was still fragrant and sweet.

"Daughters, place your baskets in the center of the pentagram along with your shoes, and then put your offerings at the feet of the gatekeeper."

The apple tree, like each of the other four magical gatekeepers, was positioned on one of the points of a pentagram. The Norse apple tree also happened to be the northernmost gatekeeper—spreading out from it, the other trees formed the rest of the points of a huge pentagram that encased Goodeville.

Before the trees were subtle markers that Sarah, and the generations of witches that had come after her, tended. They symbolized the invisible points of the pentagrams around the individual trees. At the Norse tree the markers were four large rocks, smoothed over by time and the elements. They were meaningless to anyone except Goode witches, who recognized them for what they were—symbols of the points of a pentagram.

Abigail's graceful gesture took in the rocks and the tree. "And why do we use the pentagram as our magical symbol?"

"Because each point symbolizes one of the five elements, which is powerful magic," said Mercy.

"Yeah, and our circle is traced around the points of the pentagram and includes everything inside it," finished Hunter.

"Well done, my beautiful girls. Now, let us begin," said Abigail.

The three women stepped within the pentagram and bared their feet. Then Mercy took the apple pie she'd baked for her goddess from her basket and placed it amidst the roots of the huge tree as Hunter opened her bottle of beer and poured it in a circle over the hard-packed ground. Then they returned to where their mother waited.

"Now we shall set our candles." Abigail's voice had become appropriately solemn as they were about to perform a powerful ritual that guarded all of them, and their cherished town, from unspeakable horrors.

When the girls had their candles in hand, their mother took out a long box of ritual matches and a tall white candle from her basket.

The three of them separated. Mercy went to the right and Hunter to the left, with their mother going forward to the great apple tree. Abigail reached the tree and then turned to watch her daughters place two candles each atop the smooth boulders that marked the other four points of their imagined pentagram. She lifted her candle and struck the match, saying, "First, I set the white candle in its place at the top of the pentagram. White symbolizes spirit. And with it I invoke the presence of my goddess, Athena, whose path I follow on my journey. This lifetime, that path has led me to be a Wise Woman and Kitchen Witch." She lit the white candle and held it before her, as if offering it to the tree.

Mercy loved it when her mom did ritual work. She always looked so powerful and beautiful—and more than a little mysterious when she invoked Athena and opened the sacred pentagram with the spirit candle. Nerves roiled Mercy's stomach. She could hardly believe that the night had finally come when she and her sister were joining their mother in Ritual—just like so many Goodes had done for so, so many generations. The night felt special—different. There was a listening quality to the earth and plants around her that tingled through her body. She wanted to ask Hunter if she felt it, too, and when she looked across the pentagram at her sister she saw that she was gazing up at the full moon with a rapturous expression. *Hunter feels it, too! I know she does.*

Abigail carefully placed the candle in front of the tree between thick fingers of roots. Then she traced the line of the pentagram to where Mercy was standing. She was holding the first of her two candles, which she lifted. Presenting it to her mother she said, "I set the green candle in its place on the pentagram. It symbolizes the path I have chosen to follow and the goddess whose service I am in."

Her mother lit the candle and Mercy set it on top of the rock at her feet before she and Abigail together walked to her second candle, tracing more of the pentagram. Mercy liked the feel of the cool grass against her feet, but as they took their first steps her foot landed on something that was hard enough to make her ankle twist before it squished against her foot, like she'd just stepped on a raw egg that had broken and its goo leaked between her toes. Abigail instantly steadied Mercy by catching her arm while she righted herself.

"Did you hurt your ankle?" Abigail asked.

Mercy looked down. "No, I just slid on something—" She lifted her foot and under it was an immature green apple that had broken open—and was completely filled with worms. "Ugh!" She wiped her foot quickly on the clean grass, shuddering as the worms writhed in the rotten apple meat.

Her mother peered down, and then straightened abruptly. "It's fine. Reset your intention. All is well."

But Mercy noticed that her mother's face had gone so pale that in the moonlight her skin looked like milk.

Abigail continued to the rock that marked the next point of the pentagram. Mercy shook herself mentally and followed her mother. She took several breaths to re-ground herself and then she lifted the candle that waited there and proclaimed, "And I set the brown candle in its place on the pentagram. It symbolizes the path I have chosen to follow and the goddess whose service I am in."

Before Abigail lit the candle she asked, "Speak, daughter, and name your goddess."

"Freya, the great Goddess of Love, Fertility, and Divination."

"And which path will you walk with Freya?"

Mercy's voice was strong and sure. "I am a Green Witch."

Abigail lit the brown candle and bowed her head. "Welcome to The Path, Mercy Anne Goode, Green Witch and daughter of Freya."

Mercy bowed, too, and placed the brown candle on the rock that marked that tip of their pentagram. Then her mother walked through the center of the pentagram to where Hunter stood with the first of her candles across from where Mercy's first candle, the green one, cheerily burned.

Hunter presented a yellow candle to her mother. When she spoke her voice was louder than normal, and Mercy felt a little prickle of anticipation follow the line up her spine.

"I set the yellow candle in its place on the pentagram. It symbolizes the path I have chosen to follow and the god whose service I am in."

Abigail lit the yellow candle, which Hunter placed on the boulder before walking toward Mercy as they completed the final line of their five-pointed star. She picked up the blue candle that waited there and turned to face their mother.

"And I set the blue candle in its place on the pentagram. It symbolizes the path I have chosen to follow and the god whose service I am in."

Just as with Mercy, Abigail spoke the formal words before she lit the candle. "Speak, daughter, and name your god."

"Tyr, the God of the Sky."

"And which path will you walk with Tyr?"

Hunter's voice was strong and sure. "I am a Cosmic Witch."

Abigail lit the blue candle and bowed her head. "Welcome to The Path, Hunter Jayne Goode, Cosmic Witch and daughter of Tyr."

Hunter grinned when she placed the final candle on the rock by her bare feet. She and Mercy exchanged excited looks, and then they focused on their mother, who had returned to the center of the pentagram and the baskets waiting there. She shook out three quilts, made two generations ago by their great grandmother. When the girls joined their mother, Xena padded into the pentagram, purring loudly. The three women, with Abigail's familiar, sat in the center of the pentagram, marked by brightly burning candles, and wrapped the quilts around their shoulders.

From her basket, Abigail took out a stone bowl, carved with the triple moon symbol, and lit a charcoal cube, which she placed in the bowl and then sprinkled a mixture of herbs over. Instantly the smoldering herbs began filling the grassy area with fragrant smoke. She lit a piece of palo santo wood and wafted it over the three of them saying, "Incense and wood are purifiers. They change the energy around us and keep negativity at bay."

The girls used their hands to move the smoke over and around them. Their mother placed the still-smoking stick in the burner with the herbal incense.

"And now we protect ourselves. I want you each to imagine a shield—a great, glowing shield. Close your eyes. Picture it."

Mercy closed her eyes and imagined a huge round shield with a strong apple tree, much like the one in front of her, carved in the middle of it.

"Imagine it strapped to your back, so that nothing may harm you from behind."

Mercy imagined that it wasn't a quilt covering her back, but her shining shield.

"In your mind draw a circle around you, in which you are the center," Abigail continued. "Repeat after me: *This is my space.*"

"This is my space," the girls repeated together.

"*I own this space,*" Abigail intoned.

"I own this space," they said.

"Good. Now we ready ourselves to be vessels through which the energy of the earth will flow and into the gatekeeper, strengthening our tree and keeping the gate to the Norse Underworld closed.

"Breathe with me, deeply, in and out, on a four count."

Their mother led them in several deep, cleansing breaths.

"Clear your mind of thoughts. Then *acknowledge* your feelings, and as you do don't question *why* you're feeling something. Simply breathe in with acceptance of the feeling and on your next breath out, release that feeling."

Mercy cleared her mind and then drew in a deep breath and immediately was filled with nervousness. She didn't try to decipher her nerves. Instead she thought, *hello nerves—I feel you—I acknowledge you—and now I release you!* She let out a long breath and felt the tension between her shoulder blades relax.

With her next breath in Mercy was filled with fear—fear of not being good enough, smart enough, brave enough—or worse, being too self-centered to truly walk Freya's path. Again, she acknowledged—*I get it. Fear is here. That's fine and normal and natural. Fear can be healthy. It reminds me to be smart and brave and selfless instead of selfish. And now I release you, fear.* As she breathed fear out Mercy felt the sick knot in her stomach unravel and calm.

"And we begin. We are vessels, cleansed and protected, ready to be conduits for energy. Remember, we do not keep that energy. We only guide it. Visualize the gate before you, deep within the trunk of this ancient tree who has stood guardian for hundreds of years."

Mercy kept her eyes tightly closed. She knew that Hunter's eyes were open because every Feast Day of their lives until that night they'd practiced the ritual together from *outside* the pentagram while they watched their magical mother harness the energy of the earth and direct it to close the gate. Hunter always kept her eyes open to stare at the tree, but Mercy preferred to imagine the gate in her mind's eye.

"When your image of the gate is set, reach through your bodies down into the earth—find the ley lines there—see them. What color is your ley line, Mercy?"

"Green!" Mercy said, eyes still shut.

"What color is your ley line, Hunter?"

"Deep blue!" Hunter said.

"And mine is silver gray, like the eyes of Athena. Draw your ley line up through your body and push it from the center of your forehead, like a beacon, to shine against the gate hidden within your tree. If the gate seems open at all, it will be closed. If the gate seems weary, it will be strengthened. If the gate seems small, it will grow and grow and grow until it is so powerful that nothing could possibly escape through it."

Mercy imagined that when she breathed in she drew the beam of radiant green light up and into her body—along her spine—to blaze out of her third eye in the center of her forehead.

But nothing happened.

Mercy felt the pulsing power of the ley line, just like she always could. She could even feel it lifting to her, but instead of it filling her body with luminous energy, it was like a garden hose with a kink in it, and only trickles of power sluggishly moved up to her spine and hovered there with a little warmth, like someone pressed their hand to the small of her back.

She squeezed her eyelids more firmly together and focused, concentrating on the energy that was tantalizingly close. Drew a deep breath in as she called to her goddess. *Freya, my goddess, help me. Strengthen me. Allow me to guide the energy of your earth.*

Mercy felt the warmth along her spine expand a little, but there was no infilling of energy—there was no inrush of power. The pulse of the ley line had been replaced with something cold and strange and wrong.

Suddenly Xena hissed and began growling, a guttural, dangerous sound that wasn't even recognizable as coming from the sweet, nosy feline Mercy had known her entire life.

Hunter gasped and cried, "Oh! Tyr! No!"

Mercy opened her eyes. Hunter sat beside her. They faced the tree, while their mother sat cross-legged in front of them with her back to the tree. Beside Abigail, Xena had turned to face the tree as well. The huge cat's back was fully arched and her tufted ears flattened against her skull as she continued to growl menacingly.

The thick trunk of the mighty tree dripped with something disgusting—black and foul and thick. The center of the trunk quivered, like a horse trying to shake off a swarm of biting flies, but this was no horse. A snout pushed through the darkness and took form, melted wax becoming solid as it entered this world. Red eyes broke through the shuddering bark. The thing was huge—all sinew, matted fur, and claws. Its breath came in rapid pants as it pulled its body through the corrupted center of the tree. The fetid stench of it reached Mercy— thick with sulfur and rot. Mercy tasted bile as she gagged in revulsion and fear.

The creature looked directly at them and snarled, gnashing long, pointed teeth.

Five

Abigail surged to her feet. "Run!" she screamed and pushed her daughters back toward the darkness of the open field.

Hunter's feet cemented to the ground. Her mother's shoves only jarred her enough to make her dizzy. This wasn't real. None of it.

Sealskin black liquid gushed from the tree, and spurted around the slick and matted fur of the giant wolf clawing its way into their world. It flashed in and out of focus, unstable as it tried to gain hold in this new realm. Its talons dug trenches in the grass and it bared its teeth and growled, wet nose sniffing the air. This was a nightmare, sixteen years of anxiety spilling out of Hunter's subconscious and raining down on this made-up version of things to come.

Hunter reached out for Mercy. In any nightmare, she could grab hold of her sister and will herself awake. Emptiness met her fingers. Nothing but spring air and the guttural moans of the fanged beast. Hunter whirled around. The breeze tugged at the skirt of Mercy's ivory dress as she followed their mother's instructions and ran. But Mercy wouldn't leave her. That's never how it happened. Not in Hunter's dreams and especially not her nightmares.

Mercy glanced backward and skidded to a halt. "Hunter!" she shrieked and focused her wide-eyed terror past her sister.

This was all too real. Hunter felt the monster behind her. Felt the rank air tighten and heard the otherworldly liquid slosh as the creature spilled into their realm. She couldn't turn around, couldn't force herself to move. This was supposed to be peaceful, magical, the beginning of years and years of happiness and light. What had she done to deserve this?

"Stay back, vile beast!" her mother roared over the steady crackle of the charged night air.

Hunter heard the beast's heavy footsteps crack rotting apples and beat against the earth. She whirled around as her pulse battered her eardrums.

Abigail had gathered the white candle and held it in the air. "Athena, I call to you!" The wolf cowered and its ears pressed back against its wet coat. "Give me strength in battle!" Against the crackling wind Abigail scraped a match. It left behind a trail of sparking orange that ripped through the black sky like a tear in a page and doused the scene in orange light. Magic heard Abigail's cry, but Athena hadn't shown.

The beast's image flickered as its gaze swung from the tree to the flaming arc and back to Abigail. It bared its wet teeth and stalked forward as the Goode witch pressed the flaming match against the candle's wick. She gripped the wax pillar with both hands and held it in front of her. "Athena! I call to you, my goddess, my protector!" The flame shot skyward, illuminating their small space on earth.

The wolf's top lip rippled with a growl as it sprang toward Abigail. It flashed in and out of focus as its giant paw struck out and swatted her aside. She slammed into the ground and crumpled like a rag doll.

Hunter reached out, her cries for her mother strangled by the cords of fear lining her neck. "Get away!" she finally managed as the creature prodded Abigail with his enormous muzzle.

Its ears flicked in her direction. It raised his massive head and blew out a burst of mucus-specked air. Hunter's mouth went dry, her tongue turning to paste behind her teeth. The wolf's lip curled. The magical light painted its teeth a shiny orange as he stepped over Abigail and charged at Hunter.

Mercy's bare feet slapped the earth behind Hunter as she scrambled away. Hunter stumbled over fallen apples. Her arms flailed as her feet slid out from under her and she crashed onto the ground. As the beast lunged forward, Mercy wrapped her arm around Hunter's chest and tucked herself behind her sister. Hunter squeezed her eyelids shut and held up her arms. This was the end for them both. A sob tore from her throat as hot, foul breath blew back the hair that had fallen against her cheeks.

Fangs pierced Hunter's forearm. A deep, searing ache twisted around her lungs and squeezed. Blood oozed hot and wet around sharp teeth as they sunk into her flesh. Mercy's chest shook against Hunter's back as she shouted words Hunter's pulse drowned into a whisper.

Xena was there in an instant. A streak of yowling fur, the cat hurled herself at the beast. Her howls pierced the night as she wrapped herself around the wolf's snout and dug her claws into its leathery muzzle. With a roar that rattled Hunter's bones, the creature released her arm and clamored back. It whipped its head from side to side. With a shriek, Xena flew off its face. She tumbled through the air and struck a tree limb, landing in the grass with a sickly thud.

The wolf stalked back toward Hunter and her sister. Back to finish the job and end the Goode line before the new generation could step into their power.

A screech tore through the night. The wolf cocked his head and turned toward the magical rip burning against the black sky. Hunter squeezed Mercy's hand as the cool spring air turned hot and thick. Another piercing shriek rang out as the gash opened wide. An owl burst through the tear, its feathers the same jack-o'-lantern orange as the otherworldly rip in space. Massive wings beat the air as it dove at the wolf. Blood spurted from the beast's back as the owl's talons ripped its flesh.

The owl circled Hunter and Mercy and let out another scream before landing on the ground beside their mother.

Blood oozed down the wolf's back as it spun to pursue the bird. The owl hopped closer to Abigail, tipped its beak to the sky, and shrieked. A fiery bolt flashed from the tear in the night and struck Abigail's chest. In an instant, her body was aglow in orange flames. The wolf stilled as Abigail rose to her feet and the owl took perch on her shoulder. *"Fenrir!"* Another voice coated Abigail's and a glowing spear flickered to life by her side. *"This realm is not your own!"*

With a growl, Fenrir shook the blood from his coat and stalked toward Abigail, ignoring the twins. Abigail, alight with the fiery and otherworldly powers of her goddess, pressed forward toward the ancient apple tree that grew from the magic of the Norse Underworld.

Mercy pulled Hunter to her feet and clenched Hunter's hand in her own as they crept toward Xena. The cat wound around their ankles, herding them away from their mother and the wolf who'd spilled out of its realm and flickered, unstable, into their own.

Mercy dropped Hunter's hand, scooped up Xena, and ran. This time, Hunter matched her sister's stride. Her lungs burned as she sucked in gulps of magic-charged air.

"I banish you back to your Underworld!" Abigail's voice was thunder. It clapped against Hunter's back and she whirled around in time to see her mother hurl the spear. It caught the wolf's shoulder and knocked it back into the tree. Fenrir's image flickered as it fought to break free. It howled and bucked and clawed the air, but the point of the spear had pierced through the wolf, into the tree's trunk.

Foreboding gnawed at Hunter's stomach. She left Mercy and Xena and charged back to the tree. Air fled her lungs as she slowed to a stop near her mother. She could see it now. The gash in Abigail's temple. The skin hung like wet clothes pinned to a line. Athena fueled her, kept her on her feet, but Hunter's mother was not long for this world.

"Hunter!" Athena's voice shadowed Abigail's, making goose bumps flash across the back of Hunter's neck. "Something's wrong with the gates! Don't wait until Solstice to fix them. Promise me!"

Hunter blinked through a flood of tears. "I promise!"

Abigail looked at the wolf pinned to the apple tree, its form flickering under the promise of death. Then she turned and looked past Hunter to Mercy, who tripped over Xena as the cat struggled to keep the girl at a safe distance. "Take care of your sister," Abigail said. "You'll need each other now, more than ever."

Hunter wailed as Fenrir caught the billowing skirt of Abigail's dress and pulled her to him. The beast tore through Abigail's clothes. Its teeth shredded her back and stained the fabric scarlet.

The owl shrieked as Abigail faced Fenrir and pressed her palms against the beast's matted coat. It lit like dry kindling.

Athena's war cry muted Abigail's screams as flames consumed Hunter's mother and the beast.

Hunter's knees slammed into the earth as the blaze flashed out and the rip in the sky vanished as quickly as it'd come. Tears burned down Hunter's cheeks and blood seeped from her torn forearm. She had been tapped, and now she would simply pour into the earth until her time in this realm was over.

Hunter couldn't make a sound as Xena mewled and circled the charred remains of the woman who'd once brought so much light into the world. Of Fenrir, never fully in this realm, there was not a trace. Mercy threw herself against the tree, which now showed no evidence of their loss. Hunter's chin quivered as she watched her sister slide down the trunk into the grass next to their mother's body.

Maybe they'd all stay in the field at the foot of the apple tree and let the gentle Illinois breeze sweep them away.

Six

Sheriff Dearborn lifted his Chicago Bears travel mug to his lips and blew into the round O cut into the burnt orange lid before he took a drink. Hazelnut. Dearborn's favorite. He smacked his lips, puffed a cooling breath into the navy blue tumbler, and took another sip. Trish had added an extra sugar packet even though she knew he was trying to cut out the sweet stuff.

He set his coffee mug down as he approached Goodeville's last traffic signal. The red light painted the hood of his white-and-gold cruiser a pale Christmas crimson. His thick, calloused fingers drummed against the steering wheel as he waited for the light to turn green. Dearborn had only seen a few cars on his final patrol of the night. The passenger and rear seats had all been full of teenagers who'd rolled down their windows and given the sheriff big, goofy, and if he was being honest, fairly tipsy grins and waves as they passed by. The designated drivers had remained focused on the road, and that's really all he needed to see. The sheriff wasn't in the habit of busting kids for being kids. He'd leave that to their parents.

The light turned green and Dearborn left the vibrant Main Street in his rearview and slipped under the blanket of darkness that covered cornfields and country houses. He took another sip of coffee and craned his neck to peer up at the sky. Clouds had rolled in while he'd been in his office completing the day's paperwork. Another sip. That's when Trish had made his coffee. Sweet, sweet coffee. Sweet, sweet Trish. He reached up to the transceiver attached to the shoulder of his uniform and squeezed the talk button. "Two sugars?"

Trish answered immediately. "I figured it wasn't really cheating if you didn't add the sugar in yourself." The dispatcher's voice rang back clear and smooth as if the new Alexa his nephew had set up for him at home had followed him into his car.

Dearborn fumbled with the buttons on his walkie-talkie. The darned device had always been too small for his hands. "You're too good to me, Trish."

"Don't count your chickens just yet, Sheriff. I just got off the horn with old Earl Thompson. He's been snooping around the field out by Quaker Road. Said he'll meet you out there. He also said—oh dagnabit, I had it right here . . ." Papers rustled as Trish dug through her notes.

Trish's dispatch station was a mess of Post-its, origami farm animals, and photos of her Yorkie, Pepper. Over the years, Dearborn had learned that a good leader doesn't force his team to fit into a certain mold. He allows them to be themselves. He rubbed the burnt orange and navy BE YOU sticker stuck to the center of his steering wheel. He and Matt Nagy couldn't both be wrong.

"If it was a snake, it would've bitten me." Trish's laughter tinkled through the cruiser like wind chimes. "Old Earl said that *'there's a ruckus out there at that old olive tree.'*" She'd lowered her voice and made it tremble with age. "*'Not that I'm surprised. Who plants one olive tree? A twisted, mangled one, no less. Been giving me the heebie-jeebies my whole life.'* All one million years of it." She paused. "I added that last part myself."

Dearborn's barrel chest shook with a chuckle. Trish always made him laugh. "I was hoping to end my shift on time tonight, er"—he glanced down at his watch: 02:36—"this *morning,* but I'm only a couple minutes away. I'll head over and check out the ruckus."

The sheriff flipped on his high beams as he drove deeper into the dark.

"What do you make of them planting just one olive tree all those hundreds of years ago?" Papers continued to rustle as Trish spoke, and Dearborn could picture her folding the small squares into another barnyard animal for her desktop menagerie.

He took another drink and let the sweet hazelnut drift across his taste buds as he considered Trish's question. He had never much thought about it. As a high schooler, he'd go to parties out by the aging olive tree or the lone apple tree on the other side of town or the single cherry or palm that encircle Goodeville. He'd always felt strong and protected while he was out near one of the trees. But get any teenage boy liquored up and he'd be liable to feel like Superman. Now, many years older and much, much wiser, Dearborn felt a bit like one of those lone trees——waiting, guarding, aging.

A flutter of pages. "I think it's pretty neat." Trish clucked. "Adds a bit of flavor none of the other towns have. Not sure that's what the founders were aiming for when they planted them . . ."

"I tend to agree with you, Trish." It wasn't the most honest thing he could've said. Dearborn *tended to agree* with folks a lot more than he actually agreed with them, but sometimes little white lies kept the peace and helped build trust. And a team was nothing without trust.

Sheriff Dearborn's blinker lit up the night air with a Halloween glow as he turned off the main road onto the craterous drive that passed by the ancient olive. The first-aid kit he kept in his passenger seat rattled as the cruiser bounced along the gravel. Dearborn grimaced while he did his best to pass more potholes than he hit. He closed in on Earl's parked shiny red truck as the beams from his headlights bobbed against the olive tree's gnarled trunk like he was a boat at sea and it, a buoy.

He rubbed at the pain sprouting in his neck. His old U of I football injury always acted up whenever he was out on these unpaved roads. He'd have to sit down with the mayor again. Outside city limits needed just as much care as inside.

"I'm not sure why you bother checking up on everything old Earl calls in," Trish said, bringing him back to the matter at hand. "Especially with your neck the way it is. By my count, this is ruckus number thirty-two, and that's just this year. Old Earl might beat last year's Ruckus Record."

The Ruckus Record. Dearborn's clean-shaven cheeks plumped with a grin. That was another thing that cluttered Trish's desk. She'd decorated a small piece of poster board in fancy hand-drawn calligraphy she'd learned in one of the art classes down at the fancy new craft store, Glitter and Glue. After Dearborn returned from checking out the latest call from Earl, he would come back to the precinct and watch Trish light up as she chose which of her many stickers to add to the poster board. It was a small thing, childish even, but it was a thing they shared only with each other.

He pulled behind Earl's pickup and put his car in park. "It'll give us a reason to open up that new pack of stickers you bought. Big, silver disco ball–looking stars, weren't they?"

Trish's laughter made his chest tighten.

"Oh, you caught me." She giggled. "I can't hide anything from your sharp investigative skills. And I just *cannot* stay out of that darned craft store."

Dearborn dug through the first-aid kit for the aspirin and popped a couple before he unbuckled his seat belt and threw open his door. "If Earl's going to beat last year's record, we'll need all the stickers we can get."

He unclipped the flashlight from the belt fastened around his waist and shined the light through the back window of the truck. Empty.

A faint acrid, smoky scent wafted toward him on the crisp night breeze. He took a deep inhale and followed the smell into the grass away from the tree and the truck and the suspected ruckus.

Dearborn winced as he craned his neck to talk into the transceiver. "Someone's been out here smoking—probably kids. I'll take a closer look and make sure they didn't leave any cigarette butts behind. Don't want this whole field going up."

"Ten-four." Trish was silent for a moment before she came back on the radio, her voice light and airy in that hen-like way it got when she came across a juicy bit of town gossip. "You know, old Earl hasn't been the same since Debbie left him for that spin instructor over in Chicago."

Raindrops splatted against Dearborn's back and the grass swayed around his shins. Each burst of wind through the fields brought with it the steady *whoosh* of waves on a coastal shoreline. Dearborn paused and savored the moment before resuming his march through the grass.

"That was back a year or so after the town put in the train," he said as he cast his beam back and forth over the blades' puffy tops. "What was that, five years ago now?"

A whole world of changes had happened on the heels, or maybe *on the tracks* was a more fitting description, of the new commuter train that ran in a loop from Chicago through Joliet, Bloomington, Champaign-Urbana, Rantoul, and Kankakee before bisecting Goodeville. It had saved the town from a fate too many small Midwestern municipalities had succumbed to and brought with it thriving shops and train cars packed with weary city folk desperate for the sappy slow pace of picturesque Goodeville. The commuter train had also brought Trish to Goodeville. Dearborn didn't have one complaint.

Papers rustled as Trish came back over the radio. "Five whole years this August. You know, old Earl was a member of the board that decided to bring the train into Goodeville. Without it, Debbie would be home and you wouldn't have to deal with the old coot calling every other day and sending you out on wild-goose chases. If that's not old Earl's bad luck, I don't know what is."

Dearborn paused and sniffed the air. The scent had died. He took a few steps to the right, back toward Earl's empty truck and the road and the olive tree, and sniffed again. There it was. He wiggled his nose and followed the scent like a basset hound.

"Yeah, poor Earl," he murmured into his walkie-talkie as he left the grass and crossed the road.

"*Poor Earl?* If you don't mind me saying, you should really be thinking, *poor you.*" She sighed. "In as long as I've known you, you've never even come close to finding your Debbie."

Gravel crunched under his boots as he passed through the white cones of light from his high beams. "I don't need a Debbie, Trish. I have you." Through the steady hum of the radio, he could practically hear her plump cheeks flush with heat. He scratched the back of his neck as warmth pricked his own.

Dearborn cleared his throat and pressed the talk button. "I'll check in after I've sussed out the situation. I'm headed right toward the olive tree." Another sniff. "Maybe Earl stumbled onto something real this time."

"He would love that." Trish clucked. "Be safe out there."

The line went quiet as Dearborn headed into the stretch of grass. He wiped the spits of rain from his face and rubbed the tip of his square nose. The closer he got to the tree, the thicker the stench. It bit at his nose and made his eyes water.

"Earl," he called as he swept the beam from his flashlight over the grass. "Where'd you get off to?"

The gravel crunched behind him and he spun around. He squinted through his tear-swirled vision. "Earl?" he hollered once again as he shined his flashlight along his car, Earl's truck, and then the road's shoulder. The white light struck something shiny. The hairs on the back of Dearborn's neck bristled. His mouth went dry as his fingers found his gun holster. His eyes burned and tears and rain and snot leaked down his face as he quickly, expertly closed in on the glinting metal.

Sheriff Dearborn's stomach hollowed as the scene came into view. The buckles of Earl's suspenders twinkled in the flashlight beam like trapped lightning bugs. The old man's fingers threaded through the tall grass as if he laid there, peacefully staring up at the stormy night's sky. Bile burned the back of Dearborn's throat as he shined his light on Earl's face. Blood streaked the man's wrinkled brow and cheeks, and rain pooled in the raw red hollows where his eyes had been.

Hazelnut and sick coated Sheriff Dearborn's tongue and he pressed the back of his hand against his mouth. He was a leader, and with a death like this—a *murder* like this—his town would need him to lead, need him to be strong.

The sheriff leaned into his radio. "Trish, send an ambulance to Quaker Road and wake up Carter. Wake up the coroner. Everyone! We need to—" Dearborn's eyelids slammed shut as the smoky scent intensified.

Footsteps slid across the gravel behind him.

Dearborn unbuckled his holster and drew his sidearm. "Who's out there?" Tears welled and blurred his vision. *"Who's out there?!"*

A shadow crossed his beam of light and grass mashed under heavy feet.

The acrid, burning scent was palpable, stringy sizzles of electricity biting at his eyes and nostrils. Dearborn opened his mouth to bark a command and the snapping jolts surged past his parted lips. His gun and flashlight thumped against the ground as he dropped to his knees and gripped his throat.

"Sheriff, you okay?" Trish called out into the dark and rainy night. "Sheriff?" Her voice tightened with panic. *Frank?!"*

Seven

With each blink, Hunter's lids scraped against her eyes like sandpaper. She was out of tears. She hadn't known that was possible. Not until last night. Or had it been this morning? She shielded her eyes and squinted up at the gray, cloud-filled sky. It had rained sometime in the wee hours of the morning—the only evidence that the world knew it had lost the great soul of Abigail Goode.

The screen door creaked open as Mercy emerged from the house. She shuffled across the porch and clomped down the steps. She let out a sound, somewhere between a moan and a sigh and plopped next to Hunter on the bottom step.

Hunter grimaced as she ran her fingers along the scabbing wounds on her arm. So, she *was* still able to feel.

Mercy set her phone down on the walkway between their feet and rested her head on Hunter's shoulder. Mercy was heavy, a steel anvil where the feather-light young woman had once been. That was one of the strange things about grief. How it turned some into weights and reduced others to the molted skin of the person they'd been.

Hunter rubbed her cheek against Mercy's sable hair. Good thing her sister was there to keep her from blowing away.

Mercy's phone chimed and she plucked it up off the concrete.

Hunter averted her eyes from the screen. She couldn't bear to see any words about her mother. They were too powerful, too permanent.

"Kirk?" Hunter asked as Mercy's thumbs flew across the keyboard. Her sister nodded and her phone chimed again.

"And Emily?"

Another nod.

Hunter twirled the end of her ponytail. "They'll be over soon." It wasn't a question. It didn't need to be. Whenever the sisters needed their friends, they were always there. Hunter's phone buzzed in her pocket. It was Jax. She knew Mercy had told him what happened. Even in mourning, her sister was at the top of the phone tree.

A white-and-gold sheriff's cruiser turned off Main Street and onto their drive. Hunter stood as the car parked and Deputy Carter climbed out of the driver's side and straightened the tan cowboy hat he was never without. Mercy hefted herself off the bottom step and mirrored Hunter as the deputy motioned for Sheriff Dearborn to join him outside of the car.

Deputy Carter's boots squeaked in the wet grass as he and the sheriff approached the twins and the bull's blood red porch that had failed to protect their mother.

The deputy removed his hat and rubbed his thumb against the brim as he blinked down at Hunter and her sister. Emily often mentioned Deputy Chase Carter and how adorable and puppylike he looked with his round gray eyes and his lips locked in a perpetual half smile. But there was nothing to smile about today. Every bit of Deputy Carter's puppylike appeal had washed away with the rain. "Girls, I am so terribly sorry. We all loved your mother." He paused before he cleared his throat and nudged the sheriff with his elbow.

The sheriff grunted and removed his sunglasses. "Yes, your mother.

We loved her. She was a, uh, a woman." Dearborn's brown eyes scraped against Hunter and the corner of his mouth twitched. "A now deceased woman."

The deputy let out a strained barking cough as he settled his hat against his closely cropped hair. "I hate to do this, but we have to go through the events one final time before we close up Abigail's file." He removed a pen and a small notepad from his chest pocket and flipped through a few pages before coming to the right one. "Mercy, you're the one who called 911."

Mercy's hair slipped from her shoulders as she nodded. She pushed it back behind her ear and mouthed a word, but no sound came out. She hadn't spoken since they'd gotten home. There weren't words to describe what they each felt. And if there had been, Hunter wouldn't have wanted to hear them.

Carter's Adam's apple bobbed with a tight swallow. "I'm sorry to ask you to go back through this." He tapped the point of his pen against the pad.

Hunter twined her fingers around Mercy's. They were stronger together, and Hunter needed strength now more than ever.

"The three of you were out picnicking." He glanced back down at his notes. "Is that right?"

"That's right." Hunter and her sister spoke in unison.

Hunter ignored the sheriff, who shifted restlessly in her periphery, and spoke directly to Deputy Carter. "Midnight picnics are a birthday tradition. We do them every year with Mom."

A tear rolled down Mercy's pale cheek and she let out a broken sob. "We *did* them every year."

Hunter squeezed her sister's hand. She'd be strong enough for both of them. "That's why we had the candles and incense . . . They were part of the celebration." Goose bumps peaked along her arms and she shivered. That wolf had assured that the Goode sisters would never have a true celebration ever again.

The deputy's brow creased as he scribbled something onto the paper. "Those were the same candles that started the fire? The blaze that—"

Mercy's sob cracked the space between them. "She's dead!"

Hunter tensed as she steadied the sinking weight of her sister. Mercy wasn't built for grief or trauma. Until now, those had always been Hunter's burden.

The sheriff fogged his glasses, wiped the lenses with the end of his untucked shirt, and fogged them again. "She won't have died in vain if you get money out of the whole debacle." He peered up at the clouds through his lenses before sliding the glasses onto his broad nose. "You could sue. That's what people do, isn't it?"

Hunter's stomach knotted as she stared at her reflection in Sheriff Dearborn's mirrored aviators. She'd never wished for the kind of evil dark magic so many people outside of Goodeville believed was part of the Practice. But she wished for it now. Her pendant heated against her chest. It didn't matter that the sheriff was wrong about how her mother met her end. Hunter wished she could call down the cosmos and send an entire galaxy of stars ripping through him. She didn't want money. She wanted her mom.

Deputy Carter clapped the senior officer on the back. "You'll have to excuse the sheriff. He's been up a long time. Everything's got him a little rattled."

The sheriff slid his glasses to the end of his nose. "You'd be rattled if you'd seen what I saw. That dead man out there—old man Thompson—with no eyes." With his middle and pointer fingers he mimed stabbing his eyeballs.

Hunter tightened her grip on Mercy's hand as the sheriff wiggled the imaginary eyes in front of them.

"Ripped right out of his head and then, poof, disappeared." He threw up his hand. "Swallowed up by who knows what."

With a strangled laugh, Deputy Carter tugged on the tip of his hat. "As I said, he's shaken up by the scene that happened last night out off Quaker Road by the old olive tree."

"Not *at* the olive tree. The tree had nothing to do with it!" Sheriff Dearborn swiped at the beads of sweat popping along his brow. "You girls got anything to drink?"

Hunter released Mercy's hand. "I'll get you a glass."

Deputy Carter's puppy-dog face was firmly affixed as he mouthed an apology in Hunter's direction. She couldn't even muster the ghost of a polite smile in return as she leaned into her sister and whispered, "You'll be okay." It wasn't a question. It was a reminder.

The deputy's words caught Hunter as she shakily headed up the steps toward the front door. "We, uh, we also have to discuss the matter of guardianship." He took a breath. "You girls don't happen to have any family close by, do you?"

Hunter couldn't look back at her sister who remained silent as Deputy Carter continued softly prodding the details of their family tree.

Xena meowed and slapped the screen door with her furry paw, refocusing Hunter's attention.

"You want out?" Hunter asked as she opened the door. The Maine coon circled Hunter's ankles and pressed her long body against Hunter's calves, forcing her inside. Hunter closed the screen and stumbled in. She caught herself on the bannister and crouched down near the foot of the staircase that led up to Mercy's and her rooms.

Hunter combed her fingers through Xena's fur. "I know it's hard. I miss her, too." The tears came then. Their well replenished, they rushed from her eyes like strands of pearls.

Xena chittered and wove figure eights between Hunter's feet.

"And now we'll have to leave our home." Hunter sagged onto the wood floor and hugged her knees against her chest. "I wish Mom was here." She pressed her swollen lids against her knees and wept onto her ceremony dress. The dress that she'd hand dyed and chosen to wear to begin her new life, her happier life.

Xena yowled and pressed her massive front paws against Hunter's shins. With a sniffle, Hunter raised her head and rested her chin on her damp knees. Xena's whiskers dusted Hunter's cheeks as the cat leaned in. Only a sliver of Xena's amber irises encircled her dilated pupils as she let out a string of clipped meows and sneezed right in Hunter's face.

"Gah, Xena . . ." Hunter grumbled as she blindly wiped her face with the collar of her dress.

"Sorry about that. The incantation always makes me sneeze."

Hunter dropped her dress and stared at the spot in front of her where the cat had been. Now there were feet—human feet attached to human legs attached to a human torso. Hunter scrambled backward and winced when her back struck the staircase.

The naked woman before her brushed her hand through her mane of wild black, white, and brown–streaked hair. "It's like you've never seen a cat before."

"Xena?"

The woman ran her clawlike nails down her bare form and smiled. "In the flesh."

Eight

The silence stretched to an unending, uncomfortable frozen length after Hunter went inside. Usually, in a situation where adults were hanging around looking lost and awkward Mercy would've easily alleviated the tension by engaging both officers in cheerful conversation.

But Mercy did not care about their awkwardness and she didn't think she'd ever be cheerful again.

So the silence continued.

"Um, Mercy? It is Mercy and not Hunter, right?"

Mercy looked up from her phone to meet the deputy's gaze. She cleared her throat and started to say yes, but decided nodding would be fine.

"Okay, well, Mercy—as I was asking your sister, do you have family close or—"

"Thirsty!" the sheriff interrupted. "Really need that drink." He cleared his throat several times and wiped his mouth on the back of his tan sleeve. Mercy cringed at the white crusty crap that rained from the creases of his lips.

Anger bubbled strong in Mercy's chest and the words that had been dammed within her broke loose. "Sorry, but we don't have the fresh-squeezed lemonade we'd usually offer you—with a plate of cookies or a sweet little spell or two. You see, our *mom,* the Kitchen Witch every-one loved, *died.* Horribly. Last night. We're a little off our social game at the moment. But, hey, come on in. Hunter's probably curled up in a fetal position in the kitchen crying. I'm sure she won't mind being rushed by someone who is—*gasp!*—thirsty."

Mercy brushed off the butt of her dress and turned to stomp up the stairs. Anger felt good—better than despair. Better than grief that was a chasm so deep her words got lost in it. She glanced back over her shoulder from the wide double doors. The sheriff was already follow-ing her, but the deputy was shifting from foot to foot, picking at the brim of his hat.

"You gonna stay out here?" Mercy shot the words at him. Now that she'd found them again they seemed to be firing out of her.

"Well. Um. No. Ma'am. I'll come in and—"

She didn't wait for the rest of his annoying and predictable reply. She marched into the house *not* holding the door open behind her—and ran smack into a tall woman about her mom's age who was wear-ing Abigail's fluffy flowered bathrobe. Her brown, black, and white hair was thick and fell in a mass down her back. Her unusual amber eyes narrowed.

"Excuse you, Mercy!" The woman moved back gracefully instead of staggering.

"What the bloody hell—"

"Sheriff! Deputy! Sorry it took me so long." Hunter rushed from the kitchen carrying two beading glasses of iced tea. "I was distracted by our Aunt Xena."

"Our who?" Mercy felt like her head was going to explode.

Hunter stared into her eyes giving Mercy the *look.* The one the twins had been sharing since they could formulate complete sen-tences. The *look* meant *just go with it and ask questions later.*

"Aunt Xena," Hunter said briskly, pushing past Mercy and the stranger to hand the two men the tea. "You were asleep when she arrived a few hours ago. I thought I told you she was here. So much has happened." Hunter rubbed her temples and winced like she had a headache before continuing. "Sheriff, Deputy, would you like to sit?" She gestured to the couch.

The sheriff was gulping the tea so the deputy said, "No. Thank you. We won't stay long. We know you have a lot of plans to make. So, um, Xena? You came to take guardianship of the girls?"

With sinuous grace Xena made her way to the empty couch and perched on the arm, carefully covering her bare legs with the bathrobe. With the back of her hand she smoothed her hair before she spoke. "Yes. Of course. No one else is suitable to be guardian of our girls."

Mercy stared at the woman—at the multicolored riot of hair and those distinctive amber eyes—and her stomach flip-flopped.

The deputy wrote a note in his little book. "I didn't realize Abigail had a sister."

"Oh, she didn't," Hunter said quickly. "Xena is really Mom's second cousin from back East. It's just that we've always called her auntie."

"Okay. Got it. And you're planning on remaining here, in Goode-ville, with the girls?" asked the deputy.

"I will always be here for the Goode girls," said Xena. She looked at her hand and frowned before licking a speck of something off one of her long, sharp fingernails.

"We should go," said the sheriff as he handed Hunter his empty glass. "Lots to do with this murder happening and all . . ."

Deputy Carter wiped his brow with his sleeve. "Girls, we're here if you need us. And, again, please let me offer my deepest condolences on the loss of your mother. She was a wonderful woman." He placed his untouched glass of tea on the coffee table, nodded respectfully to the girls and Xena, and then followed the sheriff, who was already on the porch, out the door.

Mercy put her hands on her hips and faced the woman balancing delicately on the arm of the couch. "Who. Is. This?"

"Well, believe it or not it's—"

"Mercy Anne Goode, you've known me since that stormy night you were born three minutes before your sister. Now, I know you're not the Kitchen Witch your mother was, but could you be a darling and brew me a large cup of Abigail's analgesic tea with a heavy dose of honey? I'm terribly sore from what that horrid Fenrir did to me last night." She had to pause then and press her hand to her bow-shaped lips to stifle a sob before she continued in a broken whisper. "I do miss my sweet Abigail so very, very much."

Mercy walked over to stand directly in front of Xena. She stared into her eyes and then slowly reached out to touch her voluminous hair. "Ohmygoddess, Xena?"

"Oh, by Bast's spectacular nipples! Of course it's me. I know you aren't stupid, so I shall blame your shock on grief."

Mercy looked at Hunter. "How?"

Hunter shrugged. "Not sure, but the incantation made her sneeze all over me."

"Did you know she was a person inside a cat suit?"

"Oh, please! *I am a cat.* More specifically, I am a familiar who has been attached to the Goode family for generations. It is accurate to say that currently I am a cat wearing a person suit." She licked the back of her hand and brushed it through her spectacularly messy hair.

"I need to sit down." Mercy fell heavily onto the couch.

"Oh, no no no." Lithely, Xena stood, grabbed Mercy's wrist, and propelled her toward the kitchen with Hunter following closely. "That beast bruised me badly. First, I need healing tea. And while I'm stuck wearing this human skin I might as well eat some of the cannabis truffles your mother keeps in the freezer." When the girls stared at her without speaking she added, "What? They're medicinal. And then we need to make plans. There is much you girls must do."

Numbly, Mercy disappeared into Abigail's deep pantry, easily finding the clearly marked pain relief tea. She paused there for a moment and breathed in the scent of her mother, squeezing her eyes shut tightly to keep the tears from escaping down her cheeks. *Just do one thing at a time. Get through one moment and then the next. It will get easier—not better—but easier. It has to.*

She emerged from the pantry to find Hunter sitting at the bar staring at Xena, who was sitting *on* the bar—her long bare legs swinging over the side as she inspected her fingernails.

"Did Abigail know you could change form like this?" Mercy blurted as she filled her mother's fancy electric teapot and pressed the button to heat water for herbal tea.

"Yes, of course. My Abigail knew everything. She was a splendid witch."

Mercy felt as if she were unraveling inside. She drew a deep breath to steady herself as she held the old wood honey dipper over a mug and dripped thick golden liquid into it. She was trying to sort through her many questions when Hunter found the one that touched them all the deepest.

"Then Mom knew that you'd be here to take care of us—to be sure we wouldn't have to leave our home. She—she died knowing we'd be okay." Hunter choked out the last of the words and wiped her cheeks quickly.

Xena leaned forward and gently stroked Hunter's dark ponytail. "Yes, kitten. Abigail would never have wished to leave her girls, but last night when she realized she had to sacrifice herself to save you—to save us all—she died in peace and must have gone to the arms of Athena knowing I would watch over both of you and help you with what is to come." She brushed a tear from her own cheek. "My Abigail was a fierce protectoress."

The electric pot chimed at the same moment the front doorbell rang, making the three of them jump. Xena sniffed the air.

"It's the boy. The one whose scent was all over Mercy last night."

"Kirk! I'll, um—"

Hunter got up and took the teapot from her. "Let him in. I'll get Xena her tea."

Xena slid sinuously from the countertop. "Emily and Jax shall be here soon. We will greet them, accept their condolences, and then be rid of them. Your mother's last words told you what you must do; you have trees to check on and no time to waste in tending them."

Mercy and Hunter stared at her.

"But our friends—" Hunter began.

She fluttered her sharp-tipped fingers about dismissively. "Are not as important as the trees. As the adult in the household I shall tell them—"

"Xena, they can't know you're a cat," said Mercy.

"Seriously," agreed Hunter.

"Of course not!" Xena scoffed, batting her hands at them. "I am your auntie."

The front door echoed with vigorous knocking. "We have no choice," Mercy told Hunter, and she hurried from the kitchen. Her body felt strange—numb and ultrasensitive at the same time. If she didn't have to answer the door—to talk to people—she would just sit. And stare. And wish with everything inside her that she could go back twenty-four hours and wrap her arms around her mom and never let her go.

She opened the door to see her quarterback boyfriend, hair wet and disheveled, like he'd just gotten out of the shower, fist raised to knock again.

"Oh, babe! Come here." Kirk moved into the house and lifted her up in a hug. Mercy pressed her face to his chest and closed her eyes, hoping the scent and feel of him would erase the rest of the world, if only for a few beats of her broken heart. Then his arms unwrapped from around her and he stepped forward—toward Hunter, who was just coming into the living room. "Hunter, I don't know what else to say except I am so sorry." He scooped Mercy's twin into a gentle hug and patted her back. "Really. I'm here for you—for both of you. Anything. Anything at all I can do I will."

"Boy, you embrace the wrong twin."

Kirk released Hunter and took a step back as Xena, carrying a steaming mug of tea and a truffle, slunk past him and into the living room, where she resumed her perch on the arm of the couch.

"I—I know," he stammered. "I was just telling Hunter sorry, too. Who are you?"

Mercy took Kirk's arm and led him to the far end of the couch—away from Xena—as she said, "This is our Aunt Xena—from the East Coast." She sat beside him and Kirk put his arm around her, pulling her comfortingly close to him.

Hunter nodded and sat in one of the several chairs adjacent to the couch in their big, comfortable living room where everything faced an enormous fireplace framed by a mantel ornately carved with triple moons. "We called Aunt Xena last night and she caught the red-eye to Chicago. She just got here."

Kirk's shoulders sagged. "So, you're moving to the East Coast?" There was no way Hunter, or anyone, could miss the genuine distress on his face.

"No!" the three women said together.

There were two quick knocks on the door and then it burst open as Emily and Jax spilled into the room.

"Ohmygod! I just—I just can't. I can't!" Emily flew across the room and collapsed on the couch on the other side of Mercy as she took her best friend's hand. Her eyes were puffy and red and mascara was smeared down her tearstained cheeks. "What can I do? How can I help?"

Mercy clung to her hand. "You being here helps."

Jax went to Hunter and pulled her up out of the chair. Wordlessly, he took her place and then cradled her on his lap so that her head rested on his shoulder, childlike. His voice was gravelly and his eyes bright with unshed tears. "I don't understand. What happened?"

Mercy forced herself to sit up straight. She wiped her face on her shoulder. Kirk held one of her hands and Emily the other. She tried to pull strength from them—tried to form the right words. *What was it she and Hunter had decided to tell everyone?* Her anger at the sheriff's callousness and then the shock about Xena turning into a person had moved her forward earlier and allowed her to think normally, but it had drained away the second Kirk pulled her into his arms. Now her brain felt wrong—like she was trying to think through mud.

"There was a fire. Dear Abigail got the girls to safety, but it caught her and killed her."

Everyone turned to face Xena.

"Hello," said the human cat. "Emily and Jax, it is lovely to formally meet you." She looked down her nose briefly at Kirk. "I am the twins' Aunt Xena."

Kirk peered up at Xena, his brow furrowed. "You mean like their cat?"

"Yes. Exactly like their lovely feline."

"Abigail has a sister?" asked Jax.

Hunter slid off his lap and moved to the thick arm of the chair, keeping his hand in hers. "No, Xena is Mom's cousin. We've mentioned her before."

"Sorry, I didn't remember." Jax nodded at Xena. "It's nice to meet you, Ms. . . ."

"Call me Auntie or simply Xena."

"Oh, wait. Are you who Abigail used to visit on her trips back to Salem?" Emily asked.

"Yes," the three women lied together.

"I will be staying here—in Goodeville—with our girls," said Xena. She finished the truffle and then began delicately licking her fingers clean.

"So, that means you won't have to leave?" Kirk asked, as Emily wiped a tear from her cheek.

"We're not going anywhere," said Hunter. "Mom would never have wanted that."

Xena nodded, causing her mane of hair to bob around her shoulders. "Goode women belong here." She stood, put the half-empty mug of tea on the end table, and then stretched languidly, arching her back and lifting her hands high over her head like she was in yoga class saluting the sun. Then she shook herself, smoothed her hair with the back of her hands, and finally faced the staring group. "Now, kittens, you must leave. You may return later—perhaps tonight. The girls will use the phone devices to tell you when it is a more appropriate time to visit."

Jax, Emily, and Kirk looked from Xena to the twins, who shrugged and nodded.

"Uh, okay. We understand," said Kirk.

Emily spoke slowly. "But Dad told me to tell you that he would help you take care of, you know, *things* for Abigail." She paused and had to press one of her hands to her chest and blink rapidly. Her other hand squeezed Mercy's like a vise grip.

"Thanks, Em," said Mercy. "Hunter and I will come over. Later. Tell your dad that, 'kay?"

"Text us when he's ready," Hunter said.

Emily nodded, biting her bottom lip. "Yeah, of course." Then she wrapped her arms around Mercy and whispered, "I just don't know what else to do."

"I know, Em. Me, too. Me, too," she murmured.

Emily stood, wiping her face again with her sleeve. "I painted a special sumi-e to honor your mom." She reached into the Kate Spade glitter clutch slung over her shoulder on its long, metal-linked strap and pulled out an original watercolor the size of a postcard. It was a beautiful silver-gray owl in flight with the full moon over its wing. "I know how much Abigail loved owls."

Mercy took the painting and through tears looked up at her friend, who was a talented young artist. "Abigail would appreciate that. She loves—um, I mean *loved* your work." Mercy paused, her voice hitching on a sob. "It's so hard to talk about her in the past tense. I just—" Her words stopped then, dammed again by unimaginable grief. With a shaking hand she put the owl on the coffee table, propping it up against one of Abigail's many statuettes of Athena so that it seemed to soar.

"Oh, babe. Come here." Kirk slid his arm around her and pulled her against him.

Jax stood, still holding Hunter's hand. "My parents wanted me to tell you that they're here for you. Mom's already cooking you one of her famous casseroles—but vegetarian because I reminded her you don't eat meat. She said, *'Abigail's daughters are not going to have to worry about food,'* and then got on the phone and started calling the other moms from church."

"I will be here and will accept the offerings for the girls so that they may grieve," said Xena as she gestured at the door.

"Thanks, Jax." Hunter spoke softly, like it hurt to talk.

"And now you must go," said Xena.

Kirk stood and helped Mercy to her feet. With his arm wrapped around her, they followed Jax and Hunter and Emily to the door.

"Em, we'll see you a little later," said Mercy. She stepped out of Kirk's arm to embrace her friend again.

Emily sniffed and nodded. "'Kay. See ya. Text if you need me before then. I'll be here super fast." She hugged Hunter quickly and then went out the door.

Jax squeezed Hunter's hand. "Same with me. I'm here. So are my parents. Whatever you need. Whenever."

Hunter nodded and wiped at her face as he joined Emily who was walking slowly, dejectedly, down the sidewalk to where they'd parked their cars.

"Are you sure you want me to leave?" Kirk asked, pulling her close to him again.

"Yes," said Xena.

Mercy nodded against his chest. "I'll text you later."

He kissed her softly before turning to Hunter. "Anything you need—either of you. Just tell me. Promise?"

Hunter nodded. "Thanks, Kirk. We appreciate it."

Kirk went out the door, but paused and turned back, opening his mouth to say something. Xena slickly stepped in front of Mercy, lifted one arched eyebrow, and hissed.

Kirk took a few steps back. "Oh, um, shit! Sorry."

"As you should be, boy. It is only polite that when one is asked to depart—one *goes.*" Xena closed the door firmly. "Now." She turned to the girls, smoothing her hair with the back of her hand. "Which tree will you visit first?" But before they could respond a moth fluttered from the door, up the stairs, and past Xena who, with catlike reflexes stalked after it.

Mercy met Hunter's gaze. "It's weird."

For a moment it looked like Hunter might almost smile. "Sadly, I think *Aunt* Xena is one of the least weird things we're going to have to deal with."

Mercy felt her shoulders slump. "So, the trees?"

Hunter nodded. "The trees. Didn't the sheriff say he found old man Thompson's body not too far from the olive tree?"

"Yeah, I think so."

"Then we might as well start there," said Hunter firmly.

Mercy concentrated, trying to sift her thoughts through the fog of grief that blanketed her mind. "You—you don't think Mr. Thompson's death had anything to do with the tree, do you?"

"Mag, I don't know. That's part of what we have to figure out." She moved closer to her sister and forced Mercy to meet her gaze. "I need you to try to pull yourself together. If the gates are messed up we have got to figure out how to fix them—and I can't do that by myself."

Mercy struggled to make her mind work. "Okay. I'll help. Promise."

"So, you agree that we should check out the Greek tree first?"

Mercy fought against gravity to lift one shoulder. "Sure. Whatever you and Xena think is best. I'll wait down here while you get dressed."

Her legs gave out and she sat on the couch, staring at the cold fire-place.

Hunter put her hand on her twin's shoulder. "I'll be down in a sec and I'll bring you a change of clothes, too."

Words stopped coming again, so Mercy nodded wearily as she picked listlessly at the embroidery that decorated her grass-stained, torn dress and continued to stare at the ashes of what used to be a warm, brightly burning hearth fire.

Nine

I think I better drive," said Hunter as she studied her sister.
Mercy shrugged. "Okay with me."

"Girls, remember, what you do today is gather information. Study the trees. Bring back details about everything—how they look, smell, and feel—sense the space around them. Reach out with your minds and your hearts, as well as your senses. We need details so that we can accurately consult the grimoires for what must be done next." Xena had changed into a pair of their mom's jeans and her sweatshirt that said KALE in bold letters across the breast. The cat person had hastily grabbed the clothes from Abigail's room while Hunter and Mercy dressed. They still smelled vaguely of cinnamon and spice. Mercy had to force herself not to hug Xena and breathe in deeply. "Do you understand?"

Hunter nodded. "Yeah, we've got it. Right, Mag?"

Mercy was staring at the fireplace wishing she'd had the energy to build a fire. Maybe it would chase away the cold that had settled deep in her soul.

"Mercy, did you hear me?"

She blinked and looked up at her sister and Xena. "Sorry. What?"

"I was telling Xena we understand what we have to do at the trees."

"Yeah that. We'll check them out."

"Good," Xena said, though she sent Mercy a dubious, slit-eyed look. "Be careful. Do not let people see you. Neither of you have car papers yet."

"You mean a license," said Hunter.

"Yes. As I said, car papers. Girls, be wise. And safe. And do not be gone long. Are you sure I shouldn't go with you?"

"No, stay here," said Hunter. "People are going to start bringing by food. They should see you so they know we're not alone. An adult will keep them from being too nosy."

"You are correct, of course. I will reassure the townsfolk. I shall also bring out the grimoires and have them ready for when you return. Now, do you have any questions?" Xena licked her finger and then smoothed back a section of Hunter's hair that had escaped from her ponytail.

"Eww, Xena. Stop. No, we've got it. Really. Right, Mercy?"

Mercy managed to nod. Even though she felt almost too heavy to move she followed Hunter to the garage and climbed into the passenger side of her mom's silver Camry. The key fob was in the cup holder where Abigail always left it, and for a moment the twins just sat. Hunter's hands rested on the steering wheel—Mercy's were lifeless in her lap.

Hunter leaned forward and pressed her forehead against the steering wheel. "It smells like Mom." Her voice was strangled.

"Everything does." Mercy wiped a hand across her face, which felt numb again. Actually her life felt numb, wrong—so drastically altered that it was unrecognizable. She tilted her head and looked at her sister. "H, I don't think I can do this."

Hunter lifted her head and wiped almost violently at her damp cheeks. Then she took her sister's hand and squeezed it—hard. "I know, but you have to—*we* have to."

"Do we?"

"Of course we do. We have to make sure the trees are okay and the gates are closed. It's what Mom wanted. It's what she'd want if she were still here. That's important, Mag. More important than how sad we are."

"Okay. I know you're right. Sorry. I'll try harder to get it together." Hunter squeezed her hand again before she let it loose. It flopped down on the console that separated the front bucket seats before Mercy put it lifelessly back in her lap. She blinked fast. First, to try to keep more tears from spilling out and, second, because if she closed her eyes for even a moment more she might never open them. The truth was all Mercy wanted to do was close her eyes and sleep and sleep and sleep—and hope when she woke, *if* she woke, everything that had happened since the creature had broken through the Norse gate would be a nightmare from which she'd finally awakened.

Hunter backed the car out of the garage, but instead of turning left to take Main Street through the heart of Goodeville, she turned right, heading for the one-lane country roads that snaked around the fields that surrounded the town—roads the twins knew as well as they knew their own names.

They drove in silence. Mercy stared out the open window. It was one of those spring days in Illinois where the sun seemed to highlight every tree's bright emerald leaves like they were dressed in jewels. Everything *looked* normal, just as it had yesterday before her life had stopped, but today everything *felt* wrong. The trees that used to call to her were mute. She couldn't even hear them breathe, something she'd been able to sense since she was in kindergarten. As Hunter followed the curvy blacktop from town and snaked through the verdant fields that made up the country surrounding Goodeville, Mercy realized she also couldn't hear the whispers the corn made as the breeze rustled through it, or the chattering of the soy plants, their pods heavy with growing beans. She heard nothing. She felt nothing—nothing at all except exhaustion and grief—not even when her sister slowed as they neared the section of brilliant green fields that framed the mighty olive tree. So, Mercy stared and let her mind be completely empty like her heart and the unimaginable future.

"Oh, crap. Is that a cop car?"

Mercy forced her gaze to focus. "It looks like the sheriff's car *and* a cop car. And I think I see yellow caution tape, too."

"Roll your window up! I can't turn around. It'd be too obvious. If someone recognizes Mom's car, let's hope they think Xena's driving."

Mercy kept her face pointed forward as they drove past, but glanced to the side. "Yeah, there's that yellow crime scene tape and I think I saw the outline of a body."

Hunter shivered. "No way we can check out the tree with the sheriff here. We'll have to come back." At the next stop sign Hunter turned to her sister. "I can cut across town super fast and swing by the Hindu tree. It's on the way home. Want to go there?"

Mercy lifted a shoulder. "Yeah, okay."

Hunter sighed, but didn't comment. Instead she took a right, crossed Main Street, and wove through a quiet neighborhood and past the high school as they silently made their way to the tree that guarded the gate to the Hindu Underworld.

"I'm gonna pull into the easement so the car can't be seen from the road," Hunter said as she braked and turned off the road and onto a grassy area that was flanked by a wall of willows on one side and a bean field on the other. Mercy jumped and rubbed a hand over her face as she realized she'd almost fallen asleep. Hunter put the car in park and touched her sister's arm. "Hey, are you okay?"

It was difficult to summon enough energy to turn her head to look at her twin, but slowly Mercy did. "No," she made herself speak. "I am not okay."

"I know, Mag. Me, either. But let's get this done—for Mom. Maybe we won't find anything wrong at all. Maybe it was just the Norse tree that was messed up, and Mom fixed it, so we won't have to do anything until Solstice. But I can't do this alone. I need you."

Mercy forced herself to sit up straighter. She nodded. "I'm with you, H. Like always. We can do this." The words sounded right, but felt wrong—like everything else.

"Let's take the deer path. The one that winds away from the road and runs along the creek. I can't deal with talking to anyone right now and there's no way we can be seen from the road if we go that way." Hunter pointed to a slim ribbon of a path that led from the cleared easement area through a wall of gently swaying weeping willows.

Their joined hands anchored each other as the twins followed the path that would lead to the point of the pentagram where generations ago Sarah Goode had conjured a banyan tree to guard the gate to the Underworld of the ancient Hindus.

Sugar Creek was only a few yards to their right. The scent and sound of it drifted through the tendrils of the willows. Usually Mercy would have inhaled the rich smell of the crystal water passing over rocks and soaked in the music it made as it cascaded toward Goode Lake, but that day she walked in a bubble of grief that was so thick it didn't allow the world to touch her. She would've stopped and slumped to the ground, unmovable, had her sister's hand not propelled her forward, so when Hunter abruptly halted, Mercy stumbled and did almost fall.

"There it is. I've always thought it's the coolest looking of all of them." Hunter jerked her chin at the enormous tree that filled the area between the tall bank of the creek and the bean field that stretched up a gradual incline to meet the blacktop road. "It looks fine from here, don't you think?"

Mercy wanted to say that she was having a problem thinking about anything except their mom, but Hunter was counting on her—and she tried to never let Hunter down. She cleared her throat and swallowed the dryness in her mouth. "It seems normal."

"Right? Maybe everything *will* be okay. Let's get closer."

Hunter dropped her hand and Mercy followed directly behind her as she left the little path. No one was in sight. Mercy thought even the birdsong was subdued. They approached the enormous tree that was so out of place in the American Midwest, and could never have existed—let alone thrived—without the magic of generations of Goode witches. The trunk of the tree was really strange looking. From a distance it appeared to be one big, thick base, but closer it became clear that it was actually a whole bunch of smaller trunks butted right up against each other, like the banyan was trying to be its own forest. Vines dripped from the mushroom-shaped green canopy. Even through her grief Mercy acknowledged that her sister was right. The tree was uniquely awesome. As they entered the area under the canopy the calf-high grass became sparse and short, which was good because the banyan's roots had broken through the fertile earth and they had to pick their way over them carefully. Mercy stopped and stared up. The banyan's leaves were small for such a huge tree, and shaped like little grass-green hearts.

Her sister's voice, hushed like she was afraid of disturbing the tree, pulled at her attention. "Do you feel anything? Anything weird?"

"Not yet." Mercy stopped staring up and walked closer to the trunk. Hunter sat cross-legged facing the banyan—situated between thick fingers of roots. She closed her eyes and lifted her face to the sky as her lips moved as if in a whispering prayer.

Mercy walked slowly around the tree. She turned so that her back rested against the gnarled bark and faced the distant creek. She tried to concentrate—to open herself so she could glean information from her usually astute senses. But the fog of grief refused to thin enough to let anything through. She shook her head.

"I don't know, H. I can't seem to—" Mercy paused and sneezed. She rubbed her nose and sneezed again.

"Shh!" Hunter said. "I'm trying to pick up on any bad energy."

"Sorry, but this smell is getting to me." Then her mind caught up with her words and she craned her neck around to meet her sister's gaze. *"It stinks!"*

Hunter frowned. "Stinks?"

Mercy nodded vigorously. "Get closer."

Quickly, her sister stood and moved to within touching distance of the tree. She breathed deeply before screwing up her face and backing off several feet. "Eesh! That reeks!"

"Sulphur," Mercy said. "It smells like rotten eggs."

Hunter's face paled. "That can't be good," she whispered.

Bile burned Mercy's throat as her stomach revolted. "I don't remember any of the trees smelling bad. Ever. Do you?"

"No. Never. Well, except for last night." Hunter circled the tree with Mercy as they studied the intricate trunk.

A shiver fingered down Mercy's spine as she remembered. "Fenrir—it reeked."

Hunter nodded. "Like this, only worse." She continued to study the tree. "But it looks okay."

"Yeah, nothing *looks* wrong, but that smell is definitely coming from the tree."

"Mag, I know it's really hard for you right now, but you're the Green Witch. You usually just *know* things about plants. Can't you see if the tree will tell you anything?"

The terrible lethargy that clouded Mercy's mind also numbed her senses, but she nodded and, ignoring the rotten egg smell, faced the tree. She leaned forward and braced her hands on the rough bark. Mercy closed her eyes and pressed her palms firmly against the banyan, attempting to feel its energy—something that was usually as easy for her as drawing breath.

Today she felt nothing. She sighed and wanted to drop to her butt and sob. Everything was wrong. *Their mom was dead!* In a burst of anger she pushed against the tree, like she could shove it—and her grief—away, and a section of the bark gave way, like a scab tearing loose, to expose a nest of worms beneath that were boring into the skin of the tree.

Sick filled Mercy's mouth and she gagged.

"What is it?" Hunter rushed to her.

93

Mercy wiped her hands over and over against her jeans and pointed at the writhing parasites.

"Oh, Tyr! What are they?"

"I don't know, but they were at the apple tree, too."

"Wait, you saw them in the bark last night?" Hunter asked as she stared up at the branches of the deceptively healthy-looking banyan.

"No. I stepped on a green apple and it broke open. It was infested with those things. Hunter, Mom said it was okay—acted like it was nothing—but I saw her face go pale." She whispered the next sentence. "Like it scared her."

"We have to tell Xena about this, and we have to see if the other three trees are sick, too."

"Hang on." Mercy's hand trembled as she reached up and grabbed a low-hanging branch. She used her weight, dangling from it so that it shook up and down. Heart-shaped leaves rained around her. They were shriveled and dead.

Hunter crouched and gathered some of the leaves. "This just keeps getting worse." She shoved a handful of leaves into her pocket. "Let's get out of here. We need to go to the other trees."

With leaden feet Mercy retraced their path to the car. She couldn't shake the feeling that worms were crawling over her skin, but she was too exhausted to say anything or do much more than occasionally brush a hand down her arms.

Hunter put the car in reverse. "Should we go to the Egyptian or Japanese gate next?"

Mercy was saved from having to care enough to respond when her phone chimed with a text message. She read the message and felt another wave of sick grief wash through her. "It's Em. She says her dad's ready to see us."

Hunter blew out a long, sad breath. She put the car back into park and picked at her thumbnail. "You think we have time to check out just one of the other trees?"

Mercy met her sister's gaze. "I think we need to take care of Mom first."

Hunter nodded, wiped her bloody thumbnail on her jeans, backed onto the gravel road, and headed toward downtown Goodeville.

Mercy let grief overwhelm her as she closed her eyes and rested her head against the cool window—and tried not to think about what was going to happen next.

Ten

Hunter had never been in a funeral home before. She'd never had any reason to. When her grandmother had passed, the service had been held at their house. Hunter and Mercy were barely out of diapers. Her great-grandmother had died before she and her sister had been born. It seemed all Goode women were destined to an early end.

The heavy wooden door of Parrott Family Funeral Home creaked open in ominous, horror movie fashion. Hunter slipped inside to the foyer. Wood paneling, forest green walls, and black-and-white photos of woodland scenes greeted her. It smelled like flowers and cedar with a hint of cinnamon. Hunter didn't know what she'd expected, but she hadn't prepared herself for normalcy.

Hunter cleared her throat. "Mr. Parrott?"

It was silent for a moment before another creaky door opened. "Be right there, girls," Emily's dad and Goodeville's only funeral director called from down the hall.

Hunter took a deep breath. She felt lighter. Maybe it was the fact that the bright Illinois sun no longer burned her tender eyes. Or maybe it was because she and her sister were taking steps forward. This wouldn't be the new, happier life Hunter had envisioned, but there was something to be said for putting the past in the past.

"You ready for this?" Hunter groped the empty air beside her as she searched for Mercy's hand. She turned. No Mercy, only the ornately carved door and more black-and-white forest photos.

The old wood floors creaked under Hunter's feet as she moved toward the door and hefted it open. Mercy was waiting just on the other side. She sniffled and brushed her pink-tipped nose on her sleeve. "I can't do it." Her chin quivered and Hunter fought the urge to scoop her sister up into her arms and rush back to the car. They had to do this. Anyone who had ever lost someone they loved had to do this. It was as much a part of life as living.

Hunter propped the door open with her foot and slid the long sleeve of her shirt down over her bandaged arm. "I'll do it alone," she whispered as she reached out and took Mercy's hand in hers. The weight was back. It hadn't been the dark colors and warm light of the funeral home or the fact that she was there to move forward, begin her new life. It had been the absence of her sister.

Hunter swallowed the thought along with the knot forming in the back of her throat. "Really, Mag, you can go home. I'll have Jax—"

"Abigail wouldn't want that." Mercy dropped Hunter's hand and slipped past her into the funeral home.

Hunter sagged against the door as it shut. She wanted to say something that would make everything better, that would fix her sister, but grief wouldn't exist without love. And Mercy had loved their mother so, so much. Hunter rubbed her finger along the raw flesh that rimmed her thumbnail as she studied Mercy's slumped shoulders and the way she hugged her arms against her middle as if her insides would spill onto the floor if she didn't hold them in. Was despair a testament to love? Hunter bit down on her fingernail. It couldn't be.

She loved her mother just as much as her sister. But Hunter *had* been through more than Mercy. The teasing, the name-calling, the bullying. In eighth grade, Rachel Leech had cut off her ponytail because *dykes don't have long hair.* A jagged piece of Hunter's nail tore free and she clenched it between her teeth. Her life had been a series of devastating events, one stacked on top of the other in a perverted game of Jenga until this—the pièce de résistance. But Hunter wouldn't let her mother's death topple her. As Mercy would say, Abigail wouldn't want that.

Footsteps creaked down the hallway as Mr. Parrott neared the foyer. "Sorry to keep you two waiting, had an unexpected call that I couldn't get away from . . ." He stilled as he caught sight of Mercy. "I can't begin to tell you how sorry I am."

Mercy hiccupped and tightened her grip around her core.

Mr. Parrott dipped his fingers into his collar and pulled gently. "I've known Abigail my whole life. She introduced me to Helene . . ." He continued to tug at his collar as he spoke. "Abigail actually gave me a special cookie recipe. She said that it would make Helene's true feelings known. We were married three months later."

The floor groaned under Hunter's weight as she scooted closer to her sister. Did hearing stories like this help? Is that what Mercy needed, to relive all the good times? Or did she need to pack away her anguish and shove it in a forgotten corner of her mind? Either way, Hunter would carry on. She'd watch pieces of herself flake off and float away like she'd been doing her entire life.

Mr. Parrott rubbed his hands together and took a deep breath. "You'll have to excuse me, girls. I was shocked to get the news this morning. Haven't quite processed it yet."

"We understand how you feel, Mr. Parrott." Hunter had meant for her words to sound comforting, uniting even. Instead they fell out of her mouth bland and dry and flat.

He moved aside and motioned for the twins to step down into the sitting room. "Dominic. You both know you can call me Dominic."

Hunter did know she could call him by his first name. He'd been saying the same thing since they'd entered high school. She'd always seen it as a prize they'd been given for going through puberty. But Hunter didn't believe in being given prizes. She believed in earning respect.

Mercy let out a strained sigh and descended the stairs. Hunter followed her sister as she dragged her feet across the maroon-and-gold Turkish rug until she reached the edge of the closest settee and plopped down. The sunset yellow glow from the overhead chandelier sparkled off the round glass coffee table that separated the girls from the funeral director.

"What happens next?" The dry leaves stuffed in Hunter's pocket crunched as she sat down next to Mercy. "We've never had to do anything like this before."

Mr. Parrott straightened a stack of brochures before he removed the top folder from a pile of folders neatly arranged in the center of the coffee table. "I need both of you to sign a few documents that will allow me to proceed with funeral preparations. Then, we'll need to go by the sheriff's department to identify and claim your mother."

Mercy's sob was cut short as she clapped her hands over her mouth.

"But I have a good relationship with Sheriff Dearborn." Mr. Parrott removed a few papers from the folder and slid them across the table. "With your signatures and Goodeville being the tight-knit community that it is, I'm sure I'll be able to claim Abigail on my own and make sure everything is taken care of before I head out of town. Then, when I return, we can proceed with the funeral."

Hunter nodded and flattened her palm against Mercy's back. With each inhale, her sister trembled like the wind-battered surface of Sugar Creek.

"If you'll both sign and date the bottom of each of these pages, we can move on to the death certificate and necessary burial permit." He plucked a pen from the table and offered it to Hunter.

"Mercy." The creases of his forehead deepened as he went on, all the while speaking to the wrong twin. "Take your time. We're in no rush."

Hunter snatched the pen from the funeral director's outstretched hand. "I'm Hunter, not Mercy." Without reading the pages, she pressed the tip of the pen against the first paper and drew the loops and swishes of her practiced signature so hard the letters imprinted across the other four sheets.

"Apologies, Hunter." Mr. Parrott cleared his throat and rubbed his palms against his thighs. "You girls wouldn't happen to have your mother's birth certificate or know if she created a will, would you?"

Mercy scooted to the edge of the settee and snatched the pen off of the table. "We want Abigail buried at home. Does it say that somewhere in these?" She picked up the pages and shook them. "I won't sign anything if we can't have *our* mother buried at *our* home." Mercy's wide-eyed, panicked gaze swung to Hunter. "I won't sign these, H. I won't!" She threw the papers down and they drifted to the floor.

Hunter gripped her sister's knee. Mercy was sinking, pulled under by the anvil of grief she'd pressed into her heart.

Mr. Parrott swept up the papers and returned them to the table with an undisturbed grace that spoke to his years of handling the bereaved. "I will list the burial location when I file the permit. If there's an issue, the city will get back to me quickly."

"There won't be an issue." Tears splatted against Mercy's shirt, darkening the heather gray fabric. "Our family members have been buried at our home for hundreds of years."

The funeral director clasped his hands and nodded. "They have been, and Abigail will be, too. I'll make sure of it."

Hunter picked the pen up off the floor and handed it to Mercy. She met her twin's eyes and telegraphed *the look* to her—sending her strength and understanding through their unbreakable bond. "Here, Mag. Let's sign these and go home."

Mercy nodded, a short, jerky movement, and wiped her face on her sleeve before taking the pen and signing each of the papers. When she was finished, Hunter wrapped her arm around her sister and helped her to her feet. Hunter needed to do something for Mercy. But the one person she would have gone to for advice was now waiting at the sheriff's office to be claimed.

Eleven

The entire drive back toward their house from the Parrott Family Funeral Home, Hunter thought about how she could help Mercy and what her mother would have said. Every thought that occurred to her eventually led nowhere. She was alone and in the dark like she'd always been. By now, the stillness was a comfort, something to hold on to when the world turned inside out and true darkness fell. And it didn't get darker than the death of Abigail Goode.

Mercy said nothing, *did* nothing as Hunter flipped on the turn signal and headed down Sycamore Street to take the long way home. A part of Hunter dreaded going back to their house, the hollow skeleton that had once been the most comforting place on earth. Her mother had been the marrow, the lifeblood, the heart. But what did that make her? What did that make Mercy? Were the sisters walking shadows that took up space without giving anything back in return? Hunter rubbed her tight, dry lips together. Her mother hadn't felt that way about her daughters. And neither should Hunter. Perhaps the Goode sisters each held a piece of marrow and blood and heart. And if Hunter could bring their home back to life, she could definitely figure out a way to revive her sister.

With a sigh, Mercy blew Hunter's thoughts right out the window. She strained against her seat belt, turned to face Hunter, and folded her legs up under her before stilling again and resuming her listless stare out the window as Hunter guided the car through the quaint neighborhood that framed Main Street. Each house was a cupcake, fatter than they were tall and each decorated in a different shade of pastel. If Hunter had more experience driving, she could get them home blindfolded and without GPS.

Mercy let out another sigh and rested the back of her head on the passenger window. "How are you so okay with everything? I feel like I'm dying."

The trench in Hunter's stomach deepened. It wasn't an accusation, but it stung nonetheless. "I'm not okay with everything." Hunter kept her eyes fixed on the road like it was the only thing preventing the car from careening into one of the cupcake houses.

"You don't seem upset."

This time Hunter did look at her sister. She opened her mouth to speak but wasn't sure what to say. She wanted to slam on the brakes and throw open the door and rush out into the middle of the street and curse the sky, the earth, the gods, whichever was responsible for taking her mother. But that would do her no good. And that would leave Mercy alone in her own darkness, her *new* darkness, and she wasn't sure if Mercy could find her way out. Hunter closed her mouth and tightened her grip on the steering wheel.

"It's just . . ." Mercy sagged deeper into the seat. "Business as usual for Hunter Goode."

Hunter bit the tip of her tongue. It wasn't her fault she was better at dealing with problems than Mercy, or that Mercy had the luxury of only having to face one devastating thing. It didn't matter how many times Mercy had been there to comfort Hunter while she cried about her latest bullying tragedy, or how many times Mercy brewed Hunter a pot of healing tea and talked about problems as simple things, shimmering bubbles of pain that would eventually pop and leave no trace. Mercy had never fully understood Hunter's pain because she'd had so little of her own.

But maybe now she would.

Hunter stopped at a stop sign as Mercy popped open the glovebox and removed the pack of travel tissues their mother kept next to the car's manual and a satchel stuffed full of dried sage. Mercy pulled out a tissue and dabbed the rounded tip of her pink nose. "I wish I was more like you."

Lint clung to the beams of light shining in through the windows. A chuckle hardened in the back of Hunter's throat. She'd been wishing the exact same thing about herself for the past sixteen years. But that wish had been a compliment to Mercy and, somehow, this didn't feel the same.

Mercy balled up the tissue and dropped her hands into her lap. "It's a charm or a tincture or something, isn't it? Something that just took away all of your feelings."

Hunter's knuckles whitened as she tightened her grip on the steering wheel. "It's nothing magical, Mag," she said, pressing a bit too firmly on the gas. The car lurched forward before she let off and resumed her twenty mile per hour cruise through the innards of Goodeville. "You know that's not—" She pressed the brakes. The car jerked to a stop in front of a pale pink house guarded by plastic flamingos. "Oh my god." Hunter's fingertips flew to her pendant.

Mercy frowned and crossed her arms over her chest. "*Ess,* H. Oh my god*ess.*"

Ignoring her sister, Hunter pulled her phone out of her pocket. She *could* help Mercy, but to do so, she'd need their friends.

Twelve

Hunter tiptoed across the kitchen and peered out into the living room. Mercy remained on the couch. The same place she'd been since they'd gotten home. The grief-stricken twin picked at the gold fringe that rimmed one of the many decorative pillows that propped her up and kept her from lying with her face smashed against the sofa cushions.

Good. Hunter nodded to herself and hurried back to the sink. Well, it wasn't necessarily *good* that Mercy was back to being nearly catatonic. But it was good that her witchy twin senses weren't tingling. Hunter preferred to spring her plan on her sister intervention style.

Hunter gathered five moonstones from the kitchen's east-facing window and exchanged them for her pocketful of crunchy, shriveled leaves. They would deal with the trees as soon as she fixed her sister.

She patted her pocket and absentmindedly glossed her fingertips over her T-shaped pendant as she set her intention on her way to the pantry.

Heal Mercy. Heal Mercy. Heal—

Hunter's hand stilled on the pantry's doorknob. Her mother's basket of Kitchen Witchery was just behind the door. Her hand fell to her side. She should return the stones to the windowsill, slink upstairs, and pour her feelings onto the pages of her book, *When Darkness Rises*. It might turn a little Poe-esque, but at least the manuscript would distract her from the memories of her mother.

She clutched her pendant: her constant reminder of her god. It warmed her palm and she let out a slow breath. She had to do this. To honor herself, to honor her sister, and, most of all, to honor her mother.

Hunter restarted her mantra and opened the pantry. She squeezed her opal and stared at the wicker basket of Kitchen Witch accoutrements sitting on the bottom shelf. One day, she would celebrate that basket and all of the funny-smelling herbs and pages of handwritten recipes it contained. A grin tugged her cheeks as she refocused and took the rusted metal step stool out of its place behind the door. Her stomach fluttered with each creak and groan of the mini-ladder as she unfolded it and climbed the three steps to reach the top shelf. This was Hunter's shelf, where she kept all of her supplies. Her favorite cauldron, her astrology charts, and most importantly, her moon water. When she and Mercy turned twelve, their mother had led them, hand in hand, into the kitchen. The trio had stood before the open pantry as their mother explained to them the importance of keeping a fully stocked and impeccably organized inventory of tools for whichever type of magic the girls chose to adopt.

Hunter inhaled. Her mother's cinnamon and spice scents hung in the air like dust, nearly bringing the memory to life.

"A witch is only as effective as she is organized. Think of what would happen if you were casting and meant to grab rosemary but instead grabbed poppy because your supplies were scattered hither and yon." Abigail's shiver tickled Hunter's hand as she mirrored her mother's pinched brow and shook her head.

Hunter still wasn't quite sure where hither and yon were, but, from that moment, she'd lived her life according to her mother's advice.

Hunter's heartbeat quickened as she pulled her large copper cauldron off the shelf and ran her fingers along her jars of moon water. She'd felt this way since that very first time, four years ago, when magic brought her to the pantry. Then, she had been excited, had wanted to jump up and down and squeal with glee that her mother thought she was old enough, responsible enough, to have her own shelf and spellwork tools, but Mercy had seized the brief moment Hunter took to savor the gift. Her sister had screamed and cried and run in circles and sucked up all of the exhilaration until the space around them seemed to crack and pop like the last bits of milkshake being slurped through a straw. Now, Hunter would give anything to have that Mercy back.

Heal Mercy. Heal Mercy. Heal Mercy.

Energy pricked Hunter's fingertips, sending a jolt down her arm that morphed the gentle butterflies flitting in her stomach into a swirling cyclone of swifts. She turned the large Mason jar and read what she'd written on her custom crescent-shaped label: APACHE TEARS. She picked up the jar and studied the stone resting in the bottom. The night Hunter had filled the glass with water and set it in the grass under the light of the full moon, the single speck of white in the center of the obsidian stone had flamed to life so bright that she'd had to shield her eyes. The power of the moon had released into the water the ancient healing properties of the Apache Tears stone. It was just the thing she'd need to heal her sister.

Hunter set the jar in the empty cauldron and resumed her scan of the few remaining jugs of moon water. Again, the tips of her fingers heated as she glossed them over the final Mason jar labeled: MANGANO CALCITE. Hunter couldn't quite remember when she'd prepared this batch of moon water, but she was no stranger to its loving, compassionate, forgiving energy. It was one of her go-tos.

She placed the second Mason jar into the cauldron and balanced the heavy bowl as she descended the stepladder and shuffled to the kitchen island.

The moment she placed the cauldron on the counter, her phone vibrated. It was funny how little coincidences like that happened. Like the universe was speaking directly to her, telling her she was doing the right thing, on the right path. Hunter suppressed the smile lifting the corners of her lips and tapped the notification. Emily's latest message in the group text lit up the screen in all caps. They were here.

Hunter blew out a calming breath and brushed her ponytail off her shoulder. She could do this. She had to. She ran her hands over the bumpy outline of the moonstones in her pocket, picked up her cauldron, and hurried to the front door.

Mercy continued to tug on the pillow fringe and blankly stare at the floor while Hunter balanced her cauldron in one hand and opened the door with the other. The jars clanked as she pulled open the door, rushed out, and nearly collided with Jax.

Jax's black brows knitted and he held out his hands. "Need some help with that?"

"Yeah, definitely." Hunter's cheeks heated as Emily and Kirk stepped onto the porch and the trio swarmed her. "Thanks for coming over so quickly."

Jax took one jar of moon water and the black-and-white stone clinked against the glass. "We came the second you sounded the alarm."

Emily crossed her arms over her chest and blew a bright pink bubble. "Yep," she said as the gum popped without leaving a trace of sticky pink on her glossed lips. "*All* of us." She rolled her eyes and tilted her head in Kirk's direction.

The quarterback reached for the second jar and hiked his broad shoulders. "What? You guys came and got me because I was included in the group text, too."

Hunter rubbed her fingers over the rough outlines of the moon phases etched in the side of her cauldron. "Well, I need all of you to make this spell work, so—"

Kirk held up the jar. "Wait, wait, wait. *Spell?* Like actual witch stuff?" He handed the jar to Jax and brushed his hands on his pants.

"Duh. They're *actual* witches." If Emily kept rolling her eyes she'd puke before the sun finished setting.

Kirk ran his hand through his hair, further spiking the gelled tips. "So, what? Are we going to do a séance or something?"

"No, moron." Emily shoved the confused football star. "Hunter's text said we're here to *help* Mercy, not make everything worse."

Kirk's thin nose and round eyes scrunched as he rubbed his shoulder. "Talking to her mom's ghost could make things better."

Hunter's pendant heated against her chest. "Stop!" She clenched her jaw and flattened her palms against the cool brass cauldron. "We're doing a spell to cleanse Mercy of her grief. She—" Hunter swallowed and tucked back a strand of hair that had fallen from her ponytail. "She goes through these periods where she won't even talk. She just sits there crying, or worse, doing nothing at all." She motioned toward the large window that looked in on the couch and part of the living room. Sunlight continued to drain into the horizon, giving the group a better view of the bereaved twin. She'd remained on the couch, awash in the gentle golden glow of the setting sun and the antique chandelier.

Emily's fingertips flew to her lips. "Oh, Mercy."

Jax's smoked topaz skin smoothed as he set his jaw. "We'll do whatever you need." Rocks clanked against glass as he lifted the jars. "I'm assuming we're using these?"

Hunter nodded. "They're moon water. If I do the spell right, they'll wash away her pain."

Kirk shoved his hands into the pouch of his hoodie and took a nearly imperceptible step back.

"Kirk, I don't have time to hold your hand through this. You're either in or out. Make a decision." Hunter's pendant remained hot against her skin as she narrowed her eyes at Mercy's boyfriend.

He stiffened and lifted his chin toward the darkening sky. "We're helping Mercy, so I'm in. No question."

The moon was brighter now, its glow no longer paled by the harsh brilliance of its sister sun. Hunter's fingers itched to draw down its powers. "Good. Just don't make a big deal about it." She swept her gaze along her three friends. "Mercy has to be an active participant, but she doesn't know that yet," Hunter said as she adjusted her grip on her cauldron and turned to open the door.

Emily rushed forward and propped open the screen with her foot. "Then how do you know she *will* be an active participant?"

Jax and Kirk had followed and mirrored Emily's furrowed brow concern.

Hunter shrugged and gripped the doorknob. "There isn't a spell Mag has met that she hasn't wanted to be a part of."

"Wait." Kirk cleared his throat and scrubbed his hand down his cheek. "Your aunt isn't here, is she? I don't think she likes me very much."

Hunter bit the inside of her cheeks. She'd laugh again someday, but not today. "She's napping. She naps a lot. Very . . . catlike." She turned the handle and leaned against the heavy wood. "If it helps, she doesn't really like anyone."

Like she'd read Hunter's mind, Mercy popped up off the couch the second her twin pushed open the door. "We're doing a spell? To talk to Mom? To see her?"

For a moment, Mercy was herself again. But it faded as quickly as it came. She knew just as well as Hunter that the magic needed to lift the veil was its own form of evil.

The quarterback shoved past Jax and Emily into the house. "What'd I tell ya? My girl and I are on the same page."

Mercy dropped the tassel-rimmed pillow and stepped forward. "Kirk, what are you—"

"Hey, numb nuts," Emily began before squeezing past Hunter and extinguishing another pink bubble. "Hunter already said that's not what we're doing."

Hunter stepped aside as Jax entered and held up the jars of moon water and gave each a little shake. "We *are* doing a spell, though."

Kirk's long legs quickly carried him to Mercy's side. "Dude." He draped his arm around her shoulders and pulled her into him. "Hunter said not to make a big deal about it."

Hunter carried her cauldron to the middle of the room and set it on the floor. "Yes, Mag, we're doing a spell." She rubbed the bumpy moonstone outlines in her pocket. "All five of us. To help you."

Emily hooked her arm around Hunter's. "Because we love you."

Jax set the jars down next to the cauldron and twined his calloused fingers around his best friend's. "And care about you."

Kirk kissed the top of Mercy's head. "And want you to be okay," he said and buried his cheek in her dark waves.

Mercy chewed her lip in that dramatic way she did when she wanted to impulsively shout *yes* but instead added a few moments of silence for effect. Even in the clutches of grief Mercy knew how to command an audience. "I'll do it."

The moonstones vibrated in Hunter's pocket. They'd heard the promise of a spell, sensed Hunter's energy and the fuel from the rising moon, and were ready to get to work. Hunter dug them out and motioned for her sister and friends to gather around the cauldron.

"Mag, you're next to me. The rest of you will sit here, here, and here." She pointed to the floor in three specific areas that surrounded the copper bowl. She used her free hand to gather the jars of moon water as Jax claimed the remaining spot next to her and Emily shuffled to the open space between Jax and Kirk. If Hunter ever got a girlfriend, she hoped Jax wouldn't be as sullen about it as Emily was about Kirk. Although, none of them, Mercy excluded, were completely convinced that Kirk wasn't a cloudy bag of old douche. But none of that really mattered. If Hunter was being honest, there was zero reason for her to think that she'd have a girlfriend any time before graduation. At Goodeville High, if anyone else's sexuality landed outside of the hetero portion of the spectrum, Hunter and company definitely didn't know about it.

The moonstones thrummed and sizzled against Hunter's palms as she cupped them and held her hands over the empty cauldron. "Pick whichever stone calls to you."

Jax, Emily, and Kirk blinked at one another before each shrugged and nodded like they shared a hive mind.

Emily tucked a stray curl behind her ear, leaned forward, and plucked a stone from the pile. "Whoa. It's warm, like, *really* warm."

Jax went next. He wrapped his fingers around the pearlescent orb and smiled. "It's magic. *Real* magic."

Kirk's eyes widened as he picked up a stone and inspected it. "Have you ever seen *Sabrina*?"

Hunter ignored him as Mercy carefully stared at the final two stones. "I can't feel anything, H. I'm all blocked."

Hunter chose for her sister, handing her a lovely pink-tinted moonstone that was the smallest of the bunch. "You'll be good as new after this."

Jax rolled the charged rock between his palms. "What exactly is *this*?"

Mercy clutched the little stone against her chest and cocked her head. "You're going to scry, aren't you?"

Hunter didn't want to share with the group. What if she failed? It was quite possible she'd bitten off way more than she could chew, and they'd all end up holding warm and aggravated moonstones while staring at a basin of room temperature water. No, she wouldn't tell. She'd pull a Mercy and leave it up to her friends' imaginations.

The wood floor made a hollow clank as Kirk set his rock in front of him. "Scry? Is that what it's called when you take out an emotion, kill it, and bury it in a hole?"

Emily sucked the air from a bubble and placed her stone on the back of her hand. She spoke as she balanced the moonstone and studied her perfectly manicured nails. "It's the act of using a crystal ball or something reflective, in this case I'm assuming it's the jars of water, to see, like, the future and stuff."

Hunter clenched her teeth to keep her mouth from flopping open. Emily was right. Unfortunately, Hunter wasn't gifted enough to see into the future (at least, she wasn't gifted enough *yet*), but she could perform small spells—or, in this case, a medium-sized one.

The stone rolled off Emily's outstretched hand and she caught it before looking up. "Gawk much?" She fisted the moonstone and crossed her arms over her chest. "What? The pretty girl can't also know things?" She cocked her head and squinted at Kirk. "Try reading a book instead of streaming. There's no way H would remove an entire emotion from Mag. That's insane."

Hunter opened her mouth to agree, but Mercy's sniffle pulled her back to what mattered most. "We should begin." Hunter set her stone in her lap and picked up the first jumbo-sized Mason jar and unscrewed the lid. "So, I'm going to say a few things while I pour the water." Her mouth went dry as she spoke and she dragged her tongue across her lips. She didn't have a script or any words prepared or a book to quote. She'd only read about spells *like* this one, but they weren't exactly this one. She'd have to trust herself and her abilities, which was a lot easier to do *before* the moment as opposed to *in* it. But Hunter did know one thing they'd need to do for sure.

"It's important that we set and maintain our intention throughout the entire spell." Her voice caught. In that moment, she reminded herself of her mother, of last night. Had that only been yesterday?

Mercy folded her legs against her chest and buried her face in her knees. She felt it, too.

Hunter cleared her throat and continued, "We're here to cleanse Mercy of her grief. That is our intention. That is our focus."

The three friends nodded and leaned closer to the cauldron as Hunter set the lid on the ground and lifted the jar over the basin. "At this time and at this place we meet before Mother Moon and Father Tyr to call for the cleansing of grief from our friend and sister, Mercy Anne Goode."

She lifted the moon water toward the sky and closed her eyes as the Apache Tear clanked in the bottom of the jar. "We humbly thank the Apache Women who shed enough tears for their lifetimes and ours." Hunter opened her eyes and poured the water into the cauldron. Emily, Jax, and Kirk gasped as the moon etchings flickered to life, then went out.

Hunter repeated the same gestures and uncapped the second jar and hefted it skyward. "We thank the sweet vibrations of mangano calcite as they free us to love and let go." Again, the etchings sputtered with magical light as the water splashed into the cauldron.

Hunter looked up and was met with a wide-eyed excitement that fed her hammering pulse. "When I say, we'll all drop in our moonstones at the same time."

She pressed her fingertips against her pendant and continued, "At this time and at this place we come together, strengthened by friendship and love, to ask for the purification of heart and mind and soul and the return of peace and hope and light."

The others joined Hunter as she reached out and held her moonstone over the brimming cauldron. "Now." She nodded, and the five stones released as one.

They fell through the water with the slow, magical syrupiness of honey through a sieve. Jagged lines of power cut through the water in electric white currents. Their intention had been granted by the moon and by Tyr and by the power that had stitched Hunter back together time and time again. The frosty white charges connected the glowing moonstones in a sacred symbol, a powerful symbol.

"Is that a star?" The reflection blazed brilliant white in Kirk's eyes.

Mercy unfurled and leaned forward. "It's a pentagram." She took

Kirk's hand in hers and sat up straight and tall. "Join hands," she instructed and clasped her fingers around Hunter's. "It'll make the incantation stronger." No, there was no spell that would keep Mercy Anne Goode away.

A geyser erupted from the center of the cauldron when the five joined hands. Enchanted moon water rained into their circle like glitter.

Hunter unclasped her hand from Mercy's and placed her palm against the back of her sister's head. As Mercy closed her eyes, a single tear washed down her cheek. Hunter squeezed Jax's hand as she began the final part of the spell. "Be rid of this despair, Mercy, and come back to me." She'd intended the last words to be a beacon of strength, a clarion call through the magical haze that filled their quaint living room. Instead, they'd been a whisper, a prayer. The words had rushed from her heart and flew out of her mouth with the ease of an exhale. Hunter released Jax's hand and rolled Tyr's pendant between her fingers. She needed her sister back. Her world was unbalanced without her.

Again, Hunter took Jax's hand in hers as she guided Mercy's head down to the cauldron. The water didn't ripple as her sister's face broke the surface. It was like glass, like ice, like Goode Lake in the dead of winter—still and peaceful. Mercy's hair fell into the cauldron, raven wings beneath the calm surface. Hunter's fingers numbed as she felt her sister take one breath and then another and another.

Kirk reached out to grab Mercy but was deflected by a magical shield of glowing white light. "Get her out of there!"

Hunter had been waiting for this. She knew Kirk wasn't the type of guy to sit back if something went wrong. Not because he was a protector but because he believed he knew what was best. Plus, she *had* seen *Sabrina*. If that's what he thought of her, of them, he'd pull out his pitchfork in no time. "Maintain your focus! Breaking it will—"

Mercy sat up. Her hair arched through the air with the perfected drama and grace of a TV starlet. Hunter couldn't move, couldn't speak, couldn't force her eyes away from the glowing cauldron and the image of her sister still caught in the skin of the water.

Jax's hand went clammy. "Hunter?" He squeezed her fingers once, twice, three times before Hunter brought herself back to the present.

Mercy's face and hair dried before any water dripped onto her shirt. "Is that me?" she asked, blinking down at the cauldron.

It worked. Hunter's heartbeat hammered between her ears. It worked. It actually worked! Hunter Jayne Goode accomplished an advanced spell using only her natural gifts and the strength of the moon and her chosen god, Tyr. If Jax didn't have hold of her hand, she'd probably float away.

"No way!" Emily pointed at the Mercy trapped in the basin of water. "She blinked!"

Kirk pressed his palms against the floor and scooted back a few inches. "*She?* That's an *it*! A water creature that we're supposed to, what? Just ignore?"

Hunter's nostrils flared and she bit down on the meaty sides of her tongue before allowing herself to react. "It's not a creature. It's Mercy. A very small part of her, anyway." She sat up a little straighter. This was her spell, her *successful* spell, and she would own it. "We asked to have her grief washed away. Not the whole thing but a tiny piece of it. Enough that she could be herself again." She gestured to the image of her sister staring up at them from the cauldron. "And that's exactly what happened."

Mercy clapped and managed to sit up a tad straighter. "It *is* me! I knew it."

Kirk scooted back toward the circle and leaned into his girlfriend. "You're okay with all of this?"

Mercy cocked her head and shrugged. "Nothing we do is evil or bad. It's all based in love and light. And, like Hunter said, it was just a small piece of my grief." She turned and took Kirk's hands in hers. "Those same two things brought you here tonight to help me, and they did. You were so powerful tonight, Kirk. So perfect. This couldn't have happened without you."

Hunter's cheeks flamed. Love and light hadn't brought Kirk there; she had. She had been the beacon of peace and hope. She had wielded the power. Hunter tightened her free hand into a fist. If Kirk had left, and he almost had, she would have figured out how to make the spell work without him. He was unnecessary, trivial. A small blip in both of their lives. A high school fling. Hunter's jagged nails bit into her palm. In ten years, neither one of them would be able to remember his name. They'd call him "the quarterback" or "that guy" or maybe they wouldn't call him anything at all. Maybe Hunter *would* become a *Sabrina* witch and erase all trace of Kirk Whitfield from her sister's memory and they'd never have to speak of him again.

Warm liquid pooled in Hunter's palm and trickled down the side of her hand. She unclenched her fingers and stared down at the blood sprouting from the crescent-shaped wounds her fingernails had carved into her flesh.

Hunter let go of Jax's hand and clutched her pendant. She needed to refocus, reground herself. She would never erase Mercy's memory. She should never even think such a thing. Wielding the power, being a conduit, it was all getting to her. It had to be.

"I'm closing the spell," Hunter blurted as she clenched her hand and hid her bleeding fist behind her back. She felt four sets of eyes press against her as she closed her own and searched for the right words. The spell no longer flowed from her. Hunter was clogged up. A big, fatty, hairy clog. She'd name it *Kirk*.

"At this time and at this place we thank Mother Moon and Father Tyr for cleansing our friend and sister and purifying her heart and mind and soul. We know you will remain near, as will we." Energy pricked Hunter's fingertips and she followed her urge, her intuition, and plunged her bleeding hand into the water. The icy cold liquid shocked her and sent her eyelids fluttering open. "This rite is ended," she continued as she watched her blood eat away the blinking image of her sister before sinking down, down, down. Hunter wet her lips and shouted the final closing line she'd heard her mother use time and time again. "Merry meet and merry part and merry meet again!"

Scarlet ribbons snaked around the glowing moonstones, turning each a petal pink. Emily sucked in a breath as the rocks lifted from the cauldron's bottom, reeled into Hunter's palm by the power of her blood.

Thirteen

It was hot inside the Goodeville precinct. Too hot. The kind of hot that made every inch sweat and stick and itch. Frank Dearborn twisted the faucet knobs and let cool water splash against his swollen knuckles. How could anyone live like this? Inside all hours of the day, fake breeze blowing down from dusty vents in the ceiling. People had come so far only to imprison themselves.

He leaned over the sink and peered into the small rectangular mirror that hung from the pristine bathroom wall. "Dearborn." He ran his tongue along his teeth and smiled. "*Sheriff* Dearborn."

It was more than convincing. It was a fact.

Pain jabbed his left eye. He clapped his hand over the spikes of heat that blurred his vision and lurched forward. His forehead crashed into the mirror. "*Mother—*" He stifled a roar and pushed himself away from the reflective glass. Shards rained onto the porcelain as he ran his fingers over the tender knot forming in the center of his forehead. It'd been like this since last night, since the olive tree. Sudden shocks of increasingly devastating pain. It would be over soon. No matter where he was, he could never escape his fate.

Eye still covered, he leaned toward his splintered reflection. He sucked in a breath through clenched teeth and forced his hand away from his eye. He affixed his gaze to the faucet. He didn't want to look.

"Damn mirrors." He flinched as he gently patted his swollen eyelid.

He shouldn't blame the mirrors. It wasn't their fault they reflected the truth. He should blame that woman. The one who'd made him love her. The one who'd turned him into a monster.

He swept his gaze back up to his reflection. If he couldn't find a cure this time, he would be like this forever. Threads of milky white swirled across his dark iris. Air hissed between his clenched teeth as he rubbed at his eye, clearing away the gunk. As quickly as the clouds of white vanished, they were back again.

He sighed. There was no use fighting it. He hadn't escaped the curse. Maybe he never would.

He unhooked his aviators from the collar of his uniform and pushed them up the bridge of his nose. Seeing through the shadows was better than revealing a problem. A *difference*. People weren't good with *different*.

His stomach roiled and saliva flooded his mouth. He was going to be sick. Not from the sight of his disgusting visage. No, this was something else. Something familiar yet out of reach. His stomach seized and a wave of vomit rolled up his throat. Chunks slipped off his tongue and squelched against the empty sink. He stared at the towel dispenser, turned on the faucet, and washed the mess away. He didn't want to look at it, either.

The bathroom door creaked open and he stepped in front of the broken mirror and the freshly cleaned sink. Deputy Carter rushed in, his hands already unbuckling his belt. "Oh, Sheriff." He stiffened. "Sorry, I, uh, I didn't know anyone was in here." He let out an awkward chuckle, took off his hat, and ran his hand through his flattened hair. "Too much coffee and not enough bathroom visits." Another bleat of laughter as he shuffled to the nearest urinal.

Dearborn's lip curled as the deputy turned his back and sighed with relief when his stream hit the porcelain. At their base, they were all animals. Caged animals. The sheriff threw open the door and charged into the bullpen.

Across the open room of desks, a woman waved at him like her arms were on fire. She was the only woman in the building without a uniform, her hair tied back tight and a row of weapons around her hips.

His teeth ground together as she waddled toward him, so eager for connection, for love. But love was weakness, downfall, the beginning of everything evil or bad. He wanted no part of it.

Her name tag glinted in the harsh overhead lighting. *Trish*. That's right. If he dug down deep enough, he could uncover the sun-bleached memory of her. But the memories were fading, and fast.

A dimple made a nest in her cheek as she smiled. "There you are. I've been looking all over for you. I was worried." Stickers, sparkling hearts and fat bears framed the capital letters on her name tag. Dearborn squinted and blinked through the haziness blurring his left eye. Maybe they were beavers. All those hairy woodland creatures looked the same. "You haven't returned any of my calls and I haven't seen you since last night before . . ." She clenched and unclenched the notepad and glittery pen between her soft hands. "Well, you know." A forced grin cracked her bleak, smooth features.

All he could do was wipe the sweat from his brow and nod. He couldn't quite remember how he should respond. The Trish memories were fading away.

"It was awful." She parted the uncomfortable silence and waded closer to him. Warmth rolled off her like she was freshly baked bread. "Old Earl Thompson finally stumbled onto something real and it killed him." She shook her head. Her red curls bounced, tossing a spicy sweetness into the air.

Pie? Was that it?

His heart clamored and the tips of his fingers tingled. His body remembered something his mind no longer knew.

"I threw out the Ruckus Report." She leaned in. Her breath fogged the gold star pinned to his chest. "Didn't think it was right to keep it since he's no longer with us. Maybe it wasn't the right thing to do to begin with."

Another shake of her head. Another swirl of sugar and spice.

He brushed the tip of his nose against her curls. "Cinnamon," he murmured as a crumb of memory rolled into focus. "You bake when you're upset."

Dearborn's memories faded in and out and would soon leave his mind altogether. But some memories stayed with the body. Things like driving, shooting, not to turn his head too quickly to the left. In a lifetime long before Dearborn, he'd been a brilliant painter. But that had ended in blood and tears and more stains on his immortal soul.

Trish pressed her notepad against her chest and took a wobbly step back. "Frank, I—" She fanned herself with her free hand and fluffed the round tips of her chin-length curls. "Well, I'm not quite sure what to say." Her cheeks flamed strawberry red as she cast a glance around the bullpen.

He followed her attention, eyes narrowed and fists clenched while he took in all the darting glances and quick returns to computer monitors, stacks of paperwork, and phone calls. There had been something between Sheriff Dearborn and this Trish woman, but that was a different person, a different life. Frank Dearborn had never learned the truth about love and happiness and the pain they both brought. Now he wouldn't allow this body or these fleeting memories to betray him again.

Trish held out the notepad and tapped at the list of names and phone numbers she'd written under two column headings: *ASAP* and *After Lunch*. "I know you'd rather not fiddle with that computer program to read your call-back list, but they're in there, too, if you're so inclined."

Although she couldn't see through his mirrored sunglasses, he kept his eyes narrowed as he snatched the notepad from her hand. He wouldn't pine after Trish. Whatever Dearborn had had with her was over, dead.

Trish fiddled with the cap of her glittery pen. "Need another cup of coffee, Sheriff? I have a sneaking suspicion you're hiding some pretty dark circles under those glasses."

A dry tickle tightened the back of his throat and his stomach seized again. Only one thing could ease his pain and quiet this restless body. He had to get away from this woman, all of these people, the hot, circulated air, and the overhead lights.

Trish rested her warm hand against his bicep. "Frank, are you feeling okay?"

"I'm fine," he croaked. He'd done nothing but lie since he'd arrived. This body knew it, and it wanted him gone.

Wet coughs tore from his lungs, a thousand molten nails searing the inside of his ribs. *Frank Dearborn isn't here!* he shouted at the battle lines carved inside his chest, his gut. *He's never coming back!*

Trish steadied him as another barking explosion ripped through him. More hands were on him, different voices shouting concerns, solutions, all guiding him toward his office door. He planted his feet and sucked in a haggard breath. "I'm fine," he repeated and jerked his arms away from the horde. "Just need—" His chest quaked as he swallowed back another coughing fit. "Just need some air." He rubbed his sweaty palms against his shirt and searched for an escape. He spotted the nearest illuminated EXIT sign, fisted his hands, and blinked past the water swirling across his good eye.

"I'll go get you that coffee, Sheriff." Trish's shoes clicked as she turned and clapped her hands at the crowd. "Back to work, everyone. Back to work."

He didn't look back as he marched to the precinct's rear exit. Their concern would do him no good. Bodies like this yearned to be re-attached to their soul or given back to the earth. Bodies like Frank Dearborn's made his curse that much more unbearable. This body couldn't be fixed. It had to be fed.

Ancient words from lifetimes ago swept through his thoughts.

> *How delicious life would be*
> *If only it could make you see*
> *The hunger for what it truly is,*
> *A way to set you free.*
> *Now carry on with your cursed life,*
> *And cut their eyes out, these orbs are so rife*
> *With magic, but only one pair of these*
> *Has what it takes to end your strife.*

The memory squeezed the tattered remnants of his broken heart. Tears welled as the door slammed shut behind him. He sagged against the side of the department's dumpster. Every ounce of him ached. He wasn't a killer. And yet . . .

Cones of light bobbed against the garbage bin. He sniffled and squinted through his lenses at the headlights as they crept through the alley, closer and closer. Brakes squeaked as the car stopped short of the dumpster. The lights turned off and the car door groaned open.

He blinked the spots of light from his sight as dress shoes clicked against the pavement. "Didn't you quit smoking years ago, Frank?"

Sheriff Dearborn's stomach growled. "Stay back."

The man's cheeks lifted with a grin. "Don't worry. I won't tell any-one. Especially not Trish." He winked his right eye. His *perfect* right eye. A sparkling drop of charcoal black swimming in an endless pearl white sea.

Get away! The words wouldn't leave the sheriff's lips. They clung to the hunger tightening his throat and drenching his mouth.

The man motioned to Dearborn's mirrored shades. "Wish I could get away with wearing sunglasses. Emily's always saying that crying makes your eyes puffy." His chuckle was dry and forced. "But you know how Em gets."

"Tears make them moist," he whispered. *Heavy and juicy and—* He wiped away the saliva at the corners of his lips.

The man stepped on a soggy clump of paper. It flattened under the toe of his shiny leather shoe. "In a small town, this job is always hard. I always know who I'm preparing. If I wasn't friends with them, I was with some of their kin. Men in our positions have to stay strong. They depend on us for that."

The sheriff pushed away from the dumpster and crept closer to the man with the flawless eye. "Can I be honest with you? *Truly* honest?"

"Of course, Frank." The man's feathery lashes waved at Dearborn with each blink.

"I'm the weakest man you know." He lunged forward, caught the man by the neck, and slammed him into the pavement. Stumpy, manicured fingers clawed at the sides of Frank Dearborn's face. The wild pawing caught Frank's sunglasses and hurled them onto the concrete. Dearborn's insides thrummed. He could see more clearly now. He could watch the fight melt from those perfect eyes like the last bits of snow from the grass.

This could be it. The pair of eyes that would free him from his curse.

Blood marred the perfect white with cherry red dots and zigzags. The man's hands fell to his sides and his legs twitched in his body's last attempts to run. Finally, his jaw slackened and his pupils widened and he stilled.

Dearborn released the man's throat and slid off him. He sat on the pavement next to the body and traced the dead man's flaccid eyelids.

He leaned in and pressed his lips against the sweat streaked forehead. *"Σας τιμώ."*

I honor you.

Dearborn plunged his fingers into the eye sockets and scooped out the gems. His stomach trembled as the first warm and gooey orb touched his tongue. He stared up at the dark sky and punctured the first eyeball with his sharp canine.

Please be those I've been seeking. Please be them. Please be them. He prayed over and over as wet paste filled his mouth and washed down his throat. He dropped the second viscous ball into his mouth and quickly chewed the slippery mass.

Nothing happened.

He rubbed his cloudy eye and blinked down at the eyeless corpse.

He had done this for nothing. Frank's stomach settled as he swallowed the last bits. He'd taken a man from his family and his community for an unfulfilled dream. But he'd had to take the chance. It was the only way he could stay in this body and the only way his curse would one day come to an end.

He looked down at his wet and bloody hands and up at the back door to the sheriff's department. He wiped his hands on his pants, plucked his sunglasses from the ground, and hooked his arms under the dead man's, whose fancy shoes bounced along the pavement as Dearborn dragged him back to his car and shoved him into the driver's seat. Frank dragged his aviators along his sleeve before he slid them on over his clouded eye. He walked to the back exit, wiped his mouth, and threw open the door.

"I need help out here!"

Deputies wasted no time springing into action. He heard them scramble to their feet and rush toward the exit. He charged back to the car and he kneeled next to the open driver's side door with his head in his hands. He would sell this performance. He would dig deep and uncover each scrap of a memory. He squinted and studied the dead man's bloodied features.

Dominic Parrott.

He would use them to rebuild Frank Dearborn's friendship with Dominic. Friendship, love, created a well of excuses he could use to drown each procedural question. After all, this wasn't the first time he'd nearly been caught.

Fourteen

B abe, you already look *lots* more like yourself!" Kirk's hand slid from the hollow of the small of Mercy's back to gently cup her butt.

She sidestepped and caught his hand in hers and squelched a sigh, reminding herself to have another talk with him about how he needed to read the room better. Mercy could feel the frowns Emily and Hunter were skewering Kirk with—not that, this time, she blamed them. It'd only been an hour ago that Hunter's spell had washed the debilitating grief from her and everyone—except Kirk—was still subdued and still in awe of Hunter's magic. "Yeah, I am feeling a lot more like me. Thanks to you guys." Mercy's smile included Jax, Emily, and Hunter—along with Kirk. "But don't you and Jax have to get home? Didn't you tell me you have a chemistry test you have to study for?"

At that moment the huge pendulum clock that had been in the Goode family for generations chimed ten times.

"Oh, crap!" Jax sprang up from the couch. "Mom made me promise to be home by ten. Kirk, we gotta go."

"You can be a little late," scoffed Kirk.

Hunter narrowed her eyes and Emily manically cracked her gum. Before they could declare war on Kirk, Mercy said, "Hey, I'm super tired. This has all been a lot. I really do need to sleep."

"Of course. Sorry." Kirk put his arm around her as she led him out the front doors and onto the porch. "You know I like spending every second with you."

"Stalker much?" Emily murmured from behind them.

"Huh?" Kirk asked cluelessly.

Mercy turned Kirk so that he was on the second step facing her while she stood on the porch, which made her almost at his eye level. "Em was just calling you a big talker. But she doesn't know you as well as I do." Mercy rested her arms across his shoulders and kissed him softly. "Thanks for coming tonight. See ya tomorrow." Before he could pull her in for a more intimate kiss, Mercy squeezed his shoulders and then walked quickly to Jax, giving him a hug. "You're a good friend. Thanks for being here, Jax."

He patted her back. "No problem. Anything for Hunter and you."

She was going to hug Emily, too, but her friend had already plopped her butt down on their wide porch swing. She looked up from her phone. "I texted Dad. He said he had some stuff to do downtown and then he'll be by to get me."

"Well, hey, I could wait for Emily's dad and get a ride with him. Right, Em?" Kirk sent her friend a hopeful look, which Emily completely ignored.

Mercy sighed. She really liked Kirk, and he was being a sweetheart, but his persistence could be exhausting. She'd opened her mouth to repeat herself when Xena, in cat form, padded through the open door and across the porch. She arched her long, sleek back, slitted her eyes at Kirk, and let loose a terrifying group of sounds.

"Hiiiiiisss, mEEEwr, hiiiiiisss!"

"Shit! That cat is huge!" Kirk backed down the porch stairs after Jax. "Okay, I'm going."

"Sorry, Xena doesn't really like many people," Mercy said while Hunter covered a laugh with a cough.

"I thought that was your aunt's name," said Kirk, still backing down the sidewalk.

"She doesn't like many people, either," said Hunter.

Kirk's forehead wrinkled in confusion.

"Dude, come on! I'm not getting grounded because of you," Jax called as he opened his car door.

Kirk waved and grinned at Mercy before rounding on Jax. "You're such a wuss sometimes . . ." His words faded away as he climbed into the passenger side of Jax's car, which took off before he'd completely closed the door.

"Don't say it," Mercy said as she sat beside Emily.

Em put her phone down and shrugged. "Hey, I'm just happy you feel better."

"Yeah, me too," said Hunter. "I'm gonna go get my grimoire. I want to document that grief spell." She started to walk past Mercy and into the house, but Mercy reached out and snagged her wrist.

"Hey. Thank you. What you did tonight—it was . . ." She had to pause and swallow back her tears before continuing in a small, soft voice. "Mom would be so proud of you."

Hunter's smile was like the stars. "You really think so?"

"I know so. Thanks, H. You're the best."

Emily sneezed violently as Xena wound around her legs. "OMG, your cat is trying to kill me again!"

Mercy shared a knowing look with her sister as she said, "Xena, give Em a break. We know you really do like her."

Emily sniffed and wiped her nose on the back of her hand. "Likes me dead!" Then she cocked her head and studied the big Maine coon as if seeing her for the first time. "Hey, I just noticed she and your Aunt Xena have, like, the same hair."

"Impossible," Hunter said as she headed into the house. "Xena has fur. Our aunt has hair. But come on, Xena. There's a bowl of cream with your name on it in the kitchen. Good watchcat—good watchcat." Chattering happily, Xena trotted after Hunter, who paused in the doorway and looked back at Mercy. "You're the best, too. I'm glad you're back." Xena yowled and Hunter rolled her eyes. "*Okay,* I said I'd get you some cream. Sheesh. You're so demanding . . ." Her voice trailed off as she marched inside and headed to the kitchen.

"Aww, twin love gives me a big, warm feeling in my cold, dead heart," said Emily. Then her eyes went huge. "Oh. Shit. Sorry. I—"

Mercy bumped her shoulder. "Stop. You can't tiptoe around me and worry about everything you say. If you do—if everyone does—we'll never find our new normal."

Emily sighed in relief and brushed a strand of her hair behind her ear as she cocked her head and studied Mercy. "You *are* better, aren't you?"

She hadn't phrased it like a question, but Mercy nodded. "Yeah. I'm still sad. I miss Abigail so much that my heart feels weird and heavy, but before the spell I couldn't make my mind work. It was like I was trying to think through mud. No, not mud. Fog. My brain was all foggy. I couldn't concentrate. All I wanted to do was cry or sleep—or both. What you guys did made the fog lift."

"And now you can start feeling better?" Emily asked tentatively.

Mercy let out a long breath. "Yeah. Before I couldn't see through my grief to any future. Now I know Hunter and I *will* have a future. It'll be different than we ever imagined it would be, but at least now I can start imagining it."

Mercy pushed against the porch with her feet and the swing glided back and forth gently, soothingly, as they gazed up at the starry night sky. They didn't speak, but Emily reached over and covered Mercy's hand with her own and Mercy felt her friend's love and support flow into her.

Hunter reappeared holding a tray laden with one of their mom's many tea sets, her thick grimoire tucked under her arm. "Thought we could all use some lavender and chamomile tea."

"Great idea, H!" Mercy took the tray from her sister and put it on the wicker table that sat between the swing and the wooden rockers that were often filled with friends or Abigail's customers. Mercy spooned honey into three delicate cups before pouring the fragrant tea and passing the cups to her sister and her best friend.

Between careful sips Emily said, "Hey, um, I wanted to tell you two how cool that was."

"That?" Hunter peered up from writing in her book of spells.

Emily jerked her chin at the grimoire. "*That*. The spell thing you did tonight."

Hunter lifted one shoulder. "*We* did it. The five of us."

"But you were the witch that led us," said Mercy. "And you made the spell up yourself, didn't you?"

Hunter's cheeks flushed pink. "I didn't have time to go through all the spell books to find exactly what we needed, so I had to."

"It was perfect, H. Really," said Mercy.

Hunter met her twin's gaze. "You can be you again now."

"I can be me again now," Mercy repeated.

"You know, I forget that you two can do actual magic," said Emily.

"Well, it's not like we go around bippity-boppity-booing all the time," said Mercy.

"But you could, right? I mean, it'd be super cool if you did." Emily peered, owllike, from one twin to the other.

"An ye harm none, do what ye will." Hunter spoke the words reverently.

Mercy shared a knowing look with her sister. "Which means, Em, that what you think is super cool would make a lot of people really uncomfortable, so we don't do it."

"Like Kirk was tonight," Hunter added.

Mercy felt a jolt of surprise. "Kirk? What do you mean? He seemed fine."

Emily snorted.

"Okay, what happened?" Mercy insisted as she looked from her best friend to her sister.

Emily stirred her tea, letting the spoon clink against the porcelain cup. "He kinda freaked. Before, when Hunter was getting us ready. Setting our intention. Is that the right word?"

Mercy and Hunter nodded together. "Yeah, that's what it's called," said Mercy. "Setting the intention of a spell or a ritual is one of the most important aspects of magic." She met her twin's gaze. "What'd he do?"

"He didn't really *do* anything. He was just weird about the whole *real magic-ness* of it all. I needed him to be one hundred percent, and I wasn't sure he'd commit." Hunter shrugged nonchalantly and shifted her gaze to her spell book.

Mercy looked at her sister, who was writing in her grimoire and wouldn't meet her eyes. She sighed. "I'm sorry about that, H."

Still not looking up from her spell book, Hunter said, "The important part is that he *didn't* mess up the spell."

"No, the important part is that you included him," Mercy said, and Hunter finally met her gaze. "Thanks. Even though Kirk can be a pain in the ass—thanks."

"No problem," her sister said.

Emily pushed her feet against the porch so that the swing continued to glide back and forth. "I guess it's actually not too surprising Kirk was uncomfortable."

"How so?" asked Mercy, draping an arm over the back of the swing as she blew across the amber colored surface of her steaming tea.

"Well, Kirk hasn't been hanging around you two for long. I mean, I've known you guys since we were practically in diapers. I'm used to the fact that you're witches, but even I was shocked by how *for real magical* that spell was."

"Oh, please." Hunter's face was turned down to her grimoire again. "Practically everyone who lives in Goodeville knows we're witches."

"Knowing and seeing are two way different things," said Emily.

"I'll talk to Kirk, but he seemed okay when he left," said Mercy.

"Yeah, be sure he doesn't get the pitchforks and torches out," muttered Hunter.

Mercy frowned at her sister. "Why wasn't Jax freaked out? His parents are uber-religious."

Hunter shook her head. "His mother is. She's super Protestant. Her family has lived here since the beginning of Goodeville. He's a lot cooler, plus, we've known Jax for a million years; he accepts us. You don't need to worry about him freaking." Hunter brushed her ponytail off her shoulder. "But Kirk was never fully into the spell or okay with it, and we don't need the stress he could cause by telling people our business."

"Don't worry about Kirk. I'll take care of him," said Mercy.

Emily cleared her throat loudly, causing both girls to shift their attention to her.

"I just want to officially let you know that if you need any other help with spell stuff or ritual whatchamacallit, I'm your girl. I wasn't freaked. I thought it was amazing."

"Your energy is really good," Hunter said.

Mercy nodded. "That helped the spell's success."

Emily grinned. "Can I pretend to almost be a witch?"

From just inside the open door Xena yowled.

Emily's grin faded. "Never mind. She already wants to kill me. I'll just leave it as I'll be a substitute witch whenever you need one."

"Deal," said the twins together.

Hunter caught her sister's gaze and smiled—really smiled—at her for the first time since the night before and a little more of the grief that had cocooned around Mercy's heart loosened.

"I'm hungry!" Mercy said. "Em, do you think we have time to order pizza before your dad gets here?"

"How 'bout I text him and tell him I'm staying the night? Mom's still home until midweek and since Dad's leaving for his conference tomorrow they're spending every second getting their fight on." She paused and shuddered. "I'd way rather stay here. Can I borrow something to wear to school tomorrow?" Em froze mid-text. "Wait, are you going to school tomorrow?"

Mercy met Hunter's gaze. "What do you think, H?"

"I think people will probably treat us like freaks whenever we go back."

Mercy nodded. "Then let's do it like a Band-Aid, just get it over with." She turned to her bestie. "Yeah, we're going to school tomorrow. Text your dad and then we'll order that pizza and—"

The sheriff's car pulled into their driveway, cutting off Mercy's words. She sighed and her shoulders slumped. "Not again. Do we have to keep going over and over this with them?"

Hunter sat straight up. She snapped her grimoire shut and put it aside. "No. No, we do not. They need to leave us alone."

"Maybe you should wake up your aunt," said Emily. "She can tell them to get lost."

"Good idea," said Hunter as she stood. "Mag, I'll go get Auntie. Tell them that she'll be out in a sec."

The car door closed and Deputy Carter slowly headed up the driveway, gravel crunching under his steel-toed boots.

"At least it's just the deputy." Mercy kept her voice low. "The sheriff was kinda creepy this morning."

"Seriously," said Hunter as she hurried inside the house.

Mercy thought Deputy Carter looked unusually pale as he climbed the porch steps and took off his hat. Dark circles made his otherwise puppyish eyes look bruised and old.

"Evening, Miss Goode." He nodded at Mercy.

"I'm Mercy." She was used to supplying her name to people who couldn't seem to ever tell the two of them apart.

But the deputy had already turned his attention to Emily. "Emily, I'm going to need you to come with me."

Emily put her teacup down on the table, but she didn't move to get off the swing. "Why? Dad's supposed to be here in a little while. Actually, I was just texting him. I'm gonna stay the night with Mercy and Hunter." Then she paused and shook her head. "Wait, I don't get it. Dad sent you here? He said he had stuff to do in town. Was he at the police station? But why would he send *you* here?"

The deputy swallowed so hard that his Adam's apple bobbed. "Your father didn't send me, but you need to come with me."

As Emily started to stand Mercy covered her hand and kept her in place on the swing. "Why? What's going on?" she asked the deputy.

His eyes flicked between Mercy and Emily, coming to rest on Em. He cleared his throat again and picked at the brim of his hat with nervous fingers. "There's been an accident. Sorry, this is . . ." He paused, swallowed again, and started over. "Emily, your father is dead."

Through their joined hands Mercy felt the jolt that rocked her friend. Emily's breath rushed from her body in a terrible gasp and she began shaking her head back and forth, back and forth.

"Dead? What are you talking about? How? It has to be some kind of mix-up or mistake." Mercy gripped Em's hand.

The deputy turned his somber gray eyes to her. "There was an accident."

"No. No. That's impossible." Em spoke softly.

Mercy squeezed her hand tightly. "Like a car accident?"

Deputy Carter's gaze flitted away as he said, "Um. Not exactly.

Emily, let's get you home to your mom. She'll explain everything to you."

"No!" The word burst from Emily.

"If it wasn't a car accident, what kind of accident was it?" Mercy felt like her brain was on fire. *First Abigail and now Em's dad? How? Why?*

"Emily, let's get you home," he repeated as he shifted from foot to foot, not meeting the gaze of either girl.

"No." Emily stood, abruptly letting go of Mercy's hand. She faced the deputy and wrapped her arms around herself. "No! *No! NO!*" Her voice grew louder and more hysterical as she continued.

Mercy stood and put her arm around her friend. Emily's body was trembling like she might fly apart into a million little pieces—a feeling Mercy understood all too well. She held on to Em tightly as she shouted into the house. "Hunter! Xena! We need you!"

The deputy started forward, like he was going to help Emily from the porch. Em cringed back.

"Get away!" she screamed between soul-wracking sobs. "Don't— touch—me!"

Hunter and Xena spilled from the doorway. "What is happening out here?" Xena asked.

"There's been an, um, accident," the deputy said quickly. "Emily's father has been killed. I came to take her home to her mother."

Xena gasped. "Oh, kitten!" She brushed past the deputy imperiously to enfold Emily within her arms as the girl clung to her and wept.

Hunter joined Mercy. They faced the deputy—blocking Emily with a wall of their love. Mercy and Hunter joined hands.

"You said, '*um, accident,*' and then used the word *killed,*" said Hunter. "Which was it—an accident or a murder?"

Mercy's stomach roiled and she swallowed down bile. She knew what the deputy was going to say before he spoke.

"It, um, was a murder. Look, I am truly sorry, but Emily's mother needs her, and I have to get her home."

Emily suddenly sneezed—once, twice, three times. From the deep pocket of Abigail Goode's soft bathrobe Xena pulled out a handful of old tissues, which Em took and tried to wipe her face, but her hands were shaking too hard.

Carefully, Xena took the tissues from her and dabbed at her cheeks, though it was impossible to stop Emily's tide of tears. "Oh, kitten . . . poor little kitten," Xena murmured as she smoothed back the girl's hair.

"Is it really true?" Emily stared at the deputy, and then she looked from him to the twins. "How can it be true?" Before anyone answered, Emily's legs wobbled and she collapsed.

Xena caught her first, and then Mercy and Hunter were there, too. They lifted her, steadied her—loved her.

"We're here, Em. We're here," Mercy said as she hooked her arm around her best friend's slim waist.

The deputy picked at his hat helplessly and repeated, "I really am sorry."

Emily was sandwiched between Mercy and Hunter—while Xena stood behind her, stroking her back and murmuring softly.

"What can we do, Em? What do you need?" Mercy asked as she wiped at her face.

Emily turned her head slowly to meet Mercy's gaze. She was no longer sobbing, but silent tears poured down her smooth, fawn cheeks to soak her shirt. "I need my daddy." Then her face broke and she leaned heavily against Mercy as waves of shudders cascaded through her body.

"Emily—Miss Parrott," the deputy stuttered. "Sh-should I call your mother? Should I go get her and bring her here?"

His words seemed to give Emily strength. She looked up at him. "Mom needs me."

The deputy nodded urgently. "Yes, yes, she does."

Emily drew a deep breath and stood up straight, like her spine had turned to steel. "I'll go. Mom does need me."

"Em, do you want us to—" Mercy began.

Emily turned to her and hugged her tightly. "I have to go to Mom."

"Kittens, help our Emily to the car," Xena told the girls.

Slowly, with Mercy on one side of her and Hunter on the other, the twins guided Emily to the deputy's car and gently helped her into the passenger's seat. The deputy slid behind the wheel and silently handed a box of tissues to Emily. When she made no move to take them, even though tears still washed her face, he put them in her lap. Emily looked up at the twins.

"I don't know what to do." Her voice was strange, listless and so soft Mercy had to lean forward to hear her.

Mercy touched her tear-ravaged cheek. "Just try to breathe."

"Take it one step at a time," Hunter added from beside Mercy. "Don't think too far into the future."

Emily nodded jerkily. "Okay. Okay."

The deputy reached across Emily and closed the door. Mercy raised her hand. "We love you, Em. We're here. Remember—we're here for you!" She watched the streetlight illuminate Emily's pale, stricken face as the deputy backed down the driveway. "She looks like a ghost." Mercy whispered her thoughts as she and Hunter returned slowly to the porch.

"She's in shock," said Hunter. "We all are."

"Oh, kittens! It's just so awful." Xena put her arms around the girls and held them close.

"How could he be dead? Murdered?" Pain throbbed in Mercy's temple with her heartbeat.

"Something is wrong. Very wrong," said Xena. "First Abigail. Then Mr. Thompson, and now Mr. Parrott."

Hunter was the first to pull from Xena's embrace. "We need to go to the other trees."

"Do you really think this has something to do with the gates?" Mercy asked.

Hunter's face looked colorless in the porch light as she stared over Mercy's shoulder out into the night. "I'm beginning to believe it does."

Fifteen

"Why are people still out there? I mean, it's almost midnight!" Mercy felt like she wanted to hit something, but settled for stomping a foot against the floor of their mom's Camry as she and Hunter stared at the cluster of palm trees that guarded the gate to the Egyptian Underworld. The trees were actually one tree, which had, over the generations, sprouted into five. They were squatty with big, handlike fans of leaves that were sharp-tipped—and the palm was awash in light from the baseball diamonds that surrounded it, which were currently filled with teams and too damn many cheering spectators.

"Crap!" Hunter mirrored her annoyance. "I totally forgot about the SBA."

"SBA? What the hell is that?"

"Small Business Association—Mom was on the team for Siren's Call Art Gallery. Every spring the SBA has a tournament. The winning team gets a weekend trip to the Four Seasons in Chicago with spa services and a special dinner included, remember?"

"That's right. Abigail thought they'd win this year." Mercy sighed. "Now what? Should we just go out there anyway?"

"No way! The whole town is there. If the trees really are dying and something terrifying is happening because of it the last thing we need is to call the town's attention to the trees—any of the trees—and to us. Let's just go on to the Japanese gate. No one will be out there." Hunter shifted the car into reverse so she could back out of the lot.

"Hang on. We may not need to go all the way to the tree. Look." Mercy pointed at a group of women, all wearing pink uniforms with KINGPIN LANES blazed across their ample bosoms. They'd just passed the big clump of out-of-place-looking doum palm trees.

"They're wearing black armbands." Hunter's voice was soft.

Mercy's gaze took in the other teams who were all wearing black armbands. She felt tears clog her throat, but she rasped out, "Every team is."

"They're honoring Mom." Blindly, Hunter's right hand reached out, searching, and Mercy grabbed it.

"Abigail would like that," Mercy said. "But that's not what I wanted you to look at. Check out what the Kingpin Lanes team is doing."

"They're sneezing," said Hunter.

"And covering their mouths like something stinks," Mercy agreed.

"Oh, no—sulfur. It's here, too."

Mercy nodded. "And check out the palm leaves. The ones on the top are still green like always. But look at the lower ones."

Hunter squinted and held her hand above her eyes to shield them from the bright field lights. "They're brown!"

"The palms are sick, too." Mercy didn't think her stomach would ever feel normal again. "Let's go on to the cherry tree."

"Okay, yeah, going." Hunter backed out and headed across town.

It was late enough that there was almost no traffic, but Mercy breathed a relieved sigh when Hunter turned off Main Street and cut through the quiet neighborhood until finally coming to the one-lane blacktop that skirted that side of town. They crossed the railroad tracks and then Hunter took a hard left onto a dirt farm access road that paralleled the tracks and the corn and bean fields that bordered them. They bumped along the dark stretch of packed ground until the car's headlights illuminated a substantial tree that loomed like a phantom between the tracks and the maturing cornfield to their left.

Hunter put the car into park and left the lights on, shifting them to bright as she said, "I've always liked this tree, especially when it's blooming."

The weeping cherry tree had bloomed several weeks ago so tonight, instead of a curtain of delicate pink the long, slender boughs looked weirdly like skeletal fingers.

Mercy shivered and didn't move to leave the car. "Remember when we were super little and would come here with Abigail when she fertilized it in the spring?"

"Yeah, we'd pretend that the boughs made a curtain."

Mercy nodded. "Inside, near the trunk, was our stage."

Hunter continued the memory. "And we'd make up dances to Gaga's songs."

"'Bad Romance' is still my fav," said Mercy.

"Of course it is." Hunter turned to face Mercy. "My fav was when we performed songs from *The Sound of Music.*"

The edges of Mercy's lips tilted up. "'Sixteen Going on Seventeen'— you used to love that one."

"I had a giant crush on Liesl."

"Good times." Mercy tried to sound light and carefree, but instead her voice broke and she had to blink hard to stop the tears pooling in her eyes from escaping down her cheeks.

Hunter tugged on her hand. "Hey, we'll have good times again."

"Doesn't feel like it right now."

"I know. But we will. I'm sure of it," Hunter said firmly. "Ready to go out there?"

"No, but we have to."

"Yep."

"Yep." Mercy sighed and let loose her sister's hand. "Okay, let's go check it out. Maybe it'll be okay."

"It looks fine from here," Hunter said as they got out of the car.

Mercy didn't say anything. She was the Green Witch, and her earth-attuned senses had been tingling since the car's headlights had captured the tree. She approached more slowly than Hunter. Mercy drew several deep breaths and stretched her senses. Now that her grief fog had lifted, she was relieved that she could hear the corn whispering with the soft spring breeze. The corn felt fine—young and strong and growing.

She turned her face into the wind, which was sweeping over the bean field to her right, on the other side of the railroad tracks. The air was perfumed with green, growing things. She could sense the pods that were already beginning to swell with soybeans. All was well there, too.

Farther away, Mercy caught the scent of the eastern branch of Sugar Creek. She could smell the distant damp earth. It was normal and soothing. She drew another deep breath to steady herself. Then, resolutely, Mercy focused straight ahead at the weeping cherry that guarded the gate to the Japanese Underworld.

"I don't smell anything bad yet," Hunter called over her shoulder.

"That's good." Mercy picked up her pace so that the sisters reached the veil of boughs together. Mercy gently lifted the drape of willow strands with her hand as she listened with her sixth sense.

At first everything felt fine. The pink flowers that would've perfumed the night just a few weeks ago had already been replaced with small, lime-colored leaves that, when fully grown, reminded her of arrowheads. The leaves were there, filling the long, graceful boughs.

"It looks okay, right?" Hunter stared at the long, graceful branches.

Mercy opened her mouth to agree, and to breathe a huge sigh of relief, when the wind picked up. It caught the dripping boughs so that they swayed as if to a waltz only they could hear—and as they moved together leaves rained all around them. Mercy bent and scooped up a handful. She turned so that the car's headlights shined on her palm and the leaves curling there.

"Shit."

"What?" Hunter peered at the leaves. "I don't see any worms."

"There aren't any. Well, there aren't any in this handful of leaves. Who knows what we'll find when we look at the trunk. But this is so damn weird."

"Tell me."

"You see these leaves that are curled and yellowish?" She touched a couple with her finger.

"Yeah."

"That usually means that the tree is not getting enough water," Mercy explained.

Hunter's forehead furrowed. "But we've had normal rain this spring. That's why the corn and beans look so good."

"Yep. Now check out these other leaves." She pointed to another cluster in her palm.

"They're green. They look okay."

"That's how they seem, but touch one." She lifted her hand so Hunter could press her finger to one of the green leaves, which made it fall apart and turn to moss-colored dust.

"It's like it's autumn and it should be brown and brittle and falling off for the winter. Why's it doing that?" said Hunter.

"Cherry tree leaves stay green but get all brittle like that when the tree gets way too much water."

Hunter shook her head. "How's that possible? First, it's like it's thirsty, and then it's flooded. What the hell?"

Mercy shook her head. "I have no clue. It's wrong. It's all wrong. Come on." Mercy squared her shoulders and lifted her chin as she tried to bolster herself against what else they might find. She fished her cell phone from the boho bag she always slung over her shoulder and flipped on its flashlight.

Hunter also pulled her phone from her pocket and turned on its light.

Mercy parted the curtain-like boughs and the girls stepped inside the embrace of the tree.

"I don't smell anything, do you?" Hunter sounded breathless.

"Nope. Not yet."

Mercy led her sister to the trunk of the tree. The bark of the cherry tree wasn't rough like the other four sentinels. Mercy had always loved its smooth, almost velvety texture. She went to the tree and pressed her palm against it, closed her eyes, and concentrated.

The first thing she felt was completely normal—it was the breathing of the tree. Mercy felt the inhale and exhale against her skin in the stirring of air and a slight change of temperature. She was beginning to relax when nausea consumed her. It cramped her stomach and made her legs go weak—so weak that she suddenly dropped to her knees.

"Mag! What is it?" Hunter crouched beside her.

"She's sick. She feels awful—like that time we went to Mexico with Abigail and we got the pukes from the water. Ugh, it's terrible." Mercy took her hand from the ailing tree and leaned forward, pressing her palms against the dirt at the base of the trunk, afraid she was going to actually throw up.

And worms writhed under her hands.

"Freya! Bloody buggering hell! That's so disgusting." She wiped her hands against her jeans as she frantically skittered backward on her knees.

Hunter shined her light down and shuddered. "They're everywhere!"

Mercy stood and kept backing away. "I'm sorry. I can't stay here. It's sick. It feels—it feels. H, I'm gonna puke!" She rushed through the dangling boughs and staggered until she bent at the waist and heaved bile and tea all over the dirt road.

"Hey, it's okay. It's not you. It's the tree." Hunter soothed as she held

Mercy's hair back. "Tell yourself that. Remember? Mom always said you had to remain separate from the plants and the earth and your green stuff, even as you listened to them."

Mercy spat into the dirt and nodded, wiping her mouth with the back of her sleeve. She handed Hunter her purse. "C-could you find the bottle of w-water in there for me?" Her voice trembled with her body and her mouth filled with bile as she tried not to puke again.

"Here, Mag." Her sister broke the seal on the bottle and handed it to her. "Rinse out your mouth before you take a drink."

Mercy did as she was told and then unbent slowly. "Sod it! I hate to puke!"

"Breathe with me, okay?"

She nodded and matched her sister's breathing until the horrible sick feeling left her. "Thanks," Mercy said. "I'm okay now."

The two of them turned to stare back at the tree.

"They're all sick, aren't they?" Hunter spoke softly, almost as if she didn't want the tree to hear.

Mercy took another drink of water and then nodded. "Yeah. I don't think we need to cross the caution tape by the olive tree to be sure. The others are sick. That one has to be, too."

Hunter began to pace. "But why? They've been healthy for generations—*literally*. Why now? What's made this happen? What's different?" Before Mercy could say anything Hunter continued, "Do you have a baggie or anything like that in that giant purse of yours?"

"Uh, yeah. I keep one of those compostable green baggies in there for when I wear those dangly turquoise earrings that get too heavy. Why?"

Hunter searched through Mercy's purse until she found the baggie. "Got it! I'm going to go gather more of those dead leaves. You stay here. I don't want you to get sick again. Hang on. BRB." She hurried to the cherry tree and ducked inside its weeping boughs.

Mercy stared after Hunter, her mind whirring as it circled around and around, echoing her sister's words. *Why now? What's changed? How could trees that have been healthy and thrived for generations suddenly sicken? Why now? What's changed?*

"Oh, Tyr! This is so damn gross!"

Hunter's words drifted to her on the wind like a gift. Her sister reappeared as she rubbed her forefinger and thumb across the amulet that symbolized her god, Tyr, and Mercy felt a jolt of electric understanding.

He's what's different! Tyr, thought Mercy. *No Goode witch in our history has ever chosen a god to follow—never until now—and now the trees are infested with parasites and dying.*

The thought made Mercy dizzy. She wanted to shout down the words that whispered through her mind.

"Hey, are you still feeling sick?" Hunter hurried to her side.

Mercy nodded.

Hunter hooked her arm through Mercy's. "Let's get in the car." Hunter opened the passenger's door for her sister and helped her inside before climbing in behind the wheel. Then she turned in her seat to face Mercy. "We have to do something. Now. Like, tonight. A spell—maybe something protective? I dunno. Xena will help us figure it out." Hunter's words kept rolling from her, not giving Mercy a chance to speak. "Wait, no. How about a ritual? Like a repeat of the Beltane Ritual. You know, to make them all stronger. We could start here, and then—"

"You mean redo the ritual that killed Mom? Bloody hell, Hunter, think! It's not like you to be so impulsive—so blind."

"The world might be dissolving around us!" Hunter picked frantically at her nonexistent thumbnail, making it bleed. "Nothing is *like* me anymore. Nothing is *like* you anymore, either. This nightmare is our new norm, and we have to stop it."

"Which is why we have to be extra careful," Mercy insisted. "H, we have to figure out what's *really* gone wrong. We can't just throw spells and rituals at the trees. What if we choose wrong? What if we make it worse *or even let another monster loose*?"

Hunter breathed out a long sigh that sounded like a sob. "Okay. Okay. I hear you." She shook herself like a cat coming in out of the rain. "But we can't just sit around talking and researching. Mag, *we have to act.*"

"I know. I'm not saying we do nothing. All I'm saying is that we have to be smart and careful."

Hunter sat up straighter. "I have an idea! Tomorrow I'll go to that big nursery in Champaign."

Mercy nodded. "World of Blooms."

"Yeah, that's it. I'll take leaves from the trees and even a sample of those worms." She shuddered. "Maybe there's something mundane we can do to make them better."

"And while you're doing that Xena and I will be going through the old grimoires to research what kind of magic we need to use," Mercy said.

"Yes. That's our plan. Okay?"

"Okay. That means no school tomorrow for us." She chewed her lip and then added, "And we have to be there for Em."

"I wonder what happened to her dad?" Hunter mused as she started the car and began backing carefully to the blacktop.

"I don't know, H. Everything feels so wrong. I can't even."

"I know, Mag. I know." Hunter's bloody thumb rubbed Tyr's amulet.

Silently, they drove through town—each girl lost in her own thoughts. Mercy stared out the window, overwhelmed by a terrible foreboding that had her feeling like she might puke again. *Could Hunter's devotion to a god and not a goddess be the match that will light the fire that will burn down the gates?* She didn't want to believe it, but the more the idea circled around her mind, the more it made sense in a world that had suddenly turned dark and chaotic and strange.

Sixteen

Mercy hovered between awake and asleep—and for a few precious moments her world felt normal. Birdsong and a gentle, corn silk–scented breeze wafted in through her open window. From the crack under her closed door the rich aromas of coffee and toast slathered with homemade strawberry jam teased her, and she imagined she heard Abigail's Pandora station—perpetually set to her favorite singer, Tina Malia—drift up the wide stairway as the songstress's sweet voice told tales of this world's magic and beyond.

"Mag! Psst! Mag! Are you awake?"

Mercy rubbed sleep from her eyes as she came fully awake, and with consciousness also came reality. Abigail Goode was dead. The trees that kept this world safe from ancient evils were sick. Emily's father had been killed. The world was upside down.

And Hunter's face was peeking into her room.

"Are you awake?" her twin repeated.

"I am now," she grumbled, rubbing sleep from her eyes. "What time is it?"

"Late. Seriously. Like, past noon. You've been sleeping forever. FYI, Jax is here. He's going to take me to the nursery. Xena has about a zillion old grimoires put out for you to go through. She just discovered coffee—heavy with cream and sugar—but apparently caffeine works on a cat person the opposite of how it works on people persons. She was practically falling asleep on her feet and had to excuse herself to Mom's room to nap."

Mercy yawned. "Then why are you waking me up?"

Hunter leaned against the doorframe and crossed her arms. "Because Jax just told me your boyfriend got permission from his parents, with his coach's okay, to skip a couple of his afternoon classes and come over here to 'check on his witchy woman,'" she air quoted as she rolled her eyes. "So, he'll be here in a while. Thought you'd want to brush your teeth or whatever."

Mercy sat up and stretched like Xena—in cat *or* human form. "Aww, that's sweet of him. And as Abigail would say, if you keep rolling your eyes, someday they're going to freeze like that."

"Oh, please. Just don't let him distract you for long. I'll be back with whatever stuff the tree person—"

"Arborist," Mercy supplied.

"Yeah, that. I'll have what the *arborist* recommends as mundane help for the trees when I get back. You, Miss Green Witch, need to have the magic part ready. Tonight, we fix this mess with a double-whammy—muggle stuff and witchy power."

"Stop stressing. I already have a few ideas. Why do you think I'm so tired?" Mercy jerked her chin at the pile of old grimoires on her bedside table. They had colorful sticky notes protruding from their closed pages like paper fringe. Then her eyes widened and she reached for her phone. "Oh, bloody buggering hell! Have you heard from Em?"

"I texted her and called her. Twice. I didn't get any answer until I told her you were sleeping and that I was checking on her for you. She only answered with two words: I'm okay."

Mercy ran one hand through her hair as she squinted at her phone and read through the six texts she'd sent Emily last night and early this morning while she'd been going through the grimoires. No response. Em hadn't answered her even once. "She's not okay. No damn way. I'm texting her right now. Again."

"Hey, Mag?"

Mercy looked up from her phone. "Huh?"

"Remember that we all grieve differently. Be there for her, but don't be surprised if this changes her. Mom's death has changed us."

"You're right. I'll remember. Thanks. And good luck today."

Hunter smiled. "You, too. Later gator."

Mercy's response was automatic. "After 'while crocodile!" Then she returned her attention to her phone, texting:

EM! SORRY. I JUST GOT UP. U OK? CALL ME!

While she waited for a response Mercy brushed her teeth, piled her hair up in a loose knot, and took a quick shower before putting on her most comfy Free People boho dress. It was the color of moss with blue flowers embroidered down the bodice of it and an adorable high-low ruffle that made it sexy and cute in the front, but long enough in the back not to cause stress whenever she had to bend over.

Her phone rang as she was sliding her feet into her favorite moccasin slippers.

"Em!"

Emily's voice was muffled, like she had a cold that had completely clogged her nose. "I can only talk for a sec."

"It is awful?" Mercy asked.

There was a long pause—so long that Mercy frantically wondered if she'd asked the wrong question—when Em's shrouded voice finally replied. "Mag, his eyes are gone."

Mercy's stomach rolled in rebellion. "Your dad? *His* eyes?"

"Yes," Emily whispered. "The sheriff told Mom."

"Oh, Freya!" Mercy's legs stopped working and she sat hard on the end of her bed as bits and pieces of the sheriff's creepy words about Mr. Thompson, the dead guy he'd found by the olive tree, lifted from her memory: . . . *dead man . . . with no eyes . . . Ripped right out of his head . . .*

"It's so terrible I don't want to think about it, but I can't stop thinking about it," said Emily.

"Is *that* how he died?"

"No. He—he was strangled and then the murderer took his eyes. Mag, I just—" Emily's words ran out as she sobbed.

"Come over, Em. Just get in your car and come over here right now."

Emily took several deep breaths before she answered, and when she did she sounded broken. "I can't. Mom's not okay." She paused and then added in a whisper, "They let her see him. I wouldn't—couldn't. But I *should have. I shouldn't* have let her go in there by herself."

"*They* shouldn't have let her see him! Bloody hell, Em! What's wrong with the sheriff?"

There was a sharp sound in the background and Emily spoke quickly. "Gotta go. I think Mom just dropped another cup. She's, uh, *medicated.* Heavily. I'll text you later."

Before Mercy could say anything else the phone disconnected. Mercy finished putting on her slippers and slowly went downstairs. She hadn't imagined Abigail's music. Hunter must have flipped on the Pandora station. Mercy was glad. She stood in the kitchen and let the beautiful lyrics of "Shores of Avalon" soothe her shattered nerves as she brewed another pot of her mom's special dark roast coffee. Mercy didn't love coffee like Abigail had, but she did like the way it smelled—and if she added enough coconut milk and sugar it didn't taste too bad. But, more importantly, it was part of her usual morning ritual, and even though it was past noon Mercy craved whatever might help her feel normal, if only for a little while.

She put two slices of thick sourdough bread in the toaster and got

Abigail's homemade strawberry jam from the pantry. As she slathered sticky-sweet goo on the warm bread her thoughts spun. *Horrible things are happening in Goodeville and it all started the night Mom was killed. What if the sick trees have something to do with it?*

Mercy sat at the table in the breakfast nook, which Xena had piled high with old grimoires the night before. She moved them out of the way and texted Em again:

CALL ME WHEN U CAN! I'M HERE. LOVE U!

Then Mercy stared out the back window as her coffee went cold as she faced the thoughts she'd pushed aside the night before.

What if Hunter's choice to swear into the service of a god instead of a goddess is causing the trees to be sick? All of it—every bad thing—started that terrible night. The night Hunter officially claimed Tyr as her god. It was the only thing Mercy could think of that differed from their Beltane Ritual and the Beltane Rituals that had been successfully performed by Goode witches for hundreds of years.

But wouldn't Mom have known that Tyr was a mistake? Mercy clearly remembered the day young Hunter had first mentioned to Abigail that she was drawn to Tyr. Their mom's response had been that it was Hunter's choice, and there was no wrong answer when a witch chose her deity. *Okay, maybe Abigail hadn't known it was a problem that H had chosen a god back then, but during the three years between that day and their dedication night she definitely would've said something if it could cause problems.* From her memory Mercy replayed her mom's words to Hunter as they walked to the Beltane Ritual: *It's about time a Goode chose a god instead of a goddess.*

She shook her head and sighed as she nibbled on her toast. "No, Abigail would've known. She was an amazing witch. She would never have let Hunter make such a big mistake. It must be something else and I'm going to figure it out and fix it. I have to." Resolutely, Mercy pulled the closest grimoire to her, grabbed a stack of pink sticky notes and her favorite purple pen, and got to work.

Mercy was deep into her great-great-grandmother Janet Goode's summer 1927 entry entitled *Healing Trees from the Drought* when she pumped her fist and shouted, "Yes! That's it!" Then she wrote quickly on the sticky notes as she muttered to herself. "This will work with just a little addition from the spell Gertrude Goode cast in 1859 after the entire state of Illinois flooded and damaged all the trees big-time." She paused for a moment, chewing the end of the pen before lifting it triumphantly and proclaiming, "Plus, I'll make a big dose of my Awake and Alive Oil! That'll be my own Green Witch contribution. This is going to be perfect!"

One problem solved, Mercy picked up her phone and clicked into the texts.

> EM, HOW U DOING?
> YOU OK?
> EMILY, I'M WORRIED ABOUT YOU.

Zero response from her bestie. Mercy got it—of course she did. She completely understood about how grief could suffocate every other emotion. But H hadn't left her alone in her despair, and she wasn't going to leave Em alone, either. She tapped out another text.

> EMILY PARROTT IF YOU DO NOT ANSWER ME I AM COM-
> ING OVER THERE. NOW!

Three dots appeared almost immediately.

> CAN'T TALK RIGHT NOW. GRANDPARENTS R HERE. I'LL
> CALL LATER. PROMISE.

Mercy sighed and chewed her lip. "Okay." She spoke to the phone like Em could hear her. "But if you don't I *will* come get you. Seriously."

She drummed her fingers against the table as she turned her attention back to the grimoires and the spells she needed to combine. It was easy—comfortable—to focus on spellwork. It was something she could *do* to make at least part of the chaos around her right again.

Mercy was listing the ingredients she'd need for her oil and real-izing she should go upstairs and get her own grimoire so she could record this new protective and healing spell when several loud knocks on the front door made her jump. Momentarily confused, she glanced at the old clock in the foyer as she headed to the door and was sur-prised to see almost two hours had passed while she'd been research-ing. She didn't have to peek out the front window to see him standing there. She could feel that it was Kirk. Mercy smoothed back her long, dark hair and opened the door.

"Babe! Man, it's good to see you!" He stepped inside and engulfed her in a hug and his familiar scent of sweat mixed with Abercrombie & Fitch's cologne, Fierce.

Mercy pressed her cheek against his chest. He was so solid and strong and *normal*. He was the guy she'd crushed on since eighth grade, when he'd seemed completely out of her league. He was the guy who made her feel special *and* needed *and* wanted. He was there, with her instead of in school preparing for finals, because he cared about her as much as she cared about him. When she looked up at him she was flooded with emotions and tears filled her eyes.

He cupped her face with his hands. "Hey, don't cry. I'm here. Everything's gonna be okay now." Kirk dipped down and pressed his lips gently to hers. He didn't deepen the kiss. Instead he looked up, checking out the rooms behind them. "Is Emily here?"

"No. I wish she was here but her mom needs her. So, everyone knows about her dad?" Mercy took Kirk's hand and led him to the couch. She curled up there beside him, with her feet tucked under her. His presence and the fact that she'd figured out the spell they needed to cast to strengthen and protect the trees had her feeling lighter than she had in days.

He nodded and kissed her hand. "Yeah, the whole school's talking about it. He was murdered, which is *really* crazy."

Mercy leaned into him. "That's what Em said."

"Did she say anything else?" Kirk asked. "There're rumors about something really nasty happening to him, but no one knows what for sure."

Mercy straightened and pulled her hand from his. "Well, I haven't had a chance to talk to Emily much. She's pretty upset." The lie came out before Mercy planned it. She just wouldn't, *couldn't* gossip with Kirk about Mr. Parrott. It was already bad enough that everyone was talking about it, which Em would hate. She couldn't add to her best friend's misery.

Kirk was instantly contrite. He slid his arm around her shoulder and pulled her close to him again. "Sorry, that wasn't cool of me. So, what have you been up to?" He glanced over his shoulder at the edge of the breakfast nook table, filled with old books and notes. "Are you actually studying in there?"

"Oh. Um. No. That's Xena's stuff," she lied again and then chewed her lip. Mercy usually hated lies—and was pretty bad at them.

Thankfully, Kirk didn't notice. All he said, with a little laugh, was, "Your aunt or your cat?"

She smacked his shoulder. "The one that can read, silly."

"Speaking of—where is she?"

"The aunt or the cat?" Mercy teased.

He grinned. "The one who hates me."

"Oh, well, that would be both. They're upstairs napping."

"Whew." He pretended to wipe sweat from his forehead. "It's weird to be hissed at."

"Sorry about that. The Xenas are protective, but they'll learn that you're one of the good guys soon, and then you'll hear nothing but purrs."

His eyes widened. "From the aunt, too?"

"It's possible."

"I'm gonna have to record that for the Cats of Insta. Talk about going viral."

"Weirdly enough I'll bet Xena would like that."

"You're obviously talking about the cat now," he said.

"Obviously!" She grinned.

He touched her cheek gently. "It's good to see you smile again."

Mercy pressed her cheek into his warm palm. "I'm better after Hunter's spell. Plus, you're another kind of magic that's good for me."

His hand dropped from her face. "That spell. It was kinda uncomfortable to see you—"

She waved her hand dismissively. "Hey, forget about that spell. Or if you want to remember it think of it as homeopathic healing."

"What do you mean?"

"Well, does acupuncture make you uncomfortable?" Mercy shifted so that instead of leaning into him she faced him as she reclined across his lap.

"It did before Coach made me go last year for my shoulder injury. It didn't hurt. Actually, it helped."

"That's what Hunter's spell was—acupuncture for my emotions. I can see that it might have been strange and even kinda freaky, but it was really just a movement of energy that helped me be able to deal with my grief in a healthier way."

His brow furrowed as he considered her words, then he let out a long breath. "I guess that makes sense."

"Of course it does. And how could I be your witchy woman without actually being witchy?"

Kirk's face cleared and he pulled her closer. "Hey, I'm here for you, not me. What happened to Emily's dad must be really hard for you after your mom."

Mercy let her head rest on his shoulder. "Yeah. It feels like my world is totally falling apart."

Kirk lifted her chin with his finger. "Then hang on to me. I won't let you fall apart." He kissed her again.

Mercy sank into him. She parted her lips and met his questing tongue. He tasted like the Big Red gum he liked to chew. His strong arms held her tightly and his mouth and touch were hot and insistent. At first she returned the kiss to keep him from saying anything more about death or spellwork, but soon she realized that his desire was a roadblock to the terrible things that had happened the past several days. When Kirk's mouth was on hers all she could think about was his need. When Kirk's hands found the ruffled edge of her dress and slipped beneath to caress her thighs and her butt, his heat burned away the misery she'd been living and breathing. She pressed herself closer to him and deepened the kiss, chasing his tongue, catching it, and then sucking softly on it. His moan drove away the sounds of the sobs that came from Hunter's room every night when she pretended to be asleep.

Abruptly Kirk broke the kiss. Breathing hard, he whispered, "It wouldn't be cool if Xena—either of them—came down here to find us like this."

And Mercy suddenly knew what she wanted—what she *needed*. She took his hand and stood, pulling him up from the couch with her. "Then let's go where we can't be interrupted—by either of them."

His answering smile was as hot and sweet as his kisses.

She led him upstairs to her room and the bed she'd never, in sixteen years, let any boy so much as sit on. That wasn't because Abigail had been uptight about sex—her mom had definitely *not* been like that. Mercy had never had a guy in her room before because until Kirk she'd never been in love.

Mercy guided Kirk to the bed and then playfully pushed him down on it. Laughing, she fell on top of him as they resumed their passionate kisses. Kirk's hands quickly went under her dress again, and she was glad that she hadn't bothered with a bra as he squeezed her breasts. She let her hands roam his body. His PROPERTY OF GOODE ATHLETIC DEPARTMENT tee was easy to untuck and she loved the way his hard, smooth muscles felt under it.

Kirk broke their kiss long enough to pull off his shirt and toss it to the floor. Then he raised a brow at her. "Your turn."

Mercy hesitated.

"Hey." He touched her cheek gently again. "We won't do anything you don't wanna do. No matter what, you say stop and I stop. Promise."

She bit her lip and then spoke softly. "I—I want to, but I don't think I'm ready for more than just, you know, making out and stuff right now."

"That's okay. Seriously. You have to be into it, too. I can wait." Kirk met her gaze and said simply, "I love you, Mercy Goode. You're worth the wait." He started to reach for his T-shirt.

Mercy's hand stopped him. "I love you, too, Kirk."

"Babe, that means so much. You're the only woman I've said that to except my mom." He looked away, blinking fast. "And then she left me."

Mercy pulled him into her arms. "I won't leave you. Ever."

His kiss was deep and hot, but he broke it off, reaching for his shirt again.

Again, she stopped him, only this time she said, "Don't put that on. I want to be close to you and your skin feels so good."

Kirk dropped the tee and then plucked at the ruffled hem of her dress. He gave her a cute, cocky smile. "It would feel even better against *your* skin."

And that did it. Mercy wanted to feel something besides sadness and worry and fear. She wanted to feel warmth and happiness—she wanted to feel safe again. Kirk made her feel safe, and *he loved her.* Mercy reached down and peeled her dress over her head so that all she wore were her panties and a tentative smile.

Kirk sucked in a sharp breath as he stared at her. Slowly, he reached out and lifted one of her breasts. "Do you know how beautiful you are?"

"No," she whispered. "Tell me."

Tenderly, his thumb caressed her nipple, causing it to harden as Mercy's back arched and a jolt of pleasure sizzled through her body. "You're not a witch. You're a goddess." His breath was ragged as his lips replaced his thumb.

Mercy wrapped her arms around his bare shoulders as she straddled him. He was right. The sensation of his hot, sweat-slick flesh against her naked skin felt so incredibly good that her world narrowed and she could think of nothing except the pleasure that pulsed through her body. She moved her hips so that the warm wetness between her legs found the hardness that pressed against his jeans, and he moaned again.

"You're *so sexy*. You feel amazing."

Mercy's hands found his nipples—smaller and tighter than hers—but his sharp intake of breath as she gently teased them made her believe that they were as sensitive. Emboldened, her hands explored downward. Her fingers traveled to the six-pack that all the girls drooled over whenever he took off his shirt after football practice.

His moan was deeper. "Ah, god! You're killing me," he said as her searching fingers found his belt buckle.

"Do you want me to stop?" she whispered.

"Hell no!"

She smiled and felt unbelievably powerful as she pushed him back on the bed. Mercy moved off his lap as she unbuckled his belt and then slowly opened his jeans. As she reached inside them to touch him Kirk shifted so that his hand could explore her bare thighs.

"Do whatever you want." He sounded breathless.

Mercy did whatever she wanted. She'd seen penises before. The internet was full of them. But she'd never touched one, and the hardness of it surprised her. She ran her hand up and down the thick length of him as his hips lifted and jerked in response. Mercy was surprised by how much she liked touching him, stroking him. It was incredible and powerful and sexy how just a small touch, a soft stroke, had him moaning and sounding like he'd just run several lengths of the football field.

She was intrigued by the drops of clear liquid that dewed the head of his penis. Mercy rubbed them gently around as Kirk gasped and whispered how good it felt and how much he loved her. And when her head dipped and her tongue replaced her fingers he groaned like she really was killing him.

"Don't stop! Oh, you fucking gorgeous goddess, *do not stop!*"

So, Mercy didn't. As her mouth covered him and she experimented by sucking and licking the thick, hard length of him, Kirk's hand slipped inside her panties. She knew how to touch herself—she knew what made her orgasm—and she rocked against his searching fingers until he found the right spot and then she moved her hips in time with her mouth.

Kirk came first, surprising Mercy with the heat and force of it, but then she sank into the waves of pleasure that cascaded through her body, making her hips buck against his hand as her orgasm engulfed her. She kept sucking and licking as another orgasm and then another rippled through her until finally she was breathing so hard she had to fall limply back on the bed. She crawled up so that she lay in the crook of his sweaty arm while their breathing slowed together.

"You are a goddess. *My* goddess," he said.

Mercy's head found his shoulder. He pulled her closer to him while she stared up at the ceiling and tried to slow her breathing and sift through her tumultuous thoughts.

Kirk kissed her damp forehead. "You were amazing."

"Um, thanks." Mercy spoke softly. Her body was still humming with the aftermath of pleasure, but as passion faded the real world rushed in to take its place. *Freya, what did I just do?*

"Seriously. A-maz-ing." Kirk laughed joyously. "Like, you blew my mind!" His fingers traced up and down the side of her neck.

Mercy had no idea why, but she had a sudden urge to pull away from him. Instead, she forced herself to be calm and turned her head to stare at Kirk's handsome profile. His face was still flushed. His full lips were lifted at the corners in a satisfied smile. He obviously didn't have a worry in the world. But Mercy's world, full of sadness and worry and loss, had come flooding back. Reality washed away the last of her pleasure and she felt utterly empty, numb—like *she* hadn't just given Kirk a blowjob and had several earth-shattering orgasms herself. Someone else had done that—someone who had tried to hide from reality, to exchange grief for lust.

It hadn't worked.

Mercy lifted herself up on her elbow. She needed to talk to Kirk—to explain to him how confused she felt—that what had just happened between them had more to do with loneliness and confusion than sex. But before she could speak she heard through her open bedroom window a car's tires on their gravel driveway and then voices floated up with the breeze. "Oh, bloody, buggering hell!!" Mercy rushed to the window. "Sodding wanker! It's Jax and Hunter!"

When she turned back to Kirk he was still lying on the bed smiling at her. She hurried back to him, throwing his shirt at him before she yanked on her dress.

"Hey, what's the big deal? Hunter's not your mom."

Mercy just stared at him until he wiped a hand across his face as he realized what he'd just said. "Oh, shit. I'm sorry. That was stupid of me."

Mercy grabbed a brush from her vanity and attacked her hair. "It's okay. I know what you meant. Kirk, I don't want Hunter to know about this. Not right now."

Kirk looked up at her as he tucked in his shirt and zipped his jeans. "Are you sorry about what we just did?"

Mercy went to him and touched his shoulder as she avoided the honest answer there wasn't time for her to give. "Now isn't a good time. Mom died. Things are not normal. I—I don't know how Hunter would take this. I don't want her to think that I've forgotten about Mom—that I don't really care she's gone."

"Okay, yeah, I get it. Hey, she already doesn't like me much and this isn't gonna help that."

"H appreciates that you've been here for me—for us. The more you're around the more she'll like you." She draped her arms over his shoulders and attempted to sound normal. "I mean, how could she *not* like you?"

He waggled his eyebrows. "Seriously." He cupped her butt cheek and squeezed. "Hey, if your sister and Jax are back that means I gotta get to practice. Crap! I didn't realize it was that late. Being with a goddess definitely messed with my sense of time. Good thing Jax is here. Mom dropped me off, and I can bum a ride from him." But Kirk didn't move except to bend and kiss her passionately.

Mercy let herself relax into his arms. *Kirk loves me,* she reminded herself.

Hand in hand they hurried down the stairs. Mercy stepped into his arms one more time as they kissed slowly again. She did feel closer to him than she'd ever felt to any guy. *And I love that closeness—that specialness that only the two of us share,* Mercy told herself sternly. *Then why do I feel so empty?* The question hovered in her mind and Mercy shoved it aside.

Kirk was still kissing her when the sound of a car door slamming made her break the embrace and push him playfully out the door.

He backed onto the porch and mouthed *I love you, goddess!* before he turned to leap down the stairs.

Mercy closed the door and sighed as she leaned against it. *What is wrong with me? If Abigail were here she'd understand. Mom would help me figure this out. If Abigail were here it wouldn't have happened,* Mercy thought, though she didn't speak the words. She felt strange, like a rubber band that had been stretched too far. Mercy shook herself and spoke the rest of her thoughts to the quiet house. "I need to eat something to ground myself. That's all. And I have to believe it's all going to be okay. Hunter and I can save the trees, Emily is going to be herself again, and Kirk Whitfield finally said he loves me." Resolutely, Mercy headed to the kitchen as she repeated, "That's right. My Kirk loves me!"

Seventeen

At this time of year, when the sun camped out in the sky and gentle rains spilled from the clouds, it was easy for World of Blooms, Champaign's largest nursery, to live up to its name. The candied scents of honeysuckle and lavender reached Hunter before she and Jax had even made it to the entrance. She inhaled and let the summertime smells pull her from the nearly empty parking lot, through the nursery's sliding double doors, past the array of pots and seed packs, garden sculptures and indoor plants to the information booth set up outside the main building's back entrance. The Qs INTO As hut looked like it belonged on the beach, complete with thatched straw roof, colorful orchid-shaped lights tacked up around the bar, and sun-streaked blond attendant.

Jax ran his hand through his earth brown hair, turning his textured fringe into a messy pompadour before he smoothed down the front of his T-shirt and flicked a speck of lint from his shorts.

Was he . . . *primping*?

Hunter trailed her best friend as he glided up to the hut and rang the small bell that sat in the middle of the bar.

The attendant's soft curls bounced around her shoulders as she turned to face them. "Heya, what can I help you find?" Her voice was starshine, bright and clear and enchanting.

Hunter's mouth went dry and she wished she, too, had combed her hand through her hair, turned it into anything other than the plain ponytail that hung down her back like the densely packed flowers of a cattail.

Jax leaned against the bar and glanced over his shoulder at Hunter. "What'd you say the name of that stuff is?"

Hunter's tongue was a ball bearing pressing against her teeth. There was no point in crushing on anyone back home in Goodeville. The one time she had, Chelsea Parham had run around school screaming that Hunter was trying to turn her into a lesbian. Since that backward day in middle school, Hunter had decided that no Goodeville girl would ever be attractive.

They're all warty toads, she'd said as her mother cupped her face and pressed their foreheads together.

There's a whole world outside of Goodeville, Abigail had whispered before she'd kissed the tip of Hunter's nose.

"It's an insecticide." Hunter cleared her throat and joined Jax in front of the hut. "For tree worms."

The attendant's eyes, robin's eggs pressed into her soft, round face, shimmered when she met Hunter's gaze. "Let me get you a map. When the trees start to bloom, it can turn into a bit of a maze." She brushed a curl from her cheek and pulled a map from beneath the bar. "We're here," she said as she took a red marker from the cup next to the bell and drew a star over the info desk. "And you want to go all the way back here." She drew a line from the hut, through the bonsai tent and the section of full sun flowering plants to the back section of the property where she marked the CONTROL THOSE PESTS! hut with another star. "And this is where I usually work." She circled the EDIBLE ORGAN-ICS section twice and looked up at Hunter. The corners of her pink lips quirked as she spoke. "If you make it back in, ask for Grace."

Hunter's legs were bags of pudding as she collected the map and wobbled away from the information booth.

Gravel crunched as Jax followed his best friend. "That's Hunter. She's *amazing*," he called back to the hut. "And she'll definitely be back!"

Hunter's cheeks sizzled and her palms were slick with sweat. There *was* a whole world outside of Goodeville and Hunter hadn't had to go far to find it.

"Dude." Jax bumped Hunter's shoulder. "Why are you running away? Go back and talk to her. She's clearly interested."

Hunter paused to unfold the map she'd scrunched up in her hand. Red marker stamped the scabbed-over slivers she'd accidentally dug into her palm the night before. "I don't even know what I would say. It's not like I ever get to practice any of that stuff."

"I'll be your wingman," he said as he dodged a pollen-coated bee. "I already have my pitch down: 'This is Hunter Goode. The best, smartest, kindest, most talented girl you've ever met.'" His forehead wrinkled and he scratched his chin. "There's more, but I'll proceed on a case-by-case basis."

Hunter folded the map and crammed it into her front pocket. "What's wrong with you? I'm not a prized pig, Jax. You can't dress me up and sell me to the highest bidder." The gravel walkway smoothed into round river rocks as they entered the bonsai tent and wove around tables covered with miniature trees and shrubs.

"H!" Jax stood in the entrance of the tent, hands shoved into his pockets. "A lot's going on. I get that and I'm here for you. But I'm not an ass." The slim lines of worry sprouting from the sharp corners of his eyes vanished when his brows lifted. "I don't think you're a piece of meat I can toss out to lady-lovin' hyenas. I just want to help."

Hunter picked at the edge of her thumbnail. "I'm not ready. For flirting or a girlfriend or making out or sex. I just—" Her eyes burned, and each blink sent tears down her cheeks. She'd never admitted any of that before. Never felt the reality of it until now. It had been easier to think that she was the victim of circumstance. That, if she lived in Chicago or New York or LA, she'd have a serious girlfriend or maybe even a revolving door of torrid love affairs. Goodeville kept Hunter protected. Kept her from seeing her truth.

Jax wrapped his arms around her. He blocked out the light and the saccharine scents of flowers and the pulsing buzz of nearby bees. "Take your time." His breath tickled her ear. "I love you, Hunter Goode. When you're ready, some badass gal will be, too."

She pressed her face against his shoulder. Her best friend always smelled like clean sheets and peppermint. "I liked your line about lady-lovin' hyenas."

Jax's chest shook with a laugh. "Really painted a good picture, didn't it?"

Hunter pressed away from him and wiped her face with the back of her hand.

"Hey, H, you got any mucus removal spells up your sleeve?" Jax pulled his shirt away from his shoulder and pointed at the slimy wet spot she'd left behind.

Hunter's eyebrow rose as she smiled. "Someday, when I'm a famous witch, that snot shirt will be worth a lot of money."

Jax followed Hunter out of the tent and back into the sunny spring afternoon. "So, we're eventually posting your witchy-ness for all to see?" He jutted his chin toward a bench of bright pink flowers. "You'll be able to tell the photogs that your entourage started next to a cockscomb."

"You just wanted to say *cock*, didn't you?"

His shoulders hunched and he hid his laugh behind his hand. "I did, but only because I don't remember the name of what we're actually looking for."

Hunter pulled her phone out of her back pocket and brought up the article she'd read to Jax in the car on the way over and scrolled until she saw the name in bold. *"Bacillus thur-ing-ein-sis."* She broke down the last word the same way she did each time they discussed abiogenesis in her biology class. Something about the *sis* really tripped her up.

Jax's chuckle was interrupted by a snort as he ran his fingertips along the starlike blooms of a row of daffodils. "I'm positive you're still not saying it right."

"Well, at least I don't snort when I laugh."

Jax wrapped his arm around Hunter's shoulders and pulled her into him. "You love my laugh snorts," he teased and rubbed his knuckles against the top of her head.

Hunter couldn't help but laugh as she pushed and twisted in an attempt to wriggle free. "You're like the brother I never wanted." She grunted and reached around to Jax's right side.

"Not the Claw! Not the Claw!" He erupted into a cacophony of snorts and giggles as Hunter snapped her fingers open and shut along his ribs.

Jax released her, wrapped his arms around his middle, and stumbled backward into a table of budding hydrangeas.

"Works every time." Hunter smoothed her hand over the mess of puffy bumps Jax had inflicted on her hair and sighed. "Remember when *I* was the one who would hold you down and give you noogies?" She pulled her tie from her disheveled ponytail and shook out her hair. "Oh, that was the life . . ."

Jax lifted the bottom of his shirt and wiped his eyes. Dark hair ran in a furry track down the middle of his flat stomach and disappeared behind the waistband of his shorts. Gone was the little boy who used to stand between the swings at recess, arms stretched as wide as they could go, hands gripping the metal chains in order to save her one, or the little boy who used to climb onto a kitchen chair to help her get her ponytail just right. Her best friend had turned into a man and she hadn't even noticed.

"That was back when I sounded like Mickey Mouse and Mercy said that I'd be shorter than Kevin Hart." Jax shoved his hands into his pockets and joined Hunter back on the path that wound through the sun-drenched plants to the small hut labeled CONTROL THOSE PESTS! "You should leave your hair down more often." He nodded toward the lengths of inky black that brushed Hunter's shoulder blades. "It's really pretty."

She gathered her hair and positioned it back into her signature ponytail. "I was just wondering what a straight guy thought about my hair choices. Tell me, should I also smile more?"

"Ah, yes, you read my mind." Jax tapped his temple and nodded dramatically. "And while you're at it, you should go back to the kitchen and make me a sammich, extra mayo, no crusts."

It felt good to laugh again. To be away from her house and the ghost of her mother. It felt good to be twin-less, free from her sister and the weight of Mercy's broken pieces that Hunter kept picking up but couldn't quite fit back together.

"Holy hell!" Jax grabbed Hunter's shoulders and ducked behind her. "It's Barbara Ritter!" he said and peered up over her shoulder before hunkering down again.

"Mrs. Ritter, your neighbor?" Hunter cocked her head at the two women who were too busy looking at plants to notice the spectacle that was currently Jax Ashley. She chewed on the tip of her pinky nail and took in the suburbanites in their nearly matching tennis outfits, one pastel yellow with sensible white tennis shoes, the other a much louder neon yellow with bright, sparkling gold shoes. Barbara was the giant, glittery highlighter, which made sense since, although her oldest child wouldn't be in high school for at least another five years, she demanded to chaperone all school dances while using a bullhorn to mortify horny teens. Maybe Barbara had given the school's principal her secret to the perfect ponytail. If Mrs. Ritter gave Hunter the recipe for a long, shiny ponytail that curled at the end like an upside-down question mark, Hunter would let her do pretty much anything.

"Yes!" Jax hissed like a stuck balloon and crawled between two large pots of flowering shrubs before he disappeared under a table covered in ivy.

Hunter bent over and parted palm-sized leaves and scarlet blooms that waterfalled like spilled cranberry juice over the lip of the pot to look down at Jax. "Why are you hiding?" She looked back at Mrs. Ritter and her friend who, aside from the neon-ness of one and the spray tanned–ness of them both, were two completely normal women.

Jax pressed his finger against his lips and frantically waved for her to join him. With a groan, Hunter obliged. Ivy stems brushed against her back and her palms smashed fresh earth as she crawled under the table and squatted next to him. "This is ridiculous," she whispered and wiped the dirt from her hands. "Why are we hiding?"

Jax blew out a puff of air, leaned forward and drew the curtain of ivy closed, and settled back against the ground. "I kind of saw her ..." He moved his hands in front of him like he was juggling invisible balls. "Chest?" He winced and shook his head. "Her boobs, okay. I saw Mrs. Ritter's boobs."

Hunter clapped her hand over her mouth and nearly toppled onto her butt.

Again, Jax pressed his finger to his lips. "My dad made me fix that rotted spot in the fence. I had a few boards down and she just, you know ..."

Hunter's jaw flopped open. "What? Took off her shirt and said, *'Here Jax, please gaze upon my heaving bosoms'*?"

"No!" Another hiss. "She was tanning, *topless,* and I saw her and didn't exactly look away."

Hunter dropped her head into her hands. "Jesus, Jax!"

"I know!" he said as he ran his hands down his cheeks. "I've apologized and said I'd mow her yard this summer for free. She declined, so I decided that my best course of action is to avoid her until I move away for college."

Hunter shook her head. Her ponytail slipped off her neck and hung limply in front of her shoulder. "That's in two years."

"Exactly why we're hiding."

Barbara Ritter's sparkly tennis shoes threw white spots across

Hunter's vision as she and her friend approached the table. Jax's eyes widened and he pressed his finger against his lips so hard that the pink flesh around his nail whitened.

Plain white Keds stood directly in front of Hunter. A ring of dirt encircled the sole like chocolate meringue. "Oh, Barbara, what about these? The . . ." There was a short pause and a ruffling of leaves before the woman continued. "Bleeding amaranthus. It says they get pretty big. If you plant them right along your fence line, they should block out your neighbors."

Jax's face lit up like a stoplight.

Barbara's sparkles inched closer to the large pots just on the other side of the ivy shield. "But the name, Susan. *Bleeding* amaranthus. I couldn't bear to have anything planted on my property with the word *bleeding* in the name. Not after what I overheard this morning."

The Keds spun to face the garish sparkles. "I knew there was something you weren't telling me. You may have re-upped your Botox, but I can still see it written all over your face. Spill!"

The gold-sparkled toes wiggled like two puppy butts. "Deputy Carter was pulled up outside of the Coffee Spot this morning. Windows down, practically yelling into his phone about Dominic Parrott."

Hunter's breath caught in her throat.

Susan sighed and her Keds relaxed and parted slightly. "I've always felt so sorry for Dominic." Another sigh. "That depressing job and practically raising his daughter alone while his wife is off on all of those *business* trips doing God knows what. Although I did see him at the IGA just a few days ago. He's leaving soon for some *funeral services convention*." She paused. "I suspect that's code for *getting the H-E double hockey sticks away from my terrible wife*." Susan sucked in a breath and her heels lifted and settled back against the gravel. "Maybe I should bring him a plate of my hot sticky buns."

"Well, don't get too excited." Barbara's right foot angled outward as she settled into her story. "You know I don't like to speak ill of the dead. Or, in this case, the family of the dead, but—"

Susan took a step back. "Dominic Parrott is dead?"

Jax squeezed Hunter's arm. She wanted to cover her ears with both hands and dig into the ground like a mole, but it wouldn't have helped. Death had stitched itself to Hunter's back and rode her like wings.

"Hush now, Susan." Barbara slid closer to her friend. "It's not common knowledge, just a fact I overheard the deputy discussing. Along with another . . ."

The dramatic pause made Hunter's stomach lurch.

The sparkle-encrusted shoes wriggled as Barbara continued, "Dominic Parrott was *murdered in his own car*. Right outside the sheriff's department. If you're not safe there, I just don't know where you can be."

Susan sucked in another breath and the toes of her shoes pressed together. "It's like in one of those *CSI* shows."

The golden sparkles halted their dance and resumed their stroll along the gravel path. "Well, I wouldn't know about that. I try to stay away from graphic television dramas . . ." Barbara's voice faded and her shoes blurred into two bright blotches as she and Susan turned and made their way back to the main building.

Hunter pressed her hands into the ground. But the killings were about her, about Mercy, about the gates, weren't they? She lifted her hands and stared down at the starlike imprints in the dirt. The sheriff's department was nowhere near any of the trees. What did that mean? What did any of it mean? She crawled out from under the table and stood. She needed answers.

Eighteen

Hunter's journal lay open in her lap and she clicked and un-clicked her pen as she and Jax neared her driveway. She scrawled a note next to the name of the insecticide they had picked up from World of Blooms and let out a defeated sigh. This was her writing journal no more. It was now destined to be filled with to-do lists and random similes and metaphors she thought of throughout the day. At least, random similes and metaphors *used to* pop into her head throughout the day. But that was back when she was going to be a famous author and pen the thrilling and romantic novel, *When Darkness Rises.* Now, she was trying to stop murders, heal sick gates, survive without her mother, and keep her only remaining human family member from falling apart.

Jax slowed to a stop in the driveway and Hunter closed her journal and dropped her head back against the headrest. On the porch, Kirk closed the front door to her house and paused at the top of the steps to stretch.

Jax bumped Hunter's elbow with the side of his sweating Big Gulp cup. "Slushies fix everything." His crooked teeth poked out from between blue-stained lips.

She looked away and chewed the end of the straw. "Can we just sit for a minute? See if I can get a sugar rush before I have to entertain Kirk." Hunter pushed the switch and the window slid down a few inches before she rolled it back up. "Maybe he's leaving," she grumbled as she rolled the window down an inch and then up again.

Jax wiped his mouth on the back of his hand and shrugged at the blue smudge it left behind. "You do what you want." He unbuckled his seat belt. "I've got to pee before I head to practice." He left the car running as he got out and headed toward Hunter's front porch.

She cracked her window again as Jax intercepted Kirk on the front steps.

"Yo, Jaxie!" Kirk held up his hand for a high five. Their hands met with a loud *slap* that seemed to further invigorate the quarterback. "Today is going *so* good!"

Jax brushed his hair back and cocked his head. Hunter craned her neck, but still couldn't hear Jax's reply.

"Lookin' light and feelin' right, my man. Finally got some of Mercy's goodies, if you know what I mean." With a laugh, Kirk stuck out his tongue and held up his hand for another celebratory high five.

Jax crossed his arms over his chest.

"What?" Kirk rocked back on his heels and flicked his chin in the air. "You jealous? You'd be swimming in it, too, if you didn't spend all your time with Hunter. You do know she's never going to switch teams, right? All she is is a cockblock. Girls don't want to see you hanging with other girls. Makes them jealous and the last thing you want is some crazy jealous chick."

Jax ran his fingers along his temple. "Do you hear yourself when you talk?"

"I hear it. But I don't think you recognize that I'm spittin' gold." Kirk draped his arm around Jax and led him down the stairs. "Let me bum a ride to practice. I'll probably play like garbage. My energy is shot." Kirk unhooked himself from Jax as they neared the car. "Hey, you got a protein shake?"

The plastic Big Gulp dented under Hunter's grip as she rolled the passenger window all the way down.

"Jesus, H!" Kirk clutched his chest. "You almost gave me a heart attack." He shoved his hands into his pockets and offered a boyish half smile. "Been there long?"

"Long enough to know you're famished." She held the blue slushie out the window. "Here." It lapped against the sides of the cup as she shook it. "Have some of this." A grin stretched her lips as he walked closer, his nervousness melting back into arrogance. He underestimated the twins. He underestimated Hunter.

"Thanks. If you knew what I'd just—" he began as Jax came around the front of the car.

Blue liquid splattered against Kirk's pristine white shoes.

"What the hell, Hunter? My trainers!" Kirk lifted one foot and then the other until the large clumps of slush had splatted onto the ground.

Hunter slid out of the car and stared down at Kirk's *trainers*. "Oops." She hiked her shoulders and tipped her smile into a frown. "Slipped. My bad." She dropped the cup in the driveway next to Kirk's blue-stained shoes, waved to Jax, and skipped up the stairs.

Hunter would not feel bad about what she'd done to Kirk. He'd deserved it, hadn't he? She chewed the inside of her cheek and sagged against the heavy front door. She didn't have excess power to blame this time. That had all been her. And, if she was being honest, she'd wanted to do worse. Hunter squeezed her eyes shut. She wouldn't feel guilty. *She wouldn't.* Kirk embodied everything wrong with guys. Of course Mercy didn't see Kirk for what he was, having never had to deal with a bully herself. Yes, he'd totally deserved what Hunter had just done after saying all those things about her and boasting about "Mercy's goodies."

Mercy.

Hunter's eyelids flew open and she rushed through the living room and into the kitchen. Mercy sat at the breakfast nook on the cushy bench she and their mother had reupholstered in a swirling sixties-style lime green patterned velvet. Stacks of grimoires littered the table, pink sticky notes sprouting from the pages like petals.

Hunter set the bottle of insecticide on the counter and leaned against the kitchen island, feigning nonchalance, although she couldn't keep from picking at the jagged points of her nails. "You okay?" The casualness she'd stapled to her tone came out brassy and flat. Hunter clenched her teeth. The last thing she wanted to do was push her sister back over the edge and watch her fall into another vast, unending ocean of grief. She wasn't sure if she could do the spell again. She wasn't sure if she should.

Mercy cupped her steaming coffee mug with both hands and lifted it to her lips. "Yep. I'm good." Her gaze never quite settled on Hunter as Mercy took a sip and set her mug back down on the table.

Hunter's stomach hardened. "Are you sure? You seem—"

"Excited?" Mercy stared right at her this time, her moss-colored eyes challenging and forceful.

Guilty. Hunter's swallow was thick, a stone sliding through her chest and thudding into the hollow of her stomach.

"Hey, come here." Mercy patted the empty space at the head of the table and took another drink.

Hunter's footsteps were silent. She wouldn't ask for the truth and her sister wouldn't offer. Mercy had won, and they both knew it.

"I've figured out the spell we need to fix the trees." Mercy plucked a weathered grimoire from one of the stacks, shoved another pile to the side, and placed the manual of magic between them on the table. "The whole drought *and* flood cherry tree business gave me an idea." She drummed her fingers against the cracked cover and continued, "We need to mix together two health-boosting spells and add a little of our own magic for protection."

Hunter's face heated as she eyed the spray bottle. Mercy had done real research, magical research. All Hunter had done was google *kill tree worms.* She hid her hands under the table and resumed picking at her nails. But it could be as simple as applying the unpronounceable insecticide to the trees. Things didn't always have to be super complicated, and just because they were witches didn't mean they had to use magic to solve their problems. Magic couldn't fix everything. Abigail Goode was still gone.

Mercy opened the book to one of the marked pages and ran her fingers over the old, loopy cursive. "It says here that Janet Goode cut a stang and used it to channel healing energy into the trees when they were damaged by drought."

"Stang?" Hunter leaned forward and studied the illustration their ancestor had drawn at the bottom of the page. The ink had smeared, but Hunter could still make out the long, thin branch forked at the end like a snake's tongue. The note scrawled next to the knotted branch read, *Most powerful when cut and carved from a living being. Remember to thank the tree, for we do not understand their sacrifice and we cannot feel their pain.*

"Janet was a Green Witch, too." Mercy said it as if she and their great-great-grandmother had just exchanged texts and were now best friends and new members of an elite social club.

Hunter had yet to read the grimoire of a cosmic witch or one who had chosen a god instead of a goddess. She smoothed her pendant between her fingers and continued to study the drawing. This wasn't the first thing that made her different, and it definitely wouldn't be the last. She slipped her hand back under the table and pulled on a hangnail. She winced when she tore into fresh skin.

Mercy filled the space with the sweet scent of lilacs as she brushed her hair over her shoulders and glanced back down at the illustration. "I thought I'd use the oak that shades our cemetery."

Hunter balled her hands to hide her raw nailbeds and set her fists on the table. "If age plays into it, then that should make the stang even more powerful."

"That's what I figured." Mercy pulled another sticky note–filled grimoire from a different pile and set it open on top of her bff Janet's. "And this is the spell Gertrude Goode did after the entire state flooded in the 1800s."

Hunter read the passage and nodded. "It's really just a blessing ritual. Like what Mom does—" She squeezed her fists, rejoicing in the flash of pain that shot out from her scabbed palm. *"Did* every spring for the garden."

"It feels like a good omen, you know? Like it's what she would want us to do." A smile plumped Mercy's cheeks and her eyelids hung heavy. She was gone for a moment, lost in the silent breath of a memory. "So, yeah." Mercy licked her lips and flashed that childlike smile at her sister before refocusing on the book. "Then I'll add my Awake and Alive Oil and you can add your charged moonstones, and we'll douse the trees with it."

Hunter's attention was pulled back to the white-and-green bottle waiting on the counter. "How do you feel about *really* mixing science and magic?" Her chair groaned as she got up and hurried to the counter. "We're twenty-first-century witches, let's make twenty-first-century magic." She set the bottle in the only space between Mercy and the grimoires. "I know insecticide is, well, *killing,* and our magic is, you know, *not,* but—"

"H! You're totally right. We're modern witches and can use modern science to help us." Then she paused, chewing her bottom lip. "But which tree do we go to first?"

Hunter's fingers tingled as she and Mercy watched the pantry door creak open. It was their mom! It had to be. She was there, showing them the way. Hunter sprinted to the pantry, pulled out her rusted stepladder, and climbed to the top. Her palms heated as she gathered her tarot deck and jumped from the step stool. She untied the velvet azure satchel she kept her most prized witchy possession in and nearly bumped into Mercy on the way to the kitchen island.

"It was Abigail, wasn't it?" Mercy asked as she bounced in place next to Hunter. "I knew she would never leave us."

Hunter spread her deck out on the counter. The pearlescent silver backs of the cards showed the current waxing gibbous phase of the moon and would change each day, becoming most powerful and accurate on the day of the full moon. "We love you, Mom." Hunter breathed and flipped over the first card.

Nineteen

Hunter studied the card she'd turned over. "Huh, that's interesting. Not where I would guess we'd start, but the cards don't lie." On it was an illustration of a wide river, muddy with rich, brown silt framed by lush green banks. The vibrant colors stood out next to the moonshine silver of the backs of the rest of the deck like a Waterhouse painting hanging in the middle of a Jackson Pollock exhibit.

Mercy squinted at the card, trying to figure out what was wrong with the logs that bobbed in clumps in the river. "Um, H, what tree does that mean?"

"Easy. The hippo-filled river is the Nile, which means we need to start at the Egyptian tree, of course."

"Oh, yeah, *of course.*"

Hunter raised a brow at her sister.

Mercy lifted her hands in surrender. "I didn't mean anything except that I'm glad you're the Cosmic Witch 'cause I'm hopeless at tarot." She looked over her shoulder at the big clock in the foyer. "So, it's just a little after three thirty. I'm pretty sure I can cut and carve a stang and, with your help, get all the stuff we need for the spells together by dusk."

From the stairway they heard a long, drawn-out yawn. Xena turned the corner into the kitchen area as she stretched and yawned again. She was still wearing their mom's fluffy bathrobe. Her hair stood out around her face like the mane of an electrocuted lion.

"Good morning, kittens," she said between yawns.

"Xena, it's afternoon," said Mercy.

Xena shrugged as she headed to the fridge. "That's human time. In cat time it's morning whenever we awaken. Hunter, love, did you get me more of that extra-thick cream and delectable tuna?"

"Yeah. Cream's in the fridge. Tuna's in the pantry."

Xena's head swiveled around and her eyes skewered Hunter's. "You remembered to get me albacore, didn't you? You know I won't eat common tuna."

"Xena, we *all* know that. You're the only carnivore living in a house of vegetarian witches," Mercy said, then went on, as she continued to list what she and her sister would need to collect for the tree spell.

Xena sighed as she made her way languidly to the pantry and began pawing—literally—through the canned goods. "Yes, I am aware of your strange dietary predilections. It is the only thing my Abigail and I ever crossed words about. Ah! Here it is! Delicious albacore." She carried the can to Hunter and plopped it down in front of her. "Do be a dear and open it for me."

"How about I show you how to open it yourself. It's really easy." Hunter stood and started for the electric can opener that sat in the corner of the kitchen counter between the coffee maker and the blender.

"Oh, no, thank you, kitten. I loathe electric appliances. What if I broke a nail?" Xena batted a hand at Hunter dismissively while she peered down at the cards. Her gaze shifted from the one face-up. "Oh, excellent! You've decided on a spell *and* you'll be beginning at the Egyptian tree."

Mercy glanced up at her. "Am I the only one confused by tarot?"

"Yes!" Xena and Hunter said together.

Xena slid onto the bench seat and licked the back of her hands,

then smoothed them through her crazy hair as she leaned into Mercy and read her notes. "A stang! That's a rather good idea. Very powerful in the hands of the right witch."

Mercy paused in her list making. "Am I the right witch?"

"Of course, kitten." Xena licked the back of her hand again and tried to smooth a strand of Mercy's hair.

Mercy backed out of her reach. "Xena, it's not cool when you do that."

"I'm just trying to help you look your best. You're rather disheveled." Xena hesitated and sniffed in Mercy's direction. Her yellow eyes widened. "Mercy Anne Goode, you smell like—"

"Nothing that's your business!" Mercy said quickly, super grateful that the whirring of the can opener kept her sister from hearing their exchange. She gathered her sticky notes so that when Hunter turned with the open can of tuna Mercy held them out to her. "Could you gather these things for me while I cut the stang? Then we'll meet in my greenhouse and put everything together."

"Sure, Mag," Hunter said, and took the open can of tuna to Xena.

"You do not think I'm going to eat from a *can,* do you, Hunter? Your mother is no longer with us, but we have not yet deteriorated into barbarism."

This time Mercy and Hunter shared their eye roll. "Perish the thought," Hunter murmured, detouring to the cabinet that held Abigail's collection of bone china.

"I suppose you want us to pour the cream for you, too?" Mercy asked, though she'd already taken a wine goblet from another cabinet.

"I do so love it when my kittens take care of me," said Xena, smiling and making a humming sound that was eerily purr-like.

Mercy had to smile, too, when she and her sister put the bowl of tuna—albacore with a small silver fork—and the crystal goblet of cream in front of Xena, who forked through the tuna delicately, still purr-humming with pleasure.

"Now, shoo, kittens!" Xena said, "Get ready for your spell. And

remember, as you gather the items, hold your intention. That was one of the reasons my Abigail was such a powerful witch. She was wonderful at setting intentions."

Hunter read the list Mercy had given her. "These things are all in Mom's pantry, right?"

Mercy nodded. "Yeah, but I think we should add fresh herbs along with the oils made from them. The rosemary, mint, and thyme are in the garden. Want me to get them?"

"Nah, I'll harvest them for you and wash them. I need to cleanse the moonstones while I add intention to them anyway. Plus, you'll be busy carving the stangs," said Hunter.

"Stangs? As in more than one?" Mercy's fingers drummed against the old grimoire she held. "You really think we can't use the same one for each tree?"

Hunter opened her mouth to answer, but Xena interceded before she could speak. "You must have unique spellwork items for each tree. The power needs to be fresh and focused—not shared. Think of the Egyptian tree only as you prepare. Once you are successful with healing that tree, then you shift your intent to the next."

"But shouldn't we be moving quicker?" Hunter asked. "The trees are getting worse and worse."

"Which is why you must concentrate on one at a time. Do not fragment your powers. Be clear. Be strong. Be decisive. That is the advice your mother would give you. If you're in a hurry stop complaining and get to work." Xena poured the cream from the wine goblet over the tuna, dipped her head, and began to lap delicately at it.

"Gross, Xena!" Hunter disappeared into the pantry.

"Oh, bloody hell that's disgusting." Mercy gagged as she hurried out the back door and headed for the pretty little greenhouse that had been an early birthday gift from Abigail.

Mercy stood the ladder against the wide trunk of the ancient oak that had watched over the Goode Cemetery for more than two centuries.

She'd fashioned a strap around the well-sharpened hedge trimmers, which she slung over her shoulder, much like her giant boho purse. Before she began to climb the ladder Mercy went to the tree and pressed both of her hands against her trunk. She breathed deeply, catching the scent of the newly blooming lilac bushes, big as trees, that framed the little wrought-iron fence enclosing the cemetery. She listened carefully, hearing the cardinals that loved the oak so much, as well as the whirring of dragonfly wings as the helicopter-like insects darted from the water feature that decorated the other side of their spacious backyard. And then Mercy felt it—the inhale and exhale of the mighty tree that vibrated softly against her palms.

"Hi there, Mother Oak." Mercy spoke with familiarity to the tree because she knew the tree well. She'd grown up in her shade and spent uncounted hours in the deep V where the massive boughs first split from the trunk, reading and hiding from weekend chores. Mercy's lips lifted in remembrance. "It's me again. Mercy. I need your help today. I'm going to cast a heal-and-protect spell over the Egyptian palms, and a stang will channel the energy of the spell. So I need your permission to harvest a living bough. I brought wax to seal the wound." She paused and patted one of the deep pockets in her dress that held a small candle and a box of matches. "And I'll be very careful. I wouldn't ask if it wasn't important. May I have your permission, Mother Oak?" Mercy pressed her palms more firmly against the skin of the oak, closed her eyes, and opened herself.

She didn't have to wait long for the tree's response. Almost immediately the bark against her palms warmed and Mercy was flooded with a wave of affection. She imagined it was a lot like being engulfed in a hug by a grandma.

"Thank you, Mother Oak. I promise to use your energy only for good and will tend to the wound I cause you." She decided not to mention that if the spell was successful she'd be back four more times. The faithful old tree probably wouldn't mind, but still . . .

Carefully, Mercy climbed the ladder, thinking of their childhood when Hunter used to boost her up to the lowest branches. She'd swing her legs hard and scramble into the arms of the oak, where she'd spend hours reading or just absorbing the warmth and strength and love of the tree. As her thoughts turned to Hunter, the breeze, which had been gentle and warm, changed—cooled—and brushed insistently against Mercy's skin. She shivered suddenly—like a dark god had walked over her grave.

God, not goddess . . .

The feeling of foreboding was so thick—so real—that Mercy paused partway up the ladder as thoughts she'd repressed for days flooded free. "Oh, Freya," she whispered. "Are you telling me that I've been right to worry about Hunter's choice of a god instead of a goddess? Is Tyr the reason our powers aren't strong enough to keep the trees healthy? Could you show me a sign—something I can understand better than symbols from a tarot deck? Something a Green Witch would get?" Mercy drew a deep breath and opened her mind to her beloved goddess, Freya.

Nothing.

Absolutely nothing came to her except the familiar sounds and scents of Grandma Oak.

Mercy sighed. "Okay, well, I promise to pay attention in case you want to send me an omen."

The warm breeze returned and Mercy shook herself, wondering if she'd imagined the cold and the foreboding. She chewed her lip contemplatively as she continued climbing.

When she got to the familiar fork in the tree, Mercy rested a moment. She centered herself again by breathing deeply. Then she focused on her intention.

I am here to harvest a bough for a magical stang that will channel healing and protective energy into the Egyptian palm trees.

Mercy recited the sentence over and over to herself as she pressed her back against the oak and let her gaze search the branches around her. Soon, her attention was captured by a thin branch growing, straight and strong, from one of the central boughs of the tree. It was forked and about an inch in diameter—and at the end, in the early spring leaves, was a circle of tangled mistletoe. Mercy grinned and nodded as she patted the skin of the bark affectionately. Mistletoe was a powerful magnifier of magic, and would be a great addition to her spell.

"That's perfect, Mother Oak! Thank you."

Mercy climbed out, straddling the thick arm like a horse, and used the shears to slice through the much smaller branch, letting it drop to the ground. Then she pulled out the candle, lit it, and dripped wax on the cut, sealing it to keep out insects and disease. She retraced her way back down the ladder and embraced the tree one last time, whispering her appreciation before she grabbed the branch with one hand and the ladder with the other. She hurried back to the greenhouse where she opened her well-organized tool chest and brought out the little folding knife she used to trim plants. Mercy kept it razor sharp so that it wouldn't cause the plant any more damage than necessary. With a sigh, she sat in the open doorway of the greenhouse and began to trim leaves as she thought about strengthening and healing the palms that guarded the gate to the Egyptian Underworld. She whittled the finishing strokes to create a spike on the bottom of the stang, and concentrated on her intention so fully that Hunter's voice made her jump.

"Hey, that looks really good!"

"Oh, bloody hell, you scared me," Mercy said.

"Sorry." Hunter sat beside her. She carried one of their mom's handwoven baskets, which she set by their feet. "Wow, you even got mistletoe."

"Yeah, Mother Oak was super generous today." Mercy touched the glossy, pointed leaves of the circle of mistletoe.

"I'm not a Green Witch," said Hunter, "but that seems like a good omen."

Mercy met her sister's gaze and nodded agreement. "A *really* good omen." She cleared her throat and added, "Hey, H, did you ever consider any other god, or goddess, to follow except for Tyr?"

Hunter's arched brows lifted in surprise. "No. Never. And that's a weird question. What makes you ask?"

Mercy shrugged. "I dunno. As I was climbing I was thinking about when we were little girls, before we thought about anything much except toys and tea parties and whatever."

Hunter snorted. "I never thought about tea parties. That was you. I always thought about books, but now you're totally the research queen."

Mercy smiled at her sister. "Sorry. That was a weird question. We shouldn't be thinking about the past right now. We should be concentrating on our spell. Speaking of—did you get all the items for my Awake and Alive Oil?"

"Yep!" Hunter opened the basket and pulled out the bottle of insecticide she'd purchased from the nursery and five vials of homemade oils, as well as the herbs she'd just harvested. Inside the basket there was also a handful of milky stones that glowed softly against the square of black velvet Hunter had lined the basket with and the sapphire-colored pouch that held her tarot.

"Awesome! Let's mix them together and then add the insecticide." Mercy frowned as she stared at the insecticide. "Hang on. This is organic, right?"

"Of course. Mag, I'm not a Green Witch, but I'm also not stupid."

"Yeah, yeah, sorry. I'm just being super careful because I want everything to be perfect. Speaking of, I have the perfect glass bottle for our oil."

Hunter followed Mercy through the glass door of the greenhouse. Abigail had built her this incredibly awesome gift several weeks ago for Mercy to fill with young plants to transplant to their vast gardens. It was already alive with hanging ferns, a tray of thriving herbs, baby tomato sprouts, and an entire shelf of happily blooming orchids.

"It smells really good in here." Hunter gently touched a wide frond of one of the hanging plants.

"Thanks, it's mostly the honeysuckle over there. I coaxed them to bloom early. Here it is!" Mercy held up a glass bottle that was the color of the ocean, like a luminous ball sealed with a tan atomizer bulb just waiting to be squeezed.

"That's pretty," Hunter said.

"Yeah, I found it in the back of Abigail's pantry. It makes me think of old-timey perfume bottles." Mercy took the top off the bottle before she placed it on the worktable. "Okay, let's do this together to make it stronger."

"Sounds good to me," agreed Hunter. "If you tell me what you need I'll hand the oils and herbs to you."

"And then you can add your insecticide at the end to fill up the bottle. Let's set our intention."

Somberly, the girls grounded themselves with three deep breaths—in and out.

"My intention is to heal the palm trees," said Mercy. "Please hand me rosemary oil."

Hunter passed her the vial of greenish-amber oil. "My intention is to protect the palm trees."

The girls worked efficiently, sharing that special bond with which they'd been born. They mixed rosemary, mint, orange, lemon, and thyme oils—and added fresh herbs to the bottle. Then Mercy passed the bottle to her sister, who poured the organic insecticide into it until it was completely full. She handed the bottle back to Mercy, who securely screwed the top on before tucking it safely within their basket. Mercy gathered the stang and the circle of mistletoe.

"Okay, I think we're ready," said Mercy.

"Me, too, but I feel like we're forgetting something," said Hunter.

Which was when Xena, still wearing the fluffy bathrobe, hair cascading in chaos around her shoulders, hurried out the back door of the house.

"Kittens! Oh, good, I caught you before you left. You need to do one more thing—ouch!" Xena lifted one of her bare feet and frowned at it as she brushed a rock from between her toes. "If I have to wear shoes I will *die*. Simply *die*!" She sat on the back porch steps and raised her foot to her mouth.

"Freya's cloak!" Mercy gasped. "Is she going to lick her foot?"

"Not while we're watching she's not. Xena! What was the one more thing?"

The cat person froze, blinked several times, and then dropped her foot. "Sorry, kittens. Being a human is very distracting. You need to make it rain."

"What?" The twins spoke together.

Xena sighed. "The Egyptian palms are in the middle of the park, correct?"

"Yeah," said Hunter.

"People will be there—even after dark. They have those horrid lights that do not allow cats to hunt at night at all. It's really very upsetting." She shook herself. "But that is not important tonight. What's important tonight is that you cast your spell without prying eyes. So—make it rain."

"Huh. She's right," Mercy said.

"Well, of course I am. Do you need me to remind you of a rain spell or—"

"No, we've got it," said Mercy. "All we need is dried heather."

"And fern leaves," finished Hunter.

"Exactly," said Xena. "I shall leave you to it." She stood and picked her way carefully to the door. "Blessed be, kittens."

"Blessed be," Mercy and Hunter responded automatically.

"I'll get the fern fronds from the greenhouse," said Mercy.

"And I just saw the dried heather hanging in the back of the pantry," Hunter said. "I'll get that and the matches and meet you in the garage. It'll be easier to call the rain to the park if we do the spell there."

"Okay. See you in a sec."

"Hey, Mag?"

Mercy hesitated at the door to the greenhouse and glanced over her shoulder at her sister.

"She was going to lick her foot!" Hunter said with a giggle.

"Right?! That cat!" Mercy shook her head, but grinned and felt a lot lighter as her sister's laughter drifted through the evening air after her.

Twenty

Hunter parked in a corner of the lot that was made shadowy by several tall, stately white oaks. The girls briskly went to the largest of the trees, whose trunk was broad enough to conceal them both from the people who were jogging around the track and playing kickball on one of the softball diamonds.

The spell was simple, but effective—and one of the first spells Abigail had taught her daughters. Mercy could hear her mom's voice lifting from her memory as Hunter struck the match against the rough side of the box. *Girls, a witch always needs a good make-it-rain spell. We must keep our Earth Mother verdant and fertile—and without rain that is impossible.*

In the car on the way there Mercy had braided the dry heather with the lush fronds of the maidenhair fern. As Hunter lifted the long, ceremonial match, she took the braid from her bottomless purse and held it to the flame. Together the twins invoked.

"Make it rain—make it rain—make it rain!" Three times, just as Abigail had taught them.

The entwined heather and fern began smoking and Mercy traced a pentagram in the air as they repeated thrice again, "Make it rain—make it rain—make it rain!"

All along Mercy's arms her tiny hairs lifted as power billowed with the smoke. The air felt noticeably thicker as it filled with magically induced humidity. The scent of spring rain tickled Mercy's nose until she sneezed.

"It's working!" Hunter fist-pumped.

Above them, the white oak swayed in a new breeze that carried the scent of heather and fern and rain. Thunder rumbled and the girls smiled at each other as they put out the smoking brand in the dirt at the base of the tree and then went back to the car and waited.

It only took fifteen minutes for the sky to open and rain to begin leaking from the billowing clouds.

"And there they go!" Hunter pointed at the last of the people who were running for their cars as thunder rumbled overhead.

"Abigail would be very pleased at how quickly that happened," said Mercy.

"Another good omen?"

Mercy nodded thoughtfully. "H, I hope so. Okay, ready to get wet?"

"Absolutely."

Alone in the parking lot, the twins gathered their spellwork supplies and headed to the center of the park where, unbeknownst to the residents of Goodeville, the clump of doum palms had protected the town from ancient Egyptian monsters for generations. Close up Mercy saw that the damage they'd glimpsed from afar the night before was worse than she'd thought. Only the uppermost palm fronds were still green and healthy. The rest were dried husks that looked like brown knife blades jutting out from thick-armed boughs. The trunks were odd, and nothing like any other Illinois tree. Mercy had long thought they looked like someone had woven together gray corn husks to form the skin of the trees. *Well, tree,* she automatically corrected herself. Though it looked like there were five big palms placed in a close circle around one another, they were actually one tree with five shoots growing from it. Abigail had told the girls that when she was a child there had only been four shoots—that the smaller of the five had sprung up when she was in elementary school. *I hope you feel healthy enough after this to sprout another tree,* Mercy silently told the doum as she pressed her hand against its rough bark. Then she turned and got to work.

The rain drizzled lazily as Mercy wiped her face with the back of her sleeve and unslung her bag from across her shoulder to drop it beside Hunter's basket. "I'm going to put the stang here." She carried the forked bough directly in front of the clump of trees. "Then I'll drape some of the mistletoe over it."

"Okay, while you're doing that I'll set a protective circle with my moonstones."

"Sounds perfect," said Mercy as she pressed the pointed tip of the stang against the hard-packed ground.

"And remember our intention—to heal and protect," said Hunter as she began to circle the palm, dropping a moonstone every three steps.

"To heal and protect," Mercy murmured. She pushed the stang against the dirt until it stood straight and strong, forked end up. Then she went to the basket and gathered the mistletoe circle and returned to the stang. There she carefully unwound the prickly ivy so that she could form three separate circles of green. Two of the circles she rested at the base of the stang. The third Mercy draped around the stang's fork so that it looked like a slender crown atop a very skinny stick drawing of a person.

Hunter rejoined her then and Mercy took the bottle of potent ancient herbs and modern insecticide from the basket. She swirled the bottle, mixing the oils. Inside the blue bottle the potion took on a moss-colored cast that appeared to be lit from within.

"It looks good," said Hunter.

"It *is* good. A mixture of us."

"And a mixture of tradition and today," added Hunter.

"Let's do this." Mercy bent and picked up both of the mistletoe wreaths. She handed one to her sister. The other she lifted and said, "I crown you with the strength and wisdom of sacred mistletoe." Hunter bowed her head so that Mercy could place the living wreath on it.

Then Hunter invoked, "I crown you with the protection and guidance of sacred mistletoe." Mercy bowed her head and Hunter placed the green circlet there.

Mercy held the bottle aloft. "I'll make the first circle, spraying as high as I can with the atomizer."

Hunter nodded. "I'll channel our intention through the stang and take the second circle."

"Perfect," said Mercy. "Just mimic what I say in your own words. Let your intuition guide you."

"Got it. I'll let Tyr guide me. He'll give me the right words."

Mercy felt a jolt at her sister's confidence in her god—the being who could be responsible for all of this—but forced the doubts from her mind and made herself refocus. *Protection and healing . . . healing and protection . . .*

The twins faced each other and breathed together—in and out—three times. Grounded to the earth, Mercy was filled with calm. Then, Hunter walked to the stang. She turned to the trees and grasped the forked ends of the green bough with her hands, and raised her head as if she spoke directly to the cosmos—a channel between earth and sky.

"Heal and protect . . . protect and heal . . . heal and protect . . . protect and heal."

With Hunter's prayer litany as background magic, Mercy began to circle the trees. She talked to the palms and her voice, amplified by her connection with the earth and the ley lines that pulsed deep beneath her feet, sounded so powerful that Mercy was reminded of her amazing mother. *"I call on the Powers of Wind and Earth—of Sun and Rain. By tree and bough, leaf and shoot, with all my heart and the workings of my hands, I bless this palm with life and love—health and growth—protection and strength."*

Mercy felt the magic swirl around her. With a feather-like caress, it shivered across her skin. Heat from the mistletoe crown flowed from her third eye and cascaded throughout her body. With every step—every word of the spell—she squeezed the atomizer bulb and misted the Awake and Alive Oil onto the dying leaves of the suffering tree. And as she did the scent of sulfur billowed with the rain-touched breeze. It burned her throat, but Mercy ignored it and joined Hunter at the stang.

Reverently, Hunter took the bottle and Mercy placed her hands on the forked ends of the stang just below the sacred mistletoe, and focused on being a channel for healing energy to flow through her body and into the earth all the way down to the roots of the ancient palms. Her hands warmed and a soft, moss-colored light illuminated the newly cut oak bough. Excitement fluttered through Mercy—*it was working!*

"Protect and heal . . . heal and protect . . . protect and heal . . . heal and protect," Mercy invoked while Hunter began her circle around the trees, spraying the potion onto its gray bark and browned leaves while she spoke her own invocation in a voice filled with power and confidence.

"I call on the Powers of Moon and Stars—of Sky and Earth. By tree and bough, leaf and shoot, with all my heart and the workings of this modern world we love so well, I bless this palm with strength and healing—growth and health—life and love."

Hunter rejoined Mercy at the stang and placed the empty bottle at their feet. Then Mercy pulled the staff from the ground. Holding it in her right hand she grasped Hunter's hand in her left and together they strode to the tree until they stood within touching distance of it. The rain had slowed to mist. The sulfuric smell was still there, but fainter. It had been diluted by the sweetness of herbs and citrus—and the sharp scent of modern magic.

Mercy lifted the stang.

"I honor you, earth's child. I honor your growth—your boughs and leaves

and thick, mighty trunk. I thank you for your protection and your energy and your spirit—may whatever ails you be gone, and never return. And may you thrive always. Blessed be!"

"Blessed be!" Hunter shouted joyfully.

The green glow intensified, and with magically enhanced power, Mercy drove the stang into the ground at the base of the tree.

There was a terrible sound like the ripping of a curtain, and all five trunks began to shiver. The ground quaked under their feet, causing the girls to stagger backward. And then the air quivered, and a veil that had until then been invisible, lifted from the center of the clump of trees to reveal a figure. His back was to them, but he whirled around, raising a spear, ready to throw.

"Foul demons! Vile monsters!" The creature lifted a shield and took a wide stance. The air before him rippled and glistened as if he were inside a fishbowl looking out, but that semipermeable barrier didn't make him appear less menacing as the power he exuded blasted at them. Then, like a bizarre version of Gandalf the Grey, he shouted, "You shall not pass!"

Together Mercy and Hunter lurched back another step, clinging to each other's hand like they needed an anchor to reality—which they definitely did because the creature in front of them defied any sense of the real that they had ever known.

His body appeared human and male. He was powerfully built. The short, woven leather skirt he wore wrapped low around his waist, and the golden protective plates that adorned his shins and forearms left most of that body exposed. He looked like a bronze statue—except for his head and neck, which were terrifying. He glared at them from behind the veil that separated his world and theirs and though the barrier between them caused his image to come in and out of focus, almost like it was pixilated, his raised spear and shield were a palpable threat.

"Tyr! What in all the hells is that?" Hunter pressed closer to Mercy.

"I don't bloody know, but I'm not going to let it get us!" Mercy closed the few feet between them and her bag that rested on the wet ground beside her sister's basket. Never taking her eyes from the creature, she frantically felt around inside her purse until her hand closed on the pepper-spray gun she always carried with her. Mercy broke the trigger seal. She held it in a two-handed grip in front of her, just like she'd seen Mariska Hargitay do a million times on *SVU.* She swallowed back the bile of her fear and began walking toward the creature that stood in the center of the glistening trees.

"Stay back! This is our world! You do not belong here!" Mercy's voice was fierce with the adrenaline that surged through her body.

Then Hunter was there beside her, so close their shoulders pressed together. Her sister was holding part of a fallen tree branch over her head, like a club.

"We guard this gate! And we are not going to let you come into our world!" Hunter sounded powerful and confident and Mercy felt a rush of pride in her sister.

The creature tilted its monstrous head. His image wavered as he appeared to study the girls with large, almond-shaped eyes that were the color of fertile earth. They were the only things in that unbelievable face recognizably human. The rest of it was definitely reptilian—like a crocodile and a dragon had been mixed together. Small, onyx scales glistened smoothly up a long, sinuous, hooded neck to a crest of crimson horns that sprouted from his head down his back. His mouth was a muzzle lined with rows of dangerous fangs that he had suddenly stopped baring at them.

"You—you are Gatekeepers?" His voice was bizarrely human—deep and masculine—and even though the barrier between worlds made their view of him go in and out of focus, his words came to them clear and strong.

Mercy kept the pepper-spray gun pointed at him. "We are. Who are you?"

The creature put the spear down, so that its flattened edge rested by his feet, which Mercy noted, were dressed in golden sandals. "I am Khenti Amenti, son of the immortal warrior Upuaut, Gate Guardian of the Realm of Osiris. And you?"

Mercy lowered the pepper-spray gun, sent a silent prayer to her goddess, *please give me the right words,* cleared her throat, and said, "I am the Green Witch, Mercy, daughter of the mighty Kitchen Witch, Abigail, Keeper of the Five Gates of Goodeville."

Beside her Hunter also lowered her club-like weapon and spoke with calm surety, like introducing herself to a half-man, half-dragon was something she did all the time. "And I am the Cosmic Witch, Hunter, also daughter of the magnificent Kitchen Witch, Abigail, and like my sister I am Keeper of the Five Gates of Goodeville."

"So we three are demi-gods, Gate Guardians between the realms of the worlds," said the creature. He took a small step back so that when he bowed his massive head it didn't cross the flickering barrier before him. "Well met, Witches."

Mercy was standing there, mouth flopped open, but Hunter recovered more quickly. She nudged her with an elbow before executing something that looked like a bow and a curtsey had had a baby. "Merry meet," said Hunter.

Mercy quickly follow suit as she, too, dipped her head and her knees and murmured, "Merry meet."

The creature put his shield down beside him. His body language instantly appeared more relaxed with the ease of his wide shoulders and the way he clasped his hands loosely in front of him.

"Forgive me for threatening you. This gate has been problematic, and when it called to me I assumed it had continued to deteriorate, perhaps allowing a beast from another realm to enter."

"Wait, the gate called you?" Mercy asked.

"And what does problematic mean?" added Hunter.

He was looking back and forth between the girls, and his eyes suddenly widened. "You are twins!"

Mercy squelched the urge to roll her eyes. "Yeah, we are." Then she added impulsively, "What are you?"

The creature's head swiveled to her and through the glowing barrier it looked as if he were a bizarre deep-sea monster moving through water. "As I said, I am Khenti Amenti, son of the immortal warrior Upuaut, Gate Guardian of the Realm of Osiris."

"No, she means *what* are you." Hunter spoke up. "Not *who*. In our world there are no people who have the heads of, um, not people."

"How odd," said Khenti.

He raised his hand and waved it in front of his reptilian face. The air before him swirled with mist, dark as his onyx scales. Mercy squinted to try to see what he was doing, but her vision of him was just too unstable, though when the mist finally cleared she blinked rapidly and her eyes managed to focus well enough through the fishbowl-like glimpse into his world to see that in place of the dragon was the head and neck of a man—*actually, not a man,* Mercy thought. *He doesn't look much older than us.* Even though his body was football-star strong and tall and muscular, his face was young and smooth. Now that the dragon head was gone, Mercy decided his skin wasn't bronze like a statue, but more acorn-colored with a golden tint like it'd been kissed, a lot, by the summer sun.

"Thanks," Hunter said. "That face is easier for us to understand."

His dark brows lifted. "You truly have no demi-gods *or* gods who use the visage of beasts in your world?"

"We truly do not," said Mercy.

"Seriously," said Hunter. "Now, what about the gate calling you and disintegrating?"

As he spoke the air between them continued to pulse and glowed, bubble-like, in the center of the trees. Even though Mercy tried to see what was behind him, it was too obscured by the strange barrier to allow her to make out more than darkness highlighted with splotches of colors. "I heard voices. I understand now they were yours,

Gatekeepers. I could not catch the words, but I felt drawn to the gate. Though I will admit I have recently remained nearby as I could tell it was weakening."

"How could you tell?" asked Mercy.

"In my world it is an orb—a glowing sphere—in a far corner of Osiris's realm, the Underworld. It is usually colored brilliantly with violets and silvers, turquoise, sapphire, and the pink of a perfect lotus bloom, but over the past several phases of the moon the colors have changed, darkened and muddied. And the scent." He wrinkled his straight nose. "It reeks of decay. So, I have remained near, standing guard so that none of those contained here can escape—and no creatures from other realms enter."

Mercy felt a shiver of fear finger down the nape of her neck. "That can happen? I mean, our gate is sick, too, but it's still standing." She gestured at the cluster of trees he'd materialized within. "These palms keep our side of the gate closed. They're not doing great, but they're still alive. Can things go back and forth even now?"

"Yes, but only if a Gatekeeper is not strong enough to stop them." He stood taller. "I am strong enough."

"That's what you heard," said Hunter. "We were casting a spell to strengthen and heal the palms."

Mercy nodded. "Yeah, we thought if we could heal the trees, the gate would be better, too. Does your side of the gate look any different since we cast the healing spell?"

The young Egyptian sighed and ran a hand through his thick, dark hair. "No, it does not."

"You called us demons and monsters," said Mercy. "Why did you assume we were enemies?"

The warrior shrugged his broad shoulders as their view of him continued to shift and pixilate. "The only beings who wish to escape from Osiris's realm are evil, those who are being punished for the wrongs they committed on earth. I assumed it was the same in your world."

"This isn't our Underworld. This is just the regular mortal realm," explained Mercy. "There are lots of different kinds of people here. Most of them aren't monsters at all."

"But you have more Gatekeepers like yourselves who protect your world, do you not?"

Hunter picked at her thumb. "Um. No. We're pretty much it."

His smooth brow wrinkled in confusion. "Did you not say you are guardians of *five* gates?"

"Yeah," said Mercy. "There're all here—in our town."

"But your mother goddess, the mighty, magnificent Abigail—she must aid you in your guardianship."

Mercy shifted from foot to foot. "She did. She died. Not long ago."

"The other gates—do they also lead to Underworlds like Osiris's realm, or do they open to mortal realms as does this one to yours?" He fired the question at them, his powerful voice in direct contrast to his wavering image.

"No," Hunter answered. "They also lead to Underworld realms like yours."

His eyes widened and he shook his head quickly, causing the barrier in front of him to shiver, like a stone dropped into a glowing pool of water. "No, that is *not* good."

"Why? What's wrong?" Mercy fisted her hands to stop them from shaking.

"It will be the same in the other Underworld realms as it is in mine. If the gates sicken there will be creatures—vile, evil things—that wish to escape their punishment. If they enter your world they will devastate your realm and spread death and chaos with them."

"Ohmygod." Hunter turned to Mercy. "The Fenrir! I looked it up after it killed Mom. He tried to devour the sun and swallowed Odin. One of Odin's sons killed him, sending him to the Norse Underworld for punishment."

Mercy's lips felt numb. "He was trying to escape. That's why he killed Abigail."

"Gatekeepers! Did he take on her form?"

"No, our mother killed him, and with her death she sealed the gate again. What do you mean, take on her form?" asked Mercy.

"That is the only way a creature can have a physical presence in the mortal realm after crossing through the barrier that divides worlds." He gestured at the bizarre veil that glowed and swirled in front of him. "We must possess the body of a being of that realm," said Khenti.

"Bloody hell! You mean wear them like a skin suit?"

He nodded. "Yes, exactly. The mortal's skin becomes a living disguise, even though the body will eventually deteriorate and they will have to choose another. That is why I remain close to our gate. Creatures must kill immediately upon entry to the other realm or they cannot remain."

Mercy grabbed Hunter's hand. "What if we cast a spell to block off the other trees and somehow keep everyone away until we figure this out?"

Hunter turned to Khenti. "Would that work? Would that give us some time?"

"Only if you can keep *all* living beings from the gates."

"You mean the creatures can take over a body that's not human?" Mercy's stomach felt sick. Again.

Khenti crossed his arms over his chest and nodded. "As you saw when first we met, many of us who exist in other realms are not fully human. It would not be difficult for an escapee to kill and then wear the body of a bird or mouse—snake or dog—or perhaps even an insect."

"Oh, shit. That's so, so bad," said Hunter.

Mercy thought she might puke. "Mr. Thompson—he was killed near the Greek tree."

"But Mr. Parrott wasn't," said Hunter. Mercy thought she looked super pale.

"He wouldn't have to be—not if whatever came out of that tree took someone else's body and is a murderer walking around in a good guy skin suit." Mercy met the Egyptian warrior's flickering gaze. "We think something from the Greek Underworld is loose in our town, killing our people. Can you help us?"

His shoulders slumped and he shook his head slowly. "I cannot, though I wish I could. Were I to cross the barrier between our worlds I would have to take on the form of someone in your realm. I, too, would have to kill to remain."

"We need to get to the Greek tree—and I mean *really* go to it this time." Hunter spoke quickly, breathlessly. "We have to figure out if something came through that gate."

"And if so, what," added Mercy. "And then we need to find out whose skin suit it's hiding in."

"Go! I give you my oath to stand guard at Osiris's gate. Nothing shall enter your world through here." Even through the shimmering divide his strength and commitment heartened Mercy.

"Thank you," Hunter said.

"I wish I could aid you more."

"Actually, you've helped us a lot," said Mercy.

Khenti smiled at her. *He's the most beautiful guy I've ever seen in my whole life.* The thought came to Mercy unbidden and she instantly pushed it aside as she felt her cheeks blaze with heat. *What in the bloody hell is wrong with me? Get it together, Mag! This isn't a time-travel rom-com!*

"That pleases me greatly." Khenti lifted his hand, passing it before his face again, which instantly shifted back to a ferocious dragon. He lifted his spear and shield. "I shall remain by the gate. Call if you have need of me again, Witches."

The air in front of him rippled, like heat rising from a boiling pot, and Khenti Amenti, Son of Upuant, Guardian of Osiris's Realm, disappeared along with the bubble that had contained him.

"That was the weirdest thing I've ever seen," said Hunter.

"I wish Abigail could've been here. She would've loved every second of it," Mercy said. "Well, except the whole creatures escaping and spreading death and destruction and chaos part."

Hunter was already picking up the basket. "Do we leave or take the stang?"

"Leave it. It might still work, right? And let's add our mistletoe crowns to the other one." Mercy went to the stang and draped her circle of mistletoe over it. "How long did they say it would take for the insecticide to kill the worms?"

"A week to ten days," said Hunter, mirroring her sister's actions.

"We might get lucky. Even though Khenti didn't see a change yet, it could still happen." Mercy said the words, but they sounded hollow even to her own ears.

Hunter nodded grimly. "Yeah, I hope so. But right now we need to get to the Greek tree."

As they hurried back to the car Mercy kept hearing the Egyptian warrior's words playing around and around in her memory. *The mortal's skin becomes a living disguise . . . The mortal's skin becomes a living disguise . . . The mortal's skin becomes a living disguise . . .*

Twenty-one

Petrichor, the earthy scent released when rain nourishes dry land, floated on the back of the cool breeze as Hunter parked the car on the gravel road near the olive tree. Hunter didn't follow Mercy as her sister charged from their mother's car into the tall grass, headed straight for the old tree. There was something in the breeze. Something more than the sweet smell. It was prickly and magical and it pulled her and her tarot in a different direction. Hunter kicked loose gravel as she walked along the side of the road, following her witchy senses.

Halfway to the tree, Mercy stopped. "H, where are you going?" she shouted, her hands in the air.

Hunter wanted to reply but thought better of it. The explanation would bring more questions than answers.

Hunter paused at the edge of the road near tire tracks from the sheriff's department vehicles that had been on the scene. Her breath caught as she raised her hand and pointed. "Over here," she called out to her sister and waded into the grass. The tall blades swayed around

Hunter's thighs and beads of water fell on her boots as the field shook free of the magical rainstorm.

Her mouth went dry and her fingers trembled as she walked through the tall, lush grasses that arched and bowed with the wind. Ahead, the grasses were crushed, flattened down long enough and by something heavy enough that the rich crimson imprint had remained even after its absence.

A wooden stake had been left behind, nestled in the ground, a scrap of yellow-and-black crime scene tape still stuck to it. When Hunter and Mercy had driven by two nights ago, the tape had been stretched around Earl Thompson's shiny red truck and extended out toward this spot. Had it not been so morbid, the whole thing would've made Hunter laugh. Silly non-magic folk trying to solve a problem that seemed more and more likely to be caused by an issue they couldn't understand much less know how to fix. But that's why Hunter and Mercy had come here: to find out if the failing gate had let something loose.

The tarot deck sizzled in her pocket as Hunter stood at the edge of the flattened red-stained grass. Earl Thompson had drawn his last breath here, had his last thought . . . What had it been? All Hunter could think about was this uneven outline his body had left. But that wasn't what he'd thought about, what kind of temporary destruction he'd leave behind. Maybe he'd thought about fear or fury or fate.

What had Hunter's mother thought when she'd lit herself on fire and left her daughters to face the world alone?

Mercy approached, her signature lilac scent catching Hunter's attention. "Don't we need to be closer to the gate?" Mercy pointed over her shoulder at the olive tree, its gnarled limbs reaching toward the last traces of clouds.

Hunter pressed the toe of her boot into the marred grass. "We have to do it here." Deep burgundy stained the earth like spilled wine. It was blood. *Human* blood. Earl Thompson's blood. Being here, this close to the scene of a crime, should make her feel *different*. Should make her feel *something*. The only things she felt were the power of the moon, the strength of Tyr, and the tarot cards burning a hole in her pocket. But those weren't emotions.

Hunter crouched down and held her hand over the bloodstain. Her palm prickled with energy. There was power in blood. That was obvious. Countries rose and fell by it. The empowered blood of kings and queens chose the heirs to the throne. But more important, more *powerful,* was the blood of their people. Shed enough of it and any tide would turn.

Their mother had never mentioned this power or the deliciously sweet way its energy lapped against each of Hunter's nerves with the steady seduction of waves on a beach. Hunter could be comfortable here, adding blood magic to her box of tools. After all, humans were made of stardust, so what was blood if not a liquid form of the cosmos?

Hunter slid her fingers along her smooth pendant and took her tarot deck out of the pocket of her oversized cardigan. The cards weren't actually hot, but their energy felt fiery, felt ready. She pulled them from their velvet pouch the same deep blue as the sky abandoned by the sun. She shielded her eyes and looked up at the azure blanket above. The moon had settled against the sun-bleached heavens like a water stain. Mother Moon was always watching, the caretaker as the sun slipped from existence each night.

Hunter ran her hand over the silver back of her deck. She felt Mercy behind her, stuffed full of questions and opinions. But this was Hunter's time to shine, and her Green Witch sister was so far out of her element that she'd sink without the safety raft of Hunter's spellwork.

"This is gross, H. Can't you work your magic anywhere else?" Mercy tented her arms and settled her hands on her hips. "Preferably at the tree since it's the actual root of the problem." Her smooth brow furrowed. "Pun not intended."

"This is a stronger site." How could Mercy not feel the energy rising from the stained earth? Hunter gripped her opal pendant. Maybe the earth hadn't called her to this spot. Maybe this was the guidance of her god. "Tyr led me here," she said and let the pendant fall back into place.

Mercy bit her lip. "Well . . ." There was that guilty look again. It wrinkled her round nose and pinched the corners of her eyes.

"You have to trust me, Mag."

"I do!" The words rushed out too quickly.

Hunter bit the inside of her cheek and turned back to the matter at hand. She'd figure out what was going on with Mercy later. Right now, magic called to her and she wouldn't keep it waiting. She situated her knees against the edge of the ring of blood and set the deck in the middle of the crushed and stained grass. Hunter didn't follow any specific tarot spreads, and neither did her cards. She did what felt right, what the deck asked her.

Reveal yourself, reveal yourself, reveal yourself. The intention chanted between her ears as she cut the deck with her right hand, rolled her amulet between the fingers of her left, and stacked the halves back together on the grass. A new set of cards was on top. The *right* set of cards.

Hunter released a measured exhale. One breath per action, one breath per question. It's what felt right, what the cards demanded. She turned over the first card and set it face-up next to the deck. She couldn't release the rest of her breath. The deck still called to her. She turned over another card and placed it face-up on the blood-stained grass. Her palm still itched, the tarot calling out for another turn, and Hunter flipped a third card. The feeling ceased and Hunter let loose the breath stored in her chest. The face of each card was milky white, held in blank suspense as they awaited further instruction. The cards would get their questions. And soon.

Another inhale and exhale to place the remaining cards on top of the velvet satchel Hunter had left on the ground outside the circle of blood.

Mercy squatted down next to Hunter. "There's nothing there," she whispered as if the cards would be offended by her comment.

Hunter's cheeks lifted with a grin. Knowing her tarot cards, they just might.

"They're waiting for questions." Hunter rubbed her palms together and exhaled as she held her hands over the three blank cards. This moment she took to double-check the readiness of her magic usually felt like warming her hands over a fire, comforting and soothing. But this time was different. This time was *more*—a fierce, blazing excitement that sent waves of need rippling from her fingertips to her toes and back again.

"We want to know if anything came through." Mercy continued to whisper. "That's what you're going to ask, right? Will all three cards tell you or—"

"Mag!" Hunter curled her hands into fists and rubbed them against her thighs. "I know what I'm doing. Let me do it in my own time."

Mercy chewed her bottom lip and nodded. "I'm just excited."

Hunter understood. Excitement dripped from her pores like sweat. She passed the back of her hand along her forehead. She needed to finish this spell and close the channels of power that lit her from the inside out.

Inhale. She pressed the fingertips of her right hand against the first card. *Exhale.* "Did a creature, a demi-god, come through this gate?"

A sound like splintering wood and the card's white face dissolved into the ghostly image of a creature hunched over, blurry fists pressed against the ground like a gorilla. Around it, each half of the split olive tree.

Mercy's brows lifted. "I'm taking that as a *yes.*"

Inhale. Hunter moved to the next card. *Exhale.* "This *thing* that came through, did it hurt anyone?"

Hunter already knew the answer. Whatever it was had killed Earl Thompson. Tyr wouldn't have led her to his blood if it hadn't.

Smoke rose from the ground beneath the cards, beneath the blood, beneath the flattened grasses. The earth sizzled and the crushed grass turned black and formed a perfect imprint of where the life had gone out of old Earl Thompson.

Mercy shrieked and hurled herself backward. She landed in the tall grass with a muffled *thud*. She held out a trembling hand and pointed at the space where she'd squatted only moments before, her jaw bobbing open and closed—the words just out of reach.

A fresh wave of smoke snaked under Hunter's nose as she followed her sister's outstretched hand. Hunter blinked once, twice, three times, her brain unwilling to process the image it received. A set of shoe prints were burned into the ground next to Hunter—*next to* the seared memory of Mr. Thompson's corpse.

Panic tightened Hunter's chest and she coughed into the magical smoke that dissipated with each gust of spring air. "Mag—" Hunter stared at the cards. The second face had changed. The image of a gnarled branch bisected the card. Above the limb, a skull nested under the smooth arch of a sickle. Below it, a puddle of skin, its face and arms slack and empty like it'd been stripped from its frame and dropped amidst the grass.

The mortal's skin becomes a living disguise.

"It wasn't just Mr. Thompson. Someone else was here." Hunter motioned to the footprints scorched into the earth. "Someone else was taken."

Ecru grass dusted Mercy's cheeks as she crawled around to Hunter's other side where the grass was unmarred by the tarot and whatever creature had slipped through the crumbling gate. "Will your cards tell you what did this?"

That's what the last card was for. It had to be. It would tell them exactly who to look for and then they could begin to put this whole mess behind them.

Inhale. Hunter's fingers found the third card. *Exhale.* "The creature, who is it?"

Mercy gripped Hunter's arm as the sisters waited for the truth.

A gurgling sound like a growl through wet paint while images slowly flicked along the card's surface as if it were scrolling through a digital contacts list: a woman with snakes piled atop her head like hair; a three-headed beast; a female rising from ocean waves, her hands cupped around her mouth; and a drooling beast with a single bulging eye and sparse hairs that stuck up from its lumpy head like question marks. The final image froze upon the face of the card.

"Oh, Freya!" Mercy pulled Hunter against her. "*His eyes are gone.* That's what Em said about her dad."

"And the sheriff said about Mr. Thompson." Hunter glossed her fingers over the image. "It's collecting eyes."

Mercy's breath left her lips in short quakes. "H-how do we stop him?"

Hunter lifted the card and squinted at the single eye glaring at her from the middle of the creature's broad forehead. *That* was the new question.

How on earth would Hunter and Mercy catch a Cyclops?

Twenty-two

Hunter passed the card to Mercy who flipped it over and examined its silver back. "So, that's it? I mean, your cards told us that it's the Cyclops, which is great, but he's not exactly walking around like this." She pointed to the strings of saliva dripping from the creature's chin and the lone eye it was best known for. "Can you do your, you know"—she waved her hand in front of Hunter as if polishing glass—"tarot thing again and ask the cards to be more specific this time?"

Hunter picked at a tender piece of skin hanging from her index finger. "That's not really how it works." She held her palm over the charred grass. "And I used up all the magic from this site." She plucked the card from Mercy's grasp. "Sometimes the tarot gives veiled answers. It would sort of be cheating if the cards just came out with a big arrow that pointed directly to what we need to know. Half of the magic is how the images are interpreted."

Mercy groaned and collapsed onto the tall grass. "It wouldn't be cheating. It would be answering the question you asked in a clear and direct manner." As she spoke, she held up her fawn hands. Her slender

214

forearms had begun to freckle under the persistence of the spring sun. "When *I* do spellwork, I know whether it's been successful or not. If it has, I get results. If it hasn't . . . well, nothing usually happens. But that *nothing* always tells me *something*. This isn't a nothing or a something. It's just—"

"A star!"

"I guess it's a start, but my point is that it could be a better one."

"Not a *start*. A *star*."

Mercy sat up as Hunter flipped the card around to face her. "I didn't notice it at first, but there's a star around his eye and another in his, um . . ."

Mercy squinted and tapped the Cyclops's left pec. "Scraggly chest hair?"

"Gross, but yes." Hunter looked at the card. "This is the answer. This is who the Cyclops is wearing."

"A star?" Mercy's brow remained pinched as she untangled a seed-pod from her hair. "You think the Cyclops is parading around town in the skin suit of a star? No one famous has ever come to Goodeville."

"Sure, but there *are* famous people here." Hunter bit down on the rugged tip of her fingernail. *Locally* famous was super close to *famous* famous. She snapped off the point of her nail and rolled it along the tip of her tongue.

A star.

A star.

A star.

"Oh!" Mercy clapped, her green eyes widening. "What about that retired Bulls basketball guy?"

Hunter nodded, flooding with ideas of her own. "Or the news anchor who was a former Miss Illinois? Or the deejay at Em's birthday who performs at all those clubs in Chicago? Or that eighth grader who plays those games on Twitch?"

Mercy rested her chin against her steepled fingers. "Any ideas how we figure out which person is no longer a person?"

Hunter clenched the jagged piece of nail between her teeth and ran her tongue along it. She was missing something. But what? "Let's go home and look at the grimoires."

"So, you're giving in to good ol'-fashioned research?" Mercy stood and offered Hunter her hand. "Welcome to the team, H."

Hunter gathered the cards and slipped them back into her pocket before taking her sister's hand and hefting to her feet. "I was on the book team *way* before you, Mag."

Mercy shrugged and skipped off toward the car, kicking chunks of dirt as she bubbled over about what information the grimoires possibly held.

Hunter paused at the black footprints burned into the grass. She and Mercy had gotten enough information to focus their hunt and start them down the right path, but Hunter had hoped for a bit more. She so desperately wanted to impress her sister and be the one to solve their problems.

"Oh, well." She sighed and spit the jagged nail onto the blackened earth before jogging to catch up to Mercy.

As Hunter's boots carried her away, a line of smoke rose from the ground, from the charred blood and dead grass and torn fingernail. The nail flamed for an instant, the same white as the full moon, before the gentle spring breeze snuffed it out and carried away the black from the burnt earth.

Twenty-three

Polyphemus sat in Sheriff Dearborn's car on a dirt road that dead ended at Goode Lake. The body he'd unzipped and removed from Dearborn's spirit had guided him here, though he wasn't sure why. His only guess was that the skin he wore still searched for its true owner like a lost lamb searched for its shepherd.

He removed his sunglasses and squinted out at the water through his one good eye. "Back to this, now." He wiggled his calloused fingers in front of his other eye. Nothing. Not even a shadow. It had completely clouded over, gone blind. "Always back to this . . . *Cyclops.*" Self-pity hardened in his stomach like a pound of gold. It was a useless, ineffective emotion, but he couldn't break free of its chains.

Goode Lake's crystal blue skin shivered with each gust of wind. He rolled his window down and hung his arm out. He knew the sun was warm just as he knew the water was wet, but he couldn't feel its pleasant rays. He only felt the sticky heat of his true form inside, pressed against the slopes and ridges of this human skin.

He flipped his hand over and cupped the sunlight in his palm. He couldn't stay in this world without nesting inside of a human form, but oh how sweet it would be to feel the sun against his own skin. Tartarus, the Greek Underworld from which he escaped, had no sun. It had no aquamarine lakes or sandy beaches. Tartarus was dark, cold, barren.

Polyphemus ran his tongue along his bottom lip and pressed his teeth against the wet flesh.

He had promised himself that this would be his last escape. Curse or not, he couldn't live as the monster these killings were turning him into. When Sheriff Dearborn's body failed and its time in this world ended, so would Polyphemus's. If this small town didn't hold the cure, this was it for him, his last hurrah before he was sucked back into darkness. He might as well live a little.

He turned off the car and opened the door. It swung open without a sound and he closed it just as quietly. He squinted back toward the road and the trees that encircled the lake as he crept toward the shoreline. He didn't want to be seen, or rather, he didn't want *Frank Dearborn* to be spotted. The townspeople liked Dearborn, *needed* him. But no one had ever needed Polyphemus. He paused and frowned at the thought. There it was again. The self-pity that kept him jailed just as well as Tartarus had. But he had escaped the hell of Tartarus, and he had done it more than once.

Polyphemus untied his boots and struggled to kick them off as he fumbled with the buttons of Dearborn's long-sleeved khaki shirt. The last time he'd felt this level of excitement, he'd been traveling to meet *her.* But that had been before she'd broken his heart and before she'd doomed him with this curse. His hands fell by his sides as a gust tented the open shirt. That was also the last time he'd been in the water.

"Nomia." He twirled the name around his tongue before it slid past his lips. Only briefly had he wondered why such a beautiful creature wanted him. He had assuaged his fears and padded his ego by saying that she was attracted to his greatness and the power that came with

being a son of Poseidon. After all, Nomia was a water nymph and he had been a prince of the seas.

His jaw ticked and he stared down at his bare feet slowly sinking into the sand.

No, he *wasn't* a prince of the seas. Nomia had reminded him of that.

"You thought I could love you?" She crouched atop the large boulder that jutted from the center of the lagoon like a tooth. Her waves of moss green hair lapped against her bare breasts as she threw back her head and laughed. One by one, Nomia's sisters rose from the depths of the lagoon. They encircled Polyphemus, their blue eyes sparkling as they fed from his anguish. "You are a bastard, Polyphemus. Denied by your father and unloved by his wife." She brushed back her hair and her iridescent skin glimmered in the sunlight. "I would never love you. As Amphitrite has proven, no woman could."

"Curse him, sister!" the nymphs chanted as one as they tightened their circle around him.

"He dared to make you his!" Their webbed hands and feet churned the cobalt depths and pinned Polyphemus in place.

"Now make him ours!" Water sloshed against his shoulders as the nymphs wrung out the space separating them from him.

Polyphemus blinked the water from the single eye pressed into the center of his forehead. His eye was the same deep brown as Nomia's, the only difference between her and her sisters. "Nomia, we're alike, you and I." He tore his hand free from the current pressing against him and patted his eyelid. "We match, remember?" His chin trembled as he stared up at the woman he loved more than he loved himself.

Nomia's talons snapped as she dug her fingers into the rock. "When I look into your eye, I see everything I hate about myself."

A howl of laughter erupted around Polyphemus. Had he not been held up by the nymphs' power, he would have sunk to the bottom of the lagoon.

"Sisters!" Nomia shouted. "Make him yours!"

Claws sliced his flesh as the nymphs pulled him beneath the water. Ribbons of blood twisted around him as he thrashed and reached for the surface. It was no use. This was their domain. And Nomia was right about his father. The great king Poseidon would never come to Polyphemus's aid.

His chest burned as he reached for the sunlight that splintered against the water's surface. His fingers broke through, then his palm, his wrist. He was almost there, almost out, almost free to take another breath—

A nymph caught his foot. She stabbed his leg with broken talons as she climbed him like a rock. Brown eyes met his when the top of his head split the water's surface.

"Nomia . . ." Her name escaped his lips on bubbles of air.

A smile lifted her full cheeks and she pressed her lips against his. She cupped his face in her hands and pressed her warm tongue between his lips.

Polyphemus welcomed the kiss. It was proof that she loved him. That she was sorry.

More webbed hands were on his feet, his legs, yanking him back down. Pain flashed against his cheeks as Nomia dug in her nails. A grin stretched her lips taut against his as she sucked air from his lungs. She pulled her mouth from his and water filled his chest. Nomia pressed against him as he convulsed. The lagoon darkened around him as Nomia whispered a curse against his ear.

> *How delicious life would be*
> *If only it could make you see*
> *The hunger for what it truly is,*
> *A way to set you free.*
> *Now carry on with your cursed life,*
> *And cut their eyes out, these orbs are so rife*
> *With magic, but only one pair of these*
> *Has what it takes to end your strife.*

One of the buttons smacked him in the face when a sharp gust pulled up his shirt. He smoothed down the fabric and took a deep breath. He wasn't drowning. He was here, at the edge of Goode Lake, sunk to his ankles in the sand. He shook his feet free, shrugged off the button-down, and stripped out of the undershirt and his pants. It was time to make new memories to take back with him to Tartarus. He shook his head. No, this time he would find a way to break free from his curse.

Polyphemus waded into the lake. He couldn't feel the cool water against his skin, not in the same way he could in his true skin, but the sound was enough to make goose bumps rise from Dearborn's arms. His heartbeat sped up and he dug his toes into the silt to keep from running back to shore. He wouldn't let Nomia continue to control him. He balled his hands and fell back. Goode Lake enveloped him. His chest shuddered as he sank deeper and watched the sunlight blur against the water's surface.

He couldn't end the curse by dying in another realm. He'd learned that time and time again. There was no quicker path back to the torment of Tartarus. And the number of humans kept growing. He couldn't kill them all. Nor did he want to. What he needed was an oracle, a vessel through which he could speak to the gods.

He tucked his feet under him and pushed himself back above water. He took a breath and ran his hands down his cheeks, pausing where he knew the scars lingered just beneath Frank Dearborn's skin.

"This world doesn't have an oracle." He shook water from his ear. Droplets rained into the lake as he set his hands on his hips and stared out at the water. "But it does have magic. The gate to Tartarus proves that."

He stiffened with realization. "This world would be overrun by vengeful, evil creatures if it wasn't being protected." He ran his hands through his hair as excitement crackled beneath his skin. He'd been so busy following the curse's instruction, he'd never stopped to look at this world.

He ran to his clothes. Water splashed with each hurried step.

No, the humans didn't have an oracle, but to protect this world, to protect this town, they must have a *witch*.

Polyphemus's hands shook as he tugged on his pants and brushed the sand from his undershirt. He could find Goodeville's witch. Like he'd watched death darken a person's eyes, he could also see within them the fire of life, and magic's flame blazed bright. He threw his shirt over his head and stuffed his sandy feet into his boots. He covered his mouth as a wet cough shook his barrel chest. He stilled and swallowed against the tickle building in his throat. It was starting again. His stomach lurched as he suppressed another cough.

Polyphemus needed to find the witch and he needed to find her fast.

Twenty-four

A Cyclops?" Xena's heart-shaped face screwed up in a grimace of disgust. She shook herself as if she could rid her body of the memory of the name. "*That* is why the eyes of the victims were missing. Polyphemus is compelled to gather them." The cat person had been sitting on the arm of the couch, but she slid off it to curl up on the cushions as she wrapped a chenille throw around herself like she suddenly felt a chill. "It's really rather horrible."

"Wait, *compelled*? Why?" Hunter asked as she sat beside Xena, redoing her ponytail.

"And who's Polyphemus?" Mercy said as she rejoined her family in the living room. She carried a tray that held three mugs of steaming hot chocolate and her cell phone. Em hadn't called or responded to the last four texts she'd sent, but Mercy wanted to be sure her phone stayed close to her for when her best friend was finally able to reach out.

"Polyphemus is a Cyclops," Xena answered matter-of-factly and then said no more while she batted at the fringed edge of the throw.

"Xena, we need more information than that," said Hunter.

The cat person looked up at the twins and sighed. "I forget how inadequate the modern public education system has become. The Cyclopes were a race of barbaric giants who terrorized ancient Greece. Polyphemus was the most human of them. I do not recall exactly how his heart was broken, but it had something to do with a nymph." Xena smoothed back her hair. "Such flighty little things. Anyway, his heart was broken and I believe he did something stupid—he was, after all, a male."

The girls nodded in mutual female understanding.

Xena finished, "And he was cursed to seek that which he was lacking until he found that which could not be discovered—meaning the second eye he was born without." She shrugged. "Or something like that. But you need not pity him. Even though he was the most human of the Cyclopes he was still a hideous, barbaric beast, and I do believe Polyphemus eats the eyeballs after he, well, *harvests* them."

"Huh. That's interesting," said Hunter.

"Interesting? It's disgusting and creepy, but less creepy than what happened out there by that tree today. Xena, you should've been there." Mercy offered the mugs of steaming cocoa to Hunter and Xena, who took them gratefully. "It made my skin crawl when the cards revealed the footprints of the killer." She shivered. "They appeared *exactly* where I was standing!"

"Thank you, kitten." Xena blew quickly across the steaming top of the cocoa. "Being able to eat, or drink, chocolate is one of my favorite things about being a person," she said.

In spite of the seriousness of everything they'd discovered that evening, Mercy couldn't help asking, "What else do you like about being a person?"

The tip of Xena's pink tongue touched the creamy cocoa. She frowned at it and blew a few breaths across it again before answering. "Well, I like my hair. It is spectacular, though that is no surprise. I have always had a lush, magnificent coat. I also do enjoy a little cannabis, especially at bedtime."

"Isn't your bedtime anytime you want to nap?" Hunter asked as she peeked up at Xena over the top of her mug of liquid chocolate and coconut cream.

"Well, yes, of course, kitten. I also am surprised by how very much I like to take a lovely bath. It almost makes up for how very much I *dislike* clothes. They are so restrictive, so binding, so *not* like fur. Well, except for my Abigail's bathrobe." Xena lifted her arm and sniffed at the fluffy, well-worn robe. "It makes me feel as if my dear girl is hugging me."

"That's really nice, Xena." Mercy curled her feet up under her and made herself comfortable in the space between her sister and Xena before she carefully blew on her own steaming chocolate.

The three of them sipped their drinks silently for a few minutes, each lost in her own thoughts, until Hunter spoke up.

"So, how do we kill the Cyclops?"

Xena tossed back her magnificent hair and said, "Killing the body it is inhabiting will be easy."

Mercy's throat closed and she put her half-empty mug down on the grimoire-laden coffee table. "I don't think killing anyone will be easy—not even someone possessed by an eyeball-eating monster."

"Kitten, as the guardian of the Egyptian gate told you, the human is already dead. What you will be killing is a reanimated body a Cyclops is using as a disguise. You must get over this foolish human squeamishness if you are to have a chance at vanquishing it."

"I agree with you, Xena," said Hunter. "But you have to understand that Mercy and I will see a human—and maybe even a friend or at least an acquaintance—when we track him down."

"Him?" Mercy asked.

Hunter nodded. "You were too freaked to notice, but those were really big boot prints—like someone who worked outside a lot would wear. It's probably a large man."

"Great . . ." Mercy muttered.

"It is great, kittens! You already know three things about the

Cyclops's skin suit." She lifted her long, slender fingers that were tipped by sharp, perfectly kept nails, and ticked off, "First, the person will be a star—symbolically not literally. Second, the person is a male. And third, he probably works, or spends a lot of time, out of doors."

"That *is* a lot more than we knew this morning." Hunter spoke firmly, confidently.

Mercy nodded and tried to sound more positive. "Yeah, that's true. I'll quit being such a downer about it. It's just really intimidating to think about needing to kill a person and a monster. Together."

Xena shook a finger in front of Mercy's face. "No, no, no. You probably will not kill them together. Well, unless you push them through the Greek gate and seal it behind them. Then the body will crumble and continue to decompose, and the Cyclops will be banished back to Tartarus."

Hunter blew out a long, sighing breath. "So, that's the best way to get rid of it?"

"Indeed," said Xena. She paused and lapped delicately at the cocoa before continuing, "Otherwise you take the risk of the Cyclops killing someone else and hiding inside his or her body."

"But before we even think about how we're gonna do all of that, don't we need to strengthen the gates?" said Mercy. "I mean, it's already super awful. The Fenrir caused Mom's death. Then the Cyclops has caused the deaths of at least three people—including whomever he's hiding inside. Think of how bad it would be if even just one more monster broke through another gate."

"It would be terrible," said Hunter.

"And very inconvenient." Xena dabbed her mouth with the back of her hand and then licked the drops of liquid chocolate from her skin. "As Goode witches you can open the gates anytime you wish by simply commanding them, so being rid of the Cyclops—once you figure out who he is and somehow get him to the Greek tree—should not be difficult. But it *will* be *extremely* difficult if you have to battle several murderous monsters at the same time."

"So, do either of you have a clue how to fix the trees? What Hunter and I did today obviously didn't work—or at least it's not working fast enough."

Hunter frowned into her hot chocolate. "The directions on the insecticide said it could take a week to ten days for the worms to die."

Xena leaned across Mercy and stroked Hunter's arm gently before she said, "Oh, kitten, I believe if the mundane part of your spell was going to work the magical part would have been effective today, if even just a little."

"Khenti said he noticed no difference on his side of the gate." Mercy picked at her lip. "And, truthfully, I didn't notice anything being any better on our side, either."

Hunter shook her head. "No, neither did I."

Mercy squared her shoulders and looked from Xena to her sister. "Do either of you have any idea at all about why the trees got sick to begin with?"

Hunter shrugged. "I'm as clueless as you are about that."

Mercy chewed the inside of her cheek to keep from blurting the thought that had been swirling around and around in her mind. *It could be because you chose a god and brought a guy to a girl party!*

"Forgive me, kittens. I am only a familiar and not the witch our Abigail was. I wish I knew what was sickening the trees, but I do not."

"It's so frustrating that none of us knows what's wrong with them," said Hunter.

"Well, what that means is that you need to look deeper and create a stronger spell to heal them," said Xena.

"That sounds logical and even like it should be easy, but Mercy's been going through those old grimoires like she's cramming for finals and what we did today was all she came up—"

"Wait! I have an idea." Mercy leaned forward, digging through the piles of grimoires. "Xena, did you pull the copies of Sarah's grimoire?"

"You mean the original Sarah Goode?" Xena asked, perking up, too.

"Yeah, that's exactly who I mean."

"Actually, I did." Xena pointed one long-tipped finger at a book that rested behind the others. It looked more like a fat folder than the other leather-bound journals. "It's good to see that my feline intuition has not left me—even while I'm in human form. It told me you might need copies of the most ancient grimoires."

Mercy grabbed the folder and sat back against the couch's cushions. She opened it carefully out of habit, even though the pages within were Xeroxed copies of the fragile originals, which remained in a temperature-controlled lockbox in a Chicago bank. Generations ago the Goode witches began copying the oldest grimoires so that the knowledge of their ancestresses would never be lost, and then sealed away the originals.

"I like to think about the fact that someday Goode witches, our great-great-granddaughters, will copy my grimoires," said Mercy as she searched for the right entry. "It makes me feel like I'm gonna live forever."

Hunter snorted softly. "It makes me stress about my handwriting."

Mercy looked up and grinned at her sister. "Well, that, too." She turned a few more pages and then pumped her fist in victory. "Yes! Here it is."

Hunter leaned closer, reading along with her. "Hey, that's the original spell that Sarah used to close the gates in the spring of 1693."

"Yep. Xena made me think of it when she said that we needed to look deeper and come up with a stronger spell. What could be stronger and deeper magic than the *first* spell?"

Hunter sat straight up. "Mag, you could be onto something!"

"Right?!" Mercy's finger traced the words as she read Sarah's loopy cursive writing. She glanced up at Xena. "Did you know Sarah had help with the first spell?"

"No. I am old, but not *that* old. I don't believe I have ever read the original spell. Like you kittens, I learned the history by listening to the Goode witches retelling it."

"Sheesh, Xena, exactly how old are you?" Mercy asked.

"One never asks a lady her age." Xena sniffed haughtily and then continued, "I assumed the original spell was almost exactly like the one the Goode witches perform during every Feast Day Ritual." She peered down at the copy of the ancient grimoire. "How interesting! Sarah had four people who aided her."

"Seriously?" Hunter scooted nearer to Mercy so she could follow along.

"Yeah, look at this," said Mercy. "Sarah was at the Norse gate, just like we were. She positioned two medicine women from the Illinois tribe at the Greek and Hindu gates, and—" Mercy paused and squinted as she struggled to make out the smudged scrawl. "I think that says Gertrude Smythe, pioneer woman and Goodeville resident, at the Japanese gate and Oceanus Martin, Pioneer Woman and Goodeville resident, at the Egyptian gate. Using smoke to signal the others, Sarah led them to begin the spell, which was almost identical to the one Abigail led us through except—" She paused and felt a jolt of surprise.

"They sealed the spell and the gates with their blood!" Hunter finished for her.

"And we need to repeat this spell as close to the original as possible." Mercy chewed her lip. "But there are no members of the Illinois tribes left here anymore. There aren't even any reservation lands in Illinois."

"Such a tragedy—such a horror what happened to the indigenous peoples," said Xena softly, sadly.

"We should add something during the ritual in remembrance of the Illinois tribe," said Hunter.

"That's a really good idea," Mercy agreed.

"Hey!" Hunter's face lit with a smile. "We do have someone very close to us who has ties to the settlers of Goodeville!"

"Ohmygoddess! Jax!" Mercy and Hunter high-fived.

"Jax would be an excellent addition, but I am in agreement with both of you that it would be wise and respectful to say a prayer for the wise women and make an offering to them during the spellwork," said Xena as she finished her chocolate, placed it on the table, and settled back to groom herself.

"We'll do that for sure, Xena," said Hunter as Mercy nodded.

"Okay, so, we have Jax who is a descendant of Goodeville's founding ancestors—and *we* can represent Sarah—all three of us. You"—Mercy jerked her chin at Hunter—"Xena, and me. But we still need one more person."

"That person should live within the Goodeville city limits," said Xena as she paused in her grooming. "She or he will also represent the pioneers who came here with Sarah."

"Em is perfect. She loved being part of the grief spell and her dad's family has run the funeral home downtown for more than a hundred years. Her grandparents *and* great-grandma just moved from here to that retirement place in Florida last year." Mercy sighed deeply. "But I don't know if she's up to it."

"If she is not, you cannot wait until her time of grief is over," said Xena. "The gates must be sealed immediately."

"You're right. I'll call her and see how she's doing."

"Has she talked to you at all today?" asked Hunter.

Mercy shrugged. "Sorta. I've been texting her. A lot. She said nothing feels right and her mom is totally not okay. Other than that she's only sent crying emoji faces."

"Do not expect her to be able to help you," said Xena.

Mercy got up and headed for her purse. She fished around inside for her phone. "Well, if she can't it'll have to be Kirk."

"Oh, hell no!" said Hunter.

Xena growled softly.

Mercy frowned and looked up from her phone. "Hey, he helped with the grief spell."

"He was *freaked out* by the grief spell and almost screwed it all up," said Hunter.

"Well, of course he was. Like Em said, he was totally inexperienced about witchy things. I talked to him and explained spellwork. He's better now. And if we have to use him I'll take full responsibility for prepping him."

Hunter rolled her eyes and Xena growled again.

Mercy put a hand on her hip. "Do either of you have a better idea?" When neither said anything Mercy continued, "Then it's settled. Emily is our first choice, but if she can't do it we'll use Kirk."

"Grandma and Grandpa are like zombies." Emily's voice sounded so, so far away as she spoke softly into the phone. "Well, scratch that. Grandpa is like a zombie—if a zombie did nothing but drink whisky and watch ESPN. Grandma is a cooking zombie. She walked in—hugged me—starting crying—ignored Mom—and went straight to the kitchen. She's been there ever since. Literally the only time she leaves is to refresh Grandpa's glass, visit the 'powder room' as she calls it, and get a new box of Kleenex. She hasn't stopped crying."

"Em, I'm so sorry. Is your mom any better?" Mercy balanced the phone on her shoulder while she rinsed the pot she'd used to make the cocoa.

"Absolutely not. Meemaw and Peepaw can't make it to the funeral, even though it won't be for four more days. They're on a Greek island cruise and said something about not being able to get a flight out from any of their ports of call. Mom thinks that's bullshit, and I have to agree. But, Mag, the truth is they never liked Dad, and they *hate* his parents. Plus, you know my parents' marriage hasn't exactly been good—not that that matters to Mom right now. She's, like, totally broken, Mag. She keeps talking about everything she should've and shouldn't have said to Dad. And then she cries so hard I swear I think she's going to puke. It's awful." Emily paused to sob softly and then blew her nose. "Sorry."

"Hey, take your time. I'm totally here for you."

"Thanks." Emily sighed deeply. "So, Mom only left her bed when

Grandma got here, and when Grandma ignored her and started cooking Mom retreated back to her bedroom and the bottle of pills the doc gave her."

"Can I please come get you? Even for just an hour or so? I made hot chocolate. I could add some witchy herbs to it to help you relax." Mercy put the pot in the dishwasher and cringed as it clanked noisily against a plate—though Em didn't seem to notice.

"Relax?" Emily's laughter was filled with sarcasm. "I can't relax. I'm the only one holding it together. I had to answer, like, a zillion funeral questions today—including stuff about Dad's casket. Jesus."

"Bloody hell, Em, can't the adults do that? You have a house full of them."

"Oh hell no. My house is filled with old people who are barely functioning. I swear if I wasn't here Dad would be on a slab in the morgue for fucking ever." She sobbed brokenly into the phone. "Wilson keeps asking me what Dad would want."

"Wilson? Isn't he just a first-year apprentice?" Mercy was sure she remembered that he was fresh out of college. Em liked to say he still looked like a very gawky, zitty teenager. "How's it okay that he's running the funeral home?"

"Oh, he's not really. Mr. Burton, from Sunset Funeral Home in Champaign, is really in charge, but Wilson keeps calling me and asking me details about Dad's service. How do I know what my father, who was murdered when he was thirty-nine years old, wanted when he died? It's not like he chatted with his sixteen-year-old daughter about his fucking funeral arrangements!"

Mercy wiped her hand on a dish towel and felt sad and sick and angry all at the same time for her friend. "Em, just tell Wilson to figure it out by himself!"

"I c-can't." Emily sniffled. "Someone has to at least *try* to do what Dad would want, and I seem to be the only somebody who cares." She started sobbing again.

"Oh, Em. I'm so sorry. I love you so much. I wish I could do something—anything."

"You can." Emily blew her nose. "Keep texting me. Even if I don't answer. Just being here for me is everything."

Mercy heard a woman's voice calling Emily's name.

"I gotta go. Grandma wants me to taste something. Again. It's disgusting, Mag. Everything she cooks has way too much salt in it—like it was made with tears."

Mercy didn't know what else to say except, "I love you, Emily Parrott."

"You, too, Mag." And the cell went dead.

Mercy walked around the corner from the kitchen. Hunter and Xena raised mirrored brows at her.

"No way she can do it." Mercy sat between them as she let out a long, disgusted exhalation. "I knew Em's mom was a flake. Not just because she's from that super rich family from New York and she always seemed to be looking down her nose at the rest of us, but because she was never here. I liked her dad a lot better. I mean, he forgot things—like school stuff."

"And her birthday," Hunter added.

Xena hissed sharply and said, "There is never any excuse for forgetting a kitten's date of birth."

"Yeah, all of that, but he was a nice man. And he told Em he was proud of her—a lot. But her mom's family isn't even coming back for the funeral—wankers."

"That's awful," said Hunter.

"Her dad's parents are here now, but they won't speak to her mom and they're so wrapped up in their own grief that they're not helping Em at all. You guys, she's having to make all the decisions for her dad's funeral."

"Oh! Poor kitten! Will she not escape to us?"

Mercy shook her head. "No. She feels like she's the only adult in the house." Mercy met her sister's turquoise gaze. "H, it's going to have to be Kirk."

Xena growled.

"Bloody hell, Xena, stop!" Mercy told the cat person, who cringed back like she was afraid Mercy would swat at her. Mercy rubbed a hand across her face. "I'm sorry, Xena. I shouldn't have yelled at you like that." Then she turned to her sister. "Seriously, H, if you can think of anyone else who already knows we're witches—and I mean *real* witches—and who we can trust, I'll totally go with you to talk to her, or him. Do you?"

"I've already thought about it. I considered Heather."

"Heather? As in the president of the drama club?"

Hunter nodded. "Yeah. Remember a few Samhains ago she came by and asked Mom for some Wiccan tips because she wanted to write a modern version of *Macbeth* and make the witches draw down the moon?"

"I remember," Mercy said. "I also remember she kept talking over Abigail the whole time she was explaining the points of a pentagram to her. Heather is one of the most arrogant people I know."

"Actually that would be Kirk," muttered Xena between licks of the last of the cocoa in her empty mug.

Mercy ignored her.

"Heather's arrogance is why I thought she might work. I figured she'd love 'playing witch,'" Hunter air-quoted. "But her family's farm is ten miles outside Goodeville city limits, and I think we really do need people to stand in for the original settlers. So it has to be someone who lives within the limits of the town."

"That's Kirk."

Her sister picked at her nonexistent thumbnail. "Okay, but you're going to have to have a serious talk with him before the spell."

"I will. And he'll be cool with it. Promise." Mercy was glad her voice sounded so sure, because her intuition wasn't nearly as convinced. She shook off the feeling—*really, we don't have a choice.* "How about you and I tell Jax and Kirk we'll meet them after football practice tomorrow? We can explain what we need the two of them to do—together. You know Kirk hates to look like any kind of a sissy in front of another guy. It should at least make him receptive enough to listen to what we have to say."

Hunter opened her mouth to speak, but Xena interrupted. "I want you to be very careful about what you disclose to those boys. Tell them only enough to set the intention to strengthen and heal the trees. They do *not* need to know the true history of Goodeville. They should *not* know about the gates."

"But, Xena, won't it be better to clue them in on—"

"No!" The cat person's eyes flashed yellow and her hair lifted as she met their gazes—all lightness gone from her expression. "I have been guardian of Goode witches for generations. Modern townspeople will not understand. Sarah Goode fled as a result of ignorance and hysteria once. That tragedy must not be repeated. Do you understand me?"

"Yes, Xena," the girls spoke together.

Xena sighed and reached out to stroke each of their cheeks. "I am sorry to be so stern with my kittens, but you must heed me on this. The less they know, the better."

"We'll only tell them enough to set their intention," said Mercy.

"Don't worry, Xena. We'll be careful," added Hunter.

"Excellent. Now, I am rather sleepy. I need a bath and my cannabis truffle or three." Xena stood and shook back her hair. "I shall see you in the morning, my lovely kittens." She leaned over and licked each of them on their foreheads before padding gracefully up the stairs.

The girls exchanged a glance. "She's a lot sometimes," whispered Mercy.

"Sometimes?" Hunter quipped with a smile. "I'll text Jax and let him know we'll be there after practice."

"Okay, I'll text Kirk, too, in a sec. I just want to be sure I've read every part of Sarah's ritual." Mercy scanned the rest of the page, making quick notes on her phone of the supplies they'd need: an offering for each and a tool for each of them to use to draw a little of their blood. Mercy chewed her lip. *Little tiny ritual knives? Where the bloody hell am I going to get some of them?*

She turned the page to the end of the spell, which was also the end of the grimoire. As she closed it, her fingernail caught on a corner of a blank page glued to the inside rear cover of the book. Mercy picked at the corner, and carefully peeled the copied sheet from the cardstock cover. It was a poem, which wasn't very shocking. Sarah's grimoires were littered with poems, though most of them were written in the margins beside spells. Their ancestress had definitely been an aspiring poet. Not a big fan of poetry, Mercy had quickly scanned Sarah's other poems as she'd concentrated on the witch's actual spellwork. But something about this particular poem pulled at her attention. It was written in bold cursive that appeared to be in Sarah's hand, but the letters had been smudged by whatever had stuck the page. Mercy smoothed her fingers over the page and squinted to make out the words.

There shall come a day

when they will sicken

with sulfur and rot

fierce and deadly

the Goode witches sworn

cannot prevent it

cannot protect them

and so the gates shall fall open

until a chosen god is forsaken

*then by parting they are mended
together again*

Mercy's breath left her in a gasp as her eyes traced the lines over and over. *How long had this poem—this prophecy—been stuck to the back cover of this old copy and ignored? And even before, in the other copies that had been made of the ancient grimoire, had anyone noticed that one of Sarah's poems was foretelling the destruction of the gates?* In the sick pit of her stomach Mercy Anne Goode knew the truth, and it made her want to puke.

"What is it, Mag?"

Still staring at the words written by their long-dead ancestress, Mercy said the first thing that came to her mind. "I don't want you to be mad at me."

Sitting beside her on the couch, Hunter turned to fully face Mercy. "Mad at you? What are you talking about? We can tell each other anything. And if this is about Kirk, I promise not to be mean. I'll just listen."

"It's not about Kirk." Mercy cleared her throat. "It's about the sick trees and the gates. I've, um, been thinking really hard about what could have started their sickness—about what's different today than in the generations before us."

Hunter nodded. "Yeah, me, too."

"Well, there's one thing that I keep circling back to. I haven't said anything because I knew it'd upset you—and I could be wrong. I *wanted* to be wrong. But what I just found at the end of Sarah's ritual makes me believe I've been on to something." Mercy chewed the inside of her cheek before blurting, "H, what if all of this is happening because you chose Tyr instead of a goddess?"

Hunter's expressive turquoise eyes narrowed and her hand automatically lifted to clutch her talisman. "If Tyr was the problem Mom would've known—would've stopped me from choosing him."

"I keep telling myself that, but what if Abigail didn't know? What if *no* Goode witch could've known because *it's never happened before?*"

"No." Hunter spoke firmly. "That's not it."

"H, just read this. I just found it on a page that was stuck to the back of the copy of Sarah's grimoire—for who knows how long. It's a poem, but it reads like more. Like it could be a warning, or even a prophecy—one that's coming true right now. And it's pretty clear that a *god,* not a *goddess,* is the problem." Mercy lifted the copy of the ancient grimoire and held it up so Hunter could see it, but her sister stood as she pushed the book away, refusing to even look at it.

"I'm not reading the old crap you found to justify whatever you've made up. Tyr's my god. We're close, unlike you and Freya."

Mercy jerked back as if Hunter had slapped her.

"Don't pretend to be shocked. It's obvious. You don't even wear Freya's talisman."

"That's not fair! I love Freya. It's different for a Green Witch. I don't need a talisman to be close to my goddess. Freya is in every tree, every flower and bush—in the earth herself. Freya is all around me." Mercy shook her head. "I can't believe you'd say something so awful to me."

"It feels shitty to have your sister question your choice of gods, doesn't it?"

Mercy stared into Hunter's eyes and within their blue-green depths she saw an unexpected anger—so fierce that it was like gazing into a tsunami.

Mercy felt her own anger stir. "Yeah, it feels shitty. But the difference is I didn't say it to hurt you."

"No, *of course* you didn't mean to hurt me. You said it without thinking about me at all—as usual, it's all about Mag."

"You're wrong. You're wrong about me and you're wrong about the poem." Mercy held up the open book again. "Just read it and *then* tell me that something written back in 1693 isn't saying that choosing a god started all of this. And it also says that you're going to have to—"

"No!" Hunter slapped the book out of Mercy's hands. "Stop talking.

I am more than done listening. Tomorrow we'll get Jax and Kirk, complete the ritual, and fix the gates. And then I *never* want to hear you say *one more word* to me about Tyr." Hunter stalked up the stairs.

"Fine!" Mercy called after her. "But when it doesn't work—again—it's going to be your fault!"

Hunter said nothing.

Mercy picked up the copy of the grimoire from where Hunter had knocked it out of her hands and onto the floor. She smoothed the page and read it again.

and so the gates shall fall open
until a chosen god is forsaken

What else could it mean? Mercy gnawed at her lip. She stared at the page, wondering what the bloody hell she should do.

And then she knew. Mercy quickly stacked all the grimoires together, even the piles that had been on the kitchen table. She carried them into the library that long ago had been built as a formal dining room, but for generations had held books and comfortable, overstuffed reading chairs instead of fine china and a gleaming wood table. She didn't bother putting them away, but piled them on a coffee table.

Then she returned to the kitchen. First, she grabbed her laptop and quickly copied the ancient ritual—translating the more difficult thee's and thou's and the other language that was confusingly archaic. She figured they'd all be on their cells together—on speaker—and one of them, *probably me 'cause I'm good at this stuff*, would lead everyone through the ritual, but with novices participating they'd need extra guidelines, especially if something happened. When she was done, Mercy printed out five copies of the ritual, as well as one of the poem or prophecy or whatever it was. She stacked the ritual instructions beside the copy of the old grimoire, folded the Xeroxed page that held the poem, and put it in her bottomless purse.

"And now one more thing that will take care of the Hunter problem," she muttered.

On the table, exactly at the spot Xena liked to perch in the morning—or whenever was morning in cat time—Mercy opened Sarah's spell book to the newly unstuck page that held the prophecy and then placed a wine goblet, the kind the cat person liked to fill with cream, on top of it.

She wouldn't have to say anything. Xena would get the message, and if she was mistaken—if she'd misunderstood the poem—if it wasn't actually a prophecy—nothing would come of it. But if she was right . . .

Mercy's feet felt weirdly heavy as she trudged up the stairs while she texted Kirk.

How bout I meet u at school tmrw after practice?

He responded right away.

k! see u then sexy!!!

Mercy texted back, *Kay!* But in her mind she knew it wasn't going to be okay. Not until they faced the truth about what was making the trees sick, whether her sister wanted to or not.

Twenty-five

The Goodeville High parking lot was full even though school had been out for a couple hours. The town never missed the Mustangs' practice. Well, they never missed a football practice or a football game as long as the Mustangs were winning and, with Kirk Whitfield as quarterback, the Mustangs always won.

Hunter hunched, her shoulders lifted to her ears, as she hid behind Mercy while they walked through the spectators slowly spilling from the bleachers now that practice was near its end. Mercy waved and bounced through the crowd, the perfect example of an up-and-coming Goodeville homecoming queen—tenacious, girlfriend of a football star, and filled with enough school spirit to kill a horse. Hunter fanned the end of her ponytail and dusted it against her lips as she dodged *hey*'s and *sorry to hear*'s. She couldn't talk to people here. She couldn't talk to people anywhere. This town thought they knew all about her because they knew her sister and her mother. These townspeople would run screaming if they learned what she'd done at the murder scene only hours before.

The memory sent pinpricks of energy across Hunter's palms. She dropped her ponytail and clenched her fists by her sides. She knew blood magic was important. She'd felt it during Mercy's grief spell and again near the old olive tree and the imprint of Earl Thompson's body. Sarah Goode's grimoire had been exactly what she'd needed to feel at ease with her new predilection. Blood magic *had* been used before, so it wouldn't be the worst thing if Hunter used it again.

Mercy grabbed Hunter's clenched fist and dragged her toward the emptying bleachers, pulling Hunter and her thoughts from the want that radiated through her fingertips to her fluttering heart.

"Are you excited?" Mercy nearly squealed. "I mean, I know this spell and everything is really serious, but I can't help but be a smidge excited. I've always wanted to be able to share my spellwork with friends."

They stopped near the metal stands. Hunter rubbed her palms together. She didn't mind keeping her spellwork to herself. However, she *did* mind that she'd have to share more of their family secret with Kirkles.

A loud *"Mustangs!"* roared from the football field followed by whoops and cheers from the crowd. Hunter blew out a puff of air. Even though she'd dodged Mercy's question and had no interest in including Kirk in their upcoming spell, she knew her sister had been correct. No matter how much Hunter disliked Kirk, he was the only other person they trusted enough to ask to participate. Hunter scrunched her nose. *Trusted* was such a strong word.

Hunter shook away the shell she'd gotten so adept at hiding in whenever she was forced to be around a crowd, and searched the throng of people for her own Hail Mary pass. She shielded her eyes against the starbursts of sunlight shooting off the players' scuffed red helmets as, one by one, the varsity players removed them and shuffled off the field. "Jax!" She lifted onto her tiptoes and waved.

"I don't see Kirk." Mercy chewed her bottom lip and searched the crowd of stinky white practice jerseys for her beloved.

Jax returned Hunter's wave and flashed her a cute, crooked-toothed grin before he slapped his teammate on his bulky shoulder pads and jogged over, his helmet in his hand.

"H! You came to a practice!" Jax's brows lifted and he enveloped her in a sweaty hug, his helmet bumping against her back with each gentle squeeze. "Hell must've finally frozen over."

"Where's Kirk?" Mercy asked before Hunter had even taken a breath to speak.

Jax scratched the back of his neck and swallowed. "He's, uh . . ." His gaze flicked across Mercy and settled on the dusty, worn gravel between his cleats. "Talking to Coach, I think."

Mercy's cheeks plumped with a smile. "I see him," she said and practically skipped over to meet the sweaty quarterback.

Hunter crossed her arms over her chest and squinted up at her best friend. "Did you pull another Mrs. Ritter and see my sister's boobs, too?"

Jax stiffened. "What? No!"

"Then what's with the weirdness? I can practically feel it pouring off you."

He picked at a clump of dirt stuck to the back of his helmet. "You're not going to like it."

She shrugged. "I don't like a lot of things."

Jax took a breath, held it for a moment, and let the words rush out with his exhale. "Yeah, but this is about your sister."

Hunter's stomach squeezed and her fingertips went cold. Someone was talking about Mercy? Hunter's attention snapped to her sister, to the people who waved and smiled at her as they passed. This didn't make sense. Everyone loved Mercy. Hunter's throat tightened. And worse, they were saying something so bad that Jax, the guy who used to pull spaghetti noodles through his nostrils like slimy dental floss, was uncomfortable?

Mercy caught Hunter's gaze, waved, and bounded back over with Kirk on her heels.

"Tell me later," Hunter said before pinning a casual smile to her lips.

Mercy wriggled into the space next to Hunter as she positioned Kirk across from her and next to Jax. "We have something mega important to ask you two!" Mercy punctuated the statement with a short series of claps. "It's serious." She dropped her hands to her sides. The words seemed to be more a reminder to herself than an explanation. "But I'm pretty sure you're both going to say yes."

"Babe, you don't even have to ask. The answer is yes. I'd do anything for you." With his sweat-soaked hair, pinched brow, the occasional *attaboy Whitfield* that came from the passersby coupled with the way he tilted his chin slightly to the side as if to say, *yeah, I'm hot, but I'm also approachable,* Kirk *attaboy* Whitfield looked like every hunky teen heartthrob in every sappy teen romance movie Hunter had ever seen. She could fault producers for being so heteronormative, but she couldn't fault them for the jock stereotype.

Mercy shuffled forward, lifted onto her tiptoes, and kissed his cheek. Hunter's lips forgot their fake smile and tugged down with a frown. She couldn't imagine liking anyone enough to kiss them through all of that sweat.

Jax set his helmet on the gravel and took Hunter's hand in his. "And, babe, I'd do anything for you. No asking. No questions. Not one. Ever." He sealed the breathy vow with a smattering of noisy kisses against the back of Hunter's hand.

Kirk bristled. "Piss off!" He wrapped his arm around Mercy's shoulders and squeezed her against his side. "You know how much I care about my little witch."

Jax rolled his eyes and steadied himself. "Sure you do," he grumbled.

Hunter would have to find out more about that, too.

Mercy hopped away from Kirk and back to her spot next to Hunter. "Actually, speaking of witches, there's this spell—"

"I knew it!" Jax snapped his fingers and shoved Kirk's shoulder. "I frickin' knew you two were going to ask us to do another spell. What is it this time? Something for Em? Oh! What about a way to ace finals? Can you do that?"

Kirk adjusted his pads and jutted his broad chin in Jax's direction. "Calm down, butterfingers."

Jax threw his hands into the air. "Dude, I dropped *one* ball."

"But it could have been *the* ball, Ashley."

"Guys!" Hunter clapped. "We're trying to ask you to participate in a spell to keep the town safe."

Jax's forehead wrinkled. "But our town is super safe," he said. "Most of the time, my dad doesn't even lock the front door." He gripped his collar with both hands and rested his forearms against his chest. "Is that because of you? Have the Goodes been, like, spell-casting vigilantes?"

Mercy dug the toe of her sneaker into the gravel. "Not exactly."

"I was gonna say, if you are, you've been doing a terrible job. Emily's dad was just murdered and so was that old guy . . ." Kirk's temples pulsed as he searched for the completion of his thought. "Oh, you know." He jabbed Jax with his elbow. "That old guy who wouldn't ever let us use his truck in the Rooster Days Parade even though it's one hundred percent Mustang red."

"Mr. Thompson?" Mercy supplied.

"Yeah, that's it." Sweat leapt from Kirk's scalp as he brushed his hand through his hair. "Wonder if we can use his truck now?"

"Anyway." Hunter didn't keep the disdain from twisting her features. "What we need you guys to do is simple."

"You'll each go to a tree and wait for our signal and then light a candle and say a few words and do some other simple, witchy stuff." Mercy continued Hunter's thought in a way only her twin sister could. "Piece of cake," she said with another clap. "Oh, this has to happen tonight. At about sunset. And you'll need to bring a gift."

Jax wrinkled his freckled nose. "For the tree?"

Mercy tugged on the hem of her pink T-shirt. "Kind of."

Kirk rubbed his hand against his barely there chin fuzz. "So, you want us to pick a tree and bring it, like, some earrings or something? And that'll keep the town safe?"

Mercy chewed her bottom lip. "Well, uh, yeah. I mean—"

Kirk shook his head. "Sorry, but you're gonna have to be more specific."

"Yeah, I'm not even sure what I'd buy a tree. Lights, maybe?" Jax rubbed the back of his neck and shrugged.

Hunter and Mercy hadn't thought this through. They were supposed to get Jax and Kirk to agree to participate in a spell by saying it would protect the town. Sure, that was a valid reason, but if she and Mercy had slowed down and really thought about it, they would have realized *help the town and get trees presents* made them sound crazy. And not *witchy* crazy, *crazy* crazy.

Hunter took a deep breath. If Mercy could get people to do almost anything, so could she. "There are five gates in Goodeville. Each is represented by a different type of super old tree that's definitely not native to Illinois. In order to keep the town safe, we have to make sure these gates stay closed. The gift we need you to bring is just a representation of the original place the tree came from. It all stems from a lot of ancient witchy magic stuff that's been going on for centuries." Hunter clasped her hands behind her back to keep from picking at her fingernails.

Jax tilted his head. "Real gates or symbolic gates?" he asked.

Hunter's fingers betrayed her, found a hangnail, and tugged. "Real gates." She winced.

Jax shared a look with Kirk before turning back to Hunter. "To actual places?"

Mercy sucked in a breath. "Well, not—"

"Yes," Hunter interrupted. At this point, it didn't matter if Jax and Kirk drove through the whole town with a bullhorn yelling about Goodeville being full of weird old trees and witchy gates. Everyone would think they were crazy crazy, too.

Jax dragged his crooked teeth along his bottom lip. "Bad places?"

Hunter rolled her answer across her tongue, smoothing out the rough edges. "Just different. What's over there doesn't belong here, and what's over here doesn't belong there."

Jax nodded. "Cool."

"Cool?" Kirk took a step back the same way he had that night on the porch before the grief spell. But that hadn't been in front of his precious *babe,* the girl he'd do anything for.

Jax hiked a shoulder. "I'm not going to pretend like I totally understand, but I know H. If she needs my help, I'm there."

Hunter crammed her hands into her pockets. She'd lied to her best friend. Her sweet, trusting, perfect best friend. It was for a good cause. She and Mercy had decided not to tell the boys the complete truth, but Hunter hadn't expected that to make lying so easy. She swallowed as guilt flooded her stomach with the same prickly swiftness as her first and only drink of vodka. But this guilt wasn't for the half-truths, the lies. This guilt that lapped hot against her stomach was for its absence. Hunter hadn't felt bad for lying. She hadn't felt anything.

Kirk shuffled back toward the group, twitching like a fly. "Yeah, of course. I mean, I'm always there for Hunter *and* Mercy."

"Whitfield!" Coach Jamison's holler made Hunter flinch.

Kirk turned and waved an acknowledgment to the stout, balding man before turning back to Mercy. "Coach needs me, but I won't be long. He'll make the JV squad stay and practice, but the A Team is done." He pressed against her like a shadow.

"You're so sweaty." Mercy giggled and made a show of pushing her hands against her boyfriend's padded chest in disgust just to lean in closer.

Hunter rolled her eyes in her best friend's direction. She'd expected Jax to return the exacerbated expression. Instead, his temples pulsed and his gaze narrowed at Kirk. The last time she'd seen him like that, he'd reached across the cafeteria table and punched Spencer Burke in the face for calling her a dykey poon bag. Jax had gotten detention and, to this day, neither he nor Hunter knew exactly what a poon bag was.

"Don't leave yet. I'll be done in a few," Kirk mumbled against the top of Mercy's head before backing away and jogging toward the field.

Mercy let out a tiny squeal as she took Hunter's hand in hers and swung it back and forth. "I told you he'd be cool with the spell. He really is awesome, right?" She sighed and watched Kirk wave at the group before he turned his attention to Coach Jamison.

Jax crossed his arms over his chest. "He really is a dick."

Hunter hiccupped back a laugh as Mercy sucked in a breath and halted her excited arm swinging.

Jax's mouth opened and closed like a suffocating fish's.

"*You're* a dick!" Mercy fired back.

Hunter squeezed Mercy's hand and bit her cheeks to stifle another chuckle.

Mercy dropped Hunter's hand and clamped her own to her waist. "Your *friend* is being an asshole because Kirk called him out about dropping those balls in practice."

With a huff, Jax threw up his hands. "It was *one* ball. And that's not why your boyfriend is a—"

"You're just jealous," Mercy spat.

"I wouldn't be jealous of Kirk Whitfield if he got drafted to the Bears."

Hunter's hand flew to her pendant. This was it. Whatever Jax had heard about Mercy had something to do with Kirk. It had to. Jax would give almost anything to play for the Bears and would be salty for years if one of his friends got to live out his dream.

Mercy leaned forward. Her hair slipped from her shoulders. "Then what is it, Jax? What's your problem with my boyfriend?"

Jax sucked in his bottom lip. His Adam's apple bobbed just above the padded collar of his practice jersey.

"Jax." Hunter bit the tip of her fingernail. "You can't clam up now."

"He told everyone, Mercy." Jax clasped his hands together. Color drained from his knuckles with each passing second. "The whole team. He told them everything."

Now Hunter was the fish. Her mouth bobbed open and closed as she struggled to put the pieces together.

Mercy took a step back. "I don't know what you're talking about." She shook her hair away from her face and dug her teeth into her bottom lip.

Jax's gaze fell to his feet. "The blowjob and the . . ." He brushed the pegs of his cleats against the gravel. "Other stuff." His dark eyes lifted. "Everyone knows, Mercy."

Mercy wrapped her arms around her core. She squeezed her stomach as if she could keep it all in, keep herself together, if she only applied enough pressure. "No," she whispered.

"I'm sorry." Jax reached out. His hand hung in the air for a moment before dropping to his side.

Mercy cleared her throat. "If he told, there had to be a reason."

Jax shook his head. "He was bragging, Mag. I swear. Big, detailed, douchebag bragging."

"You don't know him. Neither of you. Not the way I do." Mercy straightened, stiffened, and held her fists down by her sides. "I'll be at the car. Come when you're finished with . . ." She narrowed her eyes and waved a hand in front of Jax. *"This."* And stormed off.

Hunter started to go after her but Jax caught her hand. "I didn't want to tell her. Not like this."

"You did the right thing. We all know Kirk is terrible. Now she does, too."

Jax squeezed her hand before he let go and bent to pick up his helmet.

"Mercy!" Hunter called as she jogged into the parking lot after her sister. "Wait!"

Mercy whirled around, her black hair cutting the air like a scythe. "For what, Hunter? So you can tell me more lies about my boyfriend?"

"Jax wasn't lying."

Mercy slumped against the nearest car, Coach Jamison's puke green El Camino. "Kirk wouldn't do that. Not the Kirk that I know."

Hunter couldn't stop picking at her fingernails. "But the Kirk you know is the same Kirk Jax knows."

"He's just gone through so much with his mom leaving and his dad being such an awful misogynist." Mercy pressed her palm against her chest. "He thinks that the only way people will like him is if he pretends to be mister jock."

"Or maybe he *is* mister jock and he thinks the only way *you* will like him is if he pretends to be someone he's not."

Mercy's hand fell to her side. "There's no way you could ever understand. You've never even dated anyone. You're jealous! You and Jax and Em. You're jealous that someone loves me and no one loves you."

Hunter's heart squeezed. Didn't Mercy love her? Didn't that count for something?

"I'm right! Kirk is sweet and loving and kind and respectful." Mercy's left brow lifted, and she sprang away from the car. "And I know a way to prove it," she shouted and stormed back to the practice field.

Twenty-six

Mercy had to get her anger under control. Spellwork could be volatile—unpredictable—if the witch doing it wasn't calm and focused, so she forced her steps to slow and shifted her concentration from how pissed off she was to how much she loved the way the fringe that hung around the hem of her short jeans skirt felt brushing against her thighs. She shook back her hair and her lips actually lifted in a small half smile as the beads on her hoop earrings jingled musically with her movements. Mercy drew a deep breath and let it out slowly. She was still pissed, but her mind had calmed enough to work through the angry haze that colored her thoughts.

Jax was full of shit.

But her sister's best friend's words haunted her. *The blowjob and the . . . other stuff.* Her cheeks went hot. Okay, so, Kirk had said *something* to them—or at least to Jax. But it couldn't have been like Jax was making it out to be. It couldn't have been bad.

Kirk's voice seeped seductively from her memory, overpowering Jax's stupid words. *You are a goddess. My goddess. I love you.* Kirk had probably just wanted to tell Jax about the amazing thing that had happened between them—had been trying to be actual, *real* friends with him—and Jax was making a big deal out of it. Sure, Kirk could've sounded kinda douchey. No big surprise. It's not like he had any kind of a decent role model at home to show him how to treat a girlfriend. That's why Mercy had to practically teach him how to be a boyfriend—not that she minded. When they were alone Kirk was the sweetest guy ever. He just didn't know how to make that guy public.

Well, she sure as hell did. And he'd thank her later, after everyone saw the *real* Kirk Whitfield. The Kirk she knew and loved so much.

Mercy slowed as she approached the spot at the very end of the practice field where the varsity cheerleaders had set up a big table that held a giant cooler full of sports drinks and ice. It was tradition that the cheer squad practiced along with the football team, breaking at about the same time so that everyone could share the cold drinks before the boys jogged into their locker room and the cheerleaders flitted off to theirs. Mercy tended to agree with Hunter's ongoing assessment that the whole thing was a misogynistic ritual that needed to end, but the football and cheer coaches thought it was good for morale.

Giggles mixed with deep voices drifted to her on the breeze. Mercy thought what almost everyone else did—that the morale it built by the cheerleaders basically playing the role of glorified water boys caused more touchdowns in the backseat of cars than on the football field, but whatever. Today the archaic ritual was perfect for what she wanted to, *needed* to do.

She saw Hunter walking slowly to Jax, who—along with the rest of the varsity team, minus their quarterback—was downing a bottle of something that looked like it had way too much red food coloring in it to be healthy. Hunter glanced at her and Mercy motioned sharply for Hunter to join the group. Even from that distance she could see that Hunter's shoulders were bowed and her face looked pale and drawn. Mercy's stomach tightened. She hated to see Hunter upset. For years she'd been messing up anyone who hurt her sister.

And look how she paid me back today—by siding with Jax against me. She was a bitch last night when I tried to reason with her about Tyr, and she's still pissed. That's all it is.

Mercy lifted her chin. She'd show Hunter. She'd show all of them.

The fence that ringed that end of the field and the track surrounding it was lined with Thuja trees that grew side by side in pyramids of concealing evergreens, easily ten feet tall. Several yards beyond the trees and the fence the cheerleaders clustered with the football team— and her sister, who was standing beside Jax, silent and uncomfortable.

Mercy approached the wall of trees. From where she stood she could hear the sounds of voices, but was too far away and too shielded by the living wall to make out actual words.

Kirk would think anything he said to her would be private. In the shadowy protection of the evergreen hedge they couldn't even be seen, let alone heard.

But Kirk didn't actually know anything about her witchy powers, so he had zero clue what she could coax the trees to do. Well, Hunter had just decided—all on her own and against what Xena had said—to spill a bunch of stuff about them and the gates.

Now it was Mercy's turn.

She knew the perfect spell. It was simple—one of the first Green Witch spells her mom had taught her before she was even a teenager and had first shown an affinity for plants and trees and the earth. Abigail had taken her to the huge grandmother oak in their backyard and explained to her that each tree was a living being, and because of that the right witch, using the right kind of power, could ask trees for aid.

It had been a super easy spell for her to learn. She'd already been able to feel the big oak's inhalations and exhalations against her hands, and she'd been listening to the sweet whispers of the crops that surrounded their home for as long as she could remember. So, when Abigail had shown her how to focus, how to pull energy from the ley lines and be the conduit that sent that energy into the oak so that she could beseech the tree for the help she needed—it felt as natural as breathing to young Mercy.

She looked up at the wall of evergreens. They loomed above her and made her feel safe, strong, powerful even. Mercy smiled and lifted her hands, stroking the spiky, sticky upside-down Vs that were the Thuja's leaves. It was then that her mother's voice tickled across her memory. *Well done, Mag!* Abigail had said when Mercy had executed the spell so easily. *But remember, sweetheart, never use your powers for vanity or any self-serving reason. Always keep in mind the words we live by: An ye harm none, do what ye will.*

Mercy ignored the spark of intuition that all of a sudden made her palms sweaty and her stomach sick. *I'm not harming anyone. I'm showing everyone they're wrong about Kirk. I'm doing a good thing!*

She wiped her damp palms against her jeans skirt, closed her eyes, and centered herself—and found that her anger worked for her as she easily found the potent ley line that bisected the football field and ran directly under where she stood. Mercy reached down and tapped into that vein of power as she pressed her hands against the trees— ignoring the fact that their sticky leaves scratched her palms.

"I greet you, gentle giants," she murmured to them.

Instantly she felt their combined inhale and exhalation against her hands.

"I ask a favor of you, and for that favor I will draw the power beneath you up into your roots, your branches, your beautiful, lime green leaves. You will swell with health and grow taller, ever taller. Will you grant me a favor?"

From the trees rushed excitement that teased her palms and made her smile.

"Good. Here is what I ask of you . . ." Mercy bowed her head and pressed her forehead against the Thuja as she whispered her request to the line of trees.

Again, her palms tingled with excitement that was so real it reminded her of wriggling puppies. She didn't speak her thanks. Instead, she pulled the pulsing power up through the earth. The heat of it rushed into her body and through her hands to cascade into the wall of trees. They swayed as they accepted her offering like ballerinas tethered to the earth.

She stroked the thick, leafy Thuja branches and murmured, "Thank you, my friends," exactly as Abigail had trained her to do. The wall of trees swayed once more in response.

Satisfied the spell was set, Mercy rubbed her hands on her jeans skirt and headed to the break in the fence and tree line, just in time to see Kirk jogging away from the coach and the JV team, as he headed for the refreshment stand. Mercy lifted a hand and waved at him.

As soon as he saw her he grinned and changed direction, running straight to her.

"Babe! You stayed! Damn, you look good." He bent to kiss her, but she pushed against his chest with both hands—this time actually keeping him from getting close to her.

"We need to talk," she said firmly.

Jarod Frazier, the Mustangs' senior linebacker, leered at them as he crushed a Gatorade bottle in his meaty hand. "Oooh, damn! Trouble in paradise? You need some help handling her, bro?"

Mercy didn't wait for Kirk to respond. She spun on her heels and marched back through the break in the fence, leaving Kirk to jog after her—much to the jeering delight of the rest of the team.

Mercy turned to face Kirk when she reached the exact spot she'd stood earlier, hidden by the wall of trees from the view of anyone on the football field.

"Mercy, what's—"

She lifted her hand, stopping his words.

"You told Jax about what we did yesterday!"

Kirk frowned. "What the hell did he say?"

Mercy put her fists on her hips. "How about you tell me what you said instead?"

"Nothin'. Really. Just locker room talk. You know." He reached for her and she sidestepped him.

"You talked about me—about *us*—in the damn locker room? You mean the whole team knows our business?" Mercy felt her cheeks flame. Her anger was so intense she felt dizzy.

"Mercy. Babe. All us bros talk about our girlfriends. It's, like, a compliment."

"A *compliment*? Telling the 'bros,'" Mercy air-quoted, "*personal* and *private* things about our relationship is only a compliment to douchebag misogynistic pigs like your father! To normal guys—decent guys—it's a betrayal—an invasion of privacy." She shook her head, super pissed that tears had started to leak from her eyes down her cheeks. This really wasn't going the way she'd planned. To herself more than Kirk she said, "I'm such a fool. I thought you were different." She cried brokenly. "I can't believe I was so stupid." She wiped at her eyes and started to storm past him, intent on touching the trees and ending the spell, but Kirk surprised her by grabbing her wrist. As he stopped her he dropped to his knees and stared up at her.

"You gotta believe me," he begged from his knees. "I didn't mean nothing. I promise. Just—just tell me how to do better and I will."

Mercy looked down at him. His blue eyes were huge. His face had paled and he was truly upset. Had she overreacted? Kirk seemed genuinely sorry. She wiped her eyes and shook her head. "Kirk. What you did was *really* bad." She crossed her arms over her chest and waited for him to make it right—for him to be the guy she believed he was.

"Babe! Like I said, I just didn't know. But I totally get it. I'm not gonna say shit about us again. Seriously." He reached out for her and Mercy let him take her hand. He kissed it and smiled up at her. "You know I'm an idiot about this kind of stuff. Sorry, my witchy woman."

Relieved, Mercy pulled her hand from his as she started toward the line of trees. All she needed to do was to touch them to close the spell and then she and Kirk could—

But before she could reach the trees Kirk had snagged her wrist and pulled her around to face him. "No, please, don't walk away!"

Mercy meant to shake off his vise grip and touch the trees, but when she looked down at him what she saw had her frozen with shock.

He was on his knees again.

Oh, shit! He totally misunderstood!

And he was crying.

Really sobbing.

"Kirk." She spoke as softly as possible. "It's okay. We can talk about it." Her eyes darted from him to the trees as she tried to shift her body to bring herself within reaching distance of one of their sticky branches.

"Mercy, I mean it! I didn't get what I was doing. I was just happy! I wanted to tell everyone so they'd know how much you love me, and how much I love you." On his knees, he lurched forward and wrapped his arms around her waist. He pressed his cheek against the softness of her stomach as his sobs made his voice hitch. "Y-you know h-how much I n-need you."

Mercy felt the beginnings of panic. She'd expected him to apologize—to have a good excuse for what he'd done—to reassure her and react like a sweet guy who'd made one stupid mistake.

She hadn't expected him to be so clueless, and then to fall apart and cry.

Mercy tried to break the hold he had on her waist so she could get around him and be close enough to the trees so that she could close the spell, but Kirk was too big, too strong. The harder she tried to pry away from him—the tighter he clung to her.

"Okay, okay," Mercy tried to soothe. She stopped pulling at his arms and instead stroked his sweaty hair. "I—I overreacted." Her eyes darted from him to the trees as she tried to shift her body closer.

Through streaming tears he looked up at her. His eyes widened as he misread her worried expression.

His arms tightened around her.

"No, you can't do this!" Tears flooded his voice with desperation. "You know how much I love you."

"Kirk! It's okay. I forgive you!"

"I need you! You can't leave me."

"Kirk, shh." Mercy pressed her fingers against his lips, physically trying to dam the tide of his words. "It's hard for me to listen to you if you won't let me go."

Abruptly, he released her. She staggered backward until she touched the trees and surreptitiously stroked their sharp leaves. They quivered once more in response, and then stilled. Breathing a sigh of relief, she turned to Kirk.

He'd remained on his knees, hands held out as if he beseeched her blessing while he continued to snot cry. "H-how do I fix this? Want me to kick Jax's ass?"

Mercy shook her head, ready to tell him—not for the first time—that he couldn't blame other people for his bad choices, when Jarod's sarcastic voice came from behind Kirk.

"Dude! Are you *seriously* crying?"

"Right?!" Derek, the varsity center, a big, meaty kid who looked like a chubby Hitler youth, mimicked Kirk as he scrunched up his fat pink face and pretended to cry. "Babe! Don't leave me! Babe, I love you!"

Kirk rocketed to his feet and whirled around. The entire varsity football squad, and cheerleaders, had poured through the break in the fence and were *laughing* at Kirk. Jax and Hunter stood a little apart from the group, speechlessly staring from Mercy to Kirk.

Mercy narrowed her eyes and glared at the gawking group. She knew her words were hypocritical. It was because of her spell that the trees had amplified everything she and Kirk had said and broadcasted it to the varsity football team and the cheerleading squad, but she was too panicked to think of anything else to say—anything else to do.

"Oh, shut up! This is between Kirk and me, and none of your damn business."

"Uh, if it wasn't our business the two of you shouldn't have been yelling like that," quipped Jarod.

"Yeah, you were super loud. We heard everything," added Derek.

Kirk wiped violently at his face. His shoulders were slumped. He fisted his hands by his sides and for a moment Mercy thought he was going to stand up for her—stand up for them—and take on the mocking team. But his body language changed before he faced her. He put a hand on his hip and slouched like he was oh, so cool. Then he turned to look at her and his cute, full lips—the lips she'd kissed so, so many times—twisted in a sneer.

"Well, shit. I guess the cat's outta the bag now—or I should say the *pussy's* out of the bag." His laughter was cruel, and this time Jarod and Derek joined in, laughing *with* not *at* him. His voice was hard and cold with sarcasm. "Can't blame a guy for tryin' to get more than a bj, though, right?"

Mercy felt frozen. She swallowed hard before she could form words. "Kirk? What are you saying?"

Hunter took a step toward Mercy. Her blue/green eyes looked old and tired as she spoke low in a tight voice. "Come on, Mag. Let's go home."

Kirk sneered at Hunter. "For once I agree with the dyke. Go home, *Mag.*" He made her nickname sound like an insult.

Mercy couldn't move. The coldness inside had frozen her to the earth. "But you love me." Even to her ears she sounded like a stupid little girl.

Kirk laughed. "Love you? It was fun for a while, but you're too damn much work." He jerked his chin at the gleefully watching team. "Ask any of them. After what they just heard they know it's true, too." Then his brows lifted into his hairline. "Wait, they *shouldn't* have been able to hear us. It was you, wasn't it? You did some witch shit—like your sister did at your house the other night. You set me up, you bitch!"

Mercy stared at Kirk—at the cruel stranger he'd become. *No, he's always been this person. I just chose not to see it.*

Hunter ignored Kirk. She gestured at her sister and repeated, "Come on. Let's go."

Thawed by her twin's voice, Mercy nodded jerkily, and started to make a wide circle around Kirk. But he stepped up to block her.

"What's wrong? Don't want your *precious* freak of a twin to hear the truth?" He shot Hunter a mean look over his shoulder before he continued. "Too late. She already knows about the bj. But her bff probably didn't tell her the rest—how you humped my hand like the bitch in heat you are. You came all over me, you slut."

Shocked gasps erupted from the cheerleaders to mix with uncomfortable chuckles from the football players.

Mercy couldn't move again. Her entire body was flushed with heat and even though her whole being was screaming *run* she kept staring at Kirk like she'd never seen him before.

Then Hunter was there, stepping between them. She seemed to grow in height as she faced down the quarterback.

Twenty-seven

Rage surged through Hunter so hot and deep that her breath sloshed out in soupy gasps. Part of her yearned to relax into the warm embrace her anger promised. In its arms, there were no consequences, no remorse, no sad sisters made even more depressed by betrayal. In fury's grasp, there was nothing but revenge. Hunter clenched her fists. Her jagged nails dug into her scabbed palm. Kirk Whitfield was over, canceled. She'd take away everything he cared about.

Beside her, Mercy slapped her palm over her mouth and whimpered.

Hunter sucked in a breath and fought through the heat clawing up her throat ready to fork her tongue, weaponize it, use it to tear the star quarterback apart. Had it not been for her sister and the despair that squeaked past her lips, Hunter would have let the rage consume her.

Her hands relaxed as each inhale of cool spring air quelled her roiling insides. The corner of Hunter's lips quirked and a chuckle scratched at the back of her throat as she stared at the blustering windbag. All machismo, no substance. She would have pitied him had he not just trampled her sister.

Kirk lifted his chin and the shocked murmurs of their peers ceased. "What are you laughing at, *dyke*?"

Hunter held out her hand and motioned for Jax to stay back as he surged forward and Mercy stiffened.

Most people went their whole lives without a good showdown, with only the fantasy of burning their ex or quitting their job to fuel them from one unsatisfying moment to the next. Hunter had only had to wait sixteen years.

"You're not worth the trouble it would take to hit you." She untethered her smile and let it roll across her lips as she recited the Yates quote from memory. *"You're not worth the powder it would take to blow you up. You're an empty, empty, hollow shell of a man."*

Right now, her library card and every book she'd ever checked out were worth their weight in gold.

Kirk rushed forward and Jax charged out in front of Hunter. This time, she didn't stop him from intervening. She wrapped her arm around her sister and guided her from the wall of trees and the uniformed spectators chanting for a fight. Jax could hold his own and, with the number of parents and coaches off in the parking lot starting the traditional after-practice tailgating extravaganza, a fight wouldn't get very far.

As they neared the bleachers, Mercy pushed away from Hunter. "I just"—she hiccupped between cries—"want to—be alone."

Hunter twisted the hem of her shirt between her fingers. "I don't think you did anything wrong, if that's what you're worried about."

"It's not about what you think, Hunter." Mercy's lip quivered as she swiped the back of her hand across her tear-streaked cheeks. "You couldn't possibly understand what this feels like. I need to be alone right now." She slipped into the shadows under the bleachers, her feet making sharp *scuff scuff* noises as she jogged the length of the metal steps.

Choked sobs echoed through the shadows and filled the space between the sisters. Like caustic fumes, they twisted Hunter's insides. After everything they'd been through, could Mercy handle another blow?

Hunter ran under the bleachers. "Mag! Wait!" she called as Mercy plunged into the sunlight on the other side. The last time she'd given Mercy space to process her grief, her sister had been nearly catatonic. Hunter charged forward, faster. "This isn't your fault!" she shouted into the shadows. This was all Kirk. Mercy had done nothing wrong. If only Kirk had been better, had actually been the guy Mercy thought he was.

Hunter's shoelace had come untied. With each rushed step, the plastic ends of the ties struck her shin.

But Hunter *had* warned her. So had Emily and Jax. Even Xena had made her disapproval known. Why hadn't Mercy listened? Did she not trust her friends and family? Did she not care for them more than she cared for Kirk? The questions stoked the graying coals in Hunter's belly.

Since the beginning of their relationship, Mercy had put Kirk first. *You were so powerful tonight, Kirk. So perfect. This couldn't have happened without you.* The words Mercy had spoken after the grief spell spit fuel on Hunter's anger. She coughed as heat surged through her chest, up her throat.

You're jealous that someone loves me and no one loves you.

Hunter shielded her eyes as she emerged from the bleachers. Until Mercy apologized for placing Kirk above everyone else, she could run off alone.

Hunter stepped on her untied shoelace. She tripped forward and caught herself before she faceplanted in the gravel. She shuffled over to the shade of the now-closed snack hut and crouched down to tie her shoe. Her stomach churned as she crossed one shoelace over the other and tugged so hard she nearly ripped them from their holes.

Maybe this time Hunter would let her rage swallow her. A dying star spitting fire into the cosmos. She'd go back to Kirk and wouldn't choose the high road. She'd choose the low road, the same road he'd just torn down, slamming into everything he could on his way to feeling like a big man. Hunter double knotted her laces and brushed her hands on her shorts as she stood. Yes, that's what she'd do. She'd find Kirk and—

A man's wracking cough pulled Hunter's attention from the molten lava pooling in her gut. Sheriff Dearborn buried his face into the crook of his arm and leaned against the lamppost on the other side of the snack hut, a plate of nachos scattered in the gravel around his feet.

Hunter chewed the inside of her cheek. She wanted to leave, wanted to let the volcano of anger burbling in her stomach erupt all over Kirk and his jock friends.

Another bout of wet coughs. Sheriff Dearborn spit a phlegm ball onto his nachos, wiped his mouth, and sagged against the metal post. Hunter wrinkled her nose. The sheriff wasn't the youngest guy, but it wasn't her responsibility to help someone who had a cold. She squinted back at the packed parking lot. She didn't think she had it in her to fix *another* situation. Hunter exhaled and half expected smoke to billow from her parted lips.

He gripped his chest and lurched forward. His sunglasses slipped from his ears as he sucked in breaths between more throat-shredding coughs.

Concern doused the anger roiling within Hunter. She ran over to the sheriff and caught him as he pitched farther forward. Spittle dangled from his chin and she averted her eyes and helped him up. "You . . . okay . . . Sheriff?" she asked between grunts as he used her shoulders as crutches and righted himself.

"Fine. Fine." His voice had the same dry coarseness as the gravel beneath her feet. "Damn chips must've gotten me."

Hunter plucked his sunglasses from the gravel and wiped the dusty lenses with the bottom of her shirt. "Mercy nearly choked on a tortilla chip once. Now she'll only eat Lay's." She handed him the sunglasses. Her breath caught in her throat.

His left eye was completely clouded over. A fresh page in a new notebook.

"Your eye . . ."

He snatched the glasses from her hand and thrust them back onto his face. "Allergies is all," he said with a sniffle.

Hunter's fingertips itched. She slid her hand into the pocket of her slouchy knit cardigan and pressed her hand against her tarot deck. Power sizzled through her palm.

A star around his eye . . .

Sunlight glinted off the points of Sheriff Dearborn's star-shaped badge.

. . . and on his chest.

Hunter's throat tightened. She clutched her amulet and fed off the strength from the symbol of her god. Her insides warmed. But not with the hungry fire of rage or the slow burn of anger. Her fingertips found the smooth moonstone pressed into her symbol of Tyr. Her god was with her now, drawing down the magic of the moon and whispering affirmations to the powerful gift entangled in the blood of the Goode women.

Sheriff Dearborn slipped his fingers under his sunglasses and rubbed his clouded eye. "Give the other one of you my regards, Bright Eyes," he said and rushed off in the direction of the parking lot.

Hunter's hands shook as she pulled out her phone and dialed her sister's number.

Bright Eyes?

Hunter pushed away the question when Mercy answered on the second ring. "Meet me at the car, Mag. I found him," Hunter blurted before her sister had a chance to speak. "I found Polyphemus."

Mercy sucked in a breath. "Are you safe? Who is it?"

A cold pang of guilt flashed through Hunter's chest as she ran to meet Mercy. Mag did care about her. Hunter needed to stop being such a bad sister, such a bad friend. Her ponytail brushed her shoulder blades as she shook her head and with it, shook away the conscience threatening to derail her focus.

Hunter hid her mouth behind her hand as she wove through hot dog–eating townspeople milling about the parking lot. "It's the sheriff! And now that we know, we can put a stop to all of this and send him back where he belongs."

Power flared within her veins and the scabs crusted against Hunter's palm ached. She didn't know how this would end, but she knew it would be bloody.

Twenty-eight

A nd Jax is meeting us at poor Emily kitten's house?" Xena's question broke the silent ride across town.

"Yeah, Xena." Hunter glanced in the rearview mirror at the cat person, who kept looking nervously out the windows. "He took a shower while we were getting the ritual stuff together. He's bringing his offering, a dove feather from his father's collection."

"That will make an appropriate gift in honor of the indigenous women." Xena shifted and tugged at the neck of the oversized blue peasant blouse she'd borrowed from their mom's closet before she smoothed, then pulled at, and smoothed again the long, silver broom skirt that had been one of Abigail's favorites.

From the passenger seat Mercy turned to look at her. "Are you okay back there?"

"No. I very much am not. I despise these horrible, soulless things." Her long fingers fluttered at the interior of the car. "And though my Abigail was a lovely woman I do not understand how she, or any of you, ever wear clothing." Xena plucked at the sleeve of her blouse.

"Xena, you're not even wearing anything under that," Mercy said. "Bras and panties are *way* more uncomfortable than real clothes."

Xena shuddered. "I do not know how you bear it. It's already quite awful." Then she leaned forward and peered from twin to twin. "But what is even more awful is whatever is going on between the two of you."

Mercy blew out a long, frustrated breath. "There's nothing going on other than Kirk is an even bigger douchebag than you two thought. We broke up. In front of the entire sodding school. And I don't want to talk about it."

Hunter's knuckles whitened on the steering wheel. Her lips pressed into a tight line and she said nothing.

"Fine, kittens. Don't talk about it. But you two need to focus. Tonight is too important for you to bring anger and resentment into the ritual."

Mercy bowed her head. She knew Xena was right. She needed to get her shit together so that if or *when* the ritual failed there would be no doubt about why. So there, in the car with her sister's silent presence beside her, Mercy closed her eyes and concentrated on her shattered heart. On one raw, bleeding piece of it she envisioned carving the name ABIGAIL into her frayed flesh. On another wounded spot she carved HUNTER. And on the last, the newest, the most jagged piece of her somehow still beating heart she carved KIRK. Then she imagined taking a roll of gauze, like the sterile one in Abigail's emergency kit that rested in a bottom shelf of the pantry, and she wrapped it around and around the lacerations until the names could no longer be seen—until all that was left was a heart-shaped organ completely cocooned, which somehow still pulsed with stubborn life.

She turned her face to her half-open window and inhaled deeply the scents of the evening—of trees and grasses, crops and spring flowers. As she drank in the soothing earth, Mercy channeled its magic within and held it tightly to her damaged heart. The ache inside her subsided and in its place there was a nothingness that was almost equally as frightening, but a lot easier to think through.

She opened her eyes as Hunter pulled up in front of Emily's meticulously landscaped corner lot. People always oohed and aahed about the huge, brick edifice, but Mercy had never liked it. She knew the coldness of the outside and the façade of perfection were all too perfectly mimicked inside.

"There's Jax." Hunter waved and Jax got quickly out of his car and jogged across the street to them.

He put one hand on the roof and ducked down to peer inside. His left eye was swollen and black and there was a dark scab on his bottom lip. "Hi, Xena."

"Hello, Jax kitten," said Xena. She cocked her head and studied him. "Were you victorious in your battle?"

He started to grin and then grimaced as his lip began to bleed again. "Yeah, actually. I was."

"Good," Hunter said firmly.

Jax's gaze shifted to Mercy. Instead of turning away, Mercy met his kind brown eyes. "Hey, Mag. You okay?"

"Yep. Fine."

His brow lifted, but he didn't say anything else to her.

Mercy wanted to ask him if he'd really kicked Kirk's ass. Somewhere deep inside she hoped he had—hoped he'd made Kirk feel just a little of the hurt she was left suffering, but the words got trapped in the gauze that held her heart together.

Jax touched Hunter's shoulder through the open window. "How you doin'?"

Hunter covered his hand for a moment with her own. "Fine," she echoed Mercy's empty word.

Xena cleared her throat. "All right then. Shall we go get our other kitten?"

"Yeah, let's go." Without waiting for any of them, Mercy got out of the car and climbed the big stone stairs that led to a small but elaborately carved entryway. No wide, comfortable porch for the Parrotts—just lots of show that was totally devoid of warmth. As Hunter, Xena, and Jax came up to stand, fortresslike, behind her, she pressed the doorbell.

Nothing happened for so long that Mercy had raised her hand to press the button again when the door finally opened.

Emily blinked and then squinted as if the light from the setting sun was too bright for her amber eyes. Her chestnut skin looked dull; her beautiful eyes were framed with circles so dark they appeared bruised. And her hair—the gorgeous mahogany mass she was so proud of—that she liked to wear in a wild curl that fell well past her shoulders—was pulled back in a severe scrunchie. She was wearing what Mercy knew she called her *watch-TV clothes*—an old yellow sweat suit and scuffed sneakers.

Emily looked awful.

"Mag?" She sounded dazed, like she'd been awakened in the middle of sleepwalking. Then her gaze caught on the small group behind Mercy and her eyes widened. "Um, hi, guys. Do you want to come in?"

"Yes, we do." Xena pushed past her to pull Emily into her arms. "Oh, kitten! I have been so, so worried about you!"

"Uh, thanks." Emily's voice was muffled by Xena's mane of hair, but she returned the cat person's hug until a sneeze rocked her body.

"I am so sorry." Xena released Emily and took a step back. "I always forget how allergic you are."

"Allergic?" Emily's forehead wrinkled.

Mercy spoke up quickly. "Em, I know this is not a good time, but we need you."

Emily shook her head a little, like she wasn't sure she'd heard her friend correctly. "But, I—"

"Emily!" A wobbly old voice drifted from the direction of the kitchen. "If that's my delivery from the IGA, have them bring the things into the kitchen."

"No, Grandma, it's not—"

"Emily Michelle, if that's my delivery from the pharmacy, tip the boy well." Her mother's voice, which Mercy had always thought sounded shrill, splintered the air from the opposite side of the house. "They're doing me a special favor."

"It's not the deliver guy, Mom, it's—"

"It's the liquor store. Tip him well, too. Good help is hard to get." Her grandfather slurred his words from a closer room.

Emily sighed and stared at the floor.

No one came out of their respective hidey-holes to actually see who was at the door. Mercy studied her best friend, who looked completely defeated. She took Emily's hand. Her friend looked up at her.

"We need you," she repeated firmly. "Please come with us. It won't take long, and I'll explain in the car, but I promise it's important. Really important."

Emily stared at her, shoulders bowed in defeat. "I can't leave."

"Yes, kitten, you can," said Xena firmly.

"We wouldn't be here if we didn't need you," said Hunter.

Jax nodded. "Yeah, what they said. And I haven't seen you since . . . since, well, you know. But I'm really sorry, Em."

"Thanks." She cleared her throat and continued, "I wanna help you guys." Emily kept her words soft as if speaking too loudly would awaken ghosts. "I really do, but I can't leave. They're a mess. Like, my mom can barely make it to the bathroom. Grandpa's drunk. Grandma's lost her mind. Someone has to take care of them."

"Oh, kitten . . ." Xena whispered.

"Emily!" Her mother's voice made them all jump. "I need those pills!"

"I thought it was the liquor store," yelled her grandpa.

"No, I told you, it's the IGA," blared from the kitchen.

With each voice—each shout—Emily seemed to shrink more and more inside herself. *They're going to make her completely disappear and the Em I know won't exist anymore.* And Mercy Anne Goode couldn't bear to lose anyone else.

"No!" Mercy shouted, splitting the air with her anger-fueled words. "No!" she repeated. "This is bullshit!" Emily opened and closed her mouth as she stared at her friend. Mercy continued to grip her hand and kept going—kept letting the truth rush from her wounded heart and fall from her lips. "Why can't anyone be who they're supposed to be? Your mom's supposed to be a *mother,* not a drugged-out, self-indulgent brat." The words spilled around Mercy, sloshing against the immaculately decorated shell of a home. "Your grandparents are supposed to be your support system—the people *you* count on for strength and love—not the people you have to prop up."

"Mag—" Hunter began softly, but Mercy spoke over her.

"And *you're* supposed to be a girl—a teenager—a daughter who gets to be sad about losing her dad without having to play grown-up for the grown-ups!" she finished, breathing hard. Her friends stared at her as the heat of her anger drained away, leaving her heart cold and broken again. "Oh. Oh, no. Em, I'm sorry. Really I shouldn't have said all of that. I—"

"Hello, Mercy. Hello, children." Emily's mother stepped into the foyer behind them. "What is it you just said?"

Emily drew a deep breath and turned to face her mom. "Mercy said that I need to get out of the house, and she's right. Mom, I need a break. I have to have a break." She blinked hard, obviously trying to keep the tears pooling in her eyes from spilling over.

Emily's mom looked from her daughter to her friends. Her eyes were glassy, but her voice didn't waver when she spoke. "Emily, you're right. Go ahead. Be with your friends."

"Emily?" Her grandma joined Emily's mother.

"Grandma, these are my friends," said Emily.

Grandma walked stiffly to Emily and rested one hand on her shoulder. "Yes, I can see that they are."

"Beatrice, Emily was just going out," said Em's mother.

The older woman looked back at her daughter-in-law. "I think that's an excellent idea. Helene, would you join me in the kitchen?"

Emily's mom's eyes filled with tears. She nodded. "Yes. I would like that. Very much."

"What's happening out there?" slurred her grandfather.

"Nothing!" The two older women yelled together, and then they shared a real smile.

"Go. Be with your friends," repeated Em's mom after kissing her daughter on the forehead. "We'll be just fine."

Emily seemed unable to speak, so Mercy tugged on her hand as Jax opened the door and they all filed out.

They all piled into the Camry Hunter had parked across the street from the Parrotts' house, and as Mercy—with occasional help from Hunter and Xena—unfolded the truth behind the settling of Goodeville and the tragic events of the past four days, the shadows under Emily's eyes lifted. From her place between Jax and Xena in the center of the backseat, she sat up straighter, her expression growing more animated until she held up a hand and stopped Mercy.

"You're *real* witches." She looked from Hunter to Mercy. "I mean, I kinda knew it before, and that grief spell made me think that there was more to your powers than just herbs to fix cramps and an occasional love potion."

"Love potions are not actually what you think they are," said Xena. "It isn't ethical to play with someone's desires. Goode witches would never—"

"Xena, I don't think that's an important point right now," interrupted Mercy. She met her friend's gaze. "What is important is that you understand the truth. Since 1693, Goode witches have been guardians of those five gates—"

"Which are really the five weird trees?" Jax broke in.

"Yes," continued Mercy, nodding at him. "And we have to close and strengthen those gates tonight—at sunset." She glanced outside at the waning light. "Which will be pretty soon. Will you help us?"

Emily didn't hesitate. "Yes. That's what friends do, right? But it's more than that. This is why your mom and my dad were killed. So, we're getting rid of the Cyclops tonight?"

Hunter spoke firmly. "I promise."

"I'm totally in."

"Jax?" Mercy asked.

"Just tell me what I need to do."

The band of tension began to release from around Mercy's chest. She dug into her purse and pulled out the six sheets of paper she'd prepared the night before. Mercy handed out four of them, keeping two for herself—leaving the sixth sheet facedown on her lap. "Okay, ask any questions you have—anything at all. It starts with setting your intention. That means that as soon as we're on our way to our trees each of us must focus. Read my instructions carefully. Hunter and I are going to be channeling powerful energy through you tonight. You have to be prepared for it."

"How are we going to—" Emily began and then had to stop as three sneezes shook her body. "OMG, bless me!" She wiped her nose on the back of her sleeve. "Gross. Sorry. I don't know what's wrong with me. I usually only sneeze like this around ..." Her words trailed off as her head swiveled to stare at Xena, who was licking the back of her hand and smoothing her hair.

"What?" Xena stopped mid-lick.

"We might as well tell them," said Hunter. "They know everything else."

Mercy shrugged. "Fine with me. Xena?"

The cat person shook herself, which sent her hair flying madly around her shoulders and made Emily sneeze again. "Emily, kitten." Xena took her hand gently between hers. "I *am* a cat. Their cat. And by theirs I mean I've been a Goode familiar for generations. Please don't ask for how many years—it's impolite." While Emily and Jax stared slack-mouthed at her, Xena nodded. "Oh, and Emily, I am truly sorry I make you sneeze. I give you my word I do not do it on purpose. I've always liked you, kitten." She dimpled at Jax and made a little purring noise. "You, too."

Emily and Jax turned their wide-eyed gazes from Xena, who went back to grooming herself, to the twins.

"It's true," answered Hunter and Mercy together—though they didn't share the intimate smile that usually accompanied their twin-speak.

Emily went back to staring at Xena. "In a completely bizarre way that makes perfect sense."

"Yup," said Jax, who shot Xena sideways glances.

"Kittens." She paused in her grooming. "Refocus on your intention. We can discuss how spectacularly magical I am another time."

"I'm gonna have to get some Benadryl. A *lot* of Benadryl," muttered Emily as her attention returned to the spell.

"Okay, so, to answer the question I think Em was starting to ask," Mercy said. "We're going to communicate through our speaker phones."

"Except for me," Hunter broke in. "There's no way to know if I'll be able to be on my phone. Mercy will use our connection to know when I'm in place. And then you'll have to trust me to keep up."

Mercy nodded. She didn't look at Hunter. *Good. She won't try to take over. I'm better at this part anyway,* Mercy told herself. "So, I'm going to lead you through the ritual, and I'll be sure I don't waste time on flowery words and such. We light candles, then seal the gates with—"

"Blood!" Emily squeaked, her eyes on the cheat sheet.

Xena patted her knee. "Yes, kitten, but not very much."

Mercy barreled on quickly. "Then you thank your tree and blow out your candle—and we're done!"

Emily raised her hand. "You said we each need an offering, but I don't have anything."

"Em, you'll be at the cherry tree that guards the Japanese gate," explained Mercy. "I brought your offering." She reached into her purse and brought out the beautiful little Japanese sumi-e Emily had painted in remembrance of Abigail Goode.

Emily took it, holding it carefully, gazing at the soaring owl. "It seems like a million years ago that I painted this."

"It is a perfect offering," Xena assured her. "Something precious created with love."

Jax waved his hand, getting their attention. "What's my offering?"

"The dove feather you got from your dad, remember?" answered Hunter.

"Oh, right! Got it in my pocket." Jax patted his jean's pocket.

Mercy turned to look at her sister. "I didn't see what offering you brought."

Her twin's emotionless eyes met hers. Her voice had a hard edge to it that bordered on anger. "I'm going to get it on my way to the tree, but you already knew that, so why did you need to ask?"

Mercy just stared at her, unable to arrange the right words to reply.

Into the sudden silence Emily spoke up. "My other question is about the, um, blood."

"Oh, I can answer that." Xena bent and brought out a small, rectangular box from below the seat in front of her. She opened it to expose five tiny daggers, each about the size of a pinky finger. They nestled on faded red velvet.

"I've never seen those before," Hunter said, peering over the front seat.

"They were in the attic," Xena said, "in Gertrude Goode's hope chest."

"What are they?" asked Mercy, intrigued by the perfection of their carved bone handles and their razor-like blades.

"Miniature athames." When Emily and Jax sent her confused

looks Xena fluttered her fingers at them and clarified. "Sorry, kittens. I keep forgetting how new all of this is to you. An athame is a witch's dagger—used only for rituals and spells. In the past, witches used a lot more bloodletting in their spellwork." She sighed nostalgically. "That seems to have gone out of style. Well, go on, each of you, take one." She passed the box around and everyone chose their athame.

"Cut yourself beneath your thumb, on that meaty part of your palm," Hunter said. She moved her shoulders uncomfortably when everyone's gaze turned to her. "What? It's not super sensitive there, and it'll be easy to just prick yourself and then squeeze it to make the blood drip."

"I already sanitized the blades," added Xena.

Emily sneezed and then thanked her.

"Okay, does anyone have any more questions?" Mercy asked. "Sunset will be in about thirty minutes."

"I think I get it," said Emily as she held her athame carefully.

"All I need to know is which one is my tree," said Jax.

"Your tree is the banyan. It guards the Hindu gate," said Mercy.

"Em, you already know that yours is the Japanese gate."

"I've always liked that tree," said Emily.

"Xena, I thought you should go to the Egyptian tree—what with Bast being an Egyptian goddess and all."

Xena nodded. "Yes, kitten, I agree. And I have the perfect offering. I shall leave a lock of my luxurious hair. I know Bast will appreciate that."

"Hunter," said Mercy, "you'll need to go to—"

"I know what I need to do."

Mercy thought she'd never seen Hunter's eyes look so blue or so cold—like someone had frozen the Caribbean Sea. She squared her shoulders and faced Hunter. It was time.

"Do you *really* know what to do?"

"I'm taking care of the Cyclops. Cleaning up the real mess. As usual."

"As usual?" Mercy frowned at Hunter.

"And you don't need to tell me what to do."

"What's going on between them?" Emily whispered from the backseat, but Xena gently shushed her.

Mercy felt one of the wounds in her heart begin to bleed, but she ignored it. *It was time.* "Whatever, Hunter. You're still not getting it." She lifted the sheet of paper that had been waiting on her lap. "You have to put aside Tyr and choose a *goddess.* It's your *god* that caused this. Your god that made the trees sick." Mercy struck twice with her words, drew a breath, and then slashed the third and most devastating wound. *"Your god caused the Fenrir to escape."* Hunter's shoulders jerked in pain, but Mercy forced herself to go on. "Being a lesbian doesn't mean you had to choose a *god* instead of a *goddess.*" Mercy turned the page and held it so Hunter could read it.

Hunter's eyes blazed with rage as she ripped the page from Mercy's hands. "My sexuality has nothing to do with choosing Tyr. So, do you also believe that Jax is my best friend because he's a guy? Did you ever think that I'm more interested in the person, or *god,* and less concerned with their gender?" Mercy opened her mouth to speak, but Hunter didn't give her the opportunity. "And, if you'd bothered to do any real research, you'd know that they didn't see queerness as an identity back when this prophecy was written, so there's no possible way great aunt *whoever* could have been referring to me." Then she balled up the paper and threw it onto the floorboard. She jerked open her car door and grabbed her backpack from where it rested on the seat between them. Before she got out of the car, she hurled her words at Mercy.

"I'll do it," she said. "I'll betray my god and choose a goddess. I'll make this sacrifice and fix everything, not because there's something wrong with me, but because you're too weak to help yourself."

Hunter surged from the car. "Jax, I'm riding with you. Drop me off at the sheriff's." She stomped away, leaving Jax to scramble after her.

"Kitten! Do be careful!" Xena called through the window at Hunter's back.

Mercy had to swallow several times before she could speak and when she did her voice sounded hollow, like something had just gouged through her. "Em, would you drive?"

As Emily silently went to the driver's seat, Xena's soft hand stroked the back of Mercy's hair as she murmured, "Oh, my poor kittens . . ."

Twenty-nine

Goose bumps peaked along Hunter's arms as she opened the heavy glass door of the sheriff's department. It was cold. *Really* cold. Arctic tundra cold. She pulled the sleeves of her holey cardigan over her hands and rubbed them against her arms. Her boots squeaked across the shiny linoleum floor as she headed to the long, beige counter that separated the townspeople from those tasked with keeping them safe.

Trish McAlister poked up from behind the counter. Her curly red hair bounced against her pink cheeks as she hefted up a box labeled DONATE and set it on top of the Formica-covered ledge. An aluminum can spilled over the top of the box and landed on the floor with a thud.

"I got it!" Hunter welcomed the excuse to jog over and supply more heat to her body. "Only a tiny dent." She pointed to the dimple and set the can of green beans back in the box.

"They're for the elementary school's food drive." Trish brushed a few perfectly spiraled locks away from her green eyes and smiled. "I don't much think they'll care about a little dent." She shivered and zipped her puffy winter jacket up to her throat.

Hunter bounced in place and flexed her stiffening fingers. "I think your a/c has gone insane."

Trish clasped her hands in front of her and buried her chin in the collar of her coat. "The sheriff is having quite the time staying cool." Her glossed lips smoothed into a thin line. "With his hot flashes and mood swings, you'd think he was going through some type of male menopause." She grumbled before glancing up at Hunter. The color in her cheeks deepened cherry red. "But you didn't come to hear about that." She waved away the comment and lifted herself onto the stool behind the counter. "Now, what can I do for you . . . ?"

"Hunter," she supplied.

"Thank you, Hunter. It's just that you girls are so darn hard to tell apart." Trish's shoulders shook with a chuckle. "So, what can I do for you, *Hunter*?"

Hunter clenched her toes. "I need to speak with the sheriff. It's an emergency."

"Oh?" Trish pressed her hand against her chest and tilted her chin, birdlike. "I hope it's nothing serious."

"Not too serious." She cleared her throat. "Well, it *is* an emergency. Can an emergency be *un*serious?" Her toes ached and she blew out a puff of air. "I just need to see the big man in charge." Hunter bit the inside of her cheeks to keep from spouting more nonsense. If her plan was going to work, she'd have to keep from saying asinine things like *unserious emergency* and *big man in charge*.

Trish slid off her stool and straightened her puffy jacket. "I'll go see if he is taking visitors."

Hunter fought off another a/c-induced shiver. "I'm not really a visitor. I have a serious emergency."

Trish stuffed her hands into her pockets. "Hunter, dear, you are preaching to the choir." Her tennis shoes squeaked on the linoleum as she spun around and marched toward the only office with its door closed.

Except for the occasional ringing phone or *whoosh* of the printer, the sheriff's department was silent. Every few weeks, when Hunter followed Mercy in and out of the businesses along Main Street to hang flyers for the bake sales and club activities the more outgoing twin participated in, the sheriff's department pulsed with energy. Deputy Carter seemed to always be up and around, flashing a straight-toothed grin and those puppy-dog eyes at the women who stopped by to hand out sweets and innocent flirtations. There was laughter from the coffee station, somber meetings in the glass-front conference rooms, and at least one very drunk, very loud townsperson. Hunter rubbed her palms against her bare thighs and shivered. Everything was different now, colder, and it wasn't just the air conditioning. But that's what happened when the easygoing sheriff was body snatched and replaced with a murderous monster.

Hunter flinched with each of Trish's sharp knocks on the sheriff's closed wooden door. Hunter strained to hear what they were saying, but her witchy powers didn't extend to super hearing. She picked at her thumbnail and waited.

Everything rested on her. Everything always rested on her, so that wasn't really a shock, but this was so much different than pulling her sister out of her despair or making sure their mother's funeral arrangements were in order. This was huge—life ending. And then there was Tyr. Hunter swallowed.

Sheriff Dearborn yanked his door open. It slammed against the stopper with a sharp crack. Tension washed over the bullpen. Even the trilling phones quieted in Sheriff Dearborn's wake.

Hunter stiffened. She could do this. She had no choice.

She lifted onto her toes and shouted, "Sheriff!"

His head jerked from Trish to Hunter. Under the fluorescent lights, the lenses of his mirrored sunglasses looked like two starbursts.

Showtime.

Hunter knitted her brow and frowned. "Out by that old olive tree, there's a—a—" She pressed her cold fingers against her lips and sucked in a jagged breath.

The sheriff brushed past Trish and stalked toward Hunter.

Deputy Carter stood and picked up his cowboy hat off his desk. "If you take Miss Goode's statement, I'll drive out there and take a look."

"No!" Dearborn's temples flexed with each sharp clench of his jaw. "What I mean is, I need you"—he swung his gaze around the bullpen—"*all* of you, to stay here. Finish your work. Protect the town. I'll use this . . ." With another clench of his jaw, he flicked the radio attached to his shoulder. "And let you know if I need backup."

Deputy Carter's puppy face disappeared as he dropped his hat back onto his desk and sagged into his chair.

Hunter kept her damsel-in-distress mask firmly in place as she surveyed the office. None of these people had gotten to say good-bye to the real Frank Dearborn. After tonight, if everything went well for Hunter, each person's memory would be stained by the final seventy-two hours they'd spent with Polyphemus, the creature who'd stuffed himself into Frank Dearborn's skin and ruined him in more ways than one.

"Come with me, twin."

Hunter didn't flinch, didn't recoil when Polyphemus pressed his meaty paw against her back and hurried her down the hall. Instead, she surrendered, turned toward him and let him push her outside. In that moment, she needed him, needed to be rescued.

"What's out at the olive tree?" he barked as soon as the door had closed behind them.

"Sheriff, I don't know if you'd believe me if I told you." She wrung her hands. "You'd think I was crazy!" She bit the inside of her cheek until her eyes watered. "I'll have to show you." She swallowed the warm pool of copper sliding across her tongue.

He adjusted the sunglasses on the bridge of his broad nose and sniffled. "Well then, Hunter, I'll drive us on out there." He fished the keys from his pocket, pointed the fob at the cruiser, and pressed a button.

Hunter followed Polyphemus to the car as it unlocked and yellow signal lights lit up the parking lot. "Good guess with the whole *which twin* thing." Hunter could only muster a slight twitch of her lips to accompany her attempt at normalcy.

Polyphemus opened the cruiser door and paused before climbing in. He leaned forward and rested his arm on the roof of the car. "Oh, Hunter." He slid his tongue across his teeth and blew out a quaking breath. "I could never forget that spark behind those blue eyes."

Thirty

Mercy bent to look into the car through the open passenger's side window at Emily and Xena. "Okay, Em, drop Xena off at the park, and then get right to the cherry tree. You two have candles and matches, right?"

"Yes," said Emily. "Don't worry. We've got this."

"Kitten, you must focus on your intention. It is your will that holds all of us together in Ritual."

Mercy ran her hand through her long hair and shoved it back behind her ears. "That's hard to do knowing she hates me."

Xena touched her arm. "No. Hunter hates what she must do tonight. And I hate it for her, don't you? How would you feel if you knew that you must reject Freya?"

Mercy sighed. "I'd feel awful."

"Then understand her instead of judging her. Now, go." Xena paused. "And as you walk to the Norse gate, gain control over your feelings. Blessed be, my kitten."

"Blessed be, Xena," Mercy said. "Good luck, Em."

"Break a leg!" Emily said as she drove off, waving out the window.

With a sigh Mercy hefted her big purse across her shoulder and headed to their backyard and through the little gate to the fields beyond—tracing the steps she and Hunter and Abigail had taken four short nights, but an eternity, ago.

Dusk settled around the cornfields. The evening had been warm, and a soft breeze caressed the growing crops that brought to Mercy the scent of fertile earth and corn silk. The thick stalks whispered secrets she could almost hear. She relaxed into the familiarity of her world and let the earth comfort her internal wounds.

My intention is to lead this ritual to heal the trees and seal the gates with the blood of witches mixed with the representatives of those who once walked this very path—and the unique power that fills this land.

Mercy repeated her intention over and over until it became like the lyrics of a song that wouldn't leave her mind. It blocked everything else and consumed her attention.

She closed her eyes tightly before she was able to approach the mighty apple tree that guarded the Norse gate, and readied herself. She knew what she would see, though as she drew closer and closer to the wide trunk and the umbrella of ancient boughs, Mercy was surprised at how little evidence there remained of the horrible battle and their heartbreaking loss.

Only a few of the gnarled roots that pushed up from the ground like arthritic fingers showed signs of the goddess's inferno that had immolated her mother, though a dark scorch marked the skin of the tree's trunk. Mercy stared at it as her internal mantra faltered.

"Oh, thank you, Athena." Awestruck, Mercy bowed her head and pressed her hand against the blackened bark. At the place where Abigail Goode had died to save her daughters—and her town—the outline of a perfect heart had been burned into the tree.

Then she lifted her head, wiped away her tears, kicked off her shoes, and got to work—and as she prepared to open the ritual, Mercy breathed deeply, evenly, until she felt so grounded that the bare soles of her feet tingled. Then she began allowing emotions to bubble up and release—bubble and release.

Feeling invigorated, Mercy reached into her boho bag and extracted a thick white candle exactly like the ones her four impromptu coven members were, hopefully, also readying. She placed her candle at the base of the apple tree, beneath the point of the heart the goddess had scorched into its bark. She returned to her bag for matches, her phone, and the little jar filled with the last apple butter she and Abigail would ever make together. Mercy's smile was bittersweet as her finger traced the pentagram she'd painted on the side of the Mason jar last fall to mark the final batch of that season's harvest.

"I'll think of you every fall—every time I make jam or apple butter or homemade bread. I'll think of you always, Mama." Mercy placed the jar beside the white candle at the base of the tree, then she waited, repeating her intention mantra over and over.

She didn't wait long. Her phone bleeped with the first text message, a smiling cat emoji from Xena—followed by Emily's READY! And then Jax's LOCKED & LOADED!

Quickly, she joined the four of them in a group call and hit the speaker button she tucked the phone into a niche in the tree's bark.

"All right, you have placed your candles at the base of your trees?"

"Yes!" Three voices echoed back to her, like ghosts lifting from a grave.

No! No negative imagery! Mercy pushed the thought from her mind and continued.

"Your offerings are ready?"

"Yes!" they replied.

"Okay," Mercy said. "Get your matches out and give me a second. Let me find Hunter."

Mercy faced her tree and centered herself, breathing deeply once, twice, thrice, and then sent her sixth sense—that magical spark that flowed rich and thick through every sister of Salem, each daughter who carried Sarah Goode's legacy—down, down, down to find the vein of power that hummed beneath her bare feet and formed the potent pentagram that surrounded Goodeville. As she tapped into the thrumming ley lines she thought of Hunter—of everything she loved about her sister. Her generosity and kindness—her strength and wit—and above all the thing that was always there, no matter what else was happening in their world, the connection that bound them irrevocably together. The bond that had begun at their conception, forged by blood and sealed by nine months of a shared womb.

Mercy gasped as she connected with her sister. Against her closed lids Hunter swirled as a glowing sapphire orb with silver glitter as if a piece of the cosmos had come to earth, and glistened like a spot on the map of her soul.

"She's there! She's at the olive tree!" Mercy's eyes opened and she crouched before the white pillar candle. As she picked up the match she turned to the glowing face of her phone. "Okay, light your matches while I open the ritual." Mercy struck the match and lit her candle. "And so we begin. We are vessels, cleansed and protected, ready to be conduits for energy. Remember, we do not keep that energy. We only guide it. Visualize the gate before you, deep within the trunk of this ancient tree who has stood guardian for hundreds of years."

She paused to be sure the others were with her, and as she did she thought of Hunter, sending her sister an image of a brightly burning flame. *Please see me, too, Hunter! Please understand! Light your candle!* The sapphire orb in her internal map sparked suddenly brighter. *Is that it? Did you light your candle?*

Mercy's intuition demanded she continue and set the spell. All she could do was move forward and believe Hunter came with them.

"Now, place your offering near your tree. Let your intuition guide you as to where, and as you place it tell your tree that this offering is in honor of the gate it guards and the ancient world beyond. Jax, release your dove feather and thank the peoples who came before us—whose land we now call our own."

Mercy lifted the jar of apple butter. She kissed it, and then reached up and, on her tiptoes, placed it in a niche where two low-hanging limbs joined. "Thank you, mighty apple tree. I make this offering in honor of the Underworld you guard and the Norse land from which you come."

"Holy crap!" Jax's awed voice sparked through the phone. "The feather! It just lifted way, way up with the wind and then disappeared—only there isn't any wind!"

Mercy smiled. "Good. That's really good, Jax." She didn't wait for a sign from Hunter. She knew her sister's offering would be different—dangerous. The offerings at the other trees set the stage for Hunter's, heightening her power—and Mercy fervently hoped it would be enough. She drew another deep breath and continued.

"Okay, here we go. Face your trees. Ready?"

"Ready!" they chorused.

"Imagine that beneath your feet is a thick stream of power," Mercy said. "Something that runs deep and fast within the earth. Xena, what color is yours?"

Xena responded immediately. "It is the yellow of cat eyes. Rich with power."

"Jax, what color is yours?"

Jax's voice was filled with excitement. "Mine is red! Mercy! My eyes are closed, but I see it! I really see it!"

"Emily, what color is yours?"

Emily gasped and shouted, "It's pink! Just like springtime cherry blossoms! Oh, Mag, it's beautiful!"

Mercy smiled. "And mine is green, like new apples." She waited for a moment, hoping Hunter could see her sapphire blue ley line—but she had to keep going. "Think about your ley line while you take out your athames." Mercy heard the rustling as her three coven members did as she told them. "Prick your palms, just below your thumb."

Mercy didn't hesitate. She pulled the athame from the pocket of her embroidered jeans and pressed the razor-sharp blade against her flesh.

It hurt less than she thought it would—mostly it just stung—and then she squeezed the meaty part of her palm until her blood welled in fat drops. "Now, pull your ley line up through your body and push it from the center of your forehead, like a blazing star, to shine against the gate hidden within your tree." Mercy concentrated, pulling her stream of emerald power up, up, up through her body. It wasn't quite as sluggish as it had been that terrible night when Abigail had died, but it didn't fill her body with the glowing energy that always blazed from their mom during Ritual.

Mercy fisted her hands and concentrated harder. It felt like running a marathon. Sweat beaded on her face as she forced the slim stream of power up and out her third eye so that it washed the hidden gate within the tree with a pale light the color of unripe apples.

She stared at the gate, expecting it to be powerful and whole, just as it was every time their mother had shown them this ritual. It was there. It was standing. But instead of a bright, glowing gate, it had turned black, like charcoal. Mercy swallowed bile. "Are any of your gates open?"

"Yes! Mine is! It's kinda hard to see 'cause there isn't a lot of light, but it's pink, like the ley line. It looks terrible—all crumbly—and it smells bad!" Emily panted, like she'd just climbed a wall of stairs.

"Mine looks weird! Like it's made of old blood, and it reeks!" Jax, too, gasped with effort.

Xena's hiss was followed by a low, deep yowl that lifted the hair on the back of Mercy's neck.

"Xena! What's happening?" she shouted into the phone.

"Oh! That must be your Egyptian friend," Xena said. "I can see him beyond the gate. Oh, my. He does have the face of—"

"Xena, is the gate open or closed?" Mercy interrupted.

"Closed, but not well. It—it was once golden." The cat person panted. "But now it flakes like cheap jewelry and the smell is truly vile."

"All three of you—focus on your ley line! Make it shine as bright as possible from your forehead directly onto the spot where your blood dripped on your tree. The ley line power mixed with your blood will close the gate—believe it, know it, make it happen now! And then repeat after me: *By blood and offering—*"

"*By blood and offering—*" they repeated.

Mercy continued as she channeled her ley line into the tree. "*Through the power of olde—*"

"*Through the power of olde—*"

Mercy's voice rose, amplified by the energy passing through her and the generations of Goode witches that filled her DNA with magic. "*Bind this spell with our intent, set well and block this hell, block this hell—BLOCK THIS HELL!*"

The three followed her, shouting the conclusion of the spell. The power sizzled, sputtered, and finally faded as Mercy's black gate disappeared. "Now, lift your candle, ground yourselves again, thank your tree, and blow out the candle as you say, '*So I have spoken; so mote it be.*'"

Mercy completed the spell with the others.

"*So mote it be!*" chorused through the phone.

"Mag! The smell is gone!" Emily's voice trilled through the phone.

"Mine doesn't stink anymore, either!" said Jax.

"The vile odor is gone from my tree as well," said Xena. "Oh, kitten, it must have worked!"

Emily and Jax cheered and Xena's musical laughter lifted with the wind.

Mercy didn't feel triumphant. Not yet. She needed to reach Hunter. She closed her eyes and, wearily, found her ley line so that she could connect with her sister. She focused on her sister, seeking . . . seeking . . .

But found nothing.

Mercy tried again.

Nothing. No sapphire orb—no swirling stars and moons—not even the strange, psychic tickle she had *always* been able to feel, *always* been able to find.

"Emily!" she shouted into the phone. "Pick up Xena and get back here for me! Jax, meet us at the olive tree." Her voice faltered. "Hunter's gone!"

Thirty-one

Hunter's hands shook. She balled them into fists and stuffed them into her lap. She had a plan, had worked it out on the way to Emily's and finalized it in the stiff and bloated silence that now filled the inside of Sheriff Dearborn's car. All she had to do was ground and protect herself, forsake her god, and get Polyphemus before he got her. No biggie.

She blew out a puff of air. First things first. She planted her feet in the car's footwell. Grounding herself while on the move wasn't difficult. Hunter wasn't one for holding still. Unless she was writing, too much stillness meant too much thought, too much opportunity for her demons to catch up with her, and she preferred to keep them chasing.

Hunter closed her eyes and reached up, up, up, until she was nowhere. Until she was nothing. Just black and cold and stardust. Grounding didn't always mean reaching down into the soul of the earth. For Hunter, it meant grasping the heart of the cosmos.

"Can't fall asleep on me now, Hunter," he said. "I need those bright eyes of yours to lead me to this . . . what did you say it was again?"

293

Hunter flinched and her eyelids fluttered open. "By the olive tree. There's, uh . . ." She blinked through the haze clouding her vision. She'd let him pull her back too soon. She wasn't yet grounded or protected. She floated somewhere between the earth and the heavens, sinking through quicksand to get back to her body. "Burn mark. Of a person. Weird stuff. You have to see it to believe it."

He turned down the unpaved road that led to the tree and the gate and Hunter's future. He adjusted the sheriff's sunglasses and said, "I've seen some pretty weird things." His meaty paw clamped onto her thigh. "Maybe I'll tell you about them before the night is over." Moist heat seeped from his fingers and drowned every pore of her bare thigh.

"It—it's just up ahead." Hunter cursed her voice for trembling.

"I know." Polyphemus released her leg and Hunter fought the urge to wipe the ghost of his grip from her skin. His knuckles popped on the steering wheel as he guided Dearborn's cruiser onto the shoulder.

She unbuckled the seat belt and threw open her door before he'd put the car in park. "It's off the road, here," she said, tapping her phone to activate the flashlight.

His hand was back on her thigh. "Leave your phone in the car." He squeezed her flesh and a wave of nausea rippled through her stomach. "Wouldn't want to drain your battery." He let go and pulled a Maglite from his belt. "Plus, I've got this covered." He clicked it on, then off, then on again.

Hunter's throat went dry as she placed her phone on the dashboard and stepped out of the cruiser. Gravel crunched beneath her shoes as she backed away from the car, from *him*.

Polyphemus shined the cone of light across Hunter. "Where exactly is the weirdness you've been going on about?"

Hunter blinked the spots of light from her eyes and pointed at the stake the sheriff's department had left behind. He cast the light onto the field and stopped when the beam flashed on the stake and the strip of yellow caution tape fluttering in the breeze.

"You wanted to show me that they left behind some trash?"

Hunter charged into the tall grass. Polyphemus was right behind her. The flashlight's glow spilled across her left side and a half shadow stretched along the grass. Hunter looked at the sky and the sliver of moon that peeked out from behind the clouds. Mother Moon would always be with her. She couldn't say the same about Tyr. Her fingers found the pendant hanging from her neck.

She reached the stake and froze. The scorched earth was gone, vanished. "It was here." She crouched next to the grass, unstained but still crushed in the shape of Earl Thompson's body.

With a snort, Polyphemus shined the light onto the ground.

"It was right here," Hunter repeated. "I had my tarot." She mimed shuffling her deck. "I took out the cards." She drew three invisible cards and set them in the grass. "I asked each card a question and they each gave an answer. One of them burned the earth. Here." She passed her hand over Earl Thompson's imprint. "And—" Her voice caught as she turned to where the footsteps had been burned into the earth. Now, Polyphemus filled that space in the grass, the sheriff's large boots the same size as the vanished scorch marks. Hunter brushed her hands on her shorts and stood. This didn't derail her plan, it just changed it a bit.

Polyphemus stepped closer. The toe of his boot touched hers. His coppery breath warmed her face. "I'd almost lost hope, but then I found you, Bright Eyes." His palm melted against her cheek. "I've searched for you for centuries." His thumb grazed her bottom lashes, slid down the slope of her nose and pressed against her lips.

Hunter parted her lips. "I'm here now," she whispered and let her mouth graze his thumb. She watched her reflection in Sheriff Dearborn's sunglasses as she bit into his flesh.

Her teeth sunk into skin. Blood hit her tongue as Polyphemus howled. He yanked his hand free. Pain fireworked against Hunter's cheek. She hadn't heard the slap or seen it coming, but the shape of his hand now burned against her face.

Hunter scrambled backward and tripped over the flashlight he'd dropped. She caught herself as the light settled across the forest of grass. She moved backward, closer to the tree as Polyphemus stalked toward her. But this wasn't a retreat. This was a preparation.

"I am a Goode witch!" she shouted. Mangled roots jutted from the ground as Hunter neared the ancient olive. "My blood carries magic. So does yours, Polyphemus. I can feel it prick my throat like shards of glass." She spit Polyphemus's blood into her hand. "Your blood!" She pulled the athame from her pocket and sliced her blood-splattered palm. "My blood!" Scarlet gushed from the wound and swirled across Polyphemus's blood like a whirlpool against her skin. "I draw down the power of the moon and the heat of the stars!" She thrust her red palm to the sky and, for a moment, the heavens flickered.

Polyphemus roared. Hunter's pulse surged through her ears as she widened her stance and let him shorten the distance between them. With the demi-god only steps away, Hunter rushed forward. A scream scraped against the back of her throat as their bodies collided. Polyphemus grabbed her ponytail and snapped her head back.

Her hands found his shoulders, his neck, his ears. She yanked off his sunglasses and clapped her bloody palm against his good eye. "Release!" she commanded the cosmic energy she'd stored in the crimson pool that swirled against her palm. Heat shot from Hunter's palm.

With a screech, Polyphemus wrenched away. He slapped his hands over his eye and folded as he tripped backward.

Hunter ran to the base of the tree. Her hand trembled as she grabbed Tyr's pendant and yanked. The rope cord resisted. It burned the back of her neck as she pulled harder—then it snapped. Her eyes filled with tears, turning Polyphemus into a writhing blur of dark colors. She held the symbol of Tyr to her lips and whispered, "I'm sorry."

She threw the pendant to the ground and swiped the back of her hand across her eyes. "Amphitrite!" The tree's wide trunk pressed against Hunter's back as she called on a new deity—a goddess to set things right. "Wife of Poseidon and goddess of the sea, I come bearing a gift!"

Polyphemus's screams turned to growls and he charged Hunter, arms blindly thrashing the air. The flesh around his once good eye was raw, the edges charred. Hunter had blinded him, but she hadn't stopped him.

Her throat turned to barbed wire and she choked on the fear caught in the back of her mouth. "Amphitrite," she barked, her voice nearly drowned out by her thundering pulse. "I offer you Polyphemus, proof of your husband's adultery! Take him back to Tartarus and I'll submit my will to yours!"

The air cooled and the hairs along Hunter's arms bristled. Light poured from the tree, from the gate, the same cerulean as a blue giant. Polyphemus's boots beat the ground as he sped toward the brilliant glow.

Hunter pulled the athame from her pocket as the demi-god tripped on the olive tree's roots and slammed into her. Air shot out of her lungs and she lost her grip on the knife. It fell to the ground, its sharp point glinting in the blue light. Bark tore into Hunter's back as Polyphemus's weight crushed her to the ground. He roared. Spittle flew from his lips and sprayed Hunter's forehead. His hands clawed up her chest and snaked around her neck. She pawed the earth for the blade as Polyphemus squeezed her throat. The tips of her fingers brushed something cool, something metal. She gripped the hilt, raised the blade, and drove the point into his temple.

Spit showered Hunter's face as Polyphemus howled and his grip tightened on her throat.

Hunter swiped her wounded hand through the blood that leaked from his head. "We are all stardust." The words barely passed from her lips as she focused the last of her energy through her blood and into his.

Polyphemus's blood, charged with her power, sizzled against his skin. It bubbled and popped and ate through to bone. He yanked one hand from Hunter's neck and pawed at the flesh on his face that burned away into nothing.

Bursts of light flashed across Hunter's vision as Polyphemus pressed his weight against the hand still clutching her throat. The blue air coated Hunter's skin as she clawed his thick wrist. A chill tickled her spine and a woman's laughter slipped through Hunter's ears like the tongue of a snake.

Merry meet, Hunter Goode. Amphitrite's voice was like smoke, everywhere and nowhere. *I accept your offering, my child.*

Ice speared Hunter's chest. She looked down at the blue light shining through her. Amphitrite's slender arm reached out from Hunter's sternum like a spear. The goddess's laughter was a shrieking train as she grabbed Polyphemus. She sank her pointed nails into his forearm. The same blue light that shone from her skin and coated the air seeped up Polyphemus's arm. He ceased his screams and blindly blinked at Hunter. His skull, slick with blood and melted flesh, glowed as the blue light spread from one side of his body to the other.

Tartarus hath no fury like a goddess scorned. Amphitrite yanked Polyphemus's arm, and he passed through Hunter's chest as the goddess ripped him from Goodeville and cast him back into the Greek Underworld.

They vanished. Hunter fell to her knees in a fit of coughs. She sucked in air as the blue light receded back into the gate.

You are mine, now, Hunter Goode. Amphitrite's voice faded as the warm dark night retook the field.

Soft blades poked Hunter's sliced palm as she crawled through the trampled grass toward the flashlight. Her chest quaked with the memory of the otherworldly magic that had cut through her. She fumbled with the heavy flashlight and forced her legs underneath her. Her hand shook and the beam of light wavered as she guided it down the street until it landed on Sheriff Dearborn's car. She stumbled into a run. The dome lights clicked on as she opened the passenger door.

Amber light poured onto her, dirt-streaked and blood-crusted, as she swiped her phone off the dash.

With trembling hands, she dialed her sister's number. Hunter barely heard Mercy's voice over the echo of Amphitrite's words.

You are mine, now, Hunter Goode.

Epilogue

Hunter sat in the cool shadows that the palm fronds cast onto the grass. When they'd all decided to spend the afternoon at the park, she'd silently cheered. Writing outside was so much better than writing inside. But in the rush to get out of the house, she'd forgotten her journal. The worst part was that she knew exactly where it was. She closed her eyes and glided through her front door, past the living room, and into the kitchen. There it was. On top of the forgotten cooler full of seltzer and the pee-yellow tea Mag brewed and insisted tasted just like green gummy bears.

Jax's foot bumped Hunter's as he maneuvered out of the tree's shadows and back into the sun. Beside her, he closed his eyes, his lashes nearly dusting his round cheeks, and resumed tossing the football from one hand to the other while Emily and Mercy shook with girlish giggles. From now on, every day would be like this. Every day would be simple.

With an eruption of laughter, Emily threw her head back. She nearly toppled over onto the red-and-white-checkered blanket she had brought from home. She fanned her face and insisted Mercy, "Stop playing."

Hunter plucked a white clover flower and rolled the stem between the thumb and forefinger of her bandaged hand. Clover dotted the grass like patches of green fog. When the rains left and the summer sun arrived, the clover would be the only lush green in the entire park. She dusted her chin with the puffy flowers. That's what this field should be. Clover. A big, fluffy, green mattress of clover that stretched from the palm tree all the way to the playground. Hunter's neck ached as she leaned over and dropped the flower on Jax's stomach while children's laughter drifted on the breeze like faraway church bells. The scene was postcard perfect.

Hunter instinctively ran her fingertips along her sternum where Tyr's pendant had once been. Where Amphitrite had reached through her. She swallowed and dropped her hand into her lap. Well, the scene was *almost* perfect.

Mercy leapt to her feet and bounded over to Jax. "Go long!" she shouted as she stole the football and ran toward the playground. Mercy had finally gotten rid of Kirk, but no one could get rid of football.

Jax popped up. The clover flew off his shirt and landed next to Hunter's wounded hand.

Mercy jumped up and down and triumphantly waved the ball overhead. "You, too, H!" she called and added a butt wiggle to her victory dance.

Jax tapped Hunter's foot with his own. "Up and at 'em . . . or is it *Adam*?" He jutted his chin and scratched his sideburn.

Emily leaned back onto her elbows and cocked her head. "But who's *Adam*?"

"Hey!" Hunter practically heard her sister stomp her foot as Mercy cupped her hand around the side of her mouth. "You guys are taking a million years!"

With a groan, Hunter picked up the flower and got to her feet. "Doesn't Em have to play?" She tried to hide how much her muscles still ached and how much tension now hung in the air between her and her sister.

Emily scooped Mercy's giant bag onto her lap and fished out a pair of paisley-rimmed sunglasses. "I'll be the referee." She slid on the glasses and set Mercy's purse back on the blanket. "Or the cheerleader." She crossed one ankle over the other and pointed and flexed her toes. "Whichever one makes it so that I don't have to get up."

Hunter yipped as Jax launched into the air and his hip smashed into her. The sudden *thwack* of the ball against the tree was the perfect sound effect to Hunter's crash onto the grass. This time, she couldn't hide her pain.

Mercy rushed to her. "Sorry!" she squeaked, her shadow merging with the one the palms cast across the grass.

Jax offered Hunter his hand and pulled her to her feet. "H, I am so sorry!"

"I just can't stop getting beat up." She offered a heartless half smile as she glanced down at the crushed flower and brushed her hands off on her shorts.

Emily was the only one who chuckled.

Mercy clapped her hands and lifted onto her toes. "I didn't know I had such a great arm. *I* should be the Mustangs' QB."

"Yeah." Jax snorted and headed toward the ball. "Kirk wouldn't lose his mind about that."

Hunter rolled her eyes and trailed after Jax and Mercy. "Isn't most of it gone already, anyway?"

Emily pushed the borrowed sunglasses onto her head as she entered the palm's wide shadows. "It'd be really sad if what we've seen so far is him operating at one hundred percent."

Mercy stuffed her hands into the pockets of her dress. "I used to think he was smart, but when I look back, I'm like, *goddess, he was a total oaf.*"

Emily lifted her hands into the air. "Finally, she sees the light!"

Hunter draped her arm over Mercy's shoulders and pulled her in close. Mercy had not only seen the light—she'd taken a piece of it and pressed it into her heart. She glowed from the inside out. Hunter was glad to have her sister back, though Mercy's nearness no longer filled Hunter with warm fuzzies.

Jax bent over to pick up the ball and jerked to a halt before his fingers grazed the pigskin. He craned his neck and looked up, up, up. "Uh, Mag . . . ?"

Hunter stiffened. She slid her arm from Mercy's back and followed Jax's attention up one of the palm's five trunks. Cracks spiderwebbed the bark like antique porcelain.

Jax stepped back as Mercy crouched down at the base of the trunk. The football had made a divot in the tree, like a fist through drywall. Mercy sucked in a breath, pressed her fingertips against her lips, and shook her head back and forth.

Hunter's heart clicked against her ribs as her swallow lodged within her throat. "What—" She cleared her throat and started again. "What's wrong?"

"Oh, Freya!" Mercy closed her eyes and tilted her chin toward the crown of the tall palm stem. "I can barely feel it breathing."

"But we fixed them." Hunter groped at her chest for the pendant, but she'd discarded it when she threw away her god. It wasn't bad enough she'd lost her mother. She'd forsaken her god as well. But at least . . . "We healed the trees. We healed the gates. *We fixed everything.*"

Mercy's dark hair slipped from her shoulders as she reached out and pressed her hand to the trunk.

The elephant-gray bark cracked like dry earth. Hunter shielded her face as the long stem of the doum palm turned to ash and snowed down around them.

Screams ripped through the ashen air, a loud wailing that shook Hunter's bones and made her heart beat hummingbird fast. Emily gripped Jax's hand as Mercy wrapped her arms around her sister. Hunter pressed her face against Mercy's shoulder, and her spit spackled the light green fabric of Mercy's dress. It was then that Hunter realized she was the one screaming.

"It was for *nothing!*" Hunter tore away from her sister. "I betrayed

Tyr for nothing!" Her knees quaked, but she forced herself to stand. "You made me do it. You fell apart when Mom died because you've never had to face anything in your life. You dropped all of it on me. You said *I* was wrong." The rage returned. It slid through her veins like magma and cooled around her beating heart. "You're just like the rest of them." Hunter swiped the back of her hand against her cheeks. "You think if I'm not *just like* you, there's something *wrong* with me."

Tears glossed Mercy's green eyes. "But Sarah's poem said . . ." She moved closer to Hunter. Ash billowed with each step. "I thought—"

"It doesn't matter what you thought." Hunter shook her head. Papery tree bark fell around them. "What's done is done." Her gaze slid from Mercy to Jax. "Get me out of here." Hunter pressed her fingers against her chest. She wanted her pendant. She wanted her god.

Jax wrapped his arm around Hunter's shoulders and led her to the parking lot.

She ran her teeth along her bottom lip. It had all been for nothing. *She'd nearly died* for nothing. She ignored the parents and children gawking and pointing at the cloud of dust where the palm tree had been. She didn't even look back as Mercy shouted her name. Rock now encased Hunter's heart. It was better that way, safer. Hunter pressed her teeth into her lip. If she had only been stronger, maybe this would be different. Maybe this would never have happened. Maybe Hunter would have cast off the shadow of her sister and healed the gates herself.

She winced. She'd dug her teeth in too deep and bit through raw flesh. She snaked her tongue along her bottom lip. A copper tang heated the inside of her mouth and ran down her throat in a fiery blaze. A shooting star. She looked up at the blanket of sunlight overhead and pictured the stars just beyond. She hadn't known her full power before, but she knew it now. Hunter Goode held the cosmos within her blood.

She'd fix the mess that Mercy had made. And this time, nothing would stand in her way. Not even her sister.

Acknowledgments

We owe a debt of gratitude to our agents, Ginger Clark (PC) and Steven Salpeter (KC) for helping us turn an idea and a few sentences into an amazing series. Thank you!

Profound thanks to our Macmillan family. To Jennifer Enderlin, Anne Marie Tallberg, Monique Patterson, Mara Delgado-Sanchez, Sarah Bonamino, and Michelle Cashman—thank you for your support and encouragement.

Our personal publicist, Deb Shapiro, deserves accolades and applause for her imagination, innovation, patience, and hard work. You are the best!

Extra special thank-you to Sabine Stangenberg, who not only keeps my (PC) life running, but is also the talented artist who created the Goodeville map! XXXOOO

To our readers, those who have followed us for more than a decade and our lovely new fans—always remember, you are strong and smart and worthy of happiness and respect and love, always love.